Weaving A Tapestry Of Dreams
By Jess Fulton

This book is a work of fiction. Names, characters, events and places
Are products of the author's imagination. Any resemblance
to any person living or dead is coincidental.

jessfultonbooks@gmail.com

Prologue

"Hello. Good afternoon. Is this on? Can anyone hear me out there?"
The faint tapping on the top of the microphone turned to thunder in the auditorium.

"Wow! Ok. Now I can hear myself! First off I'd like to thank everyone responsible for inviting me to come and speak to this Beginners Creative Writing class. It is truly an honor. My name is..."
The nervousness of the speaker was obvious from the paper shaking in her hand. She took a deep breath to center her energy as her Yoga class instructed. It helped a little.

"Well my name is quite irrelevant actually as I don't use my real name. I am a writer. That sounded more like an AA confession. Hi my name is Joe and I'm an alcoholic. Anyway, my claim, as I said before is I am a writer. Some might say I'm an author but I prefer writer. Why? Because I write. I write because it is what I love to do. I put letters on a blank piece of paper or a computer screen and before my very eyes a story, a tale weaves itself into existence. Like some artisan weaving a tapestry from a rainbow of threads. I weave a dream from a rainbow of characters. Characters, in the dual sense, actors as well as squiggly shaped lines forming letters, But I'm straying off the subject and I only have a limited time up here I'm told. Unlike in my writing hideaway where I can take all the time I want. Ramble on and on and come back and make cuts at a later date. Today there is no rough draft, only the final copy.

"The reason I write is not for fame. I haven't come face to face with that problem yet. But I hear it's horrible. The love, that's the motivation. Someone buying your book is also nice, so the motivation can continue. Please keep that in mind if you see my book sitting all by itself on a bookstore shelf. Remember, books make a great gift for someone you don't know that well and they also make a great doorstop. One final note on being a writer, I am a writer not a talker. It seems like a contradiction in terms but it is very true. Up until a few months ago no one seemed to care one hoot about what I might have to say. Then a few books went home as doorstops and poof all of a sudden people want to hear words coming out of the whole in my head. But, I confess I am still the same person I was several months ago so I'll let you be the judge of whether I have anything important to say. Especially you there, third from the left, top row. Could someone wake him up please?"

A moment was taken to replenish the speaker's fluid level. A gulping was echoed around the room. Snickers emerged from the chairs.

"The glass of water on the podium was a great idea. Thanks. Since this is a beginner's class, I guess the best place to start is at the beginning. In the beginning God was with the word and the word was God. John 1:1. I know this is an English class not a theology class but you can't argue with the truth. The word, where it all began. And isn't it amazing how few words it takes to convey a message sometimes. And how many words it takes to describe something sometimes. I refer to my writing as a staccato form. Short and sweet. In days past people had all the time in the world to read a book, that's all they had to do. But now look how busy everyone is, going here, going there, picking up kids, picking up dinner, picking up the house. By the time they have a chance to sit and relax and pick up a book they're tired and they'll be lucky if they stay awake through the first chapter. So less is more.

"Getting back to God. I know, I know, I'll keep it brief. English not theology! God created. And we are his creation in his image. And we love to create. We have a burning desire in us to create. Art, music, dance, writing, we need to nurture our creative side. Let it grow. Let's face it we all have this beauty inside of us that wants to be on the outside of us. We want to produce something that is truly unique, one of a kind. Just like we are. Let it happen." The script was flying by now. She was on a roll. Only a few more pages and she could escape through the side door.

"A voice. I won't bring God into this topic, unless of course any of you out there wants to? OK, no hands rising. Your writing voice. You've all heard the term but what is it? A writer's voice, well it's the voice inside your head that used to talk to your imaginary friends. It's the voice that is you. But as you grew up you were taught that there was no such thing as imaginary friends, so you stopped believing in them, you stopped believing in your imagination, and you stopped talking with your voice. You still have a voice in your head but now it talks about what to fix for dinner, what to do to get a raise at work, does this one love me. Talk, talk, talk, but no imagining. Be a kid again, imagine. Dream while you're awake. If your imaginary friend is gone talk to your best friend, yourself. Look inside for that voice. My grandmother always used to say 'you can find anything you're looking for; you just need to relax and let it come to you.' Relax and listen.

"I thought there was one more reference I had with God in it, but I can't think of it right now. So on to writing discipline. Some expert writers harp, write something every day. Even if you have to erase it tomorrow write every day. Here again some people are busy. Are you busy? I get busy. Before I know it it's time to go to bed and I haven't written a word. And some people like discipline, structure. They are self- motivated and got that way by keeping a tight rein on themselves. So if you are one of those people that are obsessed with following rules; keep a note pad by your bed and before you go to sleep write two words on it. Just two words. Good Night. There, you have written for the day. A good night's sleep should await you now because you have met the criteria of writer's discipline.

But, why would a person need discipline to do what they love? And that is what this is all about. The love, the passion, you don't and you won't too often get time to write, you have to look for time to write. And it won't be something you are forcing yourself to do if it is truly your passion. A few minutes here a few minutes there, you will never be satisfied with the amount of time because you are trying to satisfy an unquenchable thirst. But that is all part of what keeps the passion alive, always wanting more.   Same thing with a relationship people, if you have to force yourself to make time to be with someone, instead of feeling you can never have enough time with someone, chances are that you are not passionate about the relationship. But now I'm way out of my league touching on psychology. Just remember, passion finds its own time and place.

"The word. How very important is the word. In the beginning of the story, as in the beginning of creation, God held one word in mind and all was created. You really didn't think I was done with the God thing did you? Well I don't know about you, but I certainly would love to know what that word was.   In all actuality I don't think it was an audible word, I think it was more a single thought a single emotion. So when I'm writing I try to keep in my mind that single thought that single emotion that I want the reader to feel. Oh there will be a variety of emotions felt through the story but the overall tone will be the sum total of all those feelings and that tone is where you need to keep your voice focused.

"Would someone please tell the gentleman in the back we are nearing the end? Yes, you. Sorry to have to wake you again. Thanks for coming. And believe me I'm not in the least offended that you're nodding off. I'd much rather be sitting out there with you than standing up here.

"Where was I? Oh yes, perfection. We all want to write the perfect story. The one and only perfect story. Sorry to burst your bubble here but they are all perfect stories. Everyone has a perfect story. And I think they should add a new genre, one of real fiction. Because let's face it. People have inhabited this planet for a long time and I don't think there is a story that hasn't somewhere, sometime, been lived. If not in entirety at least in sections. But all things have been lived, consciously or subconsciously. The goal of the writer is not in finding the perfect story but in writing it perfectly. A trip to the grocery store can be made into an enchanting love story, a horror epic or even a self-help soul discovering journey. The perfection comes from the weaver of dreams.

"My final note is on obligation. Once you have set pen to paper or fingertips to keys you have entered into an obligation. I believe if you are going to write then you need to be strong enough to fulfill that obligation. You have an obligation to the imagination, mind, and very soul of the person whom will read the words you write down. That person is entrusting you and your word to carry him or her on a journey, an adventure, a quest. You literally have that person in the palm of your hand. Your obligation is to carry them without faltering and return them safely home again. Hopefully a better person, for having embarked on your journey."

The silence roared in the speakers ears. Had everyone out there joined mister top row third from the left in a dream world of their own making? Her jaw began to tremble ever so slightly. A trait that appeared only under severe nervousness. The next part of her presentation would crumble unless she could control her jaw from shaking. She closed her eyes remembered his words echoing from her past. A calm rushed over her. She swore she could feel the brush of a hand against her cheek. She could continue. She could do this.

"Almost finished I promise. Now as the grand finale I'm going to write a story for you. Right here, right now. Nothing up my sleeve, the podium is glass, you can see through it and I don't have any more cards, no palm notes.

"When I write I relax, close my eyes and watch the story emerge in my mind. A special kind of dreaming while still awake. Could someone dim the lights please? Darkness can be a writers ally. Let the darkness caress the soul. Feel a friend walking toward you getting closer and closer, that friend is my dream, my story. Lean your head back and close your eyes. And let your imagination see what my imagination sees. Free your imagination for just the next couple of hours. Take a deep breath, let it out slowly. Let all your tension drain out. You can worry about whatever it is that is occupying your brain after class. This time is mine, to weave you a tapestry of dreams."

Assume, for the sake of argument that time, as we know it, did not exist. The same assumption to be made of space. All things happening right here right now. Furthermore assume the fact holds true in the existence of multi levels of heaven as well as hell in accordance with *Dante's Inferno*. Then there leaves but one explanation as to what makes up reality, that which truly is. That explanation would be dimensions. And what makes up dimensions but varying frequencies of vibrations. What defines vibrations, but energy. A tiny spark of light (life).

Chapter 1

On one of the higher levels of heaven, not nearly the top but a vast distance from even the first level of hell an assembly was called. There in a chamber sat 12 echelon. They are vested with the mission to pass down decisions of the utmost importance pertaining to the present level of existence and trickling down to all lower levels of vibration as well. Before them this occasion was a woman giving testimony of her cause. She was there to request permission to jump. A term used to incarnate on a lower dimension.

All in the chamber sat quiet listening to her evidence save one man standing so close to her side they would have been viewed as one except for the tiniest beam of light between them. He was tall, well proportioned for his height. He emanated power and strength. And beside him the woman fit with perfection to his side. The curve of her shoulder molded to a space under his arm. His chin came to rest on the top of her head like a last puzzle piece being put into place, nothing ever fits so perfect as the last piece. Their movement choreographed in perfect union as if they had practiced forever. She was the gentleness to his strength the grace to his power. But it was the blending of the two that radiated love between them. Separate they were fractures but together they were complete.

The woman had the floor as the man glared into the eyes of those assembled as if trying to hypnotize them into swaying the verdict in his direction. For his opinion was not in agreement with the woman by his side. A faint glow not seen by mortal eye, but this dimension did not belong to mortals, radiated around him changing from orange to crimson as the woman spoke on.

Her voice spoke not much higher than a whisper but would have lulled any normal person to sleep before the first sentence was finished. "It has been my post to witness the evolution of the race now nearly finished. As is the knowledge of all present here the time is at a close. I have many still in the race that are on the verge of passing through the curtain but the opposition gets stronger all the time. The curtain becomes denser and denser as the energy from the upcoming courser race darkens the veil."

The council sat at curved stations around the room with the man and woman in the center. Attendees could sit in the balcony surrounding the floor but only the echelon could decide the answer sought by the visitor. So she stayed focused front ignoring the audience and her partner alike.

"What is it you propose, Destiny?" The echelon in the center of the council was the appointed one to speak. He looked to each of the others to receive their minds first. With a kind melting smile he continued, his eyes giving a spark of gentleness. The light he gave forth never wavered never faltered. Only a steady white glow. "You know as well as us that it is not for us to interfere in the outcome of the race. We are to observe and let free will take its course. Let the concentration of polarity be the victor."

"But what if some cannot break through the concentration of negative energy? What if the wall is too thick? Are they to parish because the masses have chosen negatively? The time is drawing near. They deserve a chance."

"The time draws near yes, but the severity of the devastation is proportionate to the concentration of polarity. So there is a chance that those you speak of shall be the ones to inherit the planet and not parish." He echoed what he was sure she as well as all present knew.

"But these few I speak of do not want to inherit. They want to continue on. They are done with their evolution but are being held captive by forces that there are not enough of them to alter."

"Such has been the way since the beginning, Destiny. They have had multitude of chances to move onward and still they linger. The law has not suddenly changed, it has always been thus. The hour has always been drawing near. But now they panic that they have missed their ride. The universe cannot stop and wait while these few get ready for the next step."

"But isn't it written that if even one soul remains worthy that the town will be saved."

"That soul will not parish it is true. But just because a soul wants to move on is no guarantee it will happen. Life is about getting what is needed for advancement, not what is wanted. Mind you in some very rare cases the outcome is the same."

"Please sir. I implore you. I do not make excuses for their lingering. I do however have compassion for their reason. These few that I speak of have fallen in love. Not fallen in love with emotion like the others. They have not given their souls to sensation but to love. Opened their heart to another soul and become part of each other's lives. Woven together like one single tapestry. Some have fallen in love with a place a world where beauty unfolds around each corner. Life explodes from every atom. But what better place to experience the fullness of beauty and love than in a world such as theirs. Who of us here cannot remember the beauty? But they have loved too deeply. If that is possible. Become too intertwined with the physical dimension and now they are trapped. I don't see anywhere in the law where one should suffer because they have loved."

"But why jump? Is there not something that you can do from here?"

She saw a glimmer of hope for her request. The Grand Master of the Assembly was asking for details. A sign he was open for the idea.

She continued her plea. "The majority have chosen to be oblivious to any other reality of dimension or energy other than their own. Totally and completely focused on the dimension in which they view with their eyes. They are blind to what they cannot see. That's why I feel if I go back to their dimension I can influence them from there. Open their eyes. At least I can try to add to the positive energy and perhaps lesson the opposition enough for some to break through the cloud of darkness. The day is not yet upon us. I believe there is still time to make a difference. At least   I'd like to try."

Adam, the man sharing the floor with her as well as her life, spoke not to the assembly but directly to Destiny. "We do not go backwards. It isn't done." his voice thundered with authority.

Her voice even softer, only his ears could hear, a hint of sadness. "True, but unlike you I am not yet completely transmuted to this level. I can still go back if I choose."

He turned to the council to plead his case as he had no influence over her. "She lets her compassion speak for her. Lead her actions. We need to decide with logic and impartiality."

She spoke even though the comment was not directed to her. "Who are you to speak of compassion? Didn't you pull me before my time from the grips of the physical dimension?"

"I couldn't bear to see you in pain." his words soft, his tone pleading.

"Is not pain the best and fastest teacher on the lower vibrations?" she shot back still arguing her side.

With eyes closed he repeated. "I could not bear to see you in pain."

The Grand Master cleared his throat ready to give the council's decision. "This banter could go on forever. But Destiny is within her rights. And she is wise in choosing this date as there is, as she said, still time to alter the outcome and severity of devastation of the inevitable. It is in the interest of all, that we grant this visitation. Go with our blessing."

Adam made one last attempt at shifting their decision. "Her compassion will make her vulnerable. You know it will. She will have no defenses against the negative energy. And being a concentrated source of positive she will be an eminent target."

"It's true compassion makes us illogical even vulnerable, but not defenseless. We have faith for that. Have faith in her, Adam." The Master rose with the other members of the high echelon.

Adam conceded and felt guilty to hear his attitude compared with lack of faith in this woman. That was the farthest thing from the truth. But she knew that. Or at least he would have to make sure she knew that before she took her jump. Eyes the color of crystal blue carried him back to the beginning of time. She smiled up at him and all was right with the world. There was no passing of time in this reality. He was thankful for that. For upon her return it would be as if she never left his side. It would be as if he never took his eyes away, never blinked. But for her it was another matter entirely. Once she jumped she would have to fulfill the outlined life she chose for her soul to encase. Even if, and it always did in that dimension, include pain.

She broke the silence. "I have to go now."

"So soon? You've found a suitable situation then?"

"Yes actually they've found me a pod of significant positive energy. You don't have to worry." She looked up at him rather sheepishly.

"So you've been planning this a while." he tried his best at looking stern but failed miserably.

"Yes, but I really do have to go. It's my birthday."

"Happy Birthday then." he kissed her on the forehead creating a series of tiny sparks between them.

"Thanks. Could you promise me something first?"

"You don't even have to ask. I'll promise you anything."

Her face become sober with a crease of worry between her eyebrows. "Don't let me forget my way home."

He held her tighter in his embrace and the fine thread of light between them disappeared. "I'll be right here. I promise I won't let you forget. As for what the Master said, it's not a question of my faith in you. You know that?"

Dark lashes pulled a curtain over the crystal blue. Destiny nodded. And then she jumped.

A hand rested on his shoulder as the assembly dispersed. "You know it had to come to this. She was not done on the lower level yet. Her slate was not in balance." The Grand Master consoled.

"I still will not be able to bear seeing her in pain."

"Then do what you must. But give her time to do what she must. Let her complete her compassion."

"Her love is too strong for that dimension now. I should know. She could get tangled in the web just like the other souls she spoke of."

"She *is* one of those souls Adam. And now she must break the ties."

*   *   *

Forty some years had passed to Destiny. Luckily it had been nothing to Adam. He was the one to call the assemble this time.

He plead his case as passionately as she had. "The time is drawing close. Destiny has done what she set out to do. She has significantly given positive energy to the race. It is up to the scales to decide from now. I am going to bring her back, I don't need your permission I only called this assemble to inform you of my intentions."

The Grand Master spoke for the rest. "We expected her return before this. She is pushing the time limit. You know there isn't much time left. Events are happening rapidly now. The future does not look good for that dimension. It is in the hands of as they refer in that dimension, Mother Nature. The world is balancing itself. We hope she has broken her ties by now or bringing her back could prove difficult. Has she forgotten how to return on her own?"

Adam bowed his head slightly. "I don't know. I intend to find out."

"You go with our blessings of course."

A frail woman came to stand beside Adam as the assemble filed out. The woman was almost completely transparent with light. Her name was Mira. "You aren't going to jump. You can't."

"No. But I'm going to bring her back all the same."

"She has added considerably to the energy down there. The opposing darkness will not let her through easily. Her way will be barred. Darkness always tries to consume the light." short choppy sentences drifted over the waves as a bottle bobbing slowly into shore. Her tone still childlike even though her existence started long before his own.

He smiled ever so slightly."Thanks for the full color details. It won't be easy I know."

"I'm going to help you." A smile softened the worried lines of her forehead.

"Thank you but you don't have to, Mira. You are past agony and suffering. It won't be pleasant to feel and see those things again. To be subjected to the horror. I can do this alone."

"It never hurts us to be reminded of the past. That insures we keep moving forward. I'm helping you. Besides you forget the bond I have with Destiny. Perhaps I can help her remember."

"Let me try it alone first. No need in more getting tangled in a web than is necessary. But I'll call you if I need you. OK"

"I'll be here."

Chapter 2

Beep. Beep. Beep. The unanswered question since the beginning of time. Life force. What is it? If it could be seen in this very moment, reduced to its simplest form it would be a flash of light on a black monitor. Was that the essence of life then? A spark of Light in a sea of Darkness. Beep. Beep. Beep.

The rhythmic sound of an automatic door opening and closing, opening and closing, opening and closing. The rhythm ran consecutive with the air being pumped into the lungs. Air in. Air out. The tube ran down the throat into the lungs themselves. The woman was held captive by a web of tubes. Some coming in, others going out. Vital fluids, blood, food, medication, antibiotics. All trying to take over the job of the spark of light in the sea of darkness.

Two punctured lungs, a broken pelvis, both femurs shattered was the official medical term in her paperwork, eight broken ribs, and several fractured vertebrae coming dangerously close to severing the spinal cord. Ruptured spleen, bruised liver, massive concussion, fractured jaw what was left of it. Not one square inch of flesh of normal color. Reddish blue turning purple with complete black patches in between. And a coma to top it off just for good measure. But with the choice of facing this body or running into the darkness of one's subconscious the choice was a no brainier. Destiny chose the dark. Pins, plates, casts and traction tried to put this woman back together again. While the only thing playing on her private television in her private room was a spark of light on a black monitor. Beep. Beep. Beep.

A man bent over the patient. Spread one of her eyes open and cast a beam of light into it. Repeated the action with the other eye. He checked her chart. Added some notations to it. Reached down and picked up the delicate hand. It felt cold. He held it between his own to transfer his body heat. Traced the fingers from their knuckles to their ends then smiled at a private joke. She hadn't broken a fingernail. Gently as if the slightest movement would break another bone or worse cause her pain. He laid the hand to rest on her stomach.

"The family is asking again Dr. Adam." The nurse from the desk came once again to see if the family could be allowed in the room.

"OK. How many are there?"

"There's three up here. Her husband and two children. Her Father is still waiting downstairs."

"I'd prefer just one at a time. And keep an eye on the monitors. If there is any change get them out of here."

His sky blue eyes held the tiniest bit of moisture as he gazed down at the woman. This scene would contradict the title the hospital shift gave him of Iceberg Adams, when he brazenly took over the care of this patient. With his index finger he stroked the woman's cheek leaving a trail of fiery light.

The woman's husband entered the room first. Tears came more easily and more profusely to this man. He fell to the woman's side grabbing her hand and sobbing into it.

"Be careful!" the doctor snapped.

The man looked up at him as if in a drunken stupor. "I'm sorry. Is she.. Is she going to.." he couldn't continue.

The doctor turned mind reader answered as best he could. "We did, and are doing all we can. We'll have to wait and see. I'd say it's up to her now. Was your wife a strong person? Healthy?"

The man pet her hand with more care. "She's never been sick a day in her life. The only time she was in the hospital was to have the kids. And I think she probably would have preferred to have them at home had it been the popular thing to do."

"Sounds like she's tough then. That's probably a good thing."

"I don't know what to do. Nothing has ever happened to her before. She hasn't even had so much as a scratch."

"Well, sounds like she's been saving it up." he tried not to look at the woman. Not while her husband was in the room. He checked connections on the monitor, read the settings on the oxygen, traced the tube from the drip down till it came dangerously close to her hand then dropped it abruptly.

For lack of anything better to say and still being captive in his state of stupor the husband looked at the doctor with fire in his eyes. "Money is no object. Do you understand? I want her to have the best care. And if that can't happen here. We'll move her."

The doctor kept his composure, " I strongly advise against that. Moving her would be a grave mistake." then felt awkward for not searching for a better word to express himself. The man didn't seem to pay him any mind.

The husband stood as if someone else controlling his body drew him up by marionette strings. The controller thrust the man's hand out toward the doctor. "I've been brusque with you. I apologize. I'm James. Destiny, " briefly his eyes glanced down at the captive woman, "is my wife."

The grasping of hands is an odd tradition. Meant as a gesture of greeting or farewell. Often used as sign of bonding or agreement, sealing a deal. The physical implications are relaxing causing one to reduce or drop the guard. If aliens were to invade the planet no doubt the first tradition they would try to mimic would be the handshake. Once the hands parted the friendship rushed in to fill void between them.

"I'm Dr. Adams. They call me a lot of things around here. Most of them pertaining to the lower end of the Celsius scale but you can call me Adams. I'm not known for my tack. I don't see any reason to colorize the scene. But I can promise you that will in no way detract from my doing everything I can to care for your wife."

"OK. Sounds good. The truth is what I want. But I'll talk to the kids. Hannah tends toward the dramatic."

"Fine with me."

"I didn't know what to expect when I got here. She was hit by a semi. I didn't expect this. She had gone out to get the mail the neighbor said. She loved getting the mail not the e-mail type. Real honest to God mail. The semi was like it was out of control. It plowed into her center line. Took out the mail boxes and a tree. He came out without a scratch. I'm insisting on a alcohol and drug test. There was no way he could have not seen her or the tree. I'm suing of course. That's why money will be no object. You can count on that." He traced the tubes with his eyes the monitors, the ropes leading to pulleys attached to the ceiling. The Beep. Beep. Beep. Hypnotized him.

Adams looked at the woman's face, the long dark eyelashes curving upward in the air. The little ski jump of a nose now black and swollen. "It never gets easy. But actually she was pretty lucky. Did

21

you notice she didn't even break a nail?"

James looked aghast then grabbed her hand. He started to laugh. It would become his joke, his comic relief, his way of lightening the mood when the days drug on. As the weeks would pass and friends and coworkers would question how Destiny was doing he would answer. 'Hey my girls a tough one. She took a semi head on and didn't even break a nail'.

"I'd like to do something. You know to help. Is there anything I can do?" The husband was sincere with his request though he hoped the help would be minimal. He hated hospitals, and hated blood even more. A nosebleed would take him to his knees. Whether it was his or someone else's. He didn't know if he could even walk into the room. It took everything he had. He was thanking God there was no gaping holes or running blood.

"Do you pray?" The doctor inquired.

"I meant something here. To help her."

"Oh." Adams answered in surprise. That's what he was referring to with his last suggestion. He raised his eyebrows trying to think of something that the husband might possible be able to do. Something that might at least make him think he was doing something to help this woman's condition. "Maybe you could talk to her. Her brain is showing activity. She's just hiding in a dark corner of it. Maybe if you talk to her, she'll find her way back."

James looked tormented. Confused. "I don't know what you mean. I thought she was in a coma."

"That doesn't necessarily mean she can't hear. Can't register." Adams demonstrated. Standing beside her he bent down, stroked a few strands of hair from the top of her ear. The touch left a trail of fire, electric sparks. He looked up at James to see if he was watching. "Nothing too complicated. Just say her name." he turned every fiber of his attention toward Destiny and whispered in her ear. "*Destiny.*"

The warm air turned into pure energy. Like the breath of life, it passed through her ear canal electrified the nerve endings in her brain and gave a warm rush of life to her body like a slow sip of brandy to a frostbitten victim. All sense receptors aroused. Pleasure neurons stood up and took notice. Consciousness headed toward a glimmer of light on the horizon. Home. All the warmth and safety of home was right over the horizon. Home was where the light was. It wouldn't take her long now. She was almost there. She could feel the temperature rise on her face. Then a pause. A turn in the other direction. Something pulled her attention toward the darkness. When someone called your name a person had to respond. It was instinctive.

James had bent down and called her name in the opposite ear. Just as the doctor had done. "Destiny! Destiny! Come back to us. We need you." The tone of a desperate man in a desperate situation would be expected to be desperate. But not with this man either he wasn't anxious to have his wife back or he served too many years in the army. The words were blunt, almost angry if any emotion could be detected at all.   He might as well be calling for a cleanup on aisle nine.

The call was not nearly so pleasant. It felt like an order. It felt like if she turned and headed back in the direction of the darkness it would be out of obligation. Obligation instead of what her heart longed to do. She was torn. So she lay down right in the middle. Between the two voices and went into a deep sleep and began to dream.

Beep. Beep. Beep.

Chapter 3

A woman strolled down a blackened lane. No hurry to her step, the passing eye would assume the shadow following close behind held no threat, no concern, no sorrow or despair. Only a dark spot on the ground as result of the woman's form standing between the ground and the orb in the sky. Far off in the distance something kept her spellbound. Something out there that she was trying to bring into focus but just couldn't. Holding her head high she was determined to not hang her head. Bravery would get her through this day. This path to the mailbox and back, this quarter mile stretch had been walked for twenty-five years. The exact number of times could be calculated if there was any need or request. None came to mind. But even though the path had been traveled it was now different. Nothing was as it was before. The trees lining the lane were older than the pioneers but they were different now. The turn of the century two story Tudor waiting patiently at the end of the lane was different than it had been before. Everything was different. Not new different, as with the feeling that heightens every nerve ending with anticipation of the unknown. But just different as in it had never been before. Death did that to things, to people. Stole the familiarity from all that surrounded it or all that it had come into contact with. And held it captive in an unknown place.

The return trip to the house took an eternity. In a tortoise hare race she would be the last one crossing the finish line, but not care nor even realize she were in a race. No matter the time consumed by this daily ritual. Nothing demanded this woman's attention or her time. On her fortieth birthday she had sworn to make this a new beginning. A vibrant second half of her life. So they began to eat healthy, walk, and exercise regularly, even went dancing at the local dance partners club. An entire cupboard in the kitchen was dedicated to every product on the market to ward off natural decay of the body. But they had no defense against planes, trains or automobiles. The letters in her hand were becoming fewer every day. The first week after her husband's death the mail carrier drove up to the door. All the cards wouldn't fit into the mail receptacle. 'So sorry for you loss' had begun to echo in her dreams. The card companies really needed to come up with a new line. The thought was nice and considerate but the wording went on and on. Some of them being so specific as to address the *recent widow, loss of your husband, life partner*. The short ones were best.

The mail skimmed across the cherry wood dining table. Two years went into the refinishing of the sleeping treasure found at a yard sale. Each joint broken apart, new dowels made, glued, screwed and clamped to withstand a future lifetime of family gatherings. It had served its purpose with little to no complaints. The hand rubbed finish still so shiny it reflected a perfect reversal of the woman seated at the head of the table. The seat always kept for the head of the family. The reflection stared back with no readable expression as if it were strong, confident, and capable. Neatly dressed not a hair out of place. A perfect reversed image. She placed both palms on the table and rose unable to occupy this seat. Not yet, she pulled out a chair on the side of the table and attempted to sit there. The corner leg wiggled and gave a moan when asked to hold up more weight than its own. The glue that held life together was breaking down.

The mail had bumped to a stop against a flower vase. There were still some fading arrangements that needed to be disposed of. That was hard. Flowers were her favorite and hard to throw away until the last bit of fragrance had been inhaled. The ticking of the grandfather clock was deafening. She could stop the pendulum but she couldn't stop time. After the kids grew up and left the house Destiny was home alone every day. The silence was difficult at first but had found its way to becoming a welcome ally. So many thoughts and contemplations were only capable in the silence. She came to enjoy the solitude. Volunteering at the kindergarten class or the convalescent care facility was no place to think about God or how we related to the big picture. And Destiny had been thinking on this subject more and more as the time and silence passed. A break had been taken from this volunteering and in its place the writing of a book had been started. To pass the time and feed her creativity at first she told herself but now there was a road block keeping her from the end of the story.

The silence that engulfed the house was malignant. It was a fast growing tumor threatening to consume her existence. Listening to the radio or television would ward it off but only for a little while. A phone call now and then kept it at bay the longest but the truth was still evident. There would be no interruptions to the silence. No need to stop and fix dinner. Run to the dry cleaners so the suits were ready for the business trip the next week. No planning company dinners, family vacations or couples night out at the theatre. No need to attend the Cooking for Two class at the local community college. All this silence should have been banquet for her creativity to feast. However sitting at the computer screen only produced gibberish. Nonsense words flashed on the screen. Reread, highlighted and deleted. Grief starved one's creativity.

The mail could wait she thought. But it had waited two, no three days. With a cup of coffee in one hand and a knife in the other the attack began. The return labels were all familiar. They had so many friends. In the middle of the second days pile an unfamiliar letter stood at attention. It was from the Town Board of Bendline. Bendline was where she grew up. It was in the middle of the Nevada desert. A natural gravitational pull eastward had managed to get her just about as far away as possible from Bendline and still remain a citizen of this country. No one there could have heard of her loss. And the Town Board made no sense. The other cards were pushed aside as the letter from Bendline took the spotlight.

Dear Ms. Destiny Walker,

We members of the Town Board of Bendline are writing to inform you that we have started a campaign to clean up the town. It has come to our attention that the property you own by way of inheritance, on 3rd Street is in desperate need of attention. The fence is falling down as well as the structure. Your immediate help and attention to this matter would be appreciated before any legal actions would be forced to be taken.

Sincerely,

The Town Board of Bendline.

Destiny sat back in her chair. What? After reading the letter a couple more times the content still didn't make any sense. She found the envelope. Turned it over. The name and address were correct. At least it was a change from the rest of the mail she'd been getting. She'd look into it tomorrow. Tomorrow was becoming her companion. Everything could wait till tomorrow. Sometimes tomorrow was a longer time coming though. It was hard to get out of bed these days. A part of her was gone. Missing. Buried. The part was will. There was no will to do anything. Just a heavy feeling in her chest that wasn't as suffocating if the covers stayed over her head. Determination was fighting it back, keeping it from totally consuming her. In the end it was evident determination would be crowned the victor but for now the battle waged on.

Dawn broke on that tomorrow. Just as it had on all the tomorrows of her life. Sunlight spilled over the sill of her second story window. By the time the beams were horizontal in the room it was late. She had slept in, again. The thought of breakfast didn't sound any better than the thought of dinner had the night before. Coffee. Coffee had been the sustaining substance. They needed to come up with a vitamin enhanced coffee beverage. Perhaps she should work on that. Perhaps not. Today was going to be different from the previous days. Destiny had something to do. An agenda had formed. If the making of lists would have been her attribute, she finally, for the first time in weeks would have had something to put on one. But instead notes were kept in her head. She had a mental block for as long as she could remember for notebooks. If one were to read her mind today they would have read 'contact Bendline.'

E-mail would have been easier. A crack came in her voice when she least expected it. Whether talking on the phone, over the fence to a neighbor or buying groceries. Words would be trailing out of her mouth then all of a sudden like thunder that follows lightning. Crack. Then of course the crack was connected in some manner to her eyes because the rain would start to fall. But, there was no e-mail address on the letter from Bendline. A directory assistance call gave her the number of the Town Board.

"Hello."

"Hello. I'm sorry I must have dialed the wrong number I was calling the Town Board of Bendline, Nevada."

"Oh, you've got it honey. This is the right number. I just answer the phone for my husband's auto mechanic shop, my bookkeeping service and the town board. So instead of saying hello this is Cybil, from Dan's Garage, The Books Kept Right bookkeeping service and Secretary of the Town Board, I just answer hello until I see who the person on the other end wants to talk to. So you are calling for the town board? OK then. Let's back up. This is Cybil, Secretary for the Town Board of Bendline. How may I help you?"

A pause was taken to shake her head and figure out what this woman just said. "Um, yes, OK. Well my name is Destiny Walker. I received a letter yesterday, maybe the day before about a house in Bendline that needs fixing up."

"Yes, isn't it wonderful and about time too. You know we are just sick and tired of all the junk around. It's time for some beautifying. You've heard the expression just pick up and leave. Not here, they just up and leave!   Nobody does any pickin up. And we're sick of it. By we, I mean all of us here that try to keep a decent looking place. So we formed a motion and it took off like wild fire. And I guess you're calling to see about it. I see from this phone tattle tale box we just got, that you live a fair distance away, are you needing the names of some fellows that can spiff up your place for you. Because Ed's Hauling is running a special just through this month. You know to kind of do his part to help out. Do you want his number?"

This woman was exhausting just to listen to. "No that's not why I called. I think you made a mistake. I don't own any property there. I used to live there a very long time ago. But we sold everything when we left, in fact the mine bought my parents out. I just called to tell you, you need to forward this notice to the correct person."

"Oh dear! What have I gone and done. I am so sorry. Just let me get my books out. What was your name again?"

"Destiny Walker."

Pages flipped. The woman made a clucking sound with her tongue. She was either concentrating hard or calling the chickens in for breakfast.

"OK. Here you are. Destiny Walker, 437 Third Street. I have your mailing address as 780 Swan Drive. That sounds just heavenly. Is it nice there?"

"Yes, it's beautiful thank you. But what town do you show?" "Lakehead, New York. New York! Wow! Now this is what I call a long distance call. I don't recall ever talking to anybody that far away. You don't even sound like you have an accent. You sound just the same as we do out west here."

Hopefully she sounded different than this woman but in the intelligence department. "That's my address but I just don't get it. I don't own any property in Bendline."

"Well I don't know what to tell you. They just gave me this list of names and told me to send out the letters. I'm just the secretary you know, they don't give me any of the important record keeping work to do. That would be Della, I guess you could call the records office. Want me to get you the number?"

It seemed to be their error. The logical solution would be for them to call the records office. However Destiny wanted to see this resolved and the woman on the other end of the line had not done anything to gain her confidence.

"I guess so. Yes. What's the number." after a long pause she spoke again. "I'm ready I have a pen."

"Just   a minute I'm looking it up. I can't find the phone book. Oh here it is."

After seven rings the phone connected. "Records. Della."

The explanation was longer this time because Destiny had to explain the details of the prior conversation as well as the original mistake.

"Let me check. Hang on." the phone clunked on a hard surface. A snapping noise, then a local radio station came through the receiver. A talk program something about the annoyance of dogs running loose and messing in other people's yards. The announcer had opened a real can of worms. Dog owners called in perturbed stating that the state had a fence out law. If you didn't want dogs doing their business in your yard then you should fence them out. Yard manicurist called in furious at this claim stating if the owners were going to own a dog they should be responsible for keeping them contained. Just the other day a caller had a dog as big as a St. Bernard jump her fence and leave at least a one ponder. The announcer trying to keep the discussion from getting out of hand interjected that to his knowledge the fence out, law pertained to grazing animal rights not poohing rights

Destiny looked at her clock. After ten minutes she was sure Della must have taken a coffee break.

The sound of the radio snapped off in mid sentence. "OK. Got them. I had to go next door. Destiny Walker owner of said property for the last five years. Blah, blah, blah, do you want me to read all the legal jargon? Anyway you inherited the property from Pearl Appleton upon her death five years ago. It's you alright all the info matches what you told me. And I got a copy of the letter right here in front of me that the town board sent to you."

"Pearl Appleton? But how could that be I was never notified. I didn't know anything about it."

"That would explain the five years back taxes due. Well let's see who handled the affairs. Blair. Five years ago. If memory serves me correctly that was about the time he ran off to Mexico with the new school secretary and his wife's bank account and jewels she inherited from her grandmother."

"Sounds like a swell guy. Why would anyone use him to run such important affairs?"

"Actually he was a pretty nice guy and when he's the only lawyer in a couple hundred miles, what are you gonna do?"

"That was the question I was just asking myself. What am I gonna do?"

"For starters I'm afraid I've got to send you the bill for the back taxes. Let me add it up."

Destiny heard a key being punched on an adding machine, then another key, then another key then. "Damn it. Now I got to start over. New machine."

Tap. Tap. Tap. Tap.

"Would you like to call me back?"

"Shh, I've almost got it. OK $437.82."

"That's it?"

"Yea. Near as I can tell. I'll be sending you the official bill so you can check the addition yourself. It's a terrible chunk to have to come up with I'm sorry, but you know. The only things we can't escape are death and taxes."

"Yes. I do know." her voice cracked. She hung up the phone before the rain started.

Chapter 4

Beep. Beep. Beep.

Grady Murphy sat beside his daughter. Softly stroked her hand. The one that didn't have all the tubes coming out. It only had one cuff over the tip of the finger keeping track of one of her vital signs. Temperature he thought the nurse said or was it pulse? No the monitor beeping away was for that. He really wasn't listening to what the nurse had explained but it didn't really matter. He was careful not to disturb it all the same. Dr Adams had been in to check on Destiny. His news was not hopeful but not completely without hope. James had warned him about this fellow. But Grady couldn't help liking him all the same. Who couldn't like a person that held their daughters life in their hands.

He said to talk to Destiny but that was the strangest part. Usually there was never a seconds silence between them. But now for the life of him he couldn't think of a thing to say. Maybe in reflection it was because Destiny did all the talking. No denying it. She was a chatterbox. She wanted to be a writer once upon a time. That time just never seemed to have come. Maybe if he would have pushed her at it. It seems being passionate isn't enough to steer people's course sometimes. They need an outside wind blowing them in the direction they want to go.

For now he just stroked her hand softly. The right words would come. All at once they would just burst out like a stick of dynamite going off. That's what she told him one time in defense of her chattering. There's so many words inside me I can't keep them shut in sometimes. That was when she was young. Before the accident. It all changed after that.

"My little powder keg." he whispered softly

Beep. Beep. **Beep**! Her dream hit a happy note.

Chapter 5

"Dad? Hi its Destiny. Did I wake you up?"

"No. gosh no. Destiny, my little powder keg. How you holding up?"

"Honestly Dad, I feel like I've been run over by a truck. Not physically but emotionally. Every nerve ending of my psyche is screaming in agony. But you know that don't you?"

"Yea spose I do."

"Why didn't you tell us Dad? What you were going through."

"I guess I didn't have the gift of expression like you do Destiny. But your description sums it up."

"I'm sorry Dad. That I wasn't there through all of it when mom died."

"Now don't go talking like that. You are the only person I know that can think of someone else in a time her whole life is falling apart. You just worry about healing yourself and make sure the kids are doing OK too.   Are they calling you? If they don't call you, call them. That was one of my regrets. I just bottled up and didn't realize you were hurting too. I guess I figured since you had someone else in the house your heart wouldn't be hurting. But I was wrong wasn't I?"

"Let's not talk about right or wrong OK. But, yes the kids are communicating, like clockwork, e-mails several a day. Lance just started his new job. They were so good to him to let him off for the two weeks. I don't know what I would have done without him. Without both of them. But, they had their lives to get back to you know."

"Well I was hoping at least Hannah could stay with you a little while longer anyway."

"No. She had school to get back too. And a part time job. I told them I was fine. And I am Dad. It's just going to take time. And that time will go by whether they are in the house with me or not. Just one foot in front of the other isn't that what you said when mom died."

"Yea, I guess. To tell you the truth I really don't remember. It was all kind of a fog."

"I understand that. I don't know if I will ever get used to the term WIDOW. What a perfectly deplorable word. Anyway, on to the next foot, enough sad talk. I got a letter in the mail a few days ago. Seems I own a place in Bendline now."

"What are you talking about. You didn't go off and buy a place clear out there did you?"

"Buy. No, God no. especially not in Bendline, Nevada. That's a whole country away. No, a Pearl Appleton left it to me. Do you remember her?"

"Yes. I remember Pearl. Do you?"

"Not really. The name sounds familiar but the only recollection would be from stories you and mom would tell. Anyway she died five years ago. And left her place to me. I haven't the foggiest notion why."

"You were close to her Des. She had a little girl. You used to sort of baby-sit for her. I don't think she had any other family. It's nice she remembered you. I know it meant so much to her everything you did for her little girl. No   memories?"

"No bells dad. I can't recall a thing. When I called the town records to try to get to the bottom of all this mistake, wow was that an experience. There was some ridiculous story about her lawyer running off with some secretary at that time. He filed all the papers on that end just neglected to forward me any kind of notification."

"Sounds like the town is pretty much still the same."

"I don't know how we lived there for fifteen years Dad. I was blown away just trying to talk to the office help for half an hour."

"So they finally notified you about ownership?"

"Actually no. the town is on some big cleanup campaign and I guess this place I own is a real eyesore. The letter was to notify me that clean up would be appreciated or they would take legal action."

"They don't have a leg to stand on. Tell them all to go to hell."

"Whoa. Don't get your heart rate up. I wasn't calling to upset you. Actually I thought I might take a trip out there. See what the place looks like. If it looks promising I think I might stay for a while. Clean it up and maybe put a for sale sign out front. I was just calling to talk it over with you see what you thought."

"I don't know Des, I don't think it's what you need right now. It's only been what two months."

"What I need is something to do. And well at least from the sound of things there would be plenty of hard labor involved. If I stay here, I just feel like I'm being swallowed up. Everyone I see wants to talk about the accident. Give me a hug. It's wonderful of them dad, but I'm just screaming on the inside. I need some time away from all this. And there no one would know. I could just deal with it on my own and heal on my own."

"But you don't know what you'll find there Des. That conk on the head all those years ago was touch and go for a while. The trauma was so great you just checked out. Forgot it all. The doctor said in time you would probably recall the memories bit by bit, but I don't think adding total recall from thirty years ago to what you're dealing with now is such a good idea. You might have a total meltdown."

"Dad, you're being dramatic. Give me some credit. I'm not fragile. I'm your powder keg remember? Nothing's going to happen. Except maybe I'll learn how to breathe again. Besides, I think twenty five years is long enough to wait for a memory to come back Dad. If it hasn't come back yet I doubt it's going to. It's buried too deep."

"When were you thinking of going."

"I can get a flight to Vegas in two days."

"I can't talk you out of it. At least ask you to wait."

"Nope."

"Can I ask you why you called then?"

"What do you mean? I called to get your advice. To talk it over with you."

"You called to get my advice so you could ignore it?"

"Yea, I guess so. I'll keep in touch." She giggled. Then felt a pang of guilt for feeling joyous.

"Be careful Des."

"Dad you sound like I'm going to fall in a mine shaft or something."

"Once in a lifetime is enough for that."

Selective amnesia. Destiny had gone through her whole life with only half of a life. Her life began at fifteen. Not having a childhood bothered her sometimes. There was a time when she ached to know her past. What did she get for her tenth birthday, who were her friends, did she have any pets. She used to fire questions at her parents over the evening meal. Who am I? Then as time worked it's magic she started to become her own self. It didn't matter so much who she was, if she was liked or disliked. There was just the endless future ahead of her to be. So she left the past dead and gone. Perhaps she was hoping to do the same thing in this town once again. Leave another chunk of her life there and move on into the future.

Chapter 6

The thrust of her back against the seat as the jet rose higher and higher to cruising altitude resembled a feeling of freedom. Birds must feel like this all the time. No wonder they look like they never want to come back to the confines of earth. They just find an airfoil and circle round and round. Up, up, up take me away Destiny thought. As she leaned her head against the back rest. Take me away from this sorrow. At least for a little while. Let me soar.

Looking around the plane, what a marvel mass transportation was. All these people, all their separate stories intersecting for a few hours in the air. Gliding across the earth. Would there be any life changing encounters on the shared space of time? Or would everyone remain in their own private world keep the boundaries intact and pray no one tests the strength of that wall. And what about all the life changing events that would be missed. The numbers if one were privy to that universal information would be mind staggering for sure. All the chances not taken, the words unspoken. But in a few hours the chance would be gone. Passed by them all at 750 miles per hour. While they left their seat tray table in the upright and locked position.

Had Destiny and her husband taken all the chances. Spoken all the words. No. Their life had not been bad. Busy, but not bad. They could have been closer. But that was what the golden years were for. Now she'd have to settle for the silver. And she'd have to settle alone.

A child in the seat in front of her demanded her attention. Playing peek a boo over the top of the seat. Destiny let herself get carried away with the game. Children had a way of making time pass with pleasure.

The tires lurched as the monster flying whale found its way to the arrival terminal. Take offs had always been her favorite, while landings were her least favorite. What goes up, must eventually go down. Too many movies had been made of planes shooting through the end off the runway out into the dirt. Or out into the housing track at the end of the airport. All fears were laid to rest when the seatbelt sign went off and a friendly voice from the cockpit thanked everyone for flying the big blue today. And by the way the temperature was 108 with no end in sight.

108? Holy crap! Maybe the trip should have been put off for a while.

At the car rental counter the attendant was no help in giving Destiny directions to Bendline. He had never heard of the place. So she decided a car with a navigational device would suit her needs. Getting around the small town would be a snap. And there was only one road through Bendline. However Las Vegas was quite a different story. Accustom to the spider web of freeways, there was no intimidation to deal with. But the thought of getting on the wrong road with no exits in site was a catalyst to take precautions. Three hour drive awaited her departure. The sun going down would make the drive cooler. The automatic doors parted and a blast of heat hit her face. Like standing in front of a homecoming bonfire. A term her mother used to use came to mind. Destiny smiled to herself and agreed. This, must be hell.

The drive took forever. How could there be so many miles of nothing but dirt and heat waves. If she would have remembered anything about this place she never would have chosen to come back. Anything that had been left for five years unattended in this arid environment wouldn't be worth salvaging. The half way mark on the navigator screen was passed. It was too late to turn around. Into the direction of the sunset the road stretched to infinity. With each mile the skin on her face got tighter and dryer. To pass the time she stuck her hand out the window to let it surf over the oncoming air waves. The bones ached from the heat within a minute. Something caught her eye off to the side. In stride parallel to the road, a bird. Or what appeared to be a bird, spread stick legs out in front taking long jump steps. A tuft of feathers on the top of the head gave him a look of insanity. An expression of what am I doing here? And how do I cross the road? Beep. Beep. Then gone. Fading into the sagebrush, leaving behind only a question in the mind. Was it a hallucination brought on by the heat?

What started out a four lane divided freeway, turned to a two lane road with a wide shoulder, then a two lane road in serious need of repair. As the lanes narrowed the ribbon of road went from flat to following every dip and gully in the surrounding terrain. Pot holes and washouts littered the surface. The roadside crosses offered the final testimony of the less alert drivers. Dusk had absorbed the last ray of sunlight. In the distance the road disappeared from view. Two modest mountains joined softly at the base instead of a dead end a narrow passage wound through the two sentinels. Emerging from the other side of the canyon around a wide curve Bendline began to appear as if a signature was being written across a black piece of paper with sparkle ink. The lights across the valley came into view one after another.

Chapter 7

Beep. Beep. Beep.

Visiting hours were long over. The family was convinced there was nothing to be done during the hours they should be sleeping so they returned to the comfort of their own beds. Buried themselves along with their worries under homemade covers and quilts. Each stitch lovingly sewn with them in mind. The king size bed was far too big for James to sleep in alone so he pulled out the sofa sleeper in the den instead. He wondered how Destiny had slept there on the weeks he was gone on business. Maybe she didn't. Maybe she opted for the den as well. Maybe she was lonely and couldn't sleep at all. He never asked her. There was a lot he never asked her.

The lights never go out in a hospital. The shadows only get longer. Her room was the gradient of twilight. If she could have opened her eyes there would have been no sharp form she could have made out. The objects all blended into one another. A pleasant wave of warmth and love had passed through her earlier. Like the one she felt before when she heard someone call her name. Someone from the light. But it was gone now. There was only emptiness when she searched her thoughts. Not total darkness, not the light of day. Only grey, dim light. Like the room that entombed her body.

A triangle of bright light passed over the room then disappeared as the closing of a book. A darkness came closer to her. Not that the illumination in the room had changed at all but the darkness that can only be felt from the absence of light, the absence of joy and love. The void of all things good. Her brain sent a signal to her ears which did not respond. There were no sounds vibrating the bones in the inner ear. The cloud moved closer and closer. Closing in on her from every direction. She was being suffocated. Existence was being sucked out of her as the darkness stalked her deeper into a black hole of nothingness.

"Who are you? What do you want?" Her mind screamed out but the thoughts were absorbed by the abyss.

Her resolve was weakening her grip on life slipping away. The spark that was her and her alone was dimming. One last cry for help was all she had left. "Please!"

Three floors above her slouched on an office couch, Dr Adams jerked awake in a cold sweat. He raced out of the room. Down the long hall he smacked his palm against the button to the elevator stopping his forward motion. The doors did not respond, he hit the button again. Two more times. Feet spun around and decided to head down the corridor on the right. The door at the end offered no argument when hit at a dead run allowing his momentum to take the steps two and three at a time. Three floors down he swung the door open. Straight ahead the hem of a dark overcoat fluttered just as the elevator doors met in the middle. His mind was focused on other matters so only briefly recorded the scene.

Past the nurses' station, she never looked up from her computer screen. The door to Destiny's room was closed tight. Not how he had left it half an hour ago. Adams thrust it open. There lie his patient. The breathing tube ripped from her throat laying beside her on the bed. The machine still making a sucking sound. Tubes were ripped from her hands. He pushed the emergency button on the wall. The response was immediate. All available nurses and staff flooded into the room. The room turned to an ant hill some little boy had poured boiling water into just to see what would happen. Half a dozen voices shouting orders the other half dozen carrying them out. Medical supplies rushed in on cold metal carts, the room became warm with too many bodies. How many people did it take to save one life. A riddle indeed. A riddle with no answer.

He started with the breathing tube. It would be the most critical. Sliding it back down the passageway deep into the lungs. He spoke her name repeatedly as he worked to repair the damage done. The beeps were getting weaker.

"*Destiny.*" the doctor whispered her name for only her to hear.

The pleasurable feeling had returned. So warm so inviting. The hearing of the one word summed up every wonderful loving thing a person would ever want to hear. She tried to move toward the pleasure. The voice. But the darkness was so thick, quicksand made of tar holding her. The more she tried to move to the voice the stronger the quicksand pulled her down. She dared not move lest she be pulled deeper into the abyss.

"*Destiny.*"

Didn't the voice realize she could not move. It wasn't that she didn't want to. With all her heart she wanted nothing more. But she couldn't.

Beep, weaker still.

"*Destiny. Please.*" he put his mouth to her ear and sent the whisper to her soul.

If she could relax enough. Not fight the abyss but not give into it either perhaps she could slip out. The hold on her got stronger the more she fought. Like a Chinese finger trap. The way to escape was not to struggle but to relax. Relax.

"*Destiny.*"

I'm trying. Just give me a minute she thought. It was all she could do not to run for the horizon. Sprint to this voice. The promise of hope, love and safety. Be calm. Completely still. She willed every cell in her body to be still. Willed the blood to stand still. No resistance. No breathing. No heartbeat. The grip from the opposition loosen. Like a lion realizing the prey was his to do with as he would.

Her breathing stopped. The beep on the machine was gone. Nothing but a flat line across the black screen. The spark was gone.

"**Damn it! Destiny!**" tools on the tray rattled. His yell awakened the whole floor.

Beep! Beep! Beep!

She pulled free. With nothing to hold onto the tar quicksand evaporated into nothing. Went back from whence it came. The feeling Destiny returned to was not as pleasurable as she last remembered. But it would do.

The doctor turned to those standing in wait around her bed. "She's back. We've got her back. Good job everyone. Good response time. Let's get this mess cleared out of here."

The breathing machine was back to normal. The blips on the screen were steady.

The crowd of nurses and assistants returned to their normal night shift duties. The doctor satisfied himself of Destiny's condition then headed down the hall.

He slammed his hand down on the counter top of the nurses' station. "I want to know who the hell was in that room!"

The nurse that had missed his dash past the station previously jumped in her chair.

"No. No one was in the room. She didn't have any visitors Doctor." she was young her voice frail and trembling. Eyes bulging in shock.

"Someone was in there and ripped the breathing tube out of her throat."

"There was no one sir." The girl was questioning her own thoughts. But still came up with the same conclusion. No one had gone in the room. "Maybe she started thrashing."

"She's comatose!"

"Could she have woken up?"

"She could have died."

"I. I." she was near tears. "I was here the whole time I didn't see anyone go by."

"That's obvious." His voice was returning to a normal tone. He would get nowhere with her. She couldn't tell him what she didn't see. "You didn't even see me run by. Did you?"

Her tears began. She shook her head.

"Give me her chart."

He stared back at the elevator door. As he had come through the stairway doors someone was boarding the elevator. That may have been why the car was unresponsive on his floor. Was that him. The trench coat boarding the elevator?

"Are there any monitoring cameras in here?" he asked the nurse.

A folder was placed in front of him. It had a wet droplet on the cover. Wiping her nose with a tissue she answered. "I don't know of any sir."

Looking around at the ceiling all he noticed were sprinkler heads. No black domes hanging from the ceilings. There was probably an area of the hospital more secure. With a sign in desk. If he contacted the authorities of the incident there would be all kinds of inquires of the family. He wouldn't do that yet. He would try to handle it. He pushed himself away from the desk. It was going to be a long night. The chair in Destiny's room was not as comfortable as the couch in his office. But that was OK. The idea was to stay awake. He pulled a cell phone from his pocket. The number rang several times.

He spoke quietly into the mouthpiece. "I'm going to need your help after all."

His patient lay peaceful now. For all he knew she could be dreaming.

Chapter 8

The Rest Stop Motel and RV was dark when tires came to a stop. One lone light bulb illuminated a sagging screen door. Under the bulb was a sign. Obviously homemade. It was nothing more than a vinyl for sale sign turned over and marked with a wide black felt marker the word **Office**. The screen door squeaked. On the door there was an envelope taped to the glass. The front of the envelope was scribbled 'Walker #5 yer late'. Inside the envelop was a key attached to a scrap piece of red electrical wire.

With key in hand the hunt was on for #5. The office was in the center of the complex so to speak. Stepping back Destiny counted four rooms on the right of the office and four rooms on the left of the office. There didn't appear to be any additional wings. Unruly shrubs encroached most of the doors. The plaster was coming off in large chunks. And God help the place if it decided to rain. It was under a major remodel or abandonment. The latter was more likely.

First on the agenda was to find a room number. One of the eight doors surely had a number. The room just to the left of the office had a metal number four tacked to the outside of the door. It had been painted over several times but it was obviously a number four. By reasonable deduction if the numbers went from left to right that should mean the room just to the right of the office would be number five. She inserted the key. Nothing. Jiggled it. Nothing. Shouldered the door a few times but could not convince it to allow her entry. In surrender she tried the next door to the right. Bingo. Who'd have thought? The musty smell brought on a coughing attack. Exhausted she looked around outside into the dark shadows. Searching the town for another motel was an unbearable thought. A long shower and sleep was all her body called for. How bad could the room be? She flipped on a light. Flipped it off. Out in the car one of her suitcases held nothing but a sleeping bag. It was packed as a last thought, in case the house would be inhabitable. The sleeping bag was unrolled over the top of the bed in the dark. Destiny crawled deep inside, covered her head and cried herself to sleep.

Mornings used to be her time. Before her time fell apart. She had set the alarm on her watch. To start the day early. The first rays preparing the sky for the coming attraction were her favorite. While the room was still dark she dressed. A new pair of running shoes were purchased before leaving the civilization she knew so well and loved. In high school she had done some running. Cross country. It was time to start running again.

As light flooded the room through the sheer curtains the walls began to move. Her eyes had gotten tired from the drive. Such unfamiliar scenery. And the heat waves everything jiggled back and forth. Sunglasses should have been worn but they were in her suitcase instead of her purse. The effects of the eye strain were still with her. Blink. Blink, blink, blink. The motion of the wall wouldn't stop. Forcing her shoulders back as far as they would go in perfect posture, Destiny closed her eyes. Put her palms over them tight so no light would leak through then opened and closed them several times. Took her hands away. The motion was still there. She walked up close to the walls. Ants?

Where she was running to was not important. The town was not that big. Any road should lead to the surrounding foothills. Behind the motel was a dirt road. The running was soft on her feet and knees it would be a good road to start the conditioning on. She ran. The slight incline was good on her heart. Right away the blood was flowing fast. The chambers kicked into overdrive. The slight incline took her past several streets lined with mobile homes. Some had fenced yards others had wandering yards, while others had no yard at all. The road ended at the foot of the mountain. Destiny went straight. Straight up the side of the mountain. Her heart complained, her lungs gasped, her muscles cried in pain. It didn't hurt bad enough yet. Her intention was to climb midway up the hill then level off and run the rim of the hills that engulfed the town. Her lungs were bursting. The muscles right above her knees were on fire. The shoes were good. In that respect she had gotten what she paid for. Sweat came swift. Drops formed at the hairline then started to trickle down both sides of her face just in front of her ears. Her heart beat with a loud swishing sound. With one final gasp she cried out in pain and doubled over tears ran down her face.

Falling over forward on all fours. The air couldn't enter her lungs fast enough. Stars formed in front of her eyes. A ringing in her head. The breaths were taken slow and deep holding for a count of four heartbeats then exhaled expelling hard every last molecule of air. This was repeated over and over, inhale, four heart beats, exhale. The blood oxygen level raised enough to offer some relief. The sun up in full force now beat hard on her back. Taunting her 'have you had enough yet?' the temperature must have already been ninety. Seemed impossible but if the night only got down to eighty it wouldn't take long to make the climb. A sip of water and a squeeze on her face. Not quite reaching her goal in height mentally a rock was marked. It still didn't hurt bad enough. Turning to encircle the town this track was easier. She allowed herself a slower pace at first. Speeding up as her legs hurt worse and worse. Tears on her cheeks seeped back into the ear canal from the wind against her face. It still didn't hurt bad enough.

There was no animal trail to follow. The trail she found would be her own. Jumping over small sage, darting around larger ones. The ankle twisting one way with one step and the opposite direction with the other as her foothold slid over the edges of rocks. It still didn't hurt bad enough. Lizards led the way onward. This was their territory they knew it well. Rabbits darted out of hiding to take cover further up the hill and watch from a safe distance this woman inflict such torture. A cramp in her side was ignored for as long as possible. The stop was sudden. A hand grabbed her side and squeezed hard. Rain hit the ground falling from the tip of her nose. The shirt and shorts felt like a trip had been taken through the sprinkler. Every inch was soaked. The town looked fuzzy. She headed in that direction hoping the haze would clear. It still didn't hurt bad enough. She would run again tomorrow.

The shower in the motel room was wet. That was all. The metal stall stood up in the corner looked to be an afterthought. The edges where the stall met the wall were at one time sealed but after years of use or neglect the sealant was gaping and the mold was trying to fill the void. Destiny used her running shorts to stand on as the management had forgotten to leave a bath mat. The curtain was drawn across the opening with only fingernails pinching together. The water rained over her and took her away. She was surprised at how easy it was to forget, put out of her mind the disgusting surroundings of the room. She was surprised, but thankful. All the pain in her body swirled down the drain. If only life were really that easy.

The familiar squawk of the screen door announced the arrival of a customer at the Rest Stop and RV office. Hunched over a counter a man stood browsing a magazine. The soiled wife beater t-shirt hung off his boney shoulders like a potato sack. Every inhale drew the skin tighter against the outline of his collarbone. As if his body were trying to extract oxygen through the skin because the lungs were not providing enough. His cologne bore a strong resemblance to beer and sweat but was the perfect companion to the overflowing ashtray beside the man's elbow. The magazine was closed, only after he had finished the last captivating sentence. He tucked it under his elbow on the counter for safe keeping. The picture of an old playboy bunny peaked out. The title and most of the picture were rubbed through from hours of concentration.

He looked up and met Destiny's stare. Four blackened fingers threaded through a few strands of hair on top of his head. His eyebrows raised in a slight arch. A tongue covered the front teeth and a sucking sound spewed from his mouth.

"I'm Mrs. Walker." extra emphasis was implied on the Mrs. The man's eyebrows arched a bit higher. "Are you the owner?" after a long pause the question waiting in the wings to burst center stage was 'do you speak English?'

The sucking noise subsided long enough for a "Yup." he cocked his head to the side and dug at his front teeth with the little finger nail of the hand not protecting Miss October. The piece of bacon finally dislodged and he was then content to chew it like cud.

"You was late."

"I'm sorry I didn't realize there was a closing time."

A smirk revealed his sinuses were congested. "It was two for one down at Mel's. I had to go."

"I couldn't find my room. I thought if the door over there was number four then the next door must be five. But my key wouldn't work."

"How come you thought that one was four, the number was painted over. You know like when you write something then decide to scratch it out." making a back and forth motion in the air erasing a mistake.

"Sorry my mistake."

"Yup." all the flavor was finally extracted from the bacon and a decision was made to swallow. "You owe me thirty bucks."

Destiny dug in her purse to present her charge card.

"Don't take cards. Got to be cash. Read the sign."

Another masterpiece in sign painting was on the wall behind him.

"You took my card over the phone."

"That was to hold the room. Case you was late."

Retrieving the Gucci wallet deep in her bag. A Christmas gift from her daughter. All too expensive Destiny had protested but Hannah had assured her it was Dad's money anyway. This was something she would have never bought for herself but secretly she loved the fact that it was so expensive. However a wallet was enough Gucci for her, she didn't need the purse to go with it. The bill compartment was not bulging with cash. The next stop would need to be an ATM. Cash was not in the forefront of her thoughts as she prepared for the trip to nowhere land.

"I might stay another night. I haven't…"

"Then it's gonna be sixty. No multiple night discounts."

A hundred dollar bill laid on the counter.

"Care to make it three nights and a tip for the maid?" The man snickered in a rasp then broke out in a fit of coughing.

"No. Hopefully two nights will be sufficient."

A burlap curtain hung behind the man closing off living quarters. He disappeared behind the curtain tucking Miss October under his armpit. A murmuring traveled through the thin fabric. A series of numbers was slowly counted out to one hundred. The curtain was flung open, all that could be seen behind the burlap was darkness. The man put a stack of ones and fives on the counter. The magazine was laid out in front of him signaling the business transaction was over. Destiny was excused. "It's all there. I counted it."

The money felt greasy and smelled musty. Destiny stuck the bills in an outside pocket of her handbag. Not wanting to infect the Gucci. Turning to leave the screen came back and hit her on the shoulder as she turned, something she forgot to say. "There are ants in my room."

A long slow huff explained his impatience. From under the counter a yellow and red can was brought out from hiding. It resembled cleanser. With a thud it was set on the office counter and a puff of dust billowed out and hung over the top mixing gradually with the breathing air in the room. Two words caught Destiny's attention. Ant. Poison.

"Does it work?" she inquired.

"Sometimes." His free index finger gathered a dob of spit from his tongue and touched the front cover of the magazine. The page stuck to the tip of his finger and lifted with care.

The screen door slammed. Destiny was now armed and dangerous. A deep inhale before entering the room. Dust was sprinkled around the perimeter along the baseboard. Oddly enough traces of the dust were there from previous applications. Something that had escaped her attention before. She plopped down on the edge of the bed the dust particles danced in the sunlight. She drew in a deep breath not caring for the moment whether the ant poison filled her lungs or not. She could make it through this. She told herself. She'd been through worse. In fact now anything that was faced in the future there would always be that to fall back on. She had been through worse. Her husband's death had become a measuring stick for future events.

Chapter 9

The road coming into Bendline from the south took a dogleg in the middle of town at a single blinking red light. At that dogleg and the busiest corner in town sat Faye's Cafe. No one in town needed to purchase a coffee pot. Because the coffee pot was always on at Faye's. The place filled up at six in the morning and stayed full till nine. Different faces rotated in to take an empty stool. Faye, owner and operator single handedly handled the fifteen odd seats out front and husband Earl had complete domain over the back. He shouted orders to his wife and offered his two bits to the conversations out front via a single order up window. Occasionally he would step through the swinging doors that separated the kitchen from the front. Rubbing his rotund belly and dragging on a half smoked cigarette. His face was perpetually red from the heat of the grille during the day and the beer during the night. A chef's hat was cocked to the side of his balding head. A joke someone had brought back from Hollywood when they got to be a guest in the audience of a cooking show. But earl never came to the front. There was an imaginary line drawn at the swinging doors he never crossed nor did Faye cross it going from the front to the back. They had developed a system that worked for them and they saw no need to mess with it.

Ed slurped coffee from a thick rimmed coffee mug. Coke bottle glasses lifted from the morning paper to enter into the daily conversation. "Got a crazy woman in town."

He had the attention of the others at the counter.

"How's that?" one inquired.

"Saw her this morning. She looked like a jackrabbit being chased by a coyote, she was running clean around town. Only she was running in the hills. Now you tell me that ain't crazy?"

"What time was it?" Ed's partner Ed inquired just joining the conversation.

"Early. Five or better."

"How hot was it?" Asked Faye as she was making the rounds with the coffeepot.

"Ninety I'd say."

"Sounds crazy to me." Several agreed nodding their heads.

"Crazy or plumb scared. She kept looking over her shoulder like she was running away from something. Her ponytail was slapping her back like a jockey with a whip. But she looked mighty fine."

"How could you tell. You can't see two feet in front of you." Faye reminded him.

"I got me some new high powered binoculars."

"There goes the neighborhood." Chimed in partner Ed.

"Mary Clare keep your shades pulled." Earl   poked his head out of the kitchen.

Across the room Mary Clare, the school janitor, squinted her eyes. "You peak at me you'll get more than an eye full."

"Won't work for that kind of peeping. These are real high powered. For distance.   That's how I could see this crazy. I could even see the sweat dripping off her face. "

"Yea what else could you see?" A couple customers turned their stools around to face Ed. Ready for juicy details.

"Tell ya later when we don't have so much mixed company. She's got a real nice stride though. Yea a real nice bounce to her step." He jabbed his partner Ed on the stool next to him. A private joke, the whole place could guess. "There was a time or two I thought she was going to keel over though. She went down on all fours once."

"You contact the paramedics. Just in case?" Faye asked.

"Naw. I let um sleep. I saw them pretty late down at Mel's last night. It was two for one you know."

"Yea. Only his two for one's is turning out to be a quarter to one. I know he waters down." Mary Clair added her observation.

"Least it gets me out of the house. I don't need the alcohol near as much as I need the company."

Faye made a round with a full coffee pot. Topping Ed's cup she said. "Now Ed you hold it right there. Not another word like that. Doc told you to quit getting worked up your heart won't take it. And you get started on Joanie leaving with that truck driver and you'll end up in the paramedic van again."

"Faye I don't think there's a heart left in there." Ed patted his chest.

"Sure there is Ed. It just takes time." Faye said.

The little bell on the door jingled. Destiny wondered if an

angel just got its wings.   To enter the café the door had to be closed before there was room to skirt around the occupied stools.

Everyone turned to stare. Ed poked the occupied stool to his right. A faint whisper. "That's her."

Destiny felt like she was back in the theatre at high school up on stage all alone and she forgot her opening lines. She did what worked back then. She shrugged her shoulder slightly and smiled. There was a few nods and smiles then they turned their attention to other things.

A quiet table to sit and sip her morning coffee, read a little and contemplate the attack of the day was not going to be found here. A voice in her head whispered 'we're not in Starbucks any more Dorothy.' the closest stool was three feet away. And close to the door.

A tall bleach blond with cakes of eyeliner stood in front of her with a single sheet of paper, which was the menu. A coffee pot in one hand and a chipped mug hanging from her finger of the other hand.

"Oh, I'll just have a double shot latte with a splash of vanilla please." Destiny handed the menu back.

"Sorry honey, we don't have any la-te-da coffee here. It's black, cream or sugar. Or if you're feeling real adventurous, you can have cream and sugar like Whitey here." Faye nodded and smiled at the Paul Bunyan man sitting next to Destiny and infringing on her half of the airspace between the barstools.

"I'll have black thank you." Destiny managed. Still feeling front and center in a theater full of strangers.

Faye took a swipe with a damp cloth in front of Destiny dragging the prior customer toast crumbs to the floor on her side of the counter. Splashing coffee over the side of the cup as the steam swirled like a genie escaping a magic lamp. "So hon, what are you doing here? Just passing through?"

The whole café knew by now this was the crazy woman seen running the hills for dear life. If anyone could get a story out of her Faye could.

The runner looked up a bit startled at the inquiry. She didn't think to have a simple cup of coffee would entail spilling her plans and intentions. "Just visiting of sorts."

"Oh, who you visiting? Bet I know them. I know everyone in town."

"Well I'm not visiting a person I'm visiting a place." her eyes swept the room.

Earl had moseyed through the swinging doors and now all eyes were on the runner. Except Destiny noticed a small table by a window. The table only had two chairs but only one chair was occupied. Steam rose behind a copy of the Wall Street Journal. The image was like one of those games she played with her children, what's wrong with this picture? What doesn't fit? This man would be the answer. Just another person sitting in this café but somehow he was outside the boundaries of everyone else. The man dressed like them but when he was poured into the Bendline mold he over flowed it. Trying to be inconspicuous sitting in the corner reading his paper minding his own business. His dress and actions were just a facade. There was much more to this person. He was tall his graying hair showing above the paper. The outline of glasses shown just above the edge. He took a sip of coffee. Destiny looked away.

"So. Where are you visiting then? We get a lot of tourist out to the old ghost town."

"No, I'm not a tourist."

This woman was not making her job easy this morning. Faye could tell the whole place was counting on her. She decided to lay it on the line she didn't have all day.

"Well hon, we just don't have any secrets here. So who or what or where are you visiting?"

Her strategy worked. Destiny caved. How else would this woman leave her to have her coffee in peace. Besides it was no deep dark secret. "It seems I've inherited Pearl Appleton's place and I've come to look it over and clean it up I guess. I got a letter saying it was a real eyesore."

Faye stood back. Put the coffee pot on the counter and her mouth dropped open. "Destiny! Destiny Murphy!"

The man sitting alone put down his paper. The scene had his full attention.

Destiny just looked at the waitress. "I'm sorry, I don't..."

"Faye! It's me Faye Duncan. You remember." she took a step back away from the counter. Put her long arms straight up in the air. " Two bits, four bits, six bit's a dollar, all for Bendline," Faye disappeared behind the counter completely then like a rocket taking flight for the moon she jumped in the air. "stand up an holler!!!!!" Faye topped off the cheer by touching her toe to her hand high above her head. Everyone on the side of the café had a little extra spice added to the morning coffee break. Faye put both hands on the counter and leaned forward right in front of Destiny.

Faye was in great physical shape. No doubt but she had either found a way to defy natures gravity all together or the bosoms right in front of Destiny's eyes were not real. This having no bearing on the prior scene what so ever Destiny looked around at expectant faces. Faces of those waiting to greet an old friend. But none of them looked familiar. Total strangers in a strange town. She had to be honest. "I'm sorry. I don't remember."

"It's Faye. From high school. Varsity head cheerleader four years straight."

"I'm really sorry, Faye is it." Destiny's words began to crack slightly. Perhaps no one would notice. "I know, I mean I guess I used to live here. But I had an accident and to tell you the truth, I have no memory." Destiny lowered her eyes and watched the genie still trying to escape. When would he appear?

Faye just stared at her. Deflated. The man with the wall street journal spoke up. "Faye how 'bout a warm up?"

Faye walked away the café began to buzz with conversation. Destiny sat staring at her coffee mug.

Ed finished his breakfast and hit the man next to him on the shoulder. They each threw down some bills on the counter and nodded to Faye now seated opposite the Wall Street Journal.

Ed paused behind the runner, hesitated then tapped her on the shoulder. Destiny turned to see saucer size eyes looking at her behind coke bottle glasses.

"I'd like to introduce myself and give you my card." Ed spoke up.

Destiny took the card. "Ed's Hauling. The woman at the records office mentioned your name. Or was it the Town Board secretary. I don't remember. Thanks. I haven't seen the place yet. Do you think I'll need your services?"

"Definitely." the two looked at her an nodded. "You just give me Ed a call or this other number here is Ed's you can call him too." Ed gestured to the man standing beside him. He had bib overalls and a big smile. With two missing teeth.

"You're both named Ed?"

"Yea, it's easier that way. And you know what they say, two Ed's are better than one."Ed winked behind the magnifying glass, nearly doubled over laughing at his own funny. They both gave a final wave to the leftovers in the café.

The mood was lightened and Destiny laughed in spite of herself.

The other Ed with the big smile bent down close and whispered. "I got two words for you. Sports Bra." the bell jingled on the door.

Destiny quit laughing to ponder what in the world he meant by that. She scanned the room again to see if anyone else had heard what the man said or seemed to be waiting for some sort of a reaction from her. Coffee and eggs captured everyone's attention except the man with the Wall Street Journal. He smiled. Two deep indentions put his expression in parentheses. The purpose of a parentheses was to set apart, to show something was special, not within the ordinary. That was definitely the description of his smile. Her heart gave a lurch. Then mellowed to a warm glow. Destiny jerked her gaze away. What was that? Had she run too hard? Over taxed herself? Was this the prelude to a heart attack? Or was this the prelude to a memory reoccurrence? Did she have some recollection? Over her shoulder the man was facing away from her now. Talking to the waitress, the four year cheerleader. His profile was strong. There were a few small scars on his face one that cut his dark thick eyebrow nearly in half but gave a gentle raise to the brow. As quickly as it had come the feeling was gone. She turned back to her coffee.

Faye caught Destiny looking at the man. She nudged his arm. "I got to go check out Whitey. Why don't you go say hello. The worst she could do is not remember you."

Faye took the man's money that was sitting next to Destiny. Grabbing the plates and stacking them in a bin under the counter. She gave Destiny a forced smile.

Obviously Destiny had offended her. She didn't mean to but she really had no picture of her what so ever.

Someone cleared their throat next to her. Another business card? Turning to view an outstretched hand she looked up. Pale blue eyes looked into hers. The man had taken off his glasses. They must have been for reading. "I'm Adam." the smile pierced her heart again. "I grew up here too."

The hand was warm and strong. Not limp and lifeless like that of someone working behind a desk all day.

"Nice to meet you. Adam was it?" Destiny studied the man's face for a moment. Trying to picture him a teenager didn't help in recalling old memories. The only feeling out of the ordinary was when he smiled. And that could just be from over exercising. "I'm sorry. Like I told her, I really don't remember."

"No. Don't worry about it. It was a long time ago. And trust me we don't all have a memory like Faye's. I just wanted to say hello. Show you a little home town hospitality."

"Thanks. So do you still live here?"

"I come and go, it's about fifty-fifty I'd say."

The small talk was starting to get to her throat. It wasn't the same subject as at home. But too much talking made her throat crack all the same. "Speaking of going I guess I'd better do just that. According to the two Ed's I've got quite a bit of work ahead of me. I better get started. Maybe you could you tell be where Pearl Appleton's place is?"

"Sure you go straight out the door, up two blocks, turn left for four blocks. The middle one in that block. It will be on your left. You can't miss it. It's the one covered in weeds." Another smile.

"Sounds like paradise. I was hoping to be able to stay there a few nights. Maybe not. How many motels are there in town?"

"Two. The Rest Stop and the Cozy Cot. But I think the Cozy Cot is shut down for a while."

"Remodeling?

"No." The arched eyebrow pulled up further as did the corners of his mouth. "I think the sewer backed up."

"Sounds like I picked the best one then. All I have is an ant invasion. Thanks again. Bye."

Reaching into her Gucci a five dollar bill peeked out of the top. Faye appeared out of nowhere. "Keep it. For old times' sake."

Faye seemed to have overcome the immediate sting of her wounded ego. "Thanks that's very nice of you. Oh, how late are you open? I'll probably be needing some dinner."

"Till eight. Earl what's on for tonight?" Faye yelled over her shoulder.

"Meatloaf. Like every Tuesday night you know that." came a bark from the kitchen.

The bell on the door jingled. Destiny was off in search of her paradise.

Adam turned to Faye and raised his eyebrows.

"Well I don't believe a word of that memory loss crap. She's just too high and mighty anymore. Did you see that Gucci?" Faye was wiping off the counter with a vengeance.

Adam looked somewhere in the middle of the space between them as if this was the place where the past was viewed. He became quiet. "No she's not Faye. She's not high and mighty. She never put herself above anyone and I'll bet that hasn't changed."

"Saying she doesn't remember anything. I'm just not buying it. How could you lose the first part of your life? You'd think by now she would have had some kind of recall. It just doesn't make any sense."

"Maybe she'd have some recall if she wanted to."

"What do you mean?"

"Faye think about it. Would you want to remember?" His tone revealed a hint of anguish.

Detecting a hint of anguish the subject needed to be changed. Faye was after all the self-appointed jester of Bendline, the one responsible for keeping everyone happy. It wasn't considered being a busy body or nosey if the overall intention of meddling was for someone's good. "Say. Not to change the subject. But I heard her ask about a room. You still have that little vacant house don't you . Why don't you....."

He put his hand up to stop the birth of a bad idea. " I got to go."

Chapter 10

Beep. Beep. Beep.

"Adam...Adam!"

He jerked awake. Glanced at his patient a few feet away. Thinking, hoping for the briefest moment Destiny might have called his name. Checked the time. 4:30a.m. not time for shift change. He looked down at his shoulder. Then at the person responsible for his awakening. He smiled in relief. "Mira."

A woman no taller than four feet if she were wearing spike heels stood in front of him nudging his shoulder. A backpack half her size slung over her shoulder. Short stubby fingers wrapped around the strap. It hit the floor with a loud thud. "I didn't know what to bring. I couldn't recall what the season would be."

He smiled. "I must have nodded off. I'm glad to see you." he spoke in a whisper in case the ass chewing he gave the station nurse did any good for her attentiveness. Then he added. "Summer. It's Summer here. Warm."

"I might have to go shopping then."

"Don't worry you won't be spending any time out of doors. I can guarantee that."

"There must have been some trouble. Do doctors usually spend the night sleeping in the patient's room." her eyebrows arched.

"No they don't. That's what I need you for."

"What happened?"

"Last night someone, something ripped the life supports out of her. I saw someone getting on the elevator just as I reached the floor. I couldn't follow him I had to come here first. But she needs to be watched."

The frail angelic woman turned toward the patient suspended from a trapeze. With care she moved closer to Destiny's side. A hand reached toward the patient's cheek. The light beams arrived before her touch. "How's she doing. Looks like she got run over by a truck."

A slow long exhale ended with, "She did." He buried his face in his hands.

"She in a lot of pain?"

He rose to stand on the opposite side of his patient. His index finger started at her forehead and traced a line of sparks around her face to end on the corner of her mouth. "Believe me. With what's being pumped into her she can't feel a thing. She might be having some crazy dreams. But she's not in any pain."

Mira moved her focus to meet Adam's eyes. "Is she ready to go yet? Can you take her home?"

"Physically yes. In a heartbeat. But her soul is still hanging on. If I pull her now, before she's made her peace, it will all have been for nothing."

"Not all for nothing. You saw the predictions. Her being here has helped. Immensely."

"Yes. But I mean her state in the next level, the next dimension, at home hasn't changed yet. She's still entwined here. And as long as she's still attached in this dimension she can't be fully present in the next dimension."

"So you want to give her more time. To let go on her own?"

"Yes."

"But she's not safe here. She could break the ties slowly from the next level of incarnation. It would take some time but she could do it."

"I'm aware of that. But she knew what she was doing when she came down here. She had a definite agenda to make this her last trip. So that she will be equal on our plane. So she will belong." He held her hand brought it to his lips. His thought trailed off. "This truly is a beautiful dimension. It doesn't matter to me. I will wait for her forever. But on the other hand I don't know if she would understand me not letting her fulfill what she came for. She would forgive me, just like she did last time for pulling her before her time. But I've just got to let her do this."

"Then you have a plan."

He looked at her questioningly.

Mira's eyebrows raised. "You called me, so you must have a plan?" she questioned again

"First order of business is to protect her. So she can finish this life."

"Who's our opposition?"

"I don't think it's any one person. It wouldn't do me any good to question her family and alarm them by having them think someone is trying to kill her. There's no one person with a contract out on her that wants her dead. That's why it's going to take constant watching. I think it's like you said. The darkness trying to extinguish the light. Anyone in sympathy with the darkness or influenced by the darkness is her assassin. The very magnitude of her light and goodness is by magnetism drawing the opposition to her."

"So what's my job description? You look like you must be a doctor."

"That's what I've got everyone here convinced of. Yes. But I don't think I'm the hospital favorite. I thought we could pass you off as a volunteer. Just here to maybe read to her to keep the brain waves active."

"Sounds believable to me. But what is your other plan? The one that gets Destiny back home?"

"The lessons on this plane of existence are learned through life experiences. Mainly the emotions. So I plan to mentally send her all the experiences and emotions her mind can handle. To sort of speed up the process. In her comatose state she is hyper receptive to emotion and experience. So it's like giving her several lifetimes' worth of experience in one thought. Her mind weaves the experiences into story line. I have no control over the events or the outcome of the unconscious life she'll be living only the intensity of the emotions she's experiencing. To her it feels like a dream but to her soul it's a mother lode of information."

"So you are mentally pushing her and swaying her will?"

"You could put it that way."

"But that is forbidden. To tamper with another's free will."

"It's forbidden if not solicited. But she made me promise I wouldn't let her forget. I'm just keeping my promise. I'm showing her the way home. It's still up to her to follow the path."

"OK."

"OK."

The lights in the room started getting brighter. Mira looked almost transparent. Her hair was silver forming a halo around her face. She looked down at her hands out stretched. The shoes on her tiny feet could be made out through them. "I'm going to have to do something about this. I didn't want to completely materialize in this dimension. You look dense. How did you do it?"

He smirked at her. "Thanks. I think. There's some self-tanning lotion in my office. It helps.   I'll get it for you."

"Your office? You have an office?"

He smirked again. A point on his cheek indenting. "Like I said they are convinced I'm a doctor. Back to the transparency, I seem to be getting a little denser with time. Maybe it's the oxygen or something. Word to the wise though. Don't eat the food. It's got no place to go if you know what I mean."

"So I'm here to read to her. What am I supposed to read?"

"Anything. It's more the sound of your voice. That I'm after. Just put your heart into your voice. When you talk to her."

"How do I know whether it's working or not? If she's even hearing me."

"Look at the monitor. The spark of light. The halo around the spark changes. Here I'll show you.

He bent down and whispered something into Destiny's ear. The center of the spark stayed pure white but sent out a halo of crimson red.

"Wow! What did you say to her?" Mira's eyes went wide.

"That's between her and Me." he mused softly.

"I think she liked it. Whatever it was."

He smiled down on his patient. Softly stroking her temple. "The halo is not visible   to people here. It happens on too high of a frequency. But it's the monitoring tool I've been using. I was a little confused. When her husband came in the halo went dark. There's something not right. Visits from her children and her father gave off a golden halo."

"That's good right."

"It's good and its bad. If the halo is a good color from a stimulus in this dimension it means the ties are secure. That won't help her get back home."

"So you're trying to make her want to come home more than she wants to stay here."

"Yes. But in this dimension it could be viewed as wanting her to die."

Destiny felt the crimson light fading. The pleasure of the

crimson was almost too much to bear. If that was possible to feel too much emotion too much pleasure. Could one's feelings actually explode? Feeling could not be contained in a vessel of a certain size and shape, but feeling definitely had a proportion. So if their proportion was increased what was it exactly that increased. The crimson came upon her in waves, filling her, stretching her capacity to feel to the breaking point. Each time it came it stretched her capacity further and further. Like stretching the sides of a balloon. The more times it was filled up the weaker the walls became. She felt that when the boundaries finally broke she would be free. Free to be with the crimson feeling forever. But when the feeling left it left a pale trail. Like breadcrumbs through the forest. *Don't fade out of site crimson. Don't leave completely. I'm trying to follow your trail.*

This time there was another feeling in the vastness of Destiny's world. It was a pleasurable feeling. Not like the darkness from before. The darkness that tried to pull her into nothingness. It was a pleasurable feeling. Nothing like the crimson. Nothing was like the crimson. But. Blue perhaps.

The crimson always made her tired. Made her want to dream.

Chapter 11

Up two blocks and over four. A game of chess. Legs made of jello carried her to the correct spot, it was all she could do to keep from tipping over. Standing in front of the inheritance only one word came to mind. Checkmate. In was impossible. If she smoked it would have made the solution easier. A simple flick of the match. It would have been deemed an accident for sure. What was she thinking? She left her home. Her manicured yard, not a thing out of place home. To come out west, just like a pioneer, to a place sight unseen. She was no pioneer. The only reason the home back east was so manicured was because it came that way. They hadn't had to do a thing except move in some furniture and fill out change of address cards. Thinking back on the phone conversation the woman had tried in her own way to express to Destiny how run down the place was. Tried to give her the name and number of Ed's Hauling. The words fell on deaf ears. All that came through the phone line was, out west in a town called Bendline lies a house with your name on it. A get away. An escape from grief.

A realization hit her at that moment. Through her life certain truths had hit her. Like a bolt of lightning out of the sky. Hit her so hard the force made her stand at attention. Sometimes she would bonk herself on the forehead and say 'Of course how could I have been so blind'. Other times the force was not so kind. The outcome would be as if a scolding had been dished out. And her response would be one of humble submission and acceptance. Usually feeling guilty for not seeing the truth before. This realization was more the latter kind. Her guilt was a product of having wasted so much time already. She bowed her head in submission, there was a lot of work to do. Without a shadow of a doubt she knew. There was no escape from grief. It might take on a different form but it had to be worked through it could not be run away from.

Anyone passing by would have seen an odd occurrence that day in Bendline. Right in the middle of the road in the middle of the block sat a woman cross legged with her face buried in her hands. It appeared the woman was weeping.

Still, there was only one thing to do. What she came to do. She picked herself up dusted her behind and put one foot in front of the other.

The gate was open. Not inviting strangers and friends alike but broken off at the top hinge so that it lisped backward and was too warped to close even if propped upright. The yard was indeed full of weeds. Tall weeds. The fence was perhaps three feet high made of ornate heavy wire. The top of the fence used to be arched but now it sagged down between broken off wood posts. Gravity couldn't have done this alone it needed the help of broken tree branches and years of untamed weeds tangling in the wire, decaying they attempted to rejoin the earth. The trees bordered the yard on the three sides that were visible from the street. The back was hidden in the shadows cast from the dense foliage. The roof of the house took on an orient appearance as the middle was sagging but the eves held strong. A wood porch bent lower than originally intended and if a ball would be rolled across it the ball would pick up considerable speed on the right side. A match would have been a poor idea however. The walls were lath and plaster. Built to last forever. Too bad.

Blow sand covered the brick walkway from the street. There were no footprints in the sand. As if this piece of observation was needed to tell no one lived here.

Windows flanked the door on either side. Worn out decrepit soldiers. Hell bent on performing their duty till the bitter end. Wood bore faint evidence of forest green color. Screens came loose from their attachments years ago and gave invitation instead of rejection to all manner of bug life. The porch complained with loud groans of pain and torture with each step closer to the door knob.

Destiny blew dirt out of the keyhole and inserted a skeleton key into the hole below the knob. An obvious joke she was sure when the key arrived in the overnight mailer sent from Bendline with the official documents of ownership to the house. The key fit the lock, a piece of paper swung from the key like a tiny trapeze artist. The paper proclaimed *front door*. If there was a back door there was no key for it. A turn of the key woke the monster within and the door yawned open of its own accord.

Streaks of light lead a procession of dust particles into the room. The specs danced with delight to an unheard melody. Destiny followed close behind on reluctant feet. There was no real need to enter fully. Enough could be viewed to certify the project hopeless.

A few scant furnishings remained. One large overstuffed chair held down a portion of linoleum in the front room. A chrome table with one unmatched chair and an empty hutch decorated the kitchen. There was two open doors off the kitchen and a closed door off the living room. Two led to bedrooms. And the other kitchen door led to a service porch. This room was explored first.

The porch was screened in with ripped plastic flapping in the breeze. A back door to the house was through the porch but it had no lock so obviously no key was needed. The porch lie vacant except for an old ringer washing machine and a fuse box. The plastic billowed out as if taking a big breath, held it for a few moments then let it out slowly. The other room off the kitchen was devoid of furniture all together, a pile of torn up insulation with cotton and other unidentifiable articles piled one corner. Mouse droppings peppered the entire floor and crunched beneath each step. A connecting bath separated this bedroom with the front bedroom off the living room. The bathroom gave off a putrid smell as the drain traps closing off the sewer were long ago dried up. Destiny put her hand over her nose and mouth. The faucets drizzled brown sludge, but no water. Perhaps the water needed to be turned on at the main. The door was shut tight behind her.

The door off the living room opened with quiet click. Light filled the room from all directions. The walls with no windows each had a tall antique mirror so that the light bounced in a continuous play back and forth. This room was completely furnished. As if stepping back in time. An ornate iron frame bed still was dressed in pick roses with ruffles and lace all the way to the floor. A matching chair sat beside the bed with a stuffed kitten waiting patiently for playtime. The dressing table displayed mother of pearl handled hairbrush, mirror and comb. Destiny viewed these with reverence. Stroking them with fingertips. Tears filled her eyes for reasons unknown.

A shoebox sat waiting on the foot of the bed. Beckoning the inquisitive visitor. Wrapped in old wallpaper the glue began to crystallize. Words written at one time in glue with glitter adorned the lid. OUT THERE. Or something like that. Destiny sat on the edge of the bed. The old springs complained. The lid to the box lifted easily. A pungent odor drifted out of the box. Old. Dust. The smell of something sitting too long with no change of air. The lid held high enough to reveal the contents of the box. Eyebrows scrunched so tight they almost touched each other above the bridge of the nose. The leading expression of complete puzzlement. Then, Destiny's world went black.

Chapter 12

Pain pulsed through her head starting somewhere in the center and erupting out the top of her skull. Through a fog the form of a child appeared. A hand with little sausage fingers reached forward. Destiny reached out to meet the hand and it was gone. Her eyes opened convincing her it was a dream. But the little girl was so clear, and why did she know her name was Mira? Sewer gas. The gas coming out of the bathroom traps must have knocked her out. Air. Fresh air. Running shoes supported wobbly legs long enough to get out side. The porch gave comfort while normal thoughts and feelings seeped back into her brain. Once composed Destiny passed off the happening as overload. Her brain and her psyche had been through so much. Fainting and hallucinations could be considered normal. Whatever the reason , the inside of the house could be inspected later.

Sitting on the slanted porch her thoughts began to collect and clear. The box from the bedroom had somehow found its way to sitting beside her on the porch. Memory of carrying it with her outside could not be conjured. And the need to try was not present. Looking around the scene from the other angle gave her a different perspective. The clean up letter addressed the yard. A plan needed to be formulated. The inspection of the grounds began. Slowly as to be mindful of anymore fainting spells.   The outside was a shambles, but at least it was work that could be accomplished on her own. Pulling waist high weeds, trimming trees and shrubs, raking debris. The shed out back held a treasure trove of yard tools. Hoes, rakes, shovels, sickles. The last time she had seen a sickle? She had to try it out. The grass was certainly long enough.

Back and forth swipes threw grass several feet on both sides of her path. What fun! The brave jungle guide challenged the elements and nature to blaze a trail forward into the deepest darkest center of Africa to go where no man had gone, see only what the animals had witnessed. But they were sworn to secrecy. Swipe, swipe, just a little bit further, almost there! "Ouch!"

The brave jungle guide just popped a blister. Gloves would be one of the first supplies picked up at the hardware store. She called it a day.

A whole afternoon spent surmising. The rest of the time needed to be spent more productively or she would never get out of this God forsaken place.

The number five key slipped into the knob. The transition between bright sunshine outside and pitch black inside took a few moments. Gone! All of her belongings were gone! The bathroom was cleaned out. The clothes bag was gone. All of it!

The screen door hit the doorframe at the same time Destiny's hand hit the office counter. "My stuff is gone! I've been robbed!"

The burlap curtain was held back with one hand as the other lazily scratched under the man's t-shirt. Sliding noises were made as the motel clerk drug closer to the counter. "What's your beef woman?" His annoyance intensified by the long exhale of beer breath.

"All my stuff is gone from room #5. It's all gone. Everything. I need to notify someone. Can I use your phone?"

The scratching hand had just satisfied the man's armpit and was moseying toward his hind quarters. Waking up all parts of his body. "Had to move it."

"Had to move it? You moved my stuff?"

"Yep." the scratching was getting dangerously close to areas Destiny did not want to witness.

"Why?"

"Maid didn't show. We run a respectable place. Couldn't have ya stayin in a dirty room."

"Where's my stuff?"

"Six."

The scratching hand rested with three fingers now inside the front waistband of his trousers. Panicked, Destiny averted her eyes to the floor held her hand out, "Give me the key!" Once she felt the key hit her palm she spun on her heels.

"Wait. You'll be needin this." the man set something hard on the counter.

Destiny turned to see a yellow and red can waiting to be retrieved. "More ants?"

The fingers started scratching lower and lower down the stomach. He looked her in the eye daring her to break eye contact. A smile spread across his face pulling lips back far enough to expose the bread still stuck between his teeth. The remains of lunch and the start of dinner. "Roaches."

Just as her fingers wrapped around the can his hand swiped out of his pants to hold it tight to the counter. "My woman," he nodded toward the burlap, "took a fancy to the blue nighty in the bathroom. If'n you want to sell it?"

"No!"

The roach dust spilled out the top holes of the can as trembling fingers stabbed the key at the door knob. Inside the room the can was dropped to the floor. In the middle of the bed lie one big heap. All her stuff. Sitting next to her belongs on the bed she hugged the blue gown close to her body, buried her face in it. The last gift from James. It smelled of stale cigarette smoke. The flood came strong and swift like a river overflowing its banks in spring. It was useless to try to divert such a strong force of nature. It was just as useless to try to stop this force of her nature. She wept till sleep came like a shining knight and rescued her.

Running shoes followed the same course the next morning but instead of taking the course a little slower, at a gentler pace. The shoes dug harder into the rocks and dirt, climbed higher up the side of the mountain before turning to encircle the town. Lungs complained, leg muscles screamed, a heart cried out for mercy but the only response from the running shoes was, it still didn't hurt bad enough.

Chapter 13

Beep. Beep. Beep.

Adam leaned his weight against the door which gave way gratefully. Mira sat reading to the patient.

"How long have you been in here Mira?"

She gave him a look as if he had lost his faculties.

"I know how long you have been here. But have you left the room."

"No. you said to watch her and read to her. So. I watch and read."

"You're going to have to leave the room from time to time to keep up physical appearances. No human can stay in a room for the whole day without a pee break."

"But I don't have to pee. I'm not sure I can pee."

"For appearances only. The restroom is down the hall to the left. I've told the staff that you will be in here watching after Destiny. I told her you had close ties to her and you wanted to help. But you're going to have to act human."

"You didn't lie. All of that is the truth. I can act human. It's in my memory banks. Not all happy memories but there none the less." She looked at the frail broken body lying in the bed. "I don't suppose Destiny is going to want to visit these memories none too soon. If at all."

"I don't think all her memories have been bad. In fact her life here has been quite pleasant."

"And you know this how?"

"Mira, we," he gestured toward Destiny,   "are as one no matter what dimension we are in. Her memories are my memories."

"Aw. The burden of your level of mastery."

He held Destiny's hand in his. "It is no burden."

I have to be gone from here for a brief time. I have been studying the weather here. There are some patterns that concern me. The last time nature performed in this manner the humanity paid a dear price. I need to speak to the council about it. You'll be alright?"

"We will be fine. And don't worry. I'll be human. I'll rest in the restroom every two hours?"

"That should do it." he placed the hand gently back on the bed. His touch was missed as soon as he let go.

Chapter 14

Ed and Ed sat sprawled across more than their share of the counter, the classified ads propped up against the pie cases. Red circles highlighted various points of interest.

"Ed you're gonna have to move it over some if the place fills up." Faye's comment was just random conversation. The place always filled up and it always emptied out. If she would have paid closer attention in science class she would have known some Newton's law to compare the fact to.

"Yea, OK Faye. Me and Ed are just lookin to get another truck. Business is doing pretty good since the big clean-up started. We're lookin to expand."

"Well I don't have any room to expand, and this isn't your office so like I said if I need those two stools you've gotta give em up. You having ham or bacon this morning?" Faye pulled the pencil from the bouffant on top of her head.

"What did we have yesterday?"

"Ham." Faye answered

"OK give me bacon. No wait, is it still Sol's pig?"

"Yea."

"Give me the ham again then. I don't know what he does to those pigs but he comes up with the best ham I've ever had."

The other Ed answered for himself. "Well I've seen what they feed pigs, I'll have the bacon."

Ed looked at Ed, "Bacon is pig meat too you jackass."

"But it's not Sol's pig. Faye gets her bacon from the store, I've seen her. Isn't that right Faye? And don't call me a jackass."

"Yea Jimmy Dean Thick Cut is all this café will serve. Sounds like the sooner you get another truck the better. You two been spending too much time together."

"Oh, the new truck won't be for us. We're going to hire an employee."

"Employees will drive you crazy. Trust me." Whitey sat down a couple stools away but was close enough to add to the conversation.

"Hey Ed did you see any crazy people out this morning." a voice came from across the room.

"Oh, yea made the trip to the dump a whole lot more pleasant." The Wall Street Journal folded down for a moment.

"You do any hauling for her yet?" Mary Claire inquired.

"No she didn't call yet. But she will. I drove by last night on my way home. She got a bit of a start. But it would be my guess she's there through September."

"Could be a good account then."

"Why you think me and Ed are looking at the ads for?"

The place was filled to capacity. The forks clinked on plates. Earl called out order up almost as soon as Faye put up the ticket. Everyone had their usual and Earl had a good memory.

The bell on the door chimed. All the regulars were present and accounted for. That left only one person that might be ringing the bell. The Wall Street Journal was being read on the opposite side of the table this morning. If the top corner was folded over it gave a perfect view of the door. In case the bell would happen to ring.

She kept her head low and eyes to the floor. The site in the mirror that morning was not a pretty one. But everyone else's eyes raised from their plates. Looking up just far enough to see no available seats she met Faye's gaze.

Faye hit the classified ads as she walked past with a coffee pot and a clean mug. "That's it Ed I told you. It's time to move it over. Whitey slide down one." With one swipe Faye moved Whitey's plate, fork, napkin, coffee cup and crumbs down a stool. Put the mug in the center of the open spot and filled it up. The steam began to swirl out into the room. "All set for you, Destiny."

Destiny took her place at the counter and gave Faye a look of gratitude. She wished she remembered this woman. But even though she didn't remember her she was sure she was a wonderful person back then.

"Thanks."

"You don't look so hot this morning you have allergies or something." Faye scrutinized her customer's eyes.

"No. I'm not allergic to anything. But maybe it's allergies. I don't know." Destiny kept her eyes pointed down staring into the coffee cup.

The trouble with crying oneself to sleep is that one wakes up with horrible red puffy eyes. Resembling thank goodness, allergies.

The corner of the paper folded down a little further.

"Are you eating this morning? Earl stayed late last night and made some blueberry muffins. You look like you might be a blueberry muffin eater?"

"How come you didn't tell us about the muffins Faye?" Ed inquired.

"I'll take a muffin Faye." Whitey chimed in.

Two more verbal orders were called out for blueberry muffins.

"Did I ask anybody else? I'm talking to Destiny here. If you want a muffin I'll come around and take your order. For now pipe it up would ya?" She turned her attention back to the customer in front of her with the magic genie rising from her mug.

There was a few wishes on the tip of her tongue but she answered Faye's question first. "I'm really not hungry. I'm sure they're great but…"

"Well did you eat last night? You said you'd be back for meatloaf?" Faye sounded almost insulted.

"No. I'm sorry it got late, I just fell asleep. I'm not used to working that hard I guess."

"Then I'm bringing you a muffin. If you don't eat it you can take it with you."

Destiny had an urge to answer 'yes mother'.

A warm plate was presented for her inspection. In the middle of it was a giant muffin with blueberries bursting with juice seeping into the cake surrounding them. The aroma took her breath away. A fork was placed on a napkin pulled from the container. "In case you don't eat with your hands like the rest of this crowd." Faye said. She topped off Destiny's mug with more magic steam.

Destiny took one bite and her mouth exploded with pleasure. She let out a quiet "Mmm" heard by only one person in the café. .

Behind the newspaper the corners of the man's mouth turned upward. The stock market results had to be reread. The first attempt was overshadowed

The bell on the door was a steady jingle. The cash register dinged in between. The whole town started work at 9:00 and work waited for no man they said.

Ed and Ed stopped by Destiny on their way out the door. "We see you got started on the place. You still got our card, I can give you another one if you lost it."

"No. I have your card and I'll be calling you. I was planning on making a few piles first. Then maybe you could haul while I pile. I'll call you when I'm ready though."

"OK, just so you know though. We're ten bucks a load. That's our special. Usually we're twelve but with the special it's ten. But it has to be cash."

"Cash." One more anchor let loose. Her ship was sinking fast along with her determination. As if admitting defeat she continued. "Of course, I should have guessed. OK. I'll call you."

This town was living in the dark ages. Cash for everything. They didn't take checks, credit, debit, no ATM. A thief could make a killing. The hardware store had cleaned her out yesterday. She had seven dollars in her purse and hoped the heavenly muffin she was munching on was not over five dollars, plus the coffee or the tip would have to be an IOU written in blood on the napkin.

By the time the last bite of muffin went down the place was cleared out. Only the newspaper in the corner remained. But it was obvious he was engrossed.

Faye stood in front of Destiny. "OK, spill it. What's wrong?"

"What?"

"You're not allergic to anything."

"I'm not?"

"No. Honey I know allergies and you're not allergic."

"I had a bad day."

"It just got started."

"Yesterday was a bad day. And this one, with the exception of the muffin, is starting out to be its twin."

"Hear that Earl. The muffin was a hit."

A noise came from the back but was not translatable into any particular language.

Faye turned her attention back to Destiny. "I been trying to get him to make muffins for years. So what's so bad, about your days?"

Destiny stared at the steam rising from the freshly poured pot. She tried to follow one tiny particle of water as it rose, swirled then disappeared into the air absorbed into the vastness. Her red puffy eyes met with the false eyelashes batting down at her. "Look, you're busy and I've got plenty to do myself. The muffin was great. How much do I owe you?"

The heart behind the newspaper cracked just a little.

"Nothing."

"No. absolutely not. You gave me coffee yesterday that was great, but not today. Really I insist. How much?" the words came out in a wave pattern instead of straight shots.

Faye held the meal check over her heart. "Nothing, till you tell me what's wrong."

Faye had her at an unfair advantage. "OK." the words dripped slowly at first then gathered momentum as if a water main had burst. "I guess it started when I went to the hardware store yesterday. No one will take a check or a credit card. I promised the clerk I've never even been late with a payment but he said he'd love to help me but they just weren't set up to take a credit card. And they might be able to take an out of town check but definitely not an out of state, and why, hell, New York is practically out of the country. So I put back everything over my budget and left with just a few dollars in my pocket. The clerk said I might be able to cash a check at the casino across the street. I went over there but they said they'd hold my check till it cleared and give me a call. Maybe in a week. There are no ATM machines in this town. Did you know that? Of course you know that. I'm sure if I had paid for my coffee yesterday I would have discovered that you don't take credit, debit or checks either. What's wrong with this town? It's a fort Knox waiting to be heisted.

"I went back to my room. Luckily I had paid, cash of course for two nights, but my stuff was gone. All of it gone. I rushed to the office. The bum that works at the desk said he moved my stuff. To room six. Room five had ants which he gave me ant poison for. But he said the maid didn't show up to clean the room so he moved my stuff to six. And threw in a can of roach killer. Which didn't work. And he went through my stuff. He asked if I wanted to sell my night gown! And now all my stuff smells like beer and cigarettes. So this morning I showered with a roach that insisted on crawling up my leg. I loaded my stuff in the car since I didn't pay for another night. I was planning on driving to Vegas to replenish my cash supply, pamper myself with a relaxing stay in a posh hotel but I needed to fill up the car first. And guess what? The gas station only takes cash! And I hope that was not a five dollar muffin or you're out a tip!

Putting the cash issue aside, and the room switch, I brought my computer. The only way I can reach my kids back home is through e-mail. They don't pack their cell phones like every other normal young person these days. They e-mail. Oh just e-mail us mom it's too easy. So I learned to e-mail. But is there a internet provider in this town? I haven't been able to find one. Do you have internet, is this an internet café? I didn't notice a sign outside. I haven't gotten word to my kids in three days, they'll probably be sending out the search party. And last but not least Pearl Appleton's house! My assumption of a place needing fixing up was about a one on a scale of one to ten. The reality of the condition is about a hundred on a scale of one to ten. But I'm not quitting. I came out here to clean that place up and that is exactly what I'm going to do. I don't know how at this particular moment but I won't let this defeat me. I can't.   And the reason I'm not crying about all of this is because there's just no more tears left in me. You're right Faye, isn't it, I'm not allergic. There I told you my problems. Now please give me the damn check." The outpour of emotion had drained her and her limbs trembled as if starved for the oxygen used for the rapid explanation. Her head rested in her hands.

Faye stood mouth agape in front of Destiny. Holding onto the coffee pot on the counter. As if to support her from being swept downstream with this woman's troubles.

"Excuse me. I couldn't help over hearing." The voice was much lower that Faye's. Destiny's head pulled away from her hands slightly.

Enter the genie.

The Wall Street Journal lay down on the counter beside her elbow. Destiny turned to stare into eyes that carried her away. Just briefly lifted her up to hover above her troubles of the present. Carry her to a place where all the dilemma of the past few hours had no hold on her.

Faye grabbed the coffee pot mumbling as she walked away. "About time you put your paper down and got out of that damn chair."

"I might be able to help." he began.

"Oh? Are you a banker?" Unintentional sarcasm cut the air

between them.

Adam laughed. "No, but I am a landlord of sort. And I have a vacancy."

The man was only offering to help and didn't deserve another rude reply.

Destiny changed her tone to one of gratitude. "Thanks anyway but I don't need a house. I was just planning on renting a room for a week or so just to stay long enough to get the cleanup done. To fulfill my obligation."

"The vacancy I have isn't exactly a full fledged house. It's a small one roomer. You could have it on a weekly basis."

"Oh I don't know?" Destiny searched the close proximity for answers. The man's expression was expectant yet not urgent.

"If it's a money issue don't worry," he held the last part of his sentence like a seasoned actor. Timing the completion until he had the full attention of the audience. So the comment would have a strong affect. "I'll charge you rent. I could even overcharge you if you like." Then he smiled. Dimples. Was that what was so captivating about his smile? It brought the warmest feeling of de'ja vue. Were they friends? Before?

If feeling had a color this one would be crimson. Not red like a passionate love but a much deeper tone. Coming from a place and time long ago. Perhaps even the beginning of time. Then guilt flooded her thought. The color of her feelings for James was more of an orange. She would not waste time surmising colors with feeling. Her financial situation was first in line.

The gallant man's wit had her at an unfair advantage. If Destiny was to spend too much more time in Bendline she would have to toughen her defenses. At the moment given her overabundance of options, sleeping in the back seat of the rental car, or on the floor of the inherited estate. A conceded reply drifted out of her mouth. "Maybe I could come by and look at it."

His shadow towered over her as he rose from the stool. "Fine. I'll be home all afternoon. Just head south on the road in front of your place. When you've run out of road don't give up keep going a little further. That's me. I'm clear at the end of the road."

Opening his wallet he turned to Faye. "For the coffee, Faye."

He laid a stack of bills down beside Destiny. "To get you buy

in cashvi   till your check clears at the casino. Call it a loan and if the
place wil   rk out for you we could just add it to your rent." he added
with a wi   "Don't worry. I'll take your check. I trust you."
A   t of a spark was in her eyes as she looked up to tell him
thanks an   oodbye. "Then you are a banker?"
W   a nod and a smirk the bell on the door chimed and he was
gone. 'W   I come to the end of the road' she repeated in her mind.
Every mc   ng she got up lately she has felt that way. She may as well
live there

Chapter 15

Beep. Beep. Beep.

Mira kept an eye on the monitor as she read page after page to Destiny. Only a blue halo. At least it was some response.

"Who the hell are you?"

James was awestruck at the site of this stranger sitting beside his wife. The top of her head barely shown above the bed. Wisps of hair flowed in every direction. Her skin looked dirty obviously in need of a bath. Several layers of mismatched shirts were much too warm for any sane person to wear. But if rotated with each day of the week would make perfect sense to a vagrant. Beads of every color hung around her frail neck. Knee length plaid shorts would have looked in place on a golf course twenty years ago but not with one red knee high sock and another purple both rolled down over the top of clown size hiking boots.

Her age was not easily guessed. Old he would say but perhaps decay came from the quality of life rather than the quantity. She rose out of the chair but was still not much taller. Round eyes in constant expression of surprise looked at him and an outstretched hand with short sausage fingers extended in his direction which he declined.

"This is my wife's room. What are you doing here?"

The outstretched hand retracted and sought out a cell phone device in her shirt pocket. She pushed a button.

Dr. Adams came through the door, chart in hand as if on his regular rounds. He winked at Mira then turned his comment to Destiny's husband. "Oh, morning James. I see you've met Mira."

James pierced his lips tight together grabbing the doctor by the arm and escorted him out into the hall. "What kind of a circus are you running here. And what is that bag lady retard doing in my wife's room!"

"Calm down. She is not a bag lady I assure you. And she is far from retarded. A mild case of Downs but she is very capable of taking care of herself."

"I can see that by the way she dresses herself."

"Mira, tends toward bright colors."

"I don't give a damn about her likes or dislikes. I want her away from my wife!"

Adam had to think fast. He was searching James' thoughts and Destiny's memories for some direction. "Actually, James, the center sent Mira. You know, where your wife volunteers."

"I don't care if they sent the President. If she's retarded I want her away from Destiny, they can't be trusted. You can't depend on them."

"Well I don't know. I think your wife must have thought differently. Mira is only here to read to your wife. I told you her brain is active. And I think it might be advantageous to have the constant noise. I know you would if you could but you nor your family can be with her twenty four hours a day. And our staff is good here but we have other patients too. Besides it was sort of Mira's idea. I assure you your wife is safe. I'm checking on them all the time."

James shoulders softened, his fists opened, he looked back into where Destiny lay sleeping. A soft murmur of the woman reading sounded more like the purr of a contented kitten. His feet took him closer to the side of the bed.

"What are you reading?"

Mira looked up with saucer eyes. *"To Kill A Mockingbird.* It's her favorite."

"Yes. I know." he leaned down and whispered something to Destiny.

The blue halo turned dark for several beeps. Then slowly gained more blue as Mira continued her book.

James felt unease in the room. He hated hospitals but that was not the sum total of the feeling. It was more of a feeling of not belonging. Out of place. It pushed him out the door. He paused beside Dr. Adams at the nurses' station.

"She can stay. But watch her."

"I will."

Mira was massaging the digits sticking out of bandages at the ends of Destiny's feet. Staring at the beeps on the black screen the halos became pink. The doctor entered the room.

"She knew you were coming." Mira smiled at him.

"How's she doing?"

"Her feet get so cold. Her toes turn blue. Look."

"Yea her hands too." He took a hand between his. Breathed warm air into his hands. The traveled from receptors at the tips of her fingers along her arm straight into her heart. The beeps quickened and gave a crimson halo.

"I thought her husband was going to physically remove me from the room. He doesn't like me much." Mira nodded toward the vacated doorway.

Adam for the first time appraised her outfit. "He took offence at your fashion sense."

Holding out the hem of the outer layer shirt, "It was the first garments I saw. You said the situation was urgent."

"Where did you land."

"Across the street. On a little patch between some buildings. There's a little community set up there."

"That explains the clothes. I should have helped you. I wasn't thinking. I'll get you something more appropriate. He also thinks you're mentally challenged. But I think that worked to our advantage. Destiny has always been very sympathetic toward the disadvantaged."

"So you mentally convinced him to let me stay."

He smiled with a little shrug of the shoulder. "I thought you did."

Mira smiled with a little shrug of her shoulders. "Maybe we can share the flogging."

The monitor beeped steady alternating between blue and crimson halos.

Chapter 16

The knock at the front door went unanswered by man. Only beast regarded the rattle of the screen door and the regard was minimal. The pat, pat, pat of a dogs tail keeping beat to an inaudible song or a pleasant dream came through the closed door. One more attempt at a knock was all Destiny was going to give the resident to answer. She would take it as a sign, always keeping true to her name. it hadn't failed her yet. If no one showed at the door she was determined to turn tail and exit through the secret garden type yard she had just come through. The fence around the yard served as only a boundary. A legal line drawn in the dirt to show possession. The yard was hardly contained by it. The shrubs, vines and trees were not without care. In fact this yard was the exact opposite of what she had found her holdings in Bendline to be. This yard was the result of too much care. Too much water. Too much fertilizer, too much attention. But the attention was pointed in all directions except pruning and taming. The vegetation had a mind of its own and the idea on that mind was world domination. Every plant imaginable had a place here. The gardeners motto must have been, let no plant go unwanted, unable to grow. The only problem with the motto was that there was no organization to back it up. Whatever was brought home to the garden was plopped in an empty spot, watered and left to flourish. No regard to size shape, or color. Perhaps the entire yard was the outcome of migrating birds spreading seeds.

Destiny had given the person ample time to arrive at the door, even if he were at the back of the house or the other side of town for that matter. With one foot on the top step, shoulders slumped she turned to leave. A soft mumble of a voice came from behind the door. The tapping of the dog's tail increased speed and volume. The voice got louder as it approached. The door opened and the screen door creaked. A larger than life hair ball came outside and brushed against Destiny's leg. The dog was golden in color the long fur gave the appearance of floating down the stairs. The dog circled around in front of Destiny, sat down in front of her at the bottom of the stairs and gave one woof of complete authority. Sitting down the dogs head would have come above Destiny's waist. Although the tail wagging weakened his threat. Destiny offered no challenge. Not taking her eyes off the dog with one slow motion the foot was removed from the top step and placed back on top of the porch.

"Hold on. Don't go." Adam stood in the open door frame holding the screen open with one hand and a phone close to his ear with the other. The words coming out of his mouth now were directed to Destiny and the warm smile was a welcome site. "Come in, come in. Digger, leave the nice lady alone. Let her come in."

Digger stood on all fours, came around to the other side of Destiny and led her into the house, as any obedient butler would do.

"I'll be just a minute, I've got to finish this call." his eyes shown sincere apology.

Destiny nodded her understanding, looked down at the guardian now sitting close enough to her on the floor she could feel the heat from the beast breathing. She took a step backward and bumped into the wall.

An ignored command was given to the dog by his master as he turned to exit the room. "Digger! Go back to bed. You're drooling on our guest's shoe." Adam headed for an open door off the living room. Shaking his head at the dog and exclaiming to his guest as he crossed the room. "We don't get much company, she doesn't know how to act. Have a seat, I'll be right back."

He disappeared, the only evidence of his presence the low murmur of his voice coming from the open door. Destiny made her way to an overstuffed armchair keeping her eyes on the guardian now curled up on a bed by the window. The tap of the dog's tail kept time with her footsteps. Once her seat hit the chair she started sitting, and sitting and sitting. The chair enveloped her whole self. She didn't sit, she melted into the soft velour fabric. Once her butt hit bottom the warmest feeling came over her, followed by a sharp stab in the back of her throat. Her birthday chair from James felt the same. So warm, so inviting, *unparalleled comfort* the tag had said with an exclamation at the bottom of her birthday card, *now you have time to relax, LOVE, JAMES*. A furry head dropped down in her lap, as heavy as a bowling ball. All thoughts of past birthdays vanished. Two eyes stared up at her.

"Hello. Digger is it?" a quick light tap on the head. The animal was satisfied she lay down on the floor on top of Destiny's feet.

The room was large and open. All the furniture was arranged in the center. This made for better conversation she had learned in her decorating class. This room's arrangement was out of necessity alone no other options presented themselves. The wall opposite of the front door was solid windows top to bottom illuminating the other walls which were covered with book shelves, top to bottom. The sofa and armchair were colorless the books gave all the color to the room that was needed. The sun painted geometric designs on the hardwood floors. On the right was the open door her host had stepped into. Through the small rectangle of vision the room was much like this one, a bit smaller with a desk in the center, surrounded by bookshelves and a wall of windows.

Destiny leaned her head against the back of the chair and drank in the stillness of the room. It was deafening, the books sucked all the sound from the room holding it hostage inside their passages. She kept guard of her thoughts lest they could hear these too. Being in close proximity of large numbers of books had always been a place of comfort. Her favorite haunts as far back as she could remember had been libraries or bookstores, the older the better. It was mesmerizing to think of the limitless stories, tales, truths and lies, ideas and dreams that could be packaged up and bound between two pieces of cardboard placed upon a shelf waiting for just the right person to come along and claim its destiny. Someone, somewhere, cared strongly enough about an idea or story to sit for hours painstakingly writing it down, detail after detail. The intention was to come as close to perfection as humanly possible then, to put a piece of themselves between a beginning and an end, to be hidden in plane site. It was the ultimate game of hide and seek. And the most astonishing point of all, was that it all came from just twenty-six different squiggles.

Digger jumped to attention to greet the master entering the room. Destiny rose as well. Fingers found a loose string on the bottom of her shirt and wound around it. One way then the other.

"Finished. I see Digger got acquainted." he scuffed the dog's mammoth neck. The long coat rolled from side to side.

"She's big! What kind of a dog is she?"

"Nothing fancy. Golden Retriever got mixed up with a St.

Bernard. They were giving them away in front of Wal-Ma   couldn't resist such a big ball of fluff."

"She seems sweet. I guess her size alone would   p out the intruders."

"Yea, I'm not so sure she'd chase anybody off tho   . She has to spend a lot of time alone so when company comes sh   ractically sits on them to keep them from leaving. Like she did to   She was sitting on your feet wasn't she?" He directed a scowl   the dog. "Sorry."

They both looked down at a tuft of fur stuck to   top of a running shoe.

"No problem." Destiny laughed.

"I'll grab the keys to the house. It's just a ways   n the dirt lane."

Destiny stepped closer to the bookshelves to read   ne of the titles. Some of the spines were so worn the letters were   t legible. These she gently touched as if they must hold some s   d words. They had done their life duty well, been held and regarded   many an eye, now was their time to rest. The jingle of keys snappe   r head to attention.

Adam wore an understanding smile.

"Did you find what you were looking for?" Destin   quired.

The keys were in plane site so they were not   item in question. Glancing around the room the only thing out of   e was his hat carelessly tossed on the side table. Lola the houseke   had left just an hour ago, he hadn't even had a chance to g   he room comfortable yet.

"Excuse me?" he chimed with a hint of insult. "Th   s as good as it gets around here." gesturing to the furnishings.

A lump was swallowed in her throat. Talking to   gers had always been hard to master. The wrong words so often c   out. An attempt at explanation was made. "Oh, no. I mean the   oks. I've never seen so many books in someone's house before.   uld guess you are or you were looking for something."

"Or I just like books."

"I like books too."

"I would have guessed." he smiled.

He said this as if he knew her. But how could h   he didn't even kno   erself. Not now.

"]   e you read them all?"

"]   t."

"]   'e to read but I usually borrow from the library. They take
up so mu   space."

""   , but it seems like when I'm finished with a book I don't
want to p   with it. Either it was like an old friend or I wouldn't want
to give u]   hat I'd learned from it."

J&   s had always been the conversationalist. She missed that
especially   ice her throat was so uncooperative now. There was a lot
of things   t were missed. The uneasiness of talking was fading as the
subject w   ;o dear to her heart

"(you WERE searching for something?" She didn't read
right thro   1 him, like a book. Only based her surmise on her own
experienc   The state she found herself in, looking for answers, she
felt an in   ible urge to read.

"]   1y story that transparent?" his eyebrows raised as a child
with his l   l in the cookie jar.

'   1ybe I'm just a good reader."

"]   rybody's searching don't you think. Some read. Some
work. So   drink, do drugs, abuse themselves and others. Some go off
on a soli   / quest. The search takes on different scenes but it's a
search al   1e same. The only difference is that most people don't
realize it   lon't admit it. And the reason they can't admit it is that if
they say   y are searching for something that is an admission of a
lack with   1emselves. Most are too proud to admit to a lacking."

""   v, so are you a psychologist or something?" A therapist
she didn'   ed.

"]   Actually I surprised myself just then. I'm usually pretty
scotch wi   vords. I guess you must be easy to talk to."

O   . Destiny thought someone in need of a person to talk to.
"But yo   ave obviously spent some time studying the human
condition

"]   my own." He shook his head in admission.

A   irch for something had been burning inside her for quite
some tin   She had put it on the back burner due to lack of time
raising a   imily, James's busy career, her volunteer work and
obligatio   Or, perhaps it was fear of what she might see. Now the

87

time presented itself but she was afraid to look inside. Not now, not yet. It was easier to run.

"Something about knowing yourself and you will know all things? Who said that?" she pondered.

"I think it's from the Bible."

"Oh." Embarrassed color flushed her cheeks. "Well do you know yourself then?"

"Myself, no, not completely. But I know I'm happy and I wasn't before and I'd have to say I think I'm finally heading in the right direction. I took a hell of a lot of wrong turns in the past but…"

"So which one was it, which book held the road map." She panned the room with scrutiny.

"It wasn't really any one book. And I guess it was all of them. They were all pointing in the same direction."

"And that direction?"

He pointed at himself. "Inside here."

Staring at the books her hand gently traveled from one to the other. In a whisper, meant for no one's ears in particular, "I wish I could find a book to point my way."

"Is that why you run?"

She stiffened, He struck a nerve. Too many questions. And too many answers would lead to things she didn't want to say. A Caution siren sounded alarm in her. Her palms began to sweat. Knees trembled. Running was a good idea. Right now, right out the door. She looked down at her feet. A deep breath gave her the courage to stay in the room.

The running shoes must have been the giveaway. The sadness in her eyes spoke a thousand words she uttered only a few. "I'm just trying to keep my feet under me. Trying to figure out how to live." She brushed it off with nonchalance, "just like everybody else."

He knew she was not like everybody else. Never was and never could be. Not to him anyway.

Full attention returned to the book shelves. It was all the explanation that was going to be offered. The fingers continued to travel the titles, her head cocked. A waterfall of chestnut colored silk swayed as the titles drew her footsteps forward.

The man watched, amused as the forces of her destiny led her way. He longed to turn the pages of her story. Read about the roads she had traveled. Had she been happy? Did she know pain? Was her life easy? Family, friends, what were their names? Why was she here? Not just the story about the inherited house. Why did the forces that oversee our way bring her here? And a million other questions raced in the silent space between them. Did she have a dog? He wanted to read it all from cover to cover without stopping. But, he had learned one lesson well in life. Patience. "Do you have a dog?" He secretly gave himself a blue ribbon for stupidest question of the year.

A smile broke through the look of pain. "No. No, I've never had a dog. Well at least I don't think I've ever had a dog. I haven't had one since I moved from here."

"What's this?" Her hand had stopped in the middle of a shelf. It didn't rest on a book.

"It's a rock."

"That would have been my first guess." He offered no more comment so she continued with the observation. Her curiosity was peeked. He only looked into her eyes. Eyebrows slightly raised, a teacher standing at the head of the class. Not wanting to make the answer too easy on the students but realizing the correct answer means so much more if discovered on one's own. Instead of being handed out freely. Destiny was always over competitive in the classroom. An imperfect grade was unacceptable. Slowly the analysis began. "But it's displayed so reverently. Simple and plain not meaning to draw attention to itself, yet the not meaning to draw attention is exactly what makes it so noticeable. And the stone itself. A dull lump of clay. It must not be encased for its monetary value, which draws the conclusion that it must be displayed for the value it holds. The importance it holds, to you." She turned to him surrendering the floor for further response on the subject. Just as she had seen Sherlock Holmes do so many times.

"You're good Watson. But it's just a rock."

The index finger on her right hand traced the edges of the glass cube. The stone a lump of gray mud, suspended in the center of the box held in place by one tiny wire almost invisible to the naked eye.

Her curiosity would have to remain unsatisfied. This man obviously wasn't giving any more information on the subject. "I'm sorry. My dad said I was always fascinated by rocks. I didn't mean to pry. I don't like people prodding me if there's something I don't want to talk about. So the house is just up the road?"

"It's not something I don't want to talk about. The fact is I've never talked about it before. No one has ever noticed the rock before. But it's a long story. And I've never been much of a story teller." He had given her the choice. To leave or to stay. He would tell his story or he would keep it closed, tucked away on the highest shelf. It was her call. The coin had been tossed into the air. The time stretched into eternity waiting for a reply, heads or tails?

Two small squiggles. Two letters forming one word. One word that could open a door that would lead to a whole different destiny. Like the magic door in the back of the wardrobe. A whole new world was being presented. The first step would be the hardest but any journey begins with just one step. Her lips parted and she spoke the word. "So?"

"You might want to sit down. Can I get you some coffee or ice tea?"

Destiny let herself be swallowed up in the chair again as she prepared to listen to the story of Adam. Digger camped out on her feet to ensure the master had a captive audience.

Why was she so easy to talk to. He opened his mouth and the chapters of his life story poured forth.

His voice was soft and low yet rough around the edges. The tone lulled her to a place just above sleep. Aware of his talking but not aware of the exact words being spoken. A story, an idea was being transmitted but the words were not the vehicle of transport.

"The stone was a gift. From a friend. After I finished high school here I headed back east to school. I wanted to get as far away from here as my legs and summer job savings would take me. I hitched rides across the county. Wound up in Virginia. My coach at school pumped me up about being able to walk on to any team anywhere. Well after I found out what a blowhard he was and what an athlete I wasn't, my bubble was busted. I couldn't get into the scholar mode so I dropped out. One thing I knew without a doubt that I was good at was drinking beer and playing pool. I actually made a pretty good living shooting pool. I moved around a lot. Couldn't stay in one neighborhood too long or the locals would peg you for a shark and they wouldn't play you for money anymore.

"I lit in Florida my final round of pool. I had just one c note left in my wallet and wasn't about to break it for a beer. I shot my best pool when I was smashed but when you're putting money on a game you don't throw down a twenty when you need something bigger. If you tell your mark all you play for is a hundred you have to be able to show the goods. I got ahead of this guy five hundred dollars, then we go double or nothing. I was sure of myself, I should have been drunk. Like I said I play my best smashed. The whole place was gathered around the table. The joint was doing great. I thought we should have had a cut of the till for the night for bringing them in off the street. Then it all turned around. I should have quit when I was up but I got greedy. I was having my worst game ever. I couldn't get a ball to sink to save my life. My opponents smile got bigger with each shot I missed. The crowd started buying us drinks. Since I was behind in my game and behind on the drinking I started slamming. I didn't drink the hard stuff much but it hit's a lot quicker and harder than beer. My game started improving with each drink. We were just about neck and neck in the game when the lord shined down on me. The guy sunk the eight. I lifted my glass to the crowd grabbed for the money and got a cue stick across my knuckles and a fist under the chin. I became a punching bag for every guy in the place. I landed as many as I could, but the whiskey was impairing my vision by now. And luckily dulling my senses. I was thrown into the alley to be picked up with the other garbage the next day, if I lasted that long.

I don't remember much about the rest of the night. I remember losing a shoe as I was being dragged across the pavement. I opened my eyes to see a fuzzy guy with a big smile. Something smelled in bad need of a shower, either the garbage, the guy dragging me or me myself. I faded in and out of consciousness for the next few days. I'd open my eyes briefly but the light that seeped in between the swollen lids was minimal. After about a week the swelling had gone down enough to be able to get a clear vision of the man that saved my life. Roy.

Roy lived in an upper class neighborhood with a housekeeper and a gardener. He even had a driver but he said he didn't usually enlist the service of his driver when he was canvassing the alleyways for helpless souls. He had certainly hit the jackpot that night. I asked him if he was an angel trying to earn his wings. He said he just liked to help someone out every now and then.

"As I recalled my first vision of Roy in the alley though, he was an old guy with about a week's growth of beard, holes in his shirt and pants. Stinky, grubby hands and two shoes that didn't match. He swore that was him, but he did one hell of a cleanup job. On himself and me. I ended up with three broken ribs, a punctured lung, lost a tooth, seven stitches in my head and a broken hand. I still can't hold a cue stick straight, not that I would want to.

"Roy had me fixed up at ER and took me to his house from the hospital. He had an incredible library. Mine is miniscule in comparison. Roy owned several book stores. He said he got in the bookstore business because he wanted to make sure people could find the answer to what they were looking for. He took me under his wing, an angel one I'm sure. Gave me a job and an education. He was an incredible human being. When I asked him why he searched the alleyways for people in need. He said because you have to go where the need is the greatest. Besides he said everyone living on easy street are under the assumption they don't need to be saved. So you go to where the people are sure they need to be saved.

"I was sure I needed to be saved, I wasn't sure I deserved to be. When I told him that it was the only time I ever heard him raise his voice. He said everyman deserves life and all that that implies. And they shall have it as soon as they accept that fact. He said, "You my boy will just have to work a little harder when you come to the lesson on self forgiveness."

"I had lived a life no man would be proud of. Just when I thought I couldn't sink any lower, I'd find myself drowning. So I had to agree self-forgiveness was not going to be easy.

"I spent my days working in the book stores. I spent my nights reading. I was like a pilgrim crossing the dessert. My thirst for knowledge was unquenchable. Roy had every book imaginable for the seeker of the answers to life's questions. I read the Bhagavid Gita, the Tao, the Bible, all the philosopher's past and up to the present, Plato, Socrates, Leadbeater, Basant, Atkinson, Saint Germain, Ramacharaka on and on. We talked for hours on end. He taught me things about life, secrets passed down through ages. We talked of science, philosophy, religion, or what you might call religion, but it was not like the stories you learn in Sunday school, he said religion today teaches us how to worship God, we talked of knowing God and defining God. And that is why the journey is unending because God is indefinable.

"When it came time for me to leave Roy gave me that stone. He said this stone is you, a diamond in the rough. Let your journey begin. Let it be a magnet for your life to follow.

"So I started my journey. I started in Peru, went to India, studied in a monastery, crossed the Himalayas, walked the trail of the saints in upper Spain into France, and traveled on to Egypt, Jerusalem even the Stonehenge off the coast of Wales. And now here I am."

"Wow." It was all she could manage.

"I tried to warn you."

"And you finally found what you were looking for. All those places you went?"

"The real kicker is. One day I sat down in my apartment flipped on the tube. The Wizard of OZ, it hit me like a ton of bricks. I didn't have to look anywhere it was right here all along. I just had to tap into it." He tapped his chest.

"You make it sound so easy." a mournful reply.

"On the contrary, for me anyway. It's the hardest thing you'll ever do. The highest mountain you'll ever climb, the most arid dessert you'll ever cross. But you'll make it. We are assured of one thing in this life, we'll all make it. It's our, excuse the term, destiny." His eyebrows raised and cheeks indented.

The room fell silent. The books were hard at work sucking all the sound from the room. No breathing, no dog's tail tapping, not even a clock ticked to show that time was moving forward. The silence was consuming but neither one felt compelled to break it, to fill the void. For there was comfort in that void.

Destiny absorbed the story her ears had just taken in. She always knew somewhere in the gray mass at the top of her head that there was a reason for all of this, life. All the chaos, excitement, drama, pleasure, pain. Every event lead her to a place, another event. Life was one continuous chain reaction. She was just blown completely off course by the most recent of events in her life. As if she hadn't landed on solid ground yet, the blast was so strong the force still carried her further and further away. A tremendous fear rose at the thought of not knowing where her life was going to end up. Life had always been so organized, so mapped out. Summer vacations were planned two sometimes three years in advance. That was all blown

away now, a mighty dessert wind picked up all life'   lans and
scattered them across the vast expanse of space.

Adam sat calm, patient. Whether he said too   h would
remain to be seen. But it was a truth that he learned lo   go, once
something is said, the words expelled from the vocal cho   an never
be taken back in. If only they could. Lives would be diffe   . He was
completely satisfied to let this moment go on forever. N   ents that
you only let yourself dream about in the wee hours of th   ght when
something just won't let you slumber. This moment, s   g in the
company of this woman once again, was perfection. Her   so clear.
Chrystal blue like the ice that forms over a pond and refl   the deep
water as well as the sky overhead. These eyes focused o   me point
in space, darted with the slightest movement back and for s if some
scene was being watched but the picture too wide to vi   with still
eyes. It was Ok to be outside this scene. He had learned   ience, he
would wait to be invited into this story. Until then he w   d devour
this perfect moment.

All things come to pass and the moment was   different.
Destiny broke the silence. "Well my destiny for this mo   t I guess
seems to be cleaning up a very dilapidated dwelling. So I   s I better
move forward in that direction." She rose from the arms   the chair
missing their embrace the moment she stood.

"I'll show you the place."

One last glance over the shoulder at the booksh   es as the
screen door was opened for her.

"You're welcome to borrow whatever you like,   ime. I'm
not home much, just come in and grab a book. Oh, I   uld have
shown you the computer. It's in the office, where I took th one call.
You can check your e-mail there or just plug yours in if   d rather.
Same thing, I don't have to be home. The doors always   n so feel
free. Digger won't bother you. And if she wonders dow   see you
just shoo her back up to the house."

"She doesn't go with you?"

"No. she hangs out at home. She lets herself in an   t. I leave
a bag of dog food opened in the kitchen and the faucet o ack leaks
like a sieve so instead of fixing it I put a bucket under i d Digger
has fresh water anytime."

"Sounds like she's independent."

""⟩   sometimes I think the only reason she lets me hang
around is cratch behind the ears once in a while."
""⟩   l if she get's lonely she's welcome to come visit."
"(['m sure she'll do that."
""⟩   nks. For everything." The words came hard, with
hesitatior tween each one.
    A   ·een metal hat sat on top of the tiny house like a
leprechau derby. Yard work was kept to a minimum in front and
looked n existent in the back as the house was pushed right up
against tl nountain. Six foot high block walls held the slough back
on either e from wrapping around the house. The door opened with
the perst on of a bump from Adam's shoulder. A peculiar odor
exhaled n the house, damp earth. The smell was so familiar to
Destiny's ·strils but she couldn't place where or when she had ever
smelled i ·fore.
    "(good it looks like Lola made it out here. She's the
cleaning man. She'll come once a week. Just let me know if you
don't wai er to clean in here."
    "]   n't think that will be necessary. It looks like I can handle
it." she (dn't hold back a smirk. From the front door the entire
place co be viewed. A motel kitchenette sat in one corner. A
combinat stove, sink, and small refrigerator all in one compact unit.
A kitche ıble for two under the southern window and a recliner
opposite ler the north window. A room divider was pushed against
the wall ind the recliner to hide the single bed pushed up against
the back l. An armoire tucked beside the only framed room in the
place. Tv valls no longer than five feet enclosed the corner. Through
the open ır sat a yawning toilet. Destiny's eyes had gone full circle
and came ck to rest on her landlord.
    H   ıarded eyes watched her every movement. Monitored her
breathing ır any fraction of a deviance. The slightest hint of
recognitic If her memories were going to be unlocked this place
could be · key. Would they come all at once like the flash floods
across th :sert floor? Or trickle in a piece at a time giving her time
to study scene before the puzzle was complete? Her eyes were
calm stil ding some sadness deep within but the sadness did not
have roo rom the events from this place. Or at least they revealed
none. He uld give her an out all the same.

"I know, I told Faye no, when she first mentioned offering the place to you to rent. I didn't think it would work for you. It was built for an old miner needing nothing but the bare necessities and I'm afraid I haven't added anything to the place since I've moved back. These old prospectors had tunnel vision, just hell bent on finding their dream."

For no reason Destiny broke out laughing. "It's perfect, I love it. I have no idea why I love it, but I do. Who knows maybe I'll find my dream."

Destiny plopped down in the chair to see if it would fit. There was nothing like a chair that fit. An exhale escaped the chair and swirled around the woman. Tiny sparks playing a game of chase in the light streaming through the window.

"It's old and a little dusty."

"That's OK. I just can't resist a comfy chair. I have one back home. I got it...it was a gift." Too much. She was determined not to say too much. Or to think too much. "Just an outside chair but it hugs around me. I can sleep for hours in that chair pretending to read a good book. If I could have packed one thing with me it would have been my chair." she took a couple bounces to test the springs and leaned her head back. "This one isn't bad. It will do till I get back to mine."

"At least I can   promise there's no ants, roaches, mice or other vermin creeping or crawling around."

"Great! But what's that. The beams on the back wall. Looks like the place had another room that was taken off."

He held his breath. A ball appeared in the area between his stomach and his throat. It choked down by the time he stepped to the back of the shack and rubbed his hand over the bricked in area. Rough timbers bordered the bricks on three sides. Here goes nothing, "This is, or was the entrance to the mine."

Destiny's eyes went wide and her eyebrows raises up under her bangs. An expression of excitement. Not recognition. Could that be?

He continued to explain, "Yea. The old prospectors used to like to stay close to their claims. So some built their houses around the entrance."

"That's incredible! I love it even more."

"You might love it now that it's boarded up, but you should have tried to sleep in here when it was an open hole right to the center of the earth. It used to scare the hell out of me. I was sure Gollum was going to come up out of that hole and drag me down in there and keep me forever."

"The boogie man huh? And you used to sleep out here?"

"Only when my dad kicked me out of the house. So, yea. I slept out here quite a bit." He smiled, shrugging off an old memory.

The hand writing on the check didn't look like hers anymore. Good penmanship was a trademark of hers. So many thank you notes personally written out took the neatness out of her hand. A muscle still cramped in the palm when a pen was grasped. The bank would cover the check though. The president of the bank was a close friend and golf buddy of James'. All checks went across his desk if the signature looked suspicious. And lately all Destiny's checks went across his desk. "I wrote the check for a full month and the extra in cash. I don't know if it will take me the whole month, I'm praying it won't."

He was praying it would take the full month and more. There was only one God. They'd have to see which one's prayers would be granted. Who held more favor in the eye of the divine. If one believed in miracles, perhaps there would be a way they could both have their prayers answered. He handed her the keys to the castle if she felt compelled to lock the door.

"I'm going out of town tomorrow for a couple of days. But if there's anything you need let me know. I mean that, anything at all." his tone became low and hypnotic, "even if you just need to talk, I'm right up the road. I'd like to help. I get the impression you are climbing a pretty big mountain. I'd just like to say that there isn't a mountain stretched out before us that we are not capable of climbing. I've climbed my share. One of the most important lessons I learned was patience. Whatever it is you are going through. Just be patient the answers will come." Why he said that he did not know. Perhaps he was for a brief moment in time, a messenger. A servant of that power which draws to us what we need to hear. This gray darkness that enveloped her was not her. He could see deep inside her there was a glorious light waiting to escape.

Was her story so transparent? He saw into her soul. Maybe he was a good reader too. The dark cloud moved over her mind and the rain built up in her eyes. "Thanks. I might take you up on that. You seem, well you seem easy to talk to. Were we friends before? Did we talk way back when?"

"Unfortunately no." a remorseful tone made his voice all but a whisper. "You know it's not often we get a chance to right a wrong. I'd just like to try."

She looked up confused, "That sounds ominous."

"No. I didn't mean it that way. It's just part of your past. Something you don't remember. But I can't forget."

"Care to share."

"No. If you remember on your own then it's meant to be. If you don't then my prayers will be answered."

"Can you at least give me a clue?"

"I just want to say that if you ever do recall your life here. I am not the person I used to be. And I'll never be that person again."

Destiny took stock of all her emotions and intuitions. There was no ill feelings toward the man standing before her. The feelings had never been wrong before. A shrug of the shoulders, "No harm, no foul."

The comment was like a freight train steaming through the night. He didn't know what hit him. Anguish washed over him. "What did you say?!"

Puzzled by his reaction she repeated with caution. "I said no harm, no foul. I've learned to leave the past in the past. Not remembering doesn't bother me anymore. I don't remember things from here so to me they didn't happen. Whatever it is you're talking about. Well to me it didn't happen. The only problem coming back here is that you and everyone else here knows who I was. I don't know if I wish they would forget or if I'm glad they can remember."

He reached forward and with the back of his index finger he brushed her cheek as if removing a tear. A touch so soft she wasn't sure it had happened. But his hand stayed suspended in air for the briefest of moments. "You Destiny, haven't changed a bit. Thank God."

Digger's tail waved goodbye as the two companions walked down the lane.

He remembered his lesson on Patience: An audience with the Sage at the Tibetan monastery had finally been granted. After six months of weeding the garden, sweeping the floors, building fences from boulders packed from a streambed. And six months of silence. Only the sound of birds and the wind. To talk to another human being was going to be the most welcome occurrence.

The earlier the seeker of knowledge arrived at the sage's hut the better. Six months of questions had been building up. Time was critical. No one spoke of more than one audience with this sage in a lifetime. The most had to be made of this meeting. Long before the sun cast it's glow in the eastern sky the arduous trip to the mountaintop hut began. Sages always chose the highest point within sight. Perhaps symbolizing the height of illumination they had reached or perhaps the closer they were to the heavens, the clear night sky. For whatever reason the air was thin and getting thinner. Sweat beaded up on the forehead of the seeker despite the cooler temperature. A quick almost jogging pace began the trek but was slowing to a crawl. The man pushed down on the tops of his knees helping the next step be reached. The road turned to a trail, turned to a path then disappeared altogether. The only indication of being headed in the right direction was that the traveler was still going uphill. Muscles cramped, stomach pains caused the man to bend over resembling a traveler nearing the end of a long journey through life. Stopping to rest was out of the question. Stopping would only take valuable time from the end destination.

The door to the one room hut was open. The first rays of the morning orb sent splinters of light creeping reverently across the floor of the opening. In the center of the room the rays met the figure of a man seated on the floor. When the beams of light met the man's face the light seemed to reflect to all the corners of the room.

Not knowing what to do the seeker of illumination became a statue ready to be brought back to life by the magic spell of the man seated on the floor.

The magic words uttered slowly as one eye peaked open. "You're blocking my light."

The traveler jumped to one side as if leaping out of the way of a speeding bullet.

Peaking around the corner of the doorframe the traveler spoke. "I'm sorry. I didn't mean to, I saw you sitting there I didn't want to disturb you so I... I was told you would see me today so I wanted to get here early. My name is..."

A hand from the old man raised into the air to halt the babbling of the traveler. " I won't remember your name so there is no need to introduce yourself."

"OK. Well Could I, should I come in there. Or should I stay out here? I mean were you, are you done?"

"Since I am still alive, I think it safe to say that I am not yet done. But you may enter if you wish or you may stay out there. It makes no difference to me. Either way you will be sitting on the ground as the only place above ground in here is my humble bed and I am particular about keeping that only for my own use."

The old man unfolded from his position. Began to unkink like the Tin man in need of some oil. Outside of the hut he stretched out, then up, every bone in his body speaking out as it was called to attention.

"I meant were you done, meditating or whatever you were doing?"

"Doing? I was sitting in the sun. bathing in the warmth of its rays. But I am never done doing that, the sun will rise again tomorrow."

A fire pit in the middle of a small clearing held a few coals that were persuaded to flame again by the old man's gentle breath. "Would you like some coffee?"

This was not turning out to be at all what the traveler had envisioned this meeting to be. He pictured an old man with beard of white down to his naval sitting on a pedestal with torches on either side of him. A Persian rug stretching out in front of him for the seeker of knowledge to kneel before the wise man. Coffee? Did he just ask if I wanted coffee?

"I'd love some coffee."

"Pull up a rock it will only take a minute."

Not like the picture at all. This sage wore khaki pants and shirt. Sandals and was only perhaps a week from his last shave. The wrinkles on his hands and face were not an indication of his age but seemed to be rather a result of his way of life. Exposure to the elements carved crevasses in mountains as well as man. The coffee was prepared in almost a ceremonial fashion. Slow deliberate actions. As if there were nothing more important than this very action. Once the coffee was poured into cups the first sips savored. The old man spoke.

"What brings you to the top of the world."

The traveler had been rehearsing what to say all the way up the mountain. For six months he had meditated on the proper response to the sage's question. As if the wrong answer would send him tumbling back down the mountain head over heels. And secrets to all life's knowledge would be locked away from his grasp for all eternity.

Clearing his throat he began. "I seek illumination, the truth of life's secrets."   He exhaled waiting for the grades to be posted on the wall.

The old man squinted at him. Rubbed his beard. Swished away a pesky fly. Took a long slurp of coffee. Raised his face to the heavens closed his eyes and gave out a long sigh of pleasure. "Do you now?"

"Yes."

"Then why are you here?"

"To ask you to teach me sir, sage, teacher. I don't know what you want me to call you.

"Ram will be fine."

"Ram?"

"Yes, Ram, that's my name."

"OK. Ram."

"So you walked all the way up this mountain to seek life's secrets?"

"Yes."

"What did you see when you were climbing the mountain?"

"What did I see? It was dark. I didn't see anything. I was watching where I was going the climb was treacherous. And when I was climbing I was rehearsing what I was going to say to you."

The old man nearly fell over backwards with laughter.

"Well at least you're honest!"

The traveler did not let the outburst anger h   He had
learned in many prior lessons that his anger got hir   owhere.
Once he tamed his anger a door inside him began t   pen and
he didn't want to chance having the door close   jain. So
instead of being insulted and hurt, rising to his feet ir   huff and
heading down the mountain double time, he took ā   p of his
coffee and let the old man enjoy his laughter. Th   old man
probably didn't get many chances to laugh at silly   nans up
here in this world all his own.

When the old man regained some sense of   nposure
he looked back at the traveler.   A sparkle in hi   eyes the
traveler had not noticed before.

He began. "Your quest is rather broad.   o seek
illumination. To know the answer to life's secrets.   nce you
don't have a specific question for me. I can't gi   you an
answer. What was it you were looking to find up here

"I thought I could come up here and I cou   be your
student and you could teach me."

"I don't know what you need to know. Beca   e I don't
know what you already know. Therefore I can't teach   u."

The answer the traveler dreaded to hear. The   ords that
would send him back down the mountain the same   erson he
was when he came up. "You won't teach me then."

"I didn't say I won't I said I can't. I can't   ach you
anymore about life's secrets than what you learned (vhat you
could have learned climbing up this mountain."

"What do you mean?"

"I mean once you have set your mind to seel   ere is a
force, call it magnetism that brings knowledge to you   ou don't
really have to go anywhere to find what you seek t   answers
will come to you. But you have to be patient. And y   have to
pay attention. It could be in the morning paper, it   ild be a
conversation you overhear between strangers it   ould be
something you observe in nature. But the answers ā   coming.
Wait for them. The answer to life's secrets is that   s not so
secret, the answers are all around you if you look. Pā   ttention.
Relate what you see with what you seek. Tr   in the

magneti   at work in the universe. Be awake.
      S   ask you again what did you see on your hike up the
mountai
      "I   s just in a hurry I didn't see anything." he resigned to
his failur
      "1   n would you like to see what you didn't see?"
      V   a questioning look the traveler replied. "Sure. I
guess."
      "1   n close your eyes, don't think about getting to the top
of the m   tain, be patient, and pay attention."
      T   traveler cleared his mind. When his patients grew as
thin as I   vas prepared to let it a vision began to appear. The
experier   was similar to that of recalling a memory. But as he
had adn   ed he didn't remember seeing anything coming up
the mou   in. So this vision was coming from somewhere else.
Somewl   other than his short term memory. His footsteps
moved t   crawl. There was no hurry to be anywhere. There
was onl   vhat was before his eyes. Only this moment. The
world ar   d him began to glow as if it were all illuminated from
within. I   ide him in a bush a cocoon suspended from the
undersic   of a leaf. Slowly the bottom was chipped away and
from the   le of this tiny transparent casing two bright iridescent
blue wir   unfurled. Waved a greeting to the world and then
flew off   explore it. A flower which only blooms once in ten
years, s   ad its petals as the traveler neared. A mother bird
flew bac   nd forth to her nursery nest keeping mouths fed and
predatoi   way. A spider weaved an intricate pattern of lace to
silently,   iently await nature to provide for its needs. An army
of ants   orted at dawn to canvas the surrounding area and
return h   e with supplies to add to the winter cache. A bee
moved fi   one flower to the next assuring there would be seed
for the c   inuation of the circle of life. A breeze rushed though
the veg   tion surrounding the man raising a hymn to the
heavens   ove. All of this and so much more was flashing in the
travelers   nd. All he did not see.
      E   opened slowly as if coming out of a deep trance. "I
guess I   sed quite a bit."
      T   old man smiled a knowing smile. "We all do, but with

practice we learn to look in a different way. See what is in front of our eyes. Relate that to the questions haunting our dreams. And viola, we learn something!"

The chariot had pulled the sun well past the center of the sky. The traveler decided to begin his trek down the mountain as he planned on the decent taking far more time than the accent. He stood. The old man stood as well.

With an out stretched hand the traveler bid farewell. "Thank you."

The old man shook his hand. "For what?"

"For teaching me."

"I taught you nothing. No man can teach someone else. They can present information. But the student teaches himself. Or not." With this the old man laughed a hearty laugh again.

"Then thank you for presenting me with information."

"Anytime."

"You mean that?"

"Of course. Come back anytime. I enjoy the company."

"But I thought you only met with someone one time. They were not welcome back."

"All are welcome back. Most choose not to come."

This was the first of many trips up the to the top of the mountain.

With the final farewell the old man told the traveler. "Be happy, be content with the journey. That is where the answers to your questions lie. Knowledge and illumination are acquired along the path, one step at a time. Remember: The only thing at the end of your destination in this life is death. And what is death but a birth."

Chapter 17

Beep. Beep. Beep,

Mira was mashing down hard on the button on the cell phone like object in her pocket as if it would make the doctor arrive any faster.

A barrel of a man roamed around Destiny's hospital room. Coming in as if he were the health inspector. Not giving any verbal introduction. His over jacket was left unbuttoned. Not that they would meet in the middle anyway. A tie around the collar of a white shirt now yellow with age, was left pulled down to allow air to flow around the neck. It was summer and it was a stupid rule to wear a suit and tie. The sole of his shoes bulged out on either side testimony of the simple fact. When exposed to too much pressure something had to give. The sole was always the first to give way. He picked up trinkets off the metal tray, examined them in chimpanzee fashion. Then tossed them back toward the tray to form a new arrangement. Bored with what they revealed.

Mira stared up at him. She kept her hand stuffed in her pockets. The tanning lotion was wearing off. She had removed all but one layer of shirts and ditched the multi layered beads. Dr Adams had found her a smock trying to appear more hospital presentable. The boots remained and slid under her chair. The man now stood over her. Steady deliberate breaths inhaled and exhaled loudly through his congested sinuses. Moving his head from side to side. The beast readied himself to pounce. A heavy hand came down to rest on the back of her chair producing a brief complaint from the frame. Arctic air wafted across her cheek from the four hour breath mint meant to disguise the cigarette smell. Only her eyes could move. The beast picked up something from her lap. She pushed harder on the button in her pocket.

"What cha reading girlie?" the beast inquired.

"A book." she trembled. Still keeping her hands hidden.

"Well I can see that." he flipped it over to view the title. "Sure this isn't too advanced for you?"

Mira kept her eyes focused on the monitor. A strange bright orange halo was getting brighter with each beep. The beeps speeded up as a flashing light set on top of a road sign. CAUTION. CAUTION. CAUTION. She smiled to herself and sent a thought to Destiny. *"Don't worry, I can handle this Neanderthal."* The beep slowed but remained orange. Besides it could work to her advantage having everyone think she was mentally challenged. Fewer words had to come out of her mouth if the one she was talking to thought her impeded.

She raised her eyebrows high into the air. "Huh?" she answered the beast.

It worked. He tossed the book back into her lap. With a humph. From the corner her backpack peaked his attention. He unzipped the pocket and thrust in his paw. Shirts came trailing out like a clothes line. A magician's trick.

Mira tensed. Pushed the button in her pocket yet again. "Mine." she commanded to the man.

"I thought as much." He turned it upside down. Nothing remained. She rose from her station by the bed and protectively started putting the contents back into the pack.

The man moseyed back to the bedside. He gave a little tug on the cord threaded through a pulley. Traced the tubes from bags to veins. Stared hypnotically at the steady beep of the monitor. Took a pen from his shirt pocket and pocked at the breathing tube in the patients mouth.

He turned his attention back to Mira. "Know anything about an attempt to cut these machines off?"

She pushed the button in her pocket and didn't let up.

"MIRA! Once is enough! I got the first…" Dr Adams came into the room and pulled up short at the site of the stranger. Looked at Mira wearing a WHAT TOOK YOU SO LONG look on her face.

The stranger looked equally surprised to see him.

The stranger wasn't the man he saw boarding the elevator. Or at least he didn't think so. At any rate he was not wearing a trench coat.

"You must be the attending physician? I'm Lieutenant Edwards. Lakehead PD. Got a call there was an incident last night with this patient."

"Yes. But who called you?" the doctor had thought about calling but felt it would only complicate things to have policemen stationed outside Destiny's door.

"It's standard procedure for this sort of thing to be reported. You should know that."

"Of course. I was just wondering who actually made the call. I hadn't talked to the family about it yet."

"It was the on duty nurse. Just following protocol."

So the nurse wasn't as dense as he had given her credit for.

The officer took out a notepad from his pocket. "If I could ask you a few questions?"

'Of course."

"The patient chart shows you checked on her at 10:30 p.m. Then came back at 11:00 p.m. saw all the life supports removed and pushed the emergency call button."

"That's right. It took the team and I about 20 minutes to stabilize her."

"For the sake of speculation. Could it have been that you seeing such a hopeless case as this," he nodded down to Destiny, shook his head with regret, "might have come in, removed the life supports. Returned to your rounds, then started feeling guilty. Or perhaps you thought you let enough time go by so that when you put in the emergency call she would not have been revivable." Dull grey eyes tried to see through the doctor. Observe any deviation in his breathing. His focal point. When faced with the truth a suspect most generally would look away. The doctor locked eyes with him holding a juvenile staring contest. The officer broke the stare first. Turned back to see the retard pushing the last piece of clothing back into the backpack. "Just speculating of course."

Adams kept his calm. "Your speculation couldn't be farther from the truth. No one is ever hopeless. I saw someone getting onto the elevator as I was coming down the stairs. I didn't have time to follow him I was in a hurry to get here."

"And why were you in a panic to get in here?"

Adam hadn't thought far enough ahead before making this comment. In an effort to point the finger of suspicion away from him he had forgotten about the other three fingers that would be left pointing at him. "The truth is I had a feeling."

"A feeling? Care to elaborate?"

"I just had a wave come over me of urgency to get down here."

"And your feeling was right."

"Yes."

"You get these feelings very often?"

"From time to time."

"Are they right?"

"From time to time."

"One more thing doctor. Where did you go to medical school?"

It was one thing to alter someone's thoughts. Persuade a hospital to believe he was a doctor. It was an impossibility to get actual records stating that fact.

"Actually I went to school out of the country. I went to med school in India." It was the most unorganized country he could think of.

The officer made a few more notes. "Can you think of any one that would want to do this woman harm?"

"I don't know the woman officer or anything about her." he was lying through his teeth. A sin. Hopefully forgivable given the circumstances. Mira raised her eyebrows warning him the less said the better. His tone would siren the truth concerning Destiny.

"What about her family? Did they come to see her yesterday. Did they seem normal?"

"I don't know that there is a state of normal given what their mother and wife just went through. And not knowing how she will be from one minute to the next. Normal? They acted in shock. So yes I'd say they acted normal for the situation."

"You said a man was getting on the elevator? You sure it was a man?"

" Yes it was a male."

" Anyone else see him?"

"Not that I know of. I questioned the on duty nurse. He would have had to walk right past her. But she was texting or something and didn't see anything. I reprimanded her but it didn't do her memory any good,"

The officer made several laps around the small room. Nostrils flared trying to replenish the oxygen starved lungs from too much nicotine. He bent at the waist with a grunt. Looked under the patient's bed for any dropped piece of golden evidence. Spying Mira's shoes on the opposite side of the bed he raised up, shook his head and rolled his eyes. "Have you seen anything odd? Other than your reflection in the mirror?"

Mira raised her eyebrows.

Adams took liberty to answer for Mira. His tone offensive, "I really don't think that is appropriate. This is just a hospital volunteer. She comes in to read to the patient."

Officer Edwards looked down at the pathetic site on the bed. "Tell me doc. Do you honestly think it's gonna do any good?"

This emotion was so strange. Adam wanted to smash this man's face against the wall. Throw him out the three story window. And run him over with a vehicle if the fall didn't do him in. These feelings were not his. He had overcome viciousness eons ago. The negative vibrations of this dimension were getting stronger. Or else his feelings for Destiny on this dimension were drawing him into this dimension. Time was becoming a factor. To get entangled in this world now could prove to be detrimental.

This man hovering around the room was not to be hated. But rather pitied. He was a victim. A victim of too much darkness. He chose an admirable profession. No doubt he set out on a mission to help people. Not unlike Destiny's visit. He was just not strong enough or not educated enough to resist the mental pressure from a darkening world. Adam wondered if this was one of the souls Destiny had come to help. There were no chance encounters on this level or any other level. This man was here because he was supposed to be here. His evolutionary road led right to that hospital door. Who knows maybe Destiny's situation can soften this man's hardened heart to let in just enough warmth to get him out of this sea of darkness.

Adam mentally held the dark emotions at bay and whispered a reply. "There is always hope." Then he added for special effect, for no human ears, "for everyone."

"I'll send a uniformed officer around for the evening shift." he looked down at Destiny. "Doubt it will be for very long."

"Mmm." Edwards put his tablet back in his pocket. Looked at Mira. Rolled his eyes and opened the door to leave. Turning back to Adam, "Don't plan any out of town trips for a while. I can see you are tied up here. But I warn you till I get some more pieces to this puzzle,

I'm not ruling you out. And I can legally hold you at th   ation if I have to."

Mira and Adam stared at each other. Then at the t   cing light on the monitor. The halo glowed so bright it actually gave   heat.

"I think she's mad." Mira said.

Adam laughed. "I think so too. She better hurry u   r I'll end up in the electric chair."

"I don't like him. And neither does Destiny. /   it's not funny!" Mira's eyes narrowed to slits.

"No. It's not."

"That's all we need is someone nosing in. And it s   ls like he wasn't going to let you off the hook. India? Why did you s   ndia?"

"I couldn't think of a more unorganized countr   lopefully we'll be out of here by the time he discovers there are   medical school records for a Dr. Adams." he stroked the cheek o   s patient. Her blinking light turning back to a crimson. "Besides,   night add the urgency to the situation that Destiny needs. She can't   o coming to someone's rescue. I'm willing to be the person in need (scuing."

He bent closer to her ear and whispered her nam   icreasing the intensity of her experiences another level. "Dream D   iy. Keep dreaming."

Chapte 8

R
The begi
it was go
into agon
T
days. Bu
E
Destiny.
fast and
few mou
picked u
in.
E
tall cotto
at the ba
it. Warm
the life.
T
were a p
all crum
Destiny's
ants as th
feeling to
H
was the
memorie
Blinding
walked o
were spo
Mira. Th
separated
brought t
I

ing shoes chose a different path out of the little shack. ng of the run was not as steep. Destiny began to wonder if to be possible to feel the pain. It started slowly but rose But it still didn't hurt bad enough.

landlord true to his word had not been home for several jeep was in the drive that morning.

nd Ed showed up first thing to start their hauling job for ee loads were taken away by lunch. The two Ed's worked tiny was glad she had waited to call them till she was a ins ahead. The pruning, pulling, raking, swathing speed she tried to stay ahead. By lunch exhaustion had settled

nd Ed had extended a lunch invitation to Faye's but, the od in the back was irresistible. The lunch sack was tossed f the tree and a woman in a red bandana crumpled beside na sandwich washed down with hot lemonade. This was

folds in the bark of the old tree cradled her head as if it er mold. Ants scurried around the base quickly removing left from lunch. These ants were fascinating and held terest for quite some time. These were the same type of nes at the Rest Stop Inn, but it was a completely different tch them in their natural habitat.

y eyelids came to a complete close. For just a moment n. Somewhere in between wake and sleep was where ere kept. And the door to Destiny's began to crack. t came from no traceable source. The child from before f the light and reached out her hand to Destiny. No words between them but somehow Destiny knew her name was fingertips got closer and closer and just as they were a photon of light, SLAM! A truck door slammed and consciousness. The vision of the girl was scared away. iny jumped up and put on the gloves ready for the rest of her day. Her pace was not as vigorous as the haunting vision kept interrupting her work. This was the second time she had seen this girl called Mira. It meant something. But what? If the girl was an apparition this disturbed her. She had never been fond of or even believed in psychics. Let alone wanted to be one herself. Perhaps it was a memory. Something began to bubble up in her. Anticipation was the closest she could come to naming it.

Before leaving she inquired of the two Ed's if they knew the former residents of the home. Neither had lived here that long.

The next morning at Faye's Destiny grabbed her coffee mug in mid air and walked straight back to the corner table. The newspaper didn't flutter.

"Mind if I sit down?"

The corner turned down on the paper. Eyes scanned the empty seats at the counter. The paper was folded and placed on the table. Both hands wrapped around the mug of coffee in front of him. "No. Something wrong with the house?"

"No. The house is great. Can I ask you a question?" The man had offered his ear if she wanted to talk. This was not to be any confessions of her grief. There was something else creeping into the winkles of her brain. Another topic to think about except the loss of a spouse. It felt good to share her thoughts about a different subject.

"Sure."

"What do you know about a girl named Mira?" The crystal eyes shown with a glint of expectancy.

"What do you know about her?" His tone was flat.

"Not much, that's why I'm asking you."

"Are you starting to remember?"

"I think maybe I am. So what do you know about her?"

"That wouldn't be fair."

"Wouldn't be fair? To who?" She didn't expect opposition on this and was slightly offended. Was he willing to help her or not?

"To you."

"What do you mean it wouldn't be fair? I just asked you what you knew about her."

Irritation was raising in her voice. If the conversation was to continue he needed to choose his words carefully as to not scare off the timid deer exploring an unknown forest. The forest of her past.

"Yes, but if your brain is starting to remember, and I tell you everything I know, then your brain won't do the work. As long as you are grasping for memory, your mind will be forced to fill in all the blanks. That way you can be sure it's a true memory and not just something your mind is visualizing from what I say."

"Are you a shrink?"

"No."

"Something you read in a book or learned at the monastery?" sarcasm was not her strong suit but she made a stab at it for good measure.

He looked around as if trying to see if his secret had been overheard. No one's head snapped around as if in shock. He laughed, "No."

"You're enjoying this." there was a hint of enjoyment creeping into her being as well. She would wonder if it was wrong, out of place, sinful to feel enjoyment. But she would wonder later. There was some answers she was looking for right now that had nothing to do with the loss of her husband and moral issues. It had to do with a time before she knew her husband a time before she knew the person she had become.

"Yes." It was true he did enjoy any conversation with her. "So tell me what you know about Mira and I'll tell you yes or no. That way you will know if your memory is correct."

"I don't know if I like this game."

"You want to remember or not? That part of your memory has been lazy for a long time you're going to have to make it work."

"You know the funny part is. I do want to remember. Maybe it's coming back here or something. I haven't cared two cents about my memories for so long but now, it's like a quest. I want to remember."

"So start, tell me."

"There's not much. I see a child. A girl, her face is big and round with equally round eyes, a huge smile that doesn't turn up on the corners but I know it's a smile. And round sausage fingers reach out to me. As she says Desty. She lives in that house. My house now."

She looked to him for her yes or no. "Yes." He answered.

"Something is wrong with her. She's retarded?"

"Yes. It's Downs I think."

"OK. Great. And more than a yes."

"Well I thought that detail was miniscule."

"There's a box in her room. The words **Out There** are on the top."

"Not a yes or no. Can't help you there I don't know anything about a box."

"I cheated on that one anyway. I didn't see that in my mind. I saw it in her room."

"Cheaters never prosper. What else did you remember?"

"That's it."

"That's all?"

"Yea I guess I'm new at this but it's a start. I'm on my way."

"Let the journey begin." he raised his cup in a cheer.

She rested back against the chair. Folded arms across her chest nodding her head in self approval.

"Only one thing bothers me."

He had picked the paper up to finish the daily news. It froze in midair. "What's that?"

"Do you believe in ghosts?"

"Do you?"

"I don't know. It's just the vision of the little girl is so much more vivid than a memory. It's like I could really touch her."

"Does it scare you?"

"Which part? Remembering or thinking it might be a ghost?"

"Either one."

"No."

"Then I wouldn't worry about it." he was now concealed by tiny black newsprint.

She wouldn't worry about it. Right. What's to worry about. She was either getting flashes of memory that might possible drive her insane if the flood came too quickly. Or she was being visited by a little girl from across the veil separating the physical from the spiritual. And if this girl could come through. Did that mean that James could also come through? This thought had to be put out of her mind. It was hard enough to deal with James being dead. It was too much to deal with him being able to visit from the dead. An alarm sounded in her head. She held back a headache by pressing on her temples.

Looking up the lips were moving of the person across the table from her. All that came through to her awareness was a muffled noise. Trying to read the lips was useless.

Adam looked at her puzzled, "Are you alright?" "Destiny. Are you alright?" Her eyes had gone from sparkle to glazed. The color of her face drained away to a pasty white. His first thought was her morning run. It must have been too hot this morning. And probably too much on an empty stomach. She stared into his eyes. Almost pleading. Begging to know what was happening to her. Needing some reassurance that everything was going to be OK.

Pain. Piercing pain. A ringing in her ears, a pitch unbearable. Light flashing. Her own private lighting show. She waited for the crack. The crack of thunder. Pain mounting with each burst of light. She was splitting apart.

Lifeless, limp. Her head hit the table.

"Destiny!" he grabbed her arm.

The café crowd was frozen in time. No one moved. Barely breathed.

"Faye call 911!" Adam the only one able to have control of his vocal chords.

He righted her back into her chair. Her chin flopped to her chest. Still lifeless. His rough hand gently cupped under her chin. A piece of ice melted slowly over her face. Cool rivulets of water followed the contours of her cheeks, journeyed down to her jaw line then dove to the abyss. Drip.

She was somewhere in that same abyss. That place that is in between where you're going and where you've been. This place was so large. And lonely All alone. So all alone. A great expanse. Which direction to go? There were no signs. No way of knowing how far she had come nor how far was left to travel. Had she just begun this journey across this vast unknown. Was she somewhere in the middle? And it was so hot. The kind of heat that alters the senses. The heat wasn't coming from the place but rather from inside of her. Was this her crossing of the River Stix? Just a fog. A pale light shown through the fog to give enough light to navigate by. But the light came from all directions. Up, down, right, left. It was just enough light to reveal the Emptiness. Nothingness.

"Destiny. Destiny." He kept calling her name.

Mary Clare offered some smelling salts. She kept them in her purse. Just in case. Adam said they'd give her a few minutes to see if she could come around on her own.

"Destiny." he leaned over. Drew in the scent of her. Shampoo mixed with the sweat from her morning run. His lips brushed her ear as he whispered, "Destiny."

The light was getting brighter. Someone called her name. but which direction? Please call out again. I can hear you. But I don't know where you are. Her name again. Brighter. The light was definitely brighter.

Drip. Drip. Drip. Tiny splashes of melted ice pooled in the palm of her hand.

"There!" Faye called out. "Her eyelashes fluttered!"

By the time the ambulance attendant had arrived at the café Destiny was coherent once again. Which was a major disappointment to the ambulance crew. The last time they had the truck out of the garage was Christmas. When the town tree fell over and landed atop of the choir during Oh Holy Night. Destiny refused to go to the hospital. Seeing how it was in Las Vegas. It would take two days out of her schedule just to tell her what she already knew. She was fine. Just a little too much stress mixed with heat. Adam and the café group were a little harder to convince than the ambulance attendant. Ed thought she should go if for no other reason than to hear the siren blare all the way to Vegas. It's not every day you get to pass every car on the road. Looking out the window at the 1968 Wagoneer with the rear windows painted white, raised doubts that they would pass EVERY car on the road. But everyone's intentions were pure and hearts were in the right place. She promised to take it easy on the morning runs instead.

Chapter 19

Beep. Beeeeeee..............

"Nurse! Get the hell in here! Sombody! My Wife!" James hit the hallway in a panic. Running up and down slapping his fist on the counter at the nurses' station.

Mira sat outside beside the police officer. Giving James some privacy with his wife. She held down the call button in her pocket as Destiny's room once again become an anthill of excitement. Nurses rushed in with electronic equipment, bags of fluid, metal rolling trays with syringes and all manner of squiggly tools. Mira's eyes widened. Were they fixing a body or a car?

Adam rushed by. No look of disturbance from her holding the button down too long.

James was pushed out of the room. For his own good. He slid down the wall burying his face in his hands. The uniformed officer offered his chair. But the offer fell on deaf ears. He wept.

Mira eyed him curiously. Her legs swung back and forth atop the chair seat in juvenile fashion. Was this an outpour of love? These tears? If so why was the color of the halo not warmer when he came close to Destiny? This world was a confusing place. Muffled voices resonated through the door. In the background of the voices was still one long steady beep. She looked again at the crumpled man. Perhaps his agony was nearly over. Whatever the catalyst. Perhaps it was time for her and Adam to take Destiny and go home. But then would this man's tears be for himself instead of for the agony of his wife. Or were his tears for his own agony now? So many questions. So many scenarios. He needn't weep for his wife for any reason. She was assured by Adam that Destiny felt no pain. And there would be without a doubt no reason to weep for her once she left this life. So his tears may as well be for himself. Maybe she should give this sad man a glimpse of the truth as to his wife's condition. It wouldn't be very difficult. This man's mind didn't have a very strong shield to outside influence. That was one of the first things Mira had noticed about him. He was lucky to have been so close to Destiny for these years and her positive influence.

The door to the room swung open and the beep, be   beep was
once again a steady rhythm.

Squeaky wheels from the cart preceded the para   of nurses
and aids exiting the room. Instead of how many people   fit in a
phone booth the hospital plays how many people can fit i   patient's
room. Then Adam came through the doorway. He was not   py. Mira
read the words on his face. They told her why the hell   she been
out here and not in there with Destiny? She couldn'   ll Adam
Destiny and her husband needed time alone. Time to s   out their
relationship. Destiny needs to ratify the darkness of the au   hen ever
her husband is around. Leaving this world won't be   mpletely
possible until she comes to terms with the issue, whatever   .

The crumpled figure beside the door found streng   nough to
stand but not courage enough to meet the doctor's eyes.

"She's stable again. What the hell happened in the   ' Adam's
tone accusing.

"I was talking to her. Like you said I should. I wa   lding her
hand. Her hand got hotter and hotter. Then the siren start   oing off.
And the line on the monitor went flat. I ran out yelling for   ."

"She has a fever. It seems to have come on rapidly   r body if
fighting one hell of a fight. We increased the antibiotics an   uids."

"Is she going to die? Does that mean she's near the   ."

"I don't know who you've been conversing with. B   our wife
has just as good a chance to pull through as not. It's goin   be up to
her."

James looked at the body occupying the bed. "B   have to
know. Is she being kept alive right now. With all those n   ines and
tubes."

"That's a grey area. Without all the antibiotics, flu   nutrition
she might begin shutting down. But she is not totally on lif   pport."

"But why does her heart stop beating?"

That was a good question. Adam wished he knew t   nswer to
that himself. All he could do is shake his head in defeat. "   're doing
everything we can."

"You've got to promise me one thing. I just ne   to know
when it's hopeless. I just want you to promise me you'll t   me when
it gets to that point. She has a living will. Ironically she   de it out
just a couple of months ago. We had the strangest convers   n. I don't

118

even rem   ber how it all began. She made it clear there" he trailed off
into his n   iories.
"(I'll make you that promise. But I already promised you
we woul   o everything to save her and that promise comes first."
how stra   the wording the man chose. Tell him when, not if, it gets
to the po   )f hopelessness. "I have a strange request. I'd like to know
what you   re telling your wife. When the alarms started going off."
"]   ink that's a little personal. What I say to my wife is
between   wife and I. I don't see how it has anything to do with her
medical   idition." He bristled as an animal being backed into a
corner. E   darted back and forth surveying the best escape.
T   doctor held his ground. "On the contrary I think it might
play a p: n her healing and that is her medical condition. And my
business.
"]   ou are trying to see if my wife and I had any marital
problems   it might be disturbing her mental state, we didn't. I was
just talki o her about the mail that came that day. It was crazy but
she alwa   loved getting the mail. Like opening a surprise package.
Just simp   tuff like that."
"("
"s   vhat?"
"1   it was in the mail?"
"]   mestly don't know. It got scattered everywhere. I haven't
even gon   look."
A   n could tell it wasn't a complete lie. But definitely not the
whole tru   Maybe if he knew what the problem between these two
were he   uld help Destiny get through it faster. And time was
becomin;   key factor in this situation. His thoughts were not all that
different   n James. When not if. The outcome was inevitable. But
his feelin initiated from the opposite side of the situation. He would
be taking   home, James would be letting her go.
J   s looked up at the doctor as he turned to leave. "Are we
done her   have to get home to the kids. I promised them a report.
Destiny':   d should be showing up soon. We've worked out shifts."
Q   k emotions of this dimension A deep inhale tried to dull
the edge   his voice. "I'd say we're done." It hurt to hear this
woman's   nily worked out shifts to come and see her. As far as he
was conc   ed they could all go back to their too busy lives. He would

be right here, without hesitation.

He opened the door to the room with the light show in full force. Mira followed. Took her place on the opposite side of Destiny's bed. Waiting for her reprimand.

"Go ahead." she smirked at the doctor.

"Go ahead and what?"

"Give me my tongue lashing. Why was I outside and not in here?"

"It's not your fault. But yea, why were you out there and not in here?"

"Adam. Whether you like it or not these two persons are married. Joined in a physical bond. I thought they deserved some privacy. Not to mention there is something the two of them or at least Destiny needs to come to terms with in regards to that man. I thought if I left them alone maybe it might happen."

"I agree with you there, I'd like to know what he was saying to her. Did you hear anything?"

"Nope. And it wouldn't be any of my business if I did." her eyes stared at Adam. A teacher driving home the lesson of the day. The look of truth.

She was right. He was getting to entwined with Destiny's physical life. His objective was to help her break free of it. Not get stuck in the clutches himself. The details of her life, the pain, joy, sorrow were unimportant. What was important was the outcome, the end result.

His lips held tight together the ends turning upward in a smile. A sheepish smile. One that said he understood his guilt and was thankful for the insight. One that said he got caught up in the moment but was back on track now. He   nodded his head. "Thanks. I needed that."

"I think the proper response would be you're only human. But you are not."

Chapter 20

Dawn broke for most sitting at Faye's waking up slowly. For Destiny dawn cast its first rays on her trail ahead. It hurt bad but it still didn't hurt bad enough. The blisters worn from new shoes had healed and the shoes were proof of the old saying as comfortable as an old shoe. The stamina was building up in her heart and muscles and lungs. Soon she was going to have to change her time limit or be satisfied with the pain level reached in her allotted time. But for today the hour was up. There was work to be done. Slowing to a cool down walk, her mind suddenly was ablaze with a Technicolor scene. The pictures reeled into a story. In shock she bent forward. Both hands grabbed the tops of her knees to support her from tumbling forward down the mountain.

From the other side of town the sun reflected two small circles close together. Ed reached for his phone to call for help but the woman righted herself before he punched send on the phone and descended the mountain slowly.

"Good morning Faye. Do I smell blueberry muffins?" Destiny asked as she sat in the chair opposite her landlord. There was an imaginary seating chart to the café and this one appeared to have her name on it as it was the only vacant one when she came down from her mountain run for the past week and a half. A box was placed at her feet as she sat down.

"And then some. Earl begun to branch out. This morning's special is cream cheese, blueberry with crumb topping." Faye reported.

"It's not bad but you can keep the crumb top if you ask me." Ed contributed his food critique. His glasses clouding meeting the steam from the coffee.

"That's the best part. I'll take your crumbs." Ed added.

"Keep your mitts off my crumbs, jackass!"

"I'll take your crumbs Ed." Mary Clair batted her eyes from under her ball cap.

Whitey sat quiet devouring his third muffin. "I'll have another Faye, and I don't care if it comes with crumbs or not."

Stubs sat to the other side of Whitey. He was a new comer to the crowd as far as Destiny was concerned. He'd been out sick with a dog bite. Bendline's one and only mail carrier could get rid of half his deliveries showing up at the café. "You've had three muffins already Whitey. You better watch your waistline."

The door jingled. Faye's eyes grew wide. "Trixie. We haven't seen you in a month. Where have you been?"

Trixie was the only Madame in the whole county. Her place was clean. She saw to that. A doctor was flown in every two weeks to test the girls. And no drug addicts. They were allowed to booze with the clients but if they were caught with anything else they were on the bus back to Vegas. The clientele appreciated that as well as the discretion.

"I've been down with the flu. And shorthanded. But like mother Hubbard the cupboards are bare."

Adam couldn't help a smile as he folded down the corner of the paper to see Destiny regarding Trixie.

Destiny was naive but not dumb. But couldn't help being amazed at this woman. Her figure came straight out of playboy. And even at seven in the morning the woman looked remarkable. Her red sequin tank top halfway held her watermelon chest. It couldn't all be her or she should have wound up in the Ripley's Believe It Or Not. Skin tight black leather pants ended just short of three inch high heels. Windblown orange hair danced around her face and caught from time to time on her sparkle caked eyelashes.

"Coffee Trixie?" Faye asked.

"Better be decaf, I got to get back and hit the sack." The long legs mounted the stool as if straddling a horse. A sigh of joy escaped her lungs. "Oh, God it feels good to sit down."

Ed looked down the counter, glasses still fogged. "Rough night in paradise Trixie?"

"When are you gonna come out and see for yourself, Ed? What we got playing is better than anything you could get on the tube at home."

Ed gave Ed a jab in the ribs.

Mary Claire got up and left.

"How bout that muffin Faye?" Whitey asked

"I've only got one left and it's got Destiny's name on it. How bout it Destiny?"

"It smells too good to pass up. Sure. Sorry Whitey."

The whole town was represented at the café that morning. Mel from Mel's Bar, Gus the auto mechanic, Mr. Harris and son, from Harris and Sons Hardware. Frank from Frank's Food and More, Hal ran a septic and rooter service Hal He's Your Pal, even Sam, head of the town board attended coffee. When Mary Claire exited, her spot was filled by Larry. Larry didn't run a business of his own he was the 21 dealer at the local casino. All the faces were becoming as familiar to Destiny as family. With the exception of Trixie.

Someone had just told a joke and Trixie's melons bounced with laughter.

"What did you bring?" The paper still hid the man as if on a surveillance mission.

Destiny turned her head quickly with a jerk to give her attention to the Wall Street Journal.

"Me? Nothing?" Destiny answered quickly.

"Yes you did. You put a box under the table. What is it?" a corner of the paper turned down.

"It's nothing." her gaze drifted back in the direction of Trixie.

"Don't let her intimidate you. You'll get used to her."

"I'm not intimidated." in a whisper she asked, "Do you think those are real?"

He couldn't resist egging her on. "I wouldn't know. Hold on I'll ask." the chair scooted back from the table.

A hand grabbed his arm and dug into his skin. He looked down at the hand. Five slender fingers devoid of fingernail. Calluses on the palms of the hand actually scratched his skin. His heart panged that this woman would have to work so hard. A throne with servants was what she deserved, not a shovel and a rake. Then he looked into her eyes. Her face was aglow with leftover sunshine. The recent fresh air filled her lungs with rich life that radiated. No matter the price paid through the worn hands the smile on her face was worth it. He resumed his seat.

He reached out and tapped the table top. Gesturing for her to put the box on the table.

"Then show me the box. The one you described the other day. The one you found at the house. I don't think you brought it to coffee to keep it from getting stolen. I'd like to see it. "

"It can wait. I didn't think it would be this busy." wide eyes viewed Trixie rubbing the back of her neighbor at the bar. "Maybe another time. I wasn't sure you would remember my mentioning the box."

"Of course I remembered. Do you have more questions?"

"I'm not sure. Maybe, but this just felt so real I don't know if I need confirmation."

"Your memory must be improving. I'd like to hear it anyway." Her enthusiasm was wonderful to witness. Like seeing a rose bloom on a time warp video. He was safe as long as her memories concentrated on Mira. But with the recall action in motion. It was only a matter of time until total recall was reached. Would she be sitting across the table from him then. A woman anxious to share her memories. Or would she hate him for what he was. For who he was and the way he mindlessly treated her? Whatever the outcome he had this moment. This time, these precious cups of morning coffee watching crystal eyes across the table light up with joy.

The box was lifted onto the table, presented with almost reverence. "I took it home last night and was looking over the stuff inside but none of it made any sense until I was running this morning. And wow."

"I'm listening." he glanced at his watch, "I won't have to leave for another hour."

"OK. Here goes. I feel like I should prelude this with 'IN THE BEGINNING'."

"Might be a bit too strong of an intro. But what do I know? You're not starting at your birth are you, I've heard of people that remember their birth. But I don't know if an hour is going to be enough time."

"No not my birth. But the birth of a friendship."

"Who's friendship?" Ed was leaning his ear toward the side table. The volume of the whole café had been turned down a notch or two.

Stage freight sat in.

"Pipe down Ed let her talk. You'll get the details soon enough. Go ahead Destiny." Faye was self elected moderator of what would be known as the Tales of Mira.

Destiny looked over her shoulder in the direction of Trixie to see if by chance something else had her attention.

Adam tapped his finger on the top of the OUT THERE BOX followed by a clearing of his throat.

The details of a lost memory began.

"It was the first day of my freshman year in high school. I was nervous to say the least but had managed to make it from one end of the day to the other. The feeling at the end of that day was like nothing I had ever felt before. Utter and complete relief. I was practically skipping home. In fact I might have been.

I was coming up on Pearl's house. There were two people in the front yard. An older lady with graying hair pulled back in a bun. A great number of which were escaping their bondage. By her side was a young girl. I had a choice to make to cross the street or continue my charted course and risk confronting the two and perhaps even have to enter into conversation. Not one of my strengths. But the other side of the street housed Mrs. Lake's two German shepherds. I held my ground.

The older woman was explaining something to the young girl. They were by the broken gate. The woman had a long stick and she was drawing in the dirt. She drew a line and pointed to the street side of the line and said to the young girl, 'bad' Pointing to the inside of the fence she said, 'good'. The line was drawn again. This time the woman stood on the outside of the fence pointed to herself and said,' bad gram', she stood on the inside of the fence and said much gentler, 'good gram'. The last time she drew the line she held the young girls hand, brought her to the outside of the fence and said 'bad Mira.' The girl began to pucker her lips the lower one trembled. The lady then took the girl by the hand and led her across the line to the inside of the fence and said 'good Mira'. The girl opened her eyes wide, then opened her mouth just as wide in a smile. The wide eyed girl grabbed the lady's hands in hers and shook them up and down in a victory dance.

As I approached the two noticed me. The celebration halted the young girl hid behind the older lady. The hiding was a bit difficult as the girl came up to the older lady's shoulder. The young girl peeked out frequently, then darted her head back behind the lady. The woman gave her a light reassuring pat on the arm, as she spoke to me.

"Hello there," she began, "how are you?"

I stopped in front of them. A one word answer in p   ng would be rude. My forward progress paused.

"Hello." That was going to be the end of my   se I was afraid. The well of polite conversation had run dry. T   nice lady made no attempt to continue the conversation either. She   od there looking sheepish. Her eyebrows held a higher than n   al arch. Probably thinking she looked ridiculous having a young   l almost her size hiding behind her. I just stared. Tried not   but who wouldn't? No attempt at explanation was made on her p   nor was inquiry made on mine. Wide eyes peeked out from behind t   ady.

The young girl gasped as she looked down at   feet, she looked at the line still drawn in the dirt, looked at whic   de of the line my feet were on. She began yelling. "Bad! Bad! Bad   The girl continued yelling, pointing at me, looking at the lady, wait   for some response on her part. "Her bad!"

"Mira, calm down, it's all right," the lady cons   the girl. But the girl kept continuing her claim. Her insistence   w like a desert brush fire. More intense with each utterance of th   me word over and over.

"Bad, bad." the girl repeated.

The lady finally looked at me apologetically, rea   d out for my arm with one hand while still trying to pat the girl. Th   dy asked pleadingly. "Would you mind stepping into the yard   st for a moment?"

Her hand gently pulled on my arm as I stepped ac   s the line she had drawn in the dirt. The fit from the young girl ins   aneously stopped. Stepping out to stand beside the woman the   l smiled, crossed her arms over her chest and gave a swift nod to h   ead as if confirming this a personal victory.

The old woman was non-descript I would say. Esp   lly for a fifteen year old on her way home from the first day of fre   an year. Appearance details were not in the forefront of my mind.   d I been witness to a crime needing to describe her, the woman   uld have escaped.

The young girl on the other hand was, almost un   lainable. She was round, everywhere. Her face was very round. He   ms were round. Her legs were round. A bowl full of jello stom   fit tight

inside he   riped top. Chubby little fingers poked out of chubby little
hands. N   ing compared to the roundness of her eyes. Big blue
saucers i   ed rosy cheeks. The corners of her mouth drooped down
even whe   he smiled. Her smile was more of an opening of her mouth
real wide   her tiny teeth would show. Then her eyes become slits on
her roun   face instead of saucers full of questions and wonder.
Unexplai   le, this girl was unexplainable. Somehow she immediately
reached   ) my heart and touched it with a warm glow that I had
never feli   fore.
       V   1 our eyes met my heart leaped into my throat. I was spell
bound. A   ile crossed my lips. At the same time tears welled up in my
eyes. I ki   I couldn't let her see. Unable to fight them back, the tears
came. I   l never seen a retarded person before. Embarrassed, I
turned av   . A deep breath allowed my heart to return to its proper
place. Th   ld woman regarded me for quite some time.
       "   like you to meet Mira."
       Si   kept her arm wrapped around the girls shoulder as to
protect h   from the cold. Only it wasn't cold at all. The girl stood
shyly, he   mouth drooping a little, her eyes looking at me. Or, I
thought (ne. Her eyes seem to wander, each independently of the
other. Oi   ve was definitely looking at me, but I couldn't swear to the
other one   oint of focus.
       "   yo," she muttered softly.
       "   my name is Destiny," I said hesitantly reaching out my
hand, loc   g to the lady for approval.
       T.   lady nodded gently and stretched the girls arm toward me
slowly sc   at we could shake hands. When the girls hand reached
mine she   asped it firmly but not painfully. She started shaking my
hand up   l down. Slowly at first then picking up speed and altitude
with eaci   iss. I made no attempt to lead. I let my hand go along for
the ride.   iy up, then way down. Mira's head went up when our
hands wo   up. Her head went down when our hands went down. Up
high we   ild go, then quickly down again. Our feet were no longer
on the gi   id. When our hands went up we were cresting the highest
part of a   ler coaster ride. The anticipation mounting. As our hands
went zoc   ig down we were streaking down the other side of the
coaster c   to climb the back up again with equal enthusiasm. Mira
began lai   ing the higher she lifted my hand the louder she squealed.

The higher she lifted my hand the wider her eyes opened. The laughter was infectious, soon we were all on the same roller coaster ride. The hands would go up and we would squeal with excitement then the hands would come down and we would laugh even harder than the time before. It was the lady that brought a stop to our ride.

"OK, OK time to stop for now, we don't want to get too worked up, it makes us sleepy, huh?" She was pulling our hands apart and smiling brightly at the girl.

I felt a sudden let down.   I knew in my heart, a simple hand shake would never be the same.

The lady looked now at me with such gratitude in her eyes, "Well you've met Mira, my name is Pearl." She stretched her hand out in introduction to me and as I grasped her hand Mira reached for our hands to repeat the prior scene. Pearl stopped her before she could start swinging our hands. "We've had enough swinging for now Mira," she said softly. Mira returned her comment with a big smile, and a nod of understanding.

"Could you sit with us and have a glass of lemonade, we were just about to have some on the porch," Pearl gestured showing   me toward   the front porch.

Mira stared up at me with those big round eyes. No they weren't just staring at me they were pleading.

The invitation was accepted. I sat on the edge of the splintery porch. Pearl had Mira sit next to me. Then disappeared into the house. I was alone with this child.

"OK ," I said putting my hands on my knees. Mira nodded her head looking across at me and placed her hands on her knees.

"So, Mira?" she gazed at me intently, she craned her head around to look directly into my eyes, I suddenly felt I was on the hot seat, my total existence here on earth lied in my ability to communicate with this girl." How old are you?" no response. Just blue saucers staring at me.

"Ow dar?" She asked pointing with her chin in the direction that I had come.

Ow dar? What was she asking me? Ow dar.

"Wha ow dar?"   Mira tried again.

I looked around for some help with interpretation. Pearl was still beyond helping in the house. Wha ow dar? "What's? Out?

There?" I said very slowly hesitating after the utterance of each word to see if I was on the right track. Mira nodded her head exuberantly. Her eyes crossing and uncrossing as she nodded.

I was excited! I got it. I could do this, I could talk to her. But, what did she mean?

What's out there? Blind. The girl must be blind. Her eyes did look funny, and the woman kept close to her at all times. Then sat her on the porch right next to me. The woman should have told me something like that. What if she fell off the porch because I wasn't watching her carefully enough?

Ed interrupted. "Faye I thought you told me she was retarded."

All eyes were glued to Destiny. Whitey exclaimed. "Oh Ed. What did you have to go and cut in like that. Zip it up. Go ahead Mrs. Walker."

"Sorry Mrs. Walker. I won't do it again. Just trying to get the facts straight."

"Ed would you shut up. Adam said he only had an hour." Faye completed her job and returned the floor to Destiny.

"Are you blind? Can you see?" I waved my hand in front of her face.

Mira winced.

"I ee. Wha ow dar?" she repeated her question slowly as if giving me time to understand.

"I'm afraid I don't understand what you mean. What's out there? If you mean outside your yard..."

Her hands smacked together in a single clap. "Ow dar?"

"Oh. OK. Outside the yard, let me see. I guess I'd have to say everything is out there." It was the best answer I could come up with. It seemed to please her for she smiled and sort of hugged herself. I think she was as pleased with herself that she could communicate with me as I was that I could communicate with her.

When Pearl returned with the lemonade Mira smiled at her and said "Evy ting ow dar." sharing her new found knowledge of the world.

Pearl looked at me very pleased then back at Mira and said, "Why, yes that's right Mira. Everything is out there." Pearl turned to me and said, "I see you two have been visiting."

"It took a while but I finally figured out what she was asking."

I explained to Pearl.

"Yes, you did very well." Pearl began, "It's not always easy to figure out what she is trying to say, and I'm afraid she tends to get quite worked up when she can't get her point across. You witnessed a bit of that when you walked up. By the way thank you for making it easier on her and coming into the yard. Not to mention easier on me too. When she asked you what was out there, I guess I should explain. She doesn't get out much. Only when it is absolutely necessary. She has had some bad experiences when she has been out of her familiar surroundings. But, she does like to know what is out there. When I do go out I try to bring her something of what is out there. She has a special box, we call it her 'out there box'."

Mira jumped up and went into the house. She returned shortly with a large shoe box. Mira set the box down between us and with the sounds of great effort she returned to her seat beside me. She opened the box and there was her collection of 'out there'. The box contained many magical treasures. Mira picked out a feather and stroked my cheek with it. She handed me; a button, a postage stamp, a cash register tape, a gum wrapper, a penny, rock, a dried leaf, a key, half a ticket stub. I watched in awe as she showed me all the treasures in her 'out there box'. Mira watched my expression with sincere anticipation, as if she wanted these items to be as special to me as they were to her.

I tried to show the reaction she was looking for as I told her, "This is the most special treasure I have ever seen."

She seemed satisfied with my comment for she smiled and slowly started putting the items back into the box. So these were the treasures of the world, what the world was made of. All these years I thought it was just dirt, concrete, trees and bushes here and there. I guess I was wrong. It was a privilege to have been shown I was mistaken.

"You bing me ow dar?" Mira asked when she had replaced the lid on the box.

"You want to go out there?" I asked her curiously.

Without intent I had stricken horror into this fragile child. She shook her head violently and got a look of fear on her round face. Moving herself in the direction of Pearl for protection. Pearl stepped in to interpret for me, "She wants you to bring her back something from out there."

While Mira was bent over me her face inches away from mine waiting for my answer Pearl whispered. "It's OK. But if you don't mind agreeing. It will make it easier. She'll forget all about it the minute you leave."

After deliberating I said. "Sure. I'll find you something from "out there'."

Mira took the treasure back inside.

"Thank you." Pearl said. But she didn't think I meant it. And I wasn't sure either.

I headed home. Looking back over my shoulder, Mira sat rocking herself on the porch. She smiled, shrugged her shoulders way up high and sort of hugged herself.

But I must have gone back because when I was looking over this box under the lid I had written. To Mira from Destiny. Our Out There Box. I'm guessing I made it for her to keep the stuff I brought her.

Faye was the first to speak as Destiny traced the words written in glitter on top of the box. "Well I'll be. I never knew she could talk."

"I'm sure there's a lot of things we didn't know about the kid Faye." Adam was glad that the past was unfolding for Destiny. But he feared what was yet to come. This seemed to be the beginning of the inevitable. The inevitable would come, it was just a matter of time. "So what's in the box. What comprises this world of ours?"

The musty smell mixed with the aroma of toast eggs and potatoes. The lid was gently set on the table not to disturb the glitter letters. Adam peeked over the edge of the box as if viewing a precious baby sound asleep. And indeed that was what the box contained. Sleeping memories. His eyes looked at her, crystal blue orbs looked reverently at the intersection of her past and the future. A lump formed in her throat. Apologetically she named the contents of the box. As if she were sorry there was not more to the treasure chest. "A silly piece of chalk. A leaf, I'm half afraid to touch this it might crumble. A fan." a swirl of air moved between them at the fan was opened and waved. "A piece of candy, tootsie roll, one of my favorites. A feather. This empty bottle, maybe pills or something. A heart, it looks like there was something glued on it. And here's the real treasure. A penny. I've got to get on the internet and see if it's valuable. But that's it nothing else. Just some silly worthless trinkets." her shoulders shrugged as she looked out the window.

His reaction was pivotal. If he bushed it off as useless the opening door might close. But that way the past could stay where it was. In the past. The quiet grew deafening. "Worthless? I don't see anything worthless. What I see are treasures that meant the world. Meant the world to a little girl and will probably be equally priceless to you when the memory of each is unraveled."

The pivotal moment was past and he had turned in the right direction. He knew that by the smile that came across her face. "Thanks." she whispered. For what she wasn't sure.

"That's it. The end of the story?" Ed was disappointed.

Destiny smiled. "That's all I remember for now. But I think I'm on a roll. I'll keep you posted. But I got to go. I need to get a few piles of junk ahead of you and Ed."

She put the box under her arm and left a five dollar bill on the table. The box would become a part of her. It became a commonplace as her handbag. Wherever she went the box of treasures would be right there with her. Magnetizing the memories out of her subconscious.

Trixie stopped her in passing. "That was a sweet story sugar. And say if you want some more glitter to get that top looking shiny and new I can bring you some next time I come in. we got sparkles in every color under the rainbow!"

Destiny's cheeks were on fire. Keeping her head down to hide the physical signs of her embarrassment. She managed, "Oh thanks. That's nice. But I kinda like it just the way it is."

Whitey spoke up next. "You tell a real nice story Miss Destiny. You should be a writer."

She turned as red as Trixie's top for a different reason this time. Then rushed out the door.

Adam winced as if in pain. But it was true. She should be a writer.

Nine o'clock rolled around and all that was left in Faye's was dirty dishes and the Wall Street Journal deep in thought. Grabbing cups and empty muffin plates Faye sat and pulled down the paper.

"So maybe the memory loss thing wasn't a hoax. Maybe she's being truthful."

"A hoax is something you do for gain Faye. What would she possible have to gain from telling us she didn't remember."

"Well aren't you a walking dictionary. I just meant I believe her is all. You certainly have been different since she came into town. I can't even get two sentences out before you jump down my throat. And when you're not being cranky you just sit there somewhere far away with the blinds closed."

"Sorry Faye I hadn't noticed."

"Well that's better now tell me what's wrong."

"Nothing."

"That's a lie. I've known you for too long Adam. You've changed since she walked in here and I want to know why."

"We've all changed Faye."

"Over time, but not overnight." she was always good at lightening the mood. Faye hadn't really changed not that he could see. "How come you never made a pass at me Adam. You know we would have been the perfect couple. Head cheerleader, basketball captain, prom king and queen.

"I guess I was just too busy passing the ball to make a pass at you Faye." He winked.

She looked toward the kitchen. "Well I might not be the catch I used to be, but I still know a thing or two about playing the game."

His phone rang. The call to save the day. "I've got to go. My ride's here."

"You've got to open up Adam. You've been building a wall every since you moved back to Bendline. And you've put up the final bricks since her face came through the door. I'm just telling you as a friend. Let the wall down."

"It'll come down Faye. It's gonna come crashing down."

Chapter 21

Beep. Beep. Beep.

Destiny was becoming aware of the fact that she w   ı traveler in a giant labyrinth. Some of the paths she went down   ıted pain others pleasure. A familiar feeling would grow stronger   stronger as she traveled, only to come to a dead end and she would   ʹe to take a turn. Some had a tremendous draw at the beginning   ıt as the journey continued she could not wait till the nearest cro   oad. The paths were not completely dark. The light shown through   nist as if the fog rolled in to blanket the world. Visual details could   be made out she had to rely strictly on her intuition, her feelings. N   hat much unlike life itself but people tend to ignore their intuition fo   e sparkle and shine of pretties in the visual world. But, as with life t   once she chose a path there was no turning back. For as she trave   forward, the path behind fell way into oblivion. There was only   moment. The best had to be made of the turns and paths she chose.

There was no sense of time. Or space for that   tter. The labyrinth could be acres and acres or it could be the point   the head of a pin. There was no recollection as to how long sl   ıad been wandering. Searching for a memory as to when she arrive   how she arrived turned up futile. It reminded her of the first scene   f Narnia. As the world was being created. Could that be it, was   e in fact creating her world. Since the journey was taking place   ıer mind, and the funny thing was that she was aware of that, she co   create or make this anything she wished. But for now all she wishe   ıs to find the way out. The way home. For the strongest intuition   that she did not belong here.

The mist began to clear just up ahead. There w   definite blue haze migrating from the path to the right. She quicke   her pace but her feet did not move. Looking down she saw no feet   e saw no hands. Standing in front of the path there was a most   ıasurable feeling. Similar to standing on cliff looking out over the o   ı. Breeze ruffling her hair and able to see forever. This path had to l   ried. The path felt warm, kind, compassionate, faithful, it felt like   riend. At least if nothing else, it felt like the path had no end.

134

N   stroked Destiny's hand as she read on and on. Mira read
all throu; he night. She didn't require rest. Her voice was kept low
as to not turb the other patients. Two books had been finished and
she had l in a third. One of her favorites. <u>The Chronicles of Narnia</u>.
Who kne what worlds Destiny was visiting. Mira hoped the stories
could so now transfer the energy of the stories to Destiny's mind.
Somewh le same as sleep learning.

A aft of guiding light woke the new day. The curtains to the
room's c window were open wide so the rays could fall on the
patient l ng captive in the bed. The first rays of morning were
always tl est. They held the most promise and hopefully in this light
the way l le for Destiny.

T shift change was occurring as voices could be heard in the
room ne loor. The on duty nurse would check the patient for the
final tim n their shift and the new nurse would check in with the
patient lc ng them know they were taking over for the next shift.
Mira did have a watch. Six a. m. if she had to guess. With all the
machines oked up to Destiny there seemed a clock would be on one
of them. it blinking lights flashing numbers and bar codes. It had
been thii eight hours since Destiny met her destiny or rather the
grille of 8 wheeler. Hauling oranges from Florida the report said
Adam ha old her. As if these minute details were needed. They only
helped to ss the time. Give the mind something to mull over.

"(d morning. How are we today? Oh good I see you've
opened blinds. Dr Adams wrote in red on the chart. OPEN
BLINDS RST THING IN THE MORNING!" The nurse made her
stop in D ny's room.

S l hands checked the level of fluid in the bags. Traced the
tubes fro he bags to the input ports. Picked at the tape holding the
tube in I iny's throat. Pulled a piece of folded up paper from her
pocket a nade some notations as if taking the order for breakfast at
the local er. One pint of glucose, a bag of antibiotic and another
vial of m hine. That should hold her till lunch.

T nurse smiled at Mira. "I'm Faye I do the night shift most
of the we Was she a friend or family." Nodding to the bed.

" iend. But she is, not was." Mira said blankly.

T nurse flushed at her mistake. "Of course. I'm sorry. Did
you have travel far to get here. I noticed you were here all night. I

assumed you didn't live around here. Have a home to go to anyway."

"I was close by. Very close by." Mira blinked her round eyes slowly as if sleep was not too far off.

"Well I'm headed home to get some rest. You might do the same. I could have a recliner sent in so you could stretch out."

"No thank you. I'm fine. I've got to keep reading. Dr Adams said to keep her mind occupied with noise. It might bring her around."

"Well you certainly are a devoted friend. I've got the night shift again tonight so I'll see you then." Trying to add a positive note to the patient's condition to make up for the major blunder from before.

Mira continued reading as Destiny walked further down this path filled with love and warmth. The halo around the blip radiated pink.

Chapter 22

The day was the hottest without a doubt that Destiny ever remembered living through. Perhaps turning the rental car back in was a bit premature. It would have felt good to go sit in it with the windows up and turn the air on high. But, at a saving of nearly a hundred dollars a day she could use her feet. After a week of walking around town, Adam dug a bike out of his garage and asked if she might want to borrow it for transportation. Bendline was so small where ever she was headed she could get there within ten minutes on the bike. And if there was any hauling to do she felt obligated to use the two Ed's. But to keep it business she insisted on renting the bike. Two dollars a day was added to her rent.

The old chicken coop out back of the place was filled with numerous treasures. But she had to hold Ed and Ed off for a few days while she examined everything. The first day the door was opened the two Ed's came barreling out the door arms full of the contents and put it straight in the truck. It was clear they were working on volume and opening that door looked like the mother lode to a junk hauler.

From what Destiny could clean up so far though, the contents belonged in a museum instead of the dump. And that was just the items she could recognize. Some of the things she hadn't a clue what it was or used to be used for. Adam had been gone for nearly two weeks straight and Destiny had taken the opportunity to use his internet nightly. There were several antique web sites. After the digital camera arrived that she ordered online she started e-mailing pictures of the items from the chicken coop to the web sites. The e-mails were flooding in and she was learning a wealth of new knowledge about antiques. Not to mention getting great pleasure out of it. Her niche might have been found, there was practically enough stuff in the coop to start a small store.

Faye had announced during coffee there would be sun tea ready at lunch. It was after two when Destiny stopped for lunch. Warm lemonade just didn't cool her off. A hundred and twelve in the shade and probably a hundred and twenty inside the chicken coop. She made a bee line for Faye's and the ice tea.

She hopped on the bike. Not thinking it was possible to build up anymore of a sweat. She was wrong.

A cooler duct was aimed right at the front door. When cold air hit red, sweat covered face an ice cream headache was the result. Destiny wavered and grabbed for a stool.

Faye sat at the little table on the side. The café was deserted. Not even a sound from the radio in the back.

"Hey there Destiny. Come on over and join me."

The pain in her head was fading. The sweaty customer raised her head from her arms on the counter. "Hi Faye."

A large glass with ice and amber colored liquid kept Faye company. Sitting at the table counting the number of cars that passed by the window. "That's five." she said.

Destiny scooted the chair out from under the table. "Five what?"

"Five cars in one hour. But I don't know if the last one counted it was Whitey. He went by the other way half hour ago. Do you think it counts."

"Sure. Traffic is traffic." Destiny studied Faye's stare, then the amber liquid. A familiar odor carried past her from the cooler duct. "How's the tea Faye, got any left?"

"Sure. What say you help yourself? It's behind the counter in the big jar with a spout."

Beside the tea jar was a bottle of Jim Beam. The color was the same as the liquid in Faye's beverage.

"This tea is great Faye. Can I get you a refill while I'm up?"

Almost angry Faye looked at Destiny. "It's past tea time for me thanks. But the ice in my glass is getting lonely so if you could bring that bottle over?"

"Haven't you had enough."

"Not nearly enough darlin."

Destiny grabbed the bottle not knowing what else to do. The kitchen was empty. Hopefully Earl would return soon to take over the place.

"Sit with me would you Destiny?"

Destiny sat.

"I bet there's a lot of traffic where you're from huh?"

"A fair amount. But I live off the main road. So really the only vehicles I see in a day would be the ones entering or leaving my house." She would have said the only vehicles she saw was James's leaving for and returning from work. But she didn't want to get into that. Especially not with a drunk woman. The urge to talk about it had grown. The need was sprouting, bulging just beneath the surface. When it was ready to rupture the surface Destiny had decided her father would be the one she would call on.   But it wasn't that time. Not quite yet.

"Destiny. Destiny. Little Destiny Murphy. You sure shocked the hell out of me, and others when you came through that door. Who'd have thought you'd ever come back here. But look at you. You sure made something of yourself, made something of your life." Her focus was back on the street outside.

"And look at you Faye. You run this business."

She gave a sound of disgust. "More like running a prison. For myself. But I've finally given in. Quit fighting it. Just accept that this is it. This is my life, till death do us part. But there was a day. As soon as we got our diplomas, well some of us got our diplomas, some of us just got knocked up. We were gonna take the world by storm. Show people what graduates from Bendline could do for this world. But hell as soon as we hit the outskirts of town we tucked our tail between our legs and headed back for cover. Where it was safe. Good old safe Bendline. Safe because nothing ever happened here. Safe because nothing ever changed." The glass was tipped up straight. Ice hit against her teeth. The ice was lonely again.

"Don't you think maybe you've had enough?"

"Yes. But not of this." she tipped the glass toward Destiny. "I've just had enough period. Of everything. I'm ready to get out of Dodge. Like you. Go somewhere and become something. Like Adam. Fly away in some big jet every day."

"Big jet what do you mean?"

"Adam's ride. Didn't you know. He flies off in a big corporate jet. That's the ride he's always waiting for. The phone calls he gets. It's the pilot calling. Come to fly you away from little old Bendline."

"I didn't know. What does he do? Where does he go?"

Faye put her finger to her lips and made a shhh sound. "It's secret. It's hush, hush. He's so damned important he can't even tell his friends what he does. He can't even tell his friends where he went for so long after high school he keeps everything a secret. Has he told you? No. Of course not. He won't tell anybody anything. He just came back here after his dad died started fixing up the old house. Had a road crew work on the airport runway for a month. We've got a regular God Damn commercial airstrip out there. And he won't even take anybody with him. He won't even break his friends out of this prison."

The glass was emptied once again. They both reached for the bottle. Destiny reached it first. "That's enough Faye. You better save some for next time."

Faye rose from the table. Steadied herself against the counter as she made her way to the door. "Do me a favor darlin? Keep an eye on the place huh?"

"Sure Faye. I'll watch the place."

The bell jingled. "I like this bell. it reminds me of the movie. You know the one where the angel gets its wings. That's what you did. You and Adam you got your wings. Now you can fly anywhere you want to go." She turned leaning her head against the door. "I'm sorry Destiny. About before." the bell jingled again.

For an hour Destiny sat alone with her thoughts. People could be so different than one imagined them to be. Faye seemed so upbeat. A bit of a mother hen. But that was like fuel to her. It kept her going. The prior scene was disturbing, not a total surprise. But disturbing.

And Adam. Flying across the sky practically daily in a Lear. That was a shock. But Faye had been mistaken when she guessed that Adam hadn't told anyone what he did   after he left Bendline. He had told her. But there was a big chunk between his soul searching and his return to Bendline. Everyone had chunks of their lives that others didn't know about. She was no different. The box in her lap was caressed as if petting a cat.

Coughing and whizzing erupted from the kitchen. Destiny peaked through the swinging doors. Boxes were being extracted from the back of a pickup and placed in the kitchen.

"Earl?"

"Yea!"

"It's me Destiny."

"Yea?"

"Um. I came in for tea. Faye, was. She was not feeling well so she went home. She asked if I'd watch the place."

"Drunk huh?"

"Um. Well I'm going to head out now too. OK?"

"Yea."

Chapter 23

Beep, Beep, Beep.

The door to the room swung wide open with a   k. Nurse
Faye stood at the other end of the kick. Mira's eyes opene(en wider
and the halo turned to a flash of green.

"I know. I know. I was just here a few hours ag(eems the
day nurse got herself sick on too many tacos last night an   ʿ you can
believe it I'm the only one foolish enough to answer their   ne." She
wheeled in a cart with monitors, a computer and ε   w other
contraptions hanging off the sides just to look important.

"How are we doing? Has the nurse made it this far   ll."
Mira shook her head.

"Damn it! Pardon my French but don't you thin   he could
have called a little sooner. I mean you know she knew she   uldn't be
able to do her shift. The least she could have done was cal   oner so I
wouldn't be so far behind. But I know what it was. If she`   ere for at
least three hours she gets paid half a shift. Puttin her   ket book
before her patients. Now that just isn't right."

Faye came close to Destiny and started checking ε   he things
she had checked only hours before. Her breathing was lab(as if she
had completed her morning run. Her breath smelled od(Mira. A
freshness as if she had chewed on something from her gε   n. But it
was the after affect of being breathed on that Mira couldn   gure out.
Her vision got blurry and her head spun. The nurse kept   king and
talking aiming her exhale right in the direction of Mira.   st as she
thought she was going to fall off the chair Faye turned ar   valked to
the opposite side of the bed. Attached another clear bag   the pole.
Made some notes on her scrap of paper and wound u   he cords
attached to her cart.

"I'll be back just as soon as I can. But I'm not pr   sing any
speed records." She patted Destiny on the foot as she wall   by. "Just
do me a favor honey. Don't die today cuz I just don't have   time!"

T door swung closed and her voice could be heard in the
neighbor room.

N looked at Destiny then to the beep. There was a hint of
green lei en as if someone jumpstarted a car it turned crimson. In
walked m. He smiled at Mira showing small indentions in his
cheeks. n took hold of Destiny's hand. He sniffed a couple of
times. Lc d at Mira. Narrowed his eyes suspiciously.

" at?" she asked.

" e you been drinking?"

" me." she replied.

" lls like alcohol in here. Can't you smell that? Have you
left the r for any reason?"

" e." Mira didn't want to get Faye in trouble so she only
gave dire nswers. No more.

T halo on the monitor turned a playful yellow.

" ething's up." He looked at the monitor. Back to Mira.

S hrugged. Hiding a smirk. Destiny knew what she was up
to and by color of the halo, she approved.

" p your eyes open." he ordered Mira.

" "

" ent back home for what was night to you and Destiny here.
I had to recharged. This dimension wears on you. Let me know if
you need go home. I'll spell you. The council warned our time was
getting sl . The events and attitude of this world have taken a drastic
down tur)pening the door to a major influx of negativity.

I s right about the weather patterns. The council confirmed
its comin nd its going to be catastrophic. There's one hell of a storm
off the e coast and two more waiting behind it. The meteorologists
aren't sa much yet. I assume they don't want to cause panic. "

" before we came we looked at the observations and saw
the upsw ." Mira questioned.

" . That was before her accident. Before she was
unconsci ."

" ld one person make that much difference?"

")n't know. But if one person alone could, I know this
person co l be that one."

H ent down to the patient. His lips almost touching her ear.

"Keep dr iing my Destiny. Keep dreaming."

The path of her labyrinth became encased in a crimson glow. The most pleasant feeling she had ever felt. This decision was definitely the right one. The path that would lead her out of this maze and back to her life. She quickened her pace but only her thoughts obeyed.

Chapter 24

Tony was a dedicated employee. Ready to fuel the jet and fly away at a moment's notice. No complaints when he was called in the middle of the night to change the flight plan. A stop Adam had decided to make. It was time.

Grady Murphy squinted through the closed screen. "Sign on the gate says no solicitors."

"I'm not selling anything sir, Mr. Murphy. I'm Adam Barnes. I'm from, er I used to live, actually I still do live in Bendline."

A quick gasp of air made the older man stand at attention, "I remember you."

"I was wondering if I could come in, just for a minute. Or if you are busy maybe I could make an appointment for tomorrow."

The man opened the screen wide to face the visitor unobstructed. "Now's as good a time as any. Got no pressing appointments. Let me turn down the set. Have a seat."

Adam sat on the couch. Grady in the chair. The chair conformed perfectly around his frame. It must have been a family thing. Adam had gone over this conversation for days in his mind he knew what he wanted to say. Knew what he wanted to ask, just didn't know where or how to start a conversation with this man.

Grady sensed the apprehension. But was filled with reservations of his own. He remembered this name. But he didn't know if what he remembered would be good for Destiny. Not now.

"I don't know exactly where to start sir."

"How bout we start with first names."

"I'd like that sir, Grady."

The ice was broken. The meltdown could begin.

Grady started the conversation flowing. "My daughter Destiny is in Bendline. Maybe you've run into her. She's supposed to be cleaning up some dump Mrs. Appleton left to her."

"Yes I've seen her. The fact is she's renting from me. Just a small miner's shack, but the motel wasn't working out."

"That the one on your dad's place the one up against the hill?"

"That's it. I moved back after my dad died a few years ago,

I've fixed the places up. I divide my time between there and the east coast."

"Sure hope Destiny isn't planning on doing the same. She said she thought it would be good therapy to get away for a while. I'm going to strongly suggest she sell the place once it's cleaned up. Maybe you could keep an ear open for a buyer?"

"Sure. Glad to help. But you mentioned therapy. That's sort of what I wanted to talk to you about. Is she going through something with her memory?"

"Her loss of memory you mean. No. Is that how she's playing her cards out there. Keeping her hand a secret, I see."

"I'm not following."

"I'm not sure I should trip her hand if she doesn't want anybody to know."

"Your losing me Grady. I came to talk about her memory returning. She seems to be regaining fragments of her past. I just wanted you to know, oh hell I don't really know what I wanted you to know or why I'm here. I did some things in the past Sir, treated people badly and I guess this is my attempt at confession. And if and when she remembers what a son of a birch I was, I just want someone that she might still be talking to, to know I've changed and how very sorry I am."

"Why don't you tell her."

"She hasn't gotten that far yet. And why rock the boat."

"I guess I share the same attitude. Her mother and I went round and round over what to do about her amnesia. Should we push her, get her therapy, hypnosis. The time went by and she started to get a new life, one that didn't include Bendline, so we more or less put it out of our lives too. We didn't talk about it. I don't know if we did the right thing. I know she loved that little retarded girl and oddly enough she has spent half her time volunteering at a home for retarded children. Strange how things work out. Anyway right or wrong and whatever it was that brought you out here I can assure you no harm, no foul. My little powder keg was fine."

"That's exactly what she said."

"Well see there. I am concerned about a sudden memory return right now though. She's been through so much." The old man's eyes fell on a family photo on the fireplace mantle. The picture looked like the perfect family, a scene right out of Norman Rockwell. Right in the center of the picture a woman with sparkling blue eyes. Behind her stood a man his hand rested on her shoulder. Seated on either arm of the chair was a young man on one side and a young woman on the other.

Adam followed the gaze of the old man. Destiny and her family. And was that the chair, the one she loved, the one that fit her so well? A depressing cloud filled the room. The cloud eluded that this was no longer the perfect family. Something was different and this was now a scene from the past. But what part of the picture had changed? Dare he tread on sacred ground? This was Destiny's picture, her book of life. Grady had always been a strong gruff man. If the story was too private, he'd tell him to butt out.

"I'm sensing there's something more here Grady. Maybe it's none of my business but I'd like to know. If there's anything I can do."

The man's eyes glazed over still glued to the picture his voice cracked out the explanation. "She just lost her husband. Terrible car wreck. Right in front of the house. That's why I didn't protest her leaving the area for a while. Looking out at that street every day had to be hard."

Adam was speechless. An electric shock went through his body. A quick buzz sounded in his ears. His heart was falling out of his soul. Tumbling down, down, down an endless shaft. An empty void. He had to admit he wondered about this part of her life but didn't allow himself to question or speculate. The pain she must be going through. And going it alone. She was just trying to keep her feet under her she had said.

Grady continued, "I'd appreciate you not mentioning that I told you. And please don't mention to anyone else there. People try to act like they don't know, like everything is completely normal the way it has always been. But believe me you know when they know."

Normal. How could he return to Bendline and act normal? Grady was right. She'll know.

The cell phone vibrated. Tony. It was time to go.

Adam stood. Numb. Disoriented. He headed for the back of the house instead of the front door he came in.

"Thanks for seeing me Mr. Murphy."

"I do remember you from Bendline son. But what I remember

is you gave us back our Destiny. So I know if I ask you to look out for her you will."

"Absolutely Sir, Grady."

Chapter 25

Beep, beep, beep, beep, beep, beep!

Mira pushed the call button in her pocket. What was happening. The monitor was going twice as fast as it should be. The color of the halo wasn't off? She stroked the forehead of the patient. "What is it Destiny.? What's wrong?" still the monitor raced on. Mira went to the door, looked down the hall. If danger was approaching Destiny might have a premonition. No one out of place. The nurses walked in and out of rooms with trays. The officer still sat outside the room. Back at Destiny's side, she pushed the button again.

Elevators didn't move fast enough. And the delay in the door opening was completely uncalled for. If the world needed an invention, this was one. Metal plates parted, Adam squeezed through before they were even half way open. His running shoes squeaked on the freshly mopped floor.

The door to Destiny's room knew better than to offer any resistance. His expression shown no dimples this time.

"I don't know what it is. The beeps. They're so fast." Mira's heart could have been beating just as fast if she would have been completely human.

"What happen?" Adam held her wrist to make sure it wasn't machine malfunction. He checked her eyes. Blood pressure was OK. Temperature was OK.

"It just started going off the charts. So fast the machine could hardly keep up. Is it heart failure?"

He put both palms to Destiny's temples as if to read her thoughts. "No. No, I don't think so. She shows signs of… excitement? Maybe joy? What were you reading her?"

The door opened. Grady walked in. The halo was white.

"Everything OK in here? I stopped at the desk. They said if I was family I could go on in."

"Mr. Murphy? I'm doctor Adams." The two shook hands. The gesture was one of friendship from long ago.

"Yes your daughter is as good as can be expected. I was just checking on her. This is Mira. She has volunteered to stay in the room with your daughter. She reads to her or just talks. I want   brain to be stimulated as much as possible."

"She always did like anything that challenged er brain. Volunteer you say? Well I'd like to thank you for what y 're doing for my little girl." He grasped Mira's hand with both of his.

Mira was unsure of the human contact. She hadn't en in this dimension as long or as interactive as Adam had yet. Grad owed no sign of her hand feeling anything less than human. His and was warm. The palms were smooth. But from age not lac of work. Calluses still left bulges, but time had worn them down.

His attention turned to his daughter. "I could spel ou for a while if there is something you have to do."

Mira looked up in concentration. "No." There was   thing on her to do list except help Adam bring Destiny home.

Adam cleared his throat. "We'll let you have some time alone with your daughter sir." His nod toward the door gave Mira the hint. She got up from the chair.

"I'm right out here." She told Grady.

The mortal father stood over his daughter. He reached down and took her hand in his. Mira was right his hands were warm. "What have you gotten yourself into, my little powder keg?"

Her journey through the maze came to a stop. Aware of a different influence than the one at the beginning of this path. The influence was just as warm and inviting. She had the erg to laugh. But didn't know what the joke was about. Holding still on the path created an odd occurrence one of sinking. She had no feet but there was a definite feeling of being drawn downward in quicksand.

Grady sat close to his daughter. "The Doc says you need to have your brain stimulated. I guess talking to you. Well here goes." he wasn't sure where to begin or what to talk about so he gave free rein to his vocal chords they would both have to see what came out. "I guess I should be telling you all the things I never have said to you, you know in case you don't pull though this. Course I know you'll pull though, if you want to. There's never been anything you couldn't do if you wanted to. But still there are things in a lifetime that go unsaid, just because we assume the other person knows what we think or feel. But when your mother died I had a whole flood of things I wished I would have said to her but didn't. But I want you to know how proud I am of you. You have always been set apart from the crowd. There has always been something special about you. I have been in awe of you and been privileged to be the one chosen to raise you."

Destiny could not move. Her feelings of connection with this influence grew stronger and stronger, she sank deeper and deeper. But the odd thing she didn't fight the sinking. She didn't struggle to release herself from this grasp. It was too pleasant.

"We had quite a life Destiny. I know there was a hard time once your mom died but I want to thank you for getting me through it. I don't know what I would have done if you hadn't been there. That night you called to check up on me, I don't know how you knew to call but I was sitting there with a gun in my lap. The phone rang and it was my Destiny. We sure got your name right. You always did know when to call and what to say. Anyway I put the gun back in the safe and have thought about getting it out since. Thank you.

I only wish I could return the favor now. Tell you what you need to hear. To bring you back. I know you are in some limbo place. Somewhere between here and another side of reality."

The sinking continued. The surrender was nearly complete. The choice almost made. The beeps on the monitor slowed to almost nonexistent. But Grady did not notice.

"I just want you to know Destiny that if you decide not to come back here. It's ok with me. If it hurts too bad here, that's alright. I will miss your calls but I know if you go it will be because it's what you decide to do. You have always been the master of your own world the creator of your destiny. I don't know how you have done it but you have always had that gift, if you want to call it that. I know we all have to move on. I don't know a life here on earth that you have touched that isn't better, brighter for having known you. But there might just be another world you need to light up. I'll be watching for that new star in the sky." A tear splashed on Destiny's hand.

The force pulling her down was released, the rope broken. The weightlessness shot her up in full awareness of the path she was on. She was free to travel onward.

Mira took her seat right outside the door. Next to the police officer. He was young. Listening to something though plugs stuck in his ears. He texted regularly on his phone. Someone named June Bug. The picture of a blond blowing a kiss off of her hand shown on the screen every two minutes.

The door to the room slowly opened and Grady stumbled out. He put his hand on Mira's shoulder. "Could you go on in. I'm just too broke up right now. I don't think this will help her. I said my goodbyes." he paused, eyes filled to overflowing. Red rims from the night before. "Just in case." Feet that carried the weight of the world shuffled down the hall at a snail's pace.

He knows Mira thought. Their bond must have been pretty close between them. Cause he definitely knows she's not coming back to this world.

Chapter 26

The running shoes were getting holes in them. Not to mention her clothes were fitting looser than they had in some time. The yard work felt good and the running felt better.

Digger grew accustomed to her schedule. The first couple of days as she ran by the house at 5:00 in the morning Digger would just woof, wag her tail and run along side of her from one end of the fence to the other. Then take her spot on the porch to run the other direction upon the return trip.

But now Digger waited in the road and accompanied Destiny on the run. The gate was left open so Digger didn't have to barrel over the top. The company was welcome but it was harder to concentrate on the pain. And that's what the running was all about. The pain. But it still didn't hurt bad enough. So the running schedule continued.

Some mornings the agony started slow and built to a crescendo. But for this morning the pain started when the running shoes hit the floor. The night had been sleepless. A dream about James woke her and the rest of the night was hopeless. Stopping at the base of the mountain she gave it a challenging look. The ridge came fast, the pace was doubled. Digger panted with protest. Tears flowed. Digger barked as if trying to alert someone of her companion's sorry state. Calling for someone to come to the aid of the runner. Bendline that morning was encircled by a trail of tears.

The bell jingled at Faye's. All the stools were taken. Sam attempted to sit down at the small table across from the newspaper. "That seat's saved Sam." Ed announced.

"Since when has Faye been taking reservations?"

"It's OK Sam. Go ahead and sit there." Faye brought him a cup and the coffee pot.

"That's Mrs. Walker's seat Faye." Ed protested.

"She's not here yet. If she shows up before Sam's done we can bring another chair for the end of the counter. Mr. Newspaper won't mind. Will ya?"

The corner folded. "Nope."

"Besides we haven't seen Sam in a while. What's been going

on up at the hill Sam?"

"Same old. Same old. Mowing lawns. Put in a real nice border of petunias. You should come out and see."

"I'm sure I'll be out there soon enough. Old man Keller is on his last leg." Faye exclaimed.

"I heard his wife already sent all his clothes in the red cross truck that came through last month." Whitey shook his head.

"Can't fault the woman for being organized." Mary Clair added from across the counter.

The bell on the door jingled. "That's it Sam you got to go." Ed looked through the glasses apologetically.

"Ed leave Sam alone. Destiny, you're set up at the table." The man rose to relinquish his chair as Earl poked a rickety stool through the swinging doors. "This here is Sam. He's the grounds keeper at the cemetery." Faye had completed the introductions and musical chairs, the morning could continue.

Destiny walked toward the table, head down. Her eyes raised slightly to acknowledge Sam.

"Holy Cow Mrs. Walker. Are you OK? You got allergies again?"

Faye looked up. "Pipe it Ed."

"Yea, I think so Ed." Destiny admitted sniffing her nose. "Must be something blooming."

"Uh huh." uttered Faye as the cup was filled in front of the allergy prone woman. "You need some eye drops? I got some in the back."

"I'll be fine. Thanks." Destiny managed a smile. "Coffee. I need lots of it today."

The newspaper made a weak barrier against the pain of his table guest. Adam felt his heart crack open further.

Once the muffin was set in front of Destiny Ed turned to see if she looked any better. Through his glasses how could he tell? "You got any stories about the little girl for us today Mrs. Walker. We could use a Mira Tale."

"What's a Mira Tale?" Sam inquired.

"Stories about the little retarded girl that used to live here. Mira Appleton. Destiny used to know her." Whitey explained.

"Mira Appleton." Sam whispered.

"Yea, now quiet so she can tell the story." Ed turned the stool around eager to listen as a child in the library.

The man put down the paper and gave her a pleading look. Maybe a Mira story was what she needed too. Her voice was not much more than a whisper.

The words OUT THERE BOX floated in the air. A hand reached into the open box, the piece of chalk was brought out for show and tell. "I had been searching high and low for something to take to Mira for her box. Once I decided I wanted to take her something, nothing looked right. Nothing looked good enough. She wouldn't have cared what it was. A silly rock would have been fine with her."

Destiny looked through raw eyes at Adam and managed a smile.

"But I wasn't satisfied with just anything."

Approaching Mira on the steps, she looked up at me breaking her trance. "Hu yo" she said softly as her round little hand left her chin which it had been supporting. She waved slowly.

I found a seat beside Mira on the porch. Pearl came to the door, she heard voices and acknowledged my arrival. She would be out later, there were some things to attend to in the house. My heavy school bag clunked down on the porch.

"Wha da?" Mira questioned.

"This is my bag I take to school," I began to explain, then didn't continue for she probably didn't know what school was.

Mira was stretching her neck up high to see if she could spy what the bag harbored. It wasn't exactly top secret material, I began unloading it. Her eyes got very big. I explained each book and note book I extracted from the bag. She liked the history book the best. Pointing to the picture of Columbus in high feathered hat and tights, she clapped her hands together and laughed.

"This is what I do all day. This is what I do out there at school. I mostly read. And I do some writing, this is the book I write in."

It was surprising to see how careful she was with the books and how much interest she had in them. The pages with words were leafed past quickly. The pages with pictures however were turned slowly and methodically, only after careful examination of every detail. Even the pages full of fancy written words afforded more attention that just the regular typed information pages. When she was done looking at a book she would thrust it back at me and start on the next one. I let her take her time looking at all the stuff from my bag. When she had satisfied herself as to the bags contents, I told her I had something for her 'out there' box. Mira lit up like a light bulb in a basement. Her breathing got very short and fast, almost a panting. I reached into my bag for her surprise. Mira's breathing stopped altogether. Keeping the surprise hidden behind my back I turned to face her. Mira's cheeks were puffed out like a blowfish. Her eyes bugged to almost popping. Quickly I brought her surprise from behind my back and said "Here Look. Now breathe."

The blast of air let out blew her bangs up on her high forehead. Mira examined the article carefully and with great question in her expression. She fingered it softly. Rolled the item in her palm. Stroked her cheek with it. My eyes got as big as hers when she stuck out her tongue to taste it. A sour expression took over her face, she pulled it out of her mouth with a jerk.

"Dis ow dar?' she questioned. She tilted her head from side to side in disbelief. She looked at me as if I thought she had just fallen off the turnip truck. If she had better control of language skills, she would have told me, 'I may be retarded but   I'm not stupid.' Mira waited patiently for me to defend my gift.

"Yes this is out there." I took the piece of chalk from her hand and picked up a flat rock. I drew a very crude smiling face. I showed the drawing to Mira. Mira's face matched the smiling face I had drawn. Then I took my hand and erased the picture. Mira began to whimper. I drew a picture of a face with a different look. Mira smiled again. I erased the picture, drew another.

Mira took the chalk in her hand and held it carefully as if it were a new born kitten. She drew on the rock. Erased it, then drew on it again.

"See, you changed the picture." I explained to her.

Slowly, painstakingly we drew pictures. Erased pictures and drew new ones.

"I change it," she said and continued her art.   "Dis ow dar?"

"Yea, this is out there. It's called chalk. I like chalk coz if you make a mistake or you don't like the way something is, you can change it. But, I guess what I really wanted you to know about out there, is that everything out there is like this chalk."

"Everywhere ow dar chalk?"

"The whole world isn't made up of chalk, no. But life out there is like chalk You see Mira whatever is out there, you don't have to be afraid of it. You don't have to worry about being different or making a mistake. I used to be afraid of what was out there too. Until I took my piece of chalk and decided to change my picture of out there. Maybe I could help you change your picture of out there. So you're not so afraid."

"Chalk. Change it. Ow dar?" She said each word very slowly and deliberately.

I didn't really think she understood what I was trying to say. But I think I just put into words what I was coming to believe. Life was not permanent, carved in stone, but fluid and changeable. Life could take on any form I chose to put it in. And the key word was 'I' chose. There were certain constants in life. Mira's constant was the fact she was born with an extra chromosome. My constant was perhaps my looks, my family, the small town I called home. But what I did with the constants, or the hand I was dealt, was going to be up to me.

In Mira's case she would probably choose to hide in her yard forever and grasp the world one small piece at a time and put it carefully into her box of out there. Her constants were more governed by outside forces, meaning Pearl than mine. Me, on the other hand, could use the changeable part we all possess in our lives, our attitudes. Our state of mind was the real ruler of our life's outcome. I could draw the picture or erase it if it wasn't as I wished. But I was beginning to wonder if one person could use their piece of chalk to change another person's picture of the world. Maybe, just maybe if Mira couldn't change herself to be more acceptable to the world, maybe I could somehow use what I possessed to change the world to be more accepting of her.

We both stood to go put the chalk in her box. Mira looked up at me. "Tank u" she whispered. Before I could jump out of the way she had both arms wrapped tight around my waist.

I reached my arms around her and gave her back a little pat. "You're welcome" I said.

The hug continued for longer than was comfortable. I began to pull away. She squeezed me tighter. I pulled harder. Explaining to her it was alright the hug was over. "You're welcome." I repeated. "Now let go. Mira let go. Please Mira you're hurting me let go!

My stomach was being crushed, I couldn't believe strength. Maybe all of us have incredible strength we just keep it u r control. I pulled harder to get away, the harder I pulled the tigl she held. Like the power that hold the center of an atom together that of a rubber band strength. The more the particles try to spr apart the stronger the force exerted to hold them together, if the pa les are at rest no force is exerted.

I tried this idea with Mira. I relaxed her grip rela some but the small of my back still felt like it was going to break. I ldn't stay calm, I struggled harder. Just as I thought I was goin pass out Pearl came to the door.

The glasses of lemonade she was bringing for ira and I smashed to the floor. "Mira No!. Mira let go." Pearl ha lira's face between her hands trying to break her concentratio It wasn't working. Pearl tried a different strategy.

"Destiny you have to relax."

"I can't. I can't breathe. My back! It hurts!" as crying. Mira was humming.

"Destiny! You must relax!"

I tried to relax. I slowed my breathing. The gri osened. I was just ready to pull away. Pearl shouted. "No don't! nc t."

Pearl found a blade of grass and tickled just belo lira's ear. Her arms released and she giggled rubbing the spot be v her ear. "That funnies."

I was free. But trembled everywhere.

"Go put the chalk in your box Mira." Pearl said.

"Destiny. I'm so sorry. She just doesn't know." l couldn't apologize enough.

"That's OK. I just panicked. I didn't react right."

"Of course you panicked. Mira is different. It tak o much to get accustomed to how to react around her. I'm afraid I ned about her hugs the hard way. I had gotten her a small dog. I out of the room for only a moment. Mira had hugged the dog. The struggled and she squeezed harder and harder. The dog became ocious. It wasn't his fault it was self preservation. He began bitin r. When I found them he was still gripped onto her shoulder she had squeezed the life out of him."

"7   's horrible."

"}   t was."

"I   ifraid I'm mostly to blame for keeping such a small
radius for   ·a. It's just easier that way I guess."

M   ·eturned with her box. "Chalk in heya." she announced
to Pearl ν   ı wide smile.

Sh   ·ned to me. "You bring me ow dar?"

"S   Mira I'll bring you something else." I patted her
shoulder ι   felt a bulge under her sleeve. Scar tissue from too tight
of a hug.

"I   ·ny, thank you. But you don't have to bring her anything
else. You   ι young teenager. You certainly have other things to do
than this.

"7   's OK Pearl. I like her. And I'll be careful of the hug next
time."

Th   Mira gave me a gift more precious than anything I knew
of from oı   ·re. She gave me a smile.

A   ı followed the Mira Tale as before.

M   Clair shouted over. "All I can say is I've cleaned enough
chalk off   ıe sidewalk to last a life time. Those first graders. They
learn their   ;C's, the teacher sends the home with a piece of chalk to
practice   the entire length of the bus stop is covered in
masterpie(·"

Sa   oined in, "I think a child's creative side should be
encourage   [ary Clair."

"E   ıraged yes, but mark my words if they are writing and
drawing o   ·e sidewalk in first grade they'll be writing on the side of
buildings   ıgh school."

Th   ›or closed so hard the bell didn't even have a chance to
jingle.

"V   ·'s got her wound up?"

"S   ;alled the other night said the principal called the other
evening aı   ·ave her hell because there was writing all over the inside
of the stal   ι the girls bathroom." Ed said.

"V   ·'s the principal doing in the girl's bathroom?" Faye
asked.

"V   ·'s she doing calling you at night." Ed asked.

"N   of your bees wax jackass."

"Don't call me jackass."

"Then finish your doughnut. We got to get to work."

Adam and Destiny were enjoying the banter.

"You ready for us to pick up anything from the coop yet Mrs. Walker."

"Not quite. Probably Tuesday."

"OK. Faye, you and Earl going to Mel's tonight. He's gonna have a band."

"A band?"

"Yea, well Harry on the guitar and his wife on the drums."

"That's not a band."

"Close enough. Mel said Fridays have been slow so he got them to put some numbers together. He asked us to spread the word. We had to haul off a bunch of junk out of the back room. He's gonna set them up back there so people even has some place to cut it up."

"I'll talk to the old man. We'll probably stick our heads in and say hi."

"See ya there."

"You asking Mary Clair?" Ed inquired of Ed as they were paying the bill.

"Shut up Jackass."

Sam sat sipping his coffee in deep thought. He began mumbling to himself. "Mira Appleton. Yes."

Adam looked in his direction a cord in the side of his neck tensed.

Sam continued, "Up on the hill...   Holy Cripes! Faye! Watch what you're doing!" A glass of Florida Fresh Squeezed just landed in Sam's lap.

"Oh, Sam I am so sorry. Clumsy me." she winked at Adam but Destiny didn't see.

"Now I'm going to be late to work, I'll have to go home and change first."

"What do you care. You work alone. Nobody up on the hill is gonna rat you out."

He stormed out the door.

Destiny and Adam paid their bills at the same time and walked out into the new day. The world looked better than it had through red swollen eyes a while ago. The woman looked better too.

"You've worn a hole in your shoes. You need a new pair."

The big toe peaked out the front of the left shoe and gave a little wave. "No, they're just getting good."

"Digger keeping up with you."

"She had a hard time this morning. But it was a tough morning."

"It looked that way."

"But it's better now."

"Good. For the record I think you are pretty remarkable."

"What do you mean?"

"I mean the chalk. The whole truth about life is up to us, we are the artists of our lives. How did you know that? And at fifteen. I finally got around to learning the concept after beating my head against the wall or to be more truthful against someone else's fist for almost thirty years. I took the hard way. You knew all along. I could have taken the easy way. I could have just asked you."

"I'm not so remarkable. Just because a person knows something once doesn't mean they remember it. That story, the chalk. I think I told it today for me. It was something I needed to hear."

"It was something we all need to hear. Whether everyone listens or not…"

"Yea. Anyway tell Digger tomorrow we're going to take the easier road."

"OK."

Chapter 27

Beep. Beep. Beep.

The sun drug the last of its rays past the horizon. Another night with a moonless sky awaited the woman suspended on the trapeze. Mira got up to draw the curtains to keep the darkness of night outside. An imposter of daylight spread a beam of light across Destiny's face. She looked much better in the sunlight. More lifelike. This ultraviolet bulb made her look ashen. Sculpted of clay.

Inside her labyrinth the light on her path too dimmed. Vague shadows could be made out in the twilight. Soon even those would be impossible to detect and she would have to feel her way along by sense alone. Attention focused on her heart. It had never steered her wrong. Well maybe once, but that was to be forgotten. And buried.

All of a sudden she felt it. That familiar feeling. Her reason for living. The warmth grew hotter. The crimson feeling was just up ahead. She could feel it on its way. Or perhaps her way to be with it. The path was without a doubt the right one now. The warmth, the safety, the sense of belonging. All she ever wanted was just up ahead. "I'm coming." she called to whomever would listen. Whomever radiated this glow. Or caused her to radiate the crimson back.

Mira had left the room briefly. Just to keep up appearances. The policeman was still at his post. June Bug was still keeping him occupied. She went down the hall and turned into a door with the stick figure wearing a dress. Although her attire looked more like the figure on the other door. She saw females entering and exiting this door all the time.

June Bug's last message on the screen was 'Hurry home'. there was only ten minutes left on his shift. What would it hurt. Who would know. Besides that retarded girl never left the room. He passed a man in a trench coat getting off the elevator as he got on. The guy was nice enough to hold the door for him.

The hospital room looked more like command central for the space shuttle. The room had a life of its own. A heart beat. The door inhaled deep and let in a virus. It floated around the room. Circling, drifting on the air flow. Searching to find the best place to land. The best place to do it's ill intentions. Eyelids didn't flutter. The look of fear was not present. Only the steady beep, beep, beep. A green line flowing up a mountain then back down the other side. This virus could make the journey of the green line simpler. The virus could take away the mountains.

A pillow moved through the air. It came to rest on Destiny's face. The tube leading to her lungs was severed. Her body could not convulse showing signs of trauma. Lungs deflated. As weight pushed even the last of breath from them. One more bounce just to be sure. The green line went flat.

Wham! Destiny hit something. A wall. She felt right but was blocked in that direction. Left was blocked as well. The crimson was right on the other side of the wall ahead. Out of desperation she turned around. Maybe if she backtracked she could find an opening and circle around. She had not been looking for any openings along the way because this path seemed so easy. So right. There was only a few steps to be taken backwards and out of nowhere a wall appeared. She slowly moved forward again. The crimson was glowing stronger than before. She could feel the heat through the wall.

Adam saw Mira coming out of the restroom just as he turned the corner. A quick glance down the hall made his mind search for the answer to What's wrong with this picture? The officer's chair was empty. He glared at Mira and ran to the room.

The pillow was still on top of Destiny's face. Her features pressed into it as he threw it to the floor. The green line on the machine was still flat. Taunting him. He pulled the tube from her throat and began breathing his own life into her.

Destiny banged on the wall and called out. "I can't get through!"

The crimson called to her stronger. The wall got hotter. She banged again.

"Don't you understand I can't get through. I'm on the other side of this wall." frustrated and exhausted she slid down the wall in a heap. She wept.

He pushed air harder and harder into her lungs. Pushed it out with the palms of his hands. The green line still laughed, and held steady.

The crimson radiated through the wall pleading with her to

journey onward.

"I can't. I just can't. Leave me. Go on without me. I can't make it. "

He bent down beside her. Whispered in her ear. "Damn it Destiny. I can't do this alone. You've got to help me here." not knowing it was possible in this dimension. A tear fell from his cheek.

In a flash of crimson lightning picked her up from her crumpled heap and propelled her backwards. She hit the back wall.

She lay dazed for how long she didn't know. And then she said to the crimson light. "I get it. OK. There is nothing I can't do." She picked herself up. If she couldn't go right, and she couldn't go left, nor back. But she had to go forward. She would have to go through. She began the feat of tearing down the wall.

Blip. Blip. Blip.

Mira just stood by in awe. A frozen statue. Once the green line started climbing the mountain again.

Adam fell into the chair. "This being human is exhausting. These emotions are brutal." he put his hands on top of his head and leaned his head back, closed his eyes.

"Should I get the nurses to come in and fix the tube?"

"No. No we can do it. They'll just report it to the authorities again. This is nothing the authorities can do anything about. This is her personal fight. Her own demons she needs to overcome. I think she's got the idea now though." he patted her hand. The halo was the deepest crimson it had been so far.

"How long were you out of the room?" he asked Mira.

"I hadn't been gone more than five minutes. The on duty cop was in his chair when I left."

A light tap on the door was followed by it opening as if it were a secret ritual. Knock three times and the door opens.   A young uniformed officer inquired. "Did you see Ray out here. I'm suppose to take over his shift. But he's not here."

Adam spoke in a low mutter. "No. we haven't seen Ray."

Chapter 28

It was time to pay the rent again. Adam's jeep was in the drive when Destiny passed. The rent check had been in her back pocket for several days as he had been gone.

The door was open and Digger jumped against the screen before Destiny had a chance to knock.

Adam came out of the office removing his glasses along the way. "Hi. Destiny come in."

"Brought you the check. It's a few days late but I wrote it out on the first you just weren't here."

He held it out in front of him. The crease was wearing thin and the light was visible through it. "Looks like you're laundering money. That's a felony you know. Did it go through the wash?"

"No. I've had it in my pocket for a few days. In case I caught you as I passed by. I think it will still go though. If you don't think so I could write you another one."

"No. This will do." He tossed it carelessly on the side table. He hadn't deposited any of the other checks. And probably wouldn't start now.

He was amazed at the transitions Destiny had made. Not only on the cleanup project but in herself as well. When he first saw her she had a tremble to her lip as if she were always on the verge of tears. Her brow was tense and her hands would stretch out then recoil into tight fists almost constantly. Now she was calm. Her shoulders relaxed and instead of trembling her lips almost always wore a Mona Lisa smile.

"Oh, and I brought you these." she held out a small paper bag with the top rolled down. "The first harvest. Well what's left of the first harvest. I ate as I picked. Once I uncovered the strawberry patch I started watering it every day. And look! I'm a regular farmer!"

"So you are. I think I'll have some. Thanks." he returned from the kitchen with a bowl overflowing with ruby jewels. "Want to sit on the porch while I indulge?"

"Maybe for a minute."

Digger opened the door for them and waited till Destiny was seated then sat on top of her feet.

"I borrowed some of your books while you were ⟨...⟩ ."
"Good. Find anything interesting."
"Yea. It was a book about life in a monastery."
"OK. Sounds familiar."
"You said you were in a monastery for a while."
"Yea."
"Did you follow the rule of silence?"
"Yea."
"Was it hard?"
"Well no one talked so, no it wasn't too hard."
"Is that why you're so quiet now? Why you don't ⟨...⟩ much?"
"Maybe. I don't know. I just don't talk much. I d⟨...⟩ know if I ever have."
"I was talking to Faye. She said you don't ⟨...⟩ anybody anything."
"I don't talk much down there. Besides it's prett⟨...⟩ ⟨ha⟩rd to get a word in edgewise. You've seen that."
"She said you never talked about what you did ⟨...⟩ ⟨w⟩here you went after you left here." The hesitation was long. But ⟨...⟩ floor was not being turned over to him to reply. The next words w⟨...⟩ just being mulled over. "But you told me."
"Yea."
"Why did you tell me?"
"I haven't the slightest idea. Maybe because yc ⟨...⟩ ⟨ar⟩e easy to talk to."
"She said you fly away in a corporate jet every da⟨y⟩"
"Jesus. Was she drunk?"
Destiny couldn't help herself she broke out laugh⟨...⟩ 'Actually. Yes she was."
"And I was the topic for the day."
"Not the only topic."
The silence formed as a dense cloud. His irritati⟨...⟩ ⟨f⟩ueling the form. Destiny waited patiently for the cloud to disperse.
"So. Do you fly away in a jet?"
He looked at her and laughed. His cheeks flushe⟨...⟩ ⟨h⟩e figured he may as well give in it was clear this woman had sc⟨...⟩ questions that needed answering. "Yes."
Her curiosity was too peaked now to drop the ⟨...⟩ ⟨con⟩versation

166

with the a | ssion. She had to press for more information. "What do
you do. Y | e not a pilot?"
"N
"S | nat's your job?"
"It | ot a job really."
"It | ot a job. And you are not a pilot. So what is it? Are you a
secret age | hat has so much fun at his job that you don't call it
work?"
"Y | re not going to give up are you?"
"P | bly not."
He | oped a strawberry in his mouth and sat back in the chair.
The chair | a rocker and the rungs set a beat to his words. "I don't
call what | a job. Because to me it's just keeping a promise. You
asked if it | just so much fun that I didn't call it a job. I do enjoy it.
Not as mu | s I used to but I can't complain."
"E | ially the jet part."
"L | just say it never gets old."
"A | What do you do. Where do you fly off to?"
"Y | remember I told you about Roy. The man that was such
an influer | on my life. The guy in Florida. Well he contacted me
when I wa | the monastery. He said he needed to see me. He bought
me a ticke | d brought me back to the states. He was preparing for his
final days | I asked me if I would keep his oath. To make sure the
informatic | as available for those that sought it. He owned a chain of
bookstore | then and he was also into publishing. So I've been
keeping h | omise to the world and I've been keeping my promise to
him."
"Y | un the bookstores?"
"Y |
"A | he publishing?"
"T | too."
"A | where do you go?"
"N | York mostly. But other cities here and there."
"S | you run everything for a trust fund or charity?"
"N | le left it to me."
"V | !"
"It | ally not that big of a deal. I mean it is a big deal. The
man was | enerous. But the most valuable thing he gave me was a

start to life. The rest is overwhelming but not the important part of it. And I just don't want the town to know. I don't want them to think of me any differently than they do now. I just want to be the guy that comes down to coffee and listens to what's going on in town. Am I making any sense?"

"Yea. I understand. But no matter how hard you try you will never be just a regular Joe. I saw that the first time I set eyes on you."

"I hope it's because of what I've learned not because of what I've acquired. And I hope this doesn't change the way you see me."

"No. But I might ask to renegotiate my rent."

"Any time." He chuckled.

"Can I ask you something else?"

"We seem to be on a roll here. Sure."

"Do you have any regrets. Coming back giving up everything you've had to give up?"

"Who says I've had to give up anything?"

"Well you've never been married?"

"Maybe I'm not the marring kind?"

"I just thought. Well it appears you aren't married or ever been married. I don't see any pictures of children around. And I know you are not gay."

"You've got that right. Happy and content maybe, but not gay. As for family sometimes the time slips by before you have time to include everything in life that you wanted. So you have to be content with what you filled it with."

"No kids then."

"No. But I was married."

"Didn't work out?"

"No. She was a lawyer."

"I'm not surprised then. That it didn't work out, you don't seem like the lawyer type."

"Let's just say our ideas were different. I met her in New York, the city. After I came back to the states. She was a whirl wind, I didn't know what hit me. Especially after being in a monastery you know." he laughed.

"Well at least you got to keep the house." Destiny gestured to the surroundings.

"I didn't have the house yet. My dad was still alive. But the divorce was friendly. Roy gave me six months to give him a decision. He set me up in an apartment in New York so I could get a feel for things. But I met her before I gave him my decision. She was probably one of the biggest deciding factors. Anyway she got bored of me real quick. She wasn't interested in anything I had anymore. She was more interested in what the new senior partner had. She moved up in the partnership and I went back and gave Roy my answer."

"Too bad."

"Not really."

She smiled.

"And you. It's your turn."

"Me?" She hadn't planned on being called as witness to her life.

"You. What about you? Are you married?"

"Yes."

The answer hit him like a baseball bat. He nearly choked on the sweet red juice seeping down his throat.

The answer came out so quick. So automatic she didn't even have time to think about it. But the words were out there now. No further explanation was required. It was her intention after all to come to Bendline because here no one knew the truth. And the truth was the opposite of what she had just stated. She wasn't married anymore. She wasn't betrothed. A widow. Even the word sounded dark, depressing. Void of color, like a black hole sucking all the color from the rainbow. Widow. No wonder they, wore black.

"Oh. I didn't see a ring. I assumed differently. But then you know what they say about assuming."

"Yes." The answer came out flat. With an accusing air. How dare he tread on her protected feelings. But then,she felt wrong. He had been nothing but honest with her she owed him the same courtesy.

In a low almost husky voice it began. "I wasn't truthful. About being married. I was married until four months ago. I'm a widow. I hate that word. It leaves a bad taste on my tongue every time I say it. I look at myself in the mirror and try to envision myself in black. It's not my color. So I don't wear it.

"It was a car accident. James, my husband was on his way home. Pulling into the drive in fact. He was almost home. He was almost safe at home.

169

"I was in the back of the house I heard tires squeal, a hideous sound of scraping, bending metal. Then this awful silence. My chest hurt , I couldn't breathe. How awful I thought. I knew instinctively what the sound was. A horrible automobile accident. And not far away. The sirens got louder and then stopped. The accident was closer than I thought. I considered walking down to the end of our drive but I knew that was the last thing the emergency crews needed. Nosey neighbors standing around shaking their heads in horror. I stayed put. James was over an hour late. I was sure he must have gotten caught in the backed up traffic. I kept reheating the potatoes on the stove, they slowly turned to jerky. It never occurred to me to call him. It never entered my mind how strange it was that he didn't call me. I heard the click of a piece of gravel stuck in the groove of a tire as it rounded the circle drive. James always drove straight to the garage in the back. I went to the front door. The sheriff was just getting out of his car. He reached back in to grab his hat. Then my whole world turned black."

The cricket's song took over the story. Destiny shifted to an upright position in her chair. A long slow exhale. Adam sat silent afraid if he made a sound it would disturb the whole balance of the universe. The time had been so perfect this woman had brought out of hiding what needed to be revealed. Until that very moment she had not told the story in detail, only the ending result. The whole scene was pushed away and not viewed. And even now Destiny had not really been talking to anyone in particular. During the recount Adam just happened to be within hearing distance. She was just letting pain escape from her soul. Letting it seep out slowly.

He didn't know what to say and was afraid if he spoke too soon he might keep her from saying all that she needed to say.

"And that's why I run. You asked me before. That's the reason. I was getting nothing done in a whole day except crying and grieving. So I made a rule for myself. I give myself one hour a day to feel pain. When the pain creeps up in between I push it aside until its time. Then I give it all I've got. I don't hold anything back. And if that's not weird enough. You see I have this strange idea that pain can be transferred. I figure each painful experience carries with it a pre-determined amount of pain. Whether the pain is physical, mental or emotional. But I figure the pain itself can be transferred from one form to the other. So if I run hard enough and it hurts bad enough then the pain in my body can take away some of the pain in my heart. And the pain in my body only lasts for a little while."

"I don't know what to say Destiny."

"That's perfectly OK. Believe me the least said the better. It's better for me anyway."

"OK."

"I'm beginning to think that's not the only reason I run though."

It was an invitation to this man to hear the inner thinking of her mind. The secrets in her heart and soul. He was so easy to talk to. It was unexplainable. In his presence she was at peace. The universe was unfolding exactly as it should and all was right within it. Her breathing was not labored. Life giving oxygen flowed effortlessly in and effortlessly out. Useless thoughts did not flit and race through the mind but the thoughts entering were important, constructive, realization, nothing imaginary.

"Go on. I'm listening." the invitation was accepted.

"I've been doing a lot of soul searching. When the accident first happened I was numb. The mind must just shut off to avoid damage. But every since I've come to my senses I've had this awful feeling as if waking from a dream. Knowing that I have run away from home. I've been running trying to find my way back. But it's like home is inside a compound. My paradise is surrounded by walls all the way around. I always run in a circle around town. Did you know that?"

He knew. Ed reported everyday about the crazy woman running a circle around town.

" I think I'm checking to see if there is a door somewhere. The pain is a reflection of me pounding against that wall trying to break through to the other side. Break through to where I can feel at home again. Does that make any sense. Or am I a crazy woman like they said I was down at the café?"

He laughed softly. "There are no secrets in a small town are there?" she shook her head. "What you are saying makes perfect sense to me. When Roy picked me up out of the gutter and cleaned me up. He asked me when I was going to quit beating myself up. I told him in case he missed the blow by blow of the fight the other guys were beating me up. He said he saw a different picture. My whole life I had been smashing myself against other peoples fists. He told me I was just trying to beat through the wall I had built around myself. Beat down the door. He said when I finally could not take one more blow when I submitted totally, he quoted Christ "Into thy hands I commend my spirit." then and only then would I find that the door opened in. I had been beating against it all this time only to be keeping it shut. When I gave up it would swing open of its own accord. And I would feel such a joyous revelation that I would sit down on the ground and laugh so hard I would cry. But all of this cannot be written about. It cannot be told to another person, there are no directions, no how to manuals. It can only be experienced each in his own way. When I argued that he was telling me about it. He answered, And your brain doesn't have the foggiest notion of what I'm really saying. But it will. Then he raised his cup in salute to me and said here's to laughter and tears."

He let what he said linger in the air. Float around the room like the smoke from dry ice. Swirl around her feat. Drift up around her hair that was held back with a clip. Unruly pieces of hair framing her face with rings of curls. Her eyes spoke what her lips could not. Her brain, like his so many years ago, didn't have the foggiest idea what he was saying. "So here's to your laughter and tears."

Contemplating, trying to navigate through what he was saying. Some things could only be experienced. This was true. The rest she would have to let it come as it would. She looked forward to the day of laughter. "You going to eat that last strawberry?" she asked.

"It's all yours."

She rose from her chair and popped the berry into her mouth.

"Are you running tomorrow then?" Adam asked.

"Absolutely. Tell Digger to be ready. And what you said about not wanting the masses to know your secret. I'd appreciate you not telling the world what my guts just spilled."

"Your secret is safe with me."

"And yours with me."

Adam sat on the porch watching the last bit of color bleed from the sky. He had known about James. When he returned from seeing Grady he had checked the Lakehead newspaper archives on the internet. He had found a James Walker in the obituary. The surviving widow was named Destiny. It was a match. The obituary stuck to the details of the family names time of service, age and life story of the deceased. No mention was made of the reason for death. There seldom was. Just the cold hard facts. In fact Adam had often thought rather than reason for death, one should ponder the reason for life. What nurtured this life. What kept this man going day in and day out. What brought joy and laughter and love into his life. He was sure the answer to that would have been the person that just vacated his porch.

Chapter 29

Beep. Beep. Beep.

The door yawned, stretched and groaned as th   rge frame with a barrel chest entered the room. The feeling was   iliar. The smell was familiar. And neither was pleasant. Mira (1 feel his presence before the door opened. She began pushing the   ton in her pocket. The halo on Destiny's monitor indicated she   d feel the unpleasantness approaching as well. The orange got brig   with each beep. If she was that perceptive Mira thought it wou   t be long before she was ready to leave with Adam and herself. I   squeezed Destiny's hand to let her know she felt it too.

"Don't worry I called him. I'm sure he's on   vay." she whispered to Destiny just as the door gave into th   eutenant's shoulder.

"You still here Girlie?" he glared at Mira bre₂   g heavily through his nostrils clogged and swollen from too   ch smoke irritation.

"I reading." she answered in dumb fashion.

"Yea, yea. So you said last time. Have you be₁   1 here the whole time?"

Mira nodded. Wide eyes.

"The whole time? You never left?"

Mira moved her head back and forth.

"Not even to pee?"

Mira gulped. She had been found out. How did   know she went down the hall to the bathroom. Not to pea but just   ₂ around a bit.

"I peed" she confessed and stopped short I   ˙e adding 'forgive me father for I have sinned.'

The Lieutenant leaned over Destiny. The swell   had gone down remarkable. It was unbelievable how much bett₆   ₁e looked. Almost human. Almost as if she was going to pull   ough. He begrudged coming to investigate the attempt on this wo   's life the

first time ought it was a waste of his time as she was clearly
checking There was a lot of cases out there he could be working
on. But n ow she looked like she might actually be worth looking
into.
Dc y stopped chipping away at the wall she was locked
behind. T ight coming through the translucent barrier was fading.
Night wa: wning but in her suspended state there was no night or
day so it r be something else. What was that smell? How could she
smell? Sh s going to gag!
A k flash of light from behind the darkness made the smell
subside. 1 bright light pushed out the darkness. The warmth from
the light v amiliar. Home. If she could just get through this wall.
Ac nudged the lieutenant out of the way. As if on his
regular rc s he grabbed Destiny's wrist, looked at his watch.
Checked tubes. After satisfying himself as to his patient's
condition arned to the excess baggage in the room.
"B again Lieutenant?"
"Y There was another attempt on this woman's life I hear."
Ac and Mira looked at each other. The guard outside the
door was :, they hadn't told anybody. How did he know? Or did he
know?
Th utenant continued. "You didn't notify me."
"C ously someone did." Adam answered. "I have peoples'
lives to at to."
"C ously. And I have peoples' safety to attend to. I have also
been look into your records Dr. Adams. There doesn't seem to be
any recorc you in India."
"I ot surprised. There's a lot of people in India. And they
don't keej y good records."
"B his hospital does. And there doesn't seem to be any
record of here either. You don't see any other patients. Surely you
are not th ecialized. You don't collect a paycheck. Surely you are
not that gc ous." his eyes narrowed with the final word drawing out
the s like iss of a snake. His 'I've got you now' attitude made his
chest swe
Ac drew a long impatient breath. Guessing games had never
been on h vorites list. Plain and simple truth was his choice. "What
is it you a: iplying?"

"I'm not implying anything yet. But you'll have to come down to the station with me. To answer some questions." gorilla hand wrapped around the top of his arm and began to persuade him to exit the room.

"Ask your questions here. I can't leave right now."

The grip tightened. "No can do. But you can come with or without cuffs. Doesn't make any difference to me." He pulled the jacket back to reveal a set of handcuffs in a leather pouch attached to his belt, right beside his revolver.

The halo flashed more rapid. The halo was broad, almost jumped off the monitor. The orange caution was too late. The trap had been sprung. The light was leaving. "Don't go!" She cried out. "You can't leave me hear alone. I HAVE TO COME WITH YOU!" This thought washed over her like a tsunami. The truth she had been searching a lifetime for had just been revealed. She had found her golden chalice. She knew now where she belonged. Without a doubt she belonged with this light source. But something, some predator was dragging it away. She began throwing all her energy at the wall. She had to break through. It wasn't just for herself now it was to save the source of light that was on the other side. And then there was darkness. Even in the darkest night sky there is still light. This was a complete absence of light. Her heart hurt. There was a big void taking over her being. She was collapsing in on herself. Without this light there was no life in her. She couldn't die. She couldn't cease to exist. She struck out at the wall again. And again. Harder. Harder. And harder still. "I will not die! I will not let this predator take away this source of light. I will not be extinguished."

Adam looked at the monitor as he headed out the door. The halo was more a flash of lightning now. Each beep would be blinding to the average eye if it could be detected. This was a good response. What he had been waiting for. She was fighting now. This was the turning point. With a smirk he winked at Mira.

"I'm all yours lieutenant?"

Chapter 30

The front tire bulged out on either side of the rim. Instead of one inch hugging the pavement the tire hugged at least three. The lack of air gave a exaggerated swale to the bumps in the warm pavement. The incline all the way back to the house was harder to peddle due to the extra drag.

The shed behind Adam's where the bike lay hidden was home to all manner of tools and equipment. There was a large cylinder upright in the corner if memory served her correctly. A compressor. The last block was taken at a walk.

Banging strikes of metal against metal hit her eardrums before the source came into view. An old green and white truck was sitting in front of the drive door to the shed. The hood was up and the truck seemed to be eating someone alive. But not without a fight.

"Adam?" Destiny inquired of the mechanic.

A large frame in greasy overalls stuck his head out from under the truck. "Hi Destiny."

"Who's winning?"

"Definitely not me." a red rag from the back pocket was pulled out and used to wipe his hands.

"What are you doing?"

"It used to be my old truck. I pushed it out of the garage this morning just to have a peek under the hood. Found a few problems. I've made four trips to the parts store but it still won't turn over. It might be terminal. How bout you?"

"I seem to have a flat. I thought I remembered seeing a compressor in here. Does it work?"

"Yea. The back corner. The air's on and the hose is out. You might have to change the chuck. I was using the air wrench. Help yourself. Or I could do it."

"Thanks I think I can get it. You've got plenty of problems of your own."

The front tire quickly back to normal pressure the bike rolled without effort past the truck. The mechanic was in the driver's seat pumping on the accelerator. As Destiny walked past he pulled the door closed to give the bike and rider ample room. The engine caught burped and belched smoke. He pumped the throttle to keep it going. His grin was that of a school boy starting his own truck for the very first time.

Destiny smiled a congratulations to him. "Looks like you won."

"I like to win." he was still grinning ear to ear.

Rust outlined a huge hollowed out dent in the driver's door. Destiny was going to ask about the dent. Her hand traced the deepest part of the indention. Suddenly there was no need to ask about the dent. This memory was not one she would be sharing with Adam. There was no need, the answer to the memory game was a certain yes. She knew without a doubt.

Pearl had asked Destiny to sit with Mira. The weather was cooling. The leaves loosening their grips on the branches. Destiny had taken Mira outside to chase leaves.

Mira was fascinated by the falling leaves. They drifted down so slowly. She went over to one as it was coming down, it seemed she was going to try to catch it but instead put her face straight up to heaven and let the golden leaf brush softly against her cheek as if she were accepting a kiss from an angel.

She giggled and touched her cheek softly and said "Kit me." She held her hand out and a leaf floated down landing in her palm. She brought the leaf to me and brushed it across my cheek. "Kit you" she said.

Mira's fingers felt like ice cubes where they brushed across my cheek and the backs of her hands were bright red to match her glowing red face. I guess she was used to a California climate. I asked her if she was cold and told her maybe we should go inside but her reaction to going inside was fitful.

"Ow here" she stomped her foot and demanded. "Wan mo kitses"

It was fine with me to stay out there forever. I couldn't believe how anyone could get such joy from a falling leaf. Mira stood with her face pointed upward anticipating the next leaf to fall. She would squeal with delight and hold her breath as one came close enough to touch her. We walked around the house one full circle only to find the leaves were doing the same thing on all sides of the house. Then the phone rang. I left Mira at the front gate, staring across the line in the dirt. She muttered "Ow dar", as she usually did when she came the imaginary gate.

I returned from taking a message for Pearl only to find Mira not at the front gate. She must have decided to make another lap around the house without me. I traipsed around the house, no Mira. I called for her, no answer. I looked in her favorite hiding place behind the tree in the middle of the back yard, no Mira. Tiny beads of sweat began forming on my forehead. Back inside the house, maybe she went in to get her 'out there box'. She wasn't in her room, or any of the other rooms in the small house.   My breathing had quickened and I started to feel like I was going to get sick. I yelled out "Mira, it's OK to be loud, I can't find you."

No noise met my eardrums except the rustle of the falling leaves. The thought hit my mind like a bolt of lightning. There were a lot more leaves 'Ow dar' than in Mira's yard. She must have gone after more leaf kisses. I bolted through the imaginary gate yelling for Mira. I looked up and down the street. There was no sign of anyone. Which direction should I go? Where would I start looking? The dirt was too hard to leave any fresh footprints. I paused and held my breath. I could hear yelling.

There was a green and white truck at the stop sign down the street. Two men were out of the truck, one yelling at the other. The wind muffled their voices. Then Mira appeared. Walking close to the edge of the fences. Almost even with the truck. Staying as close to the fence line too I crept along eyes glued to the truck and the men.

The older of the two men was done talking with his mouth. He began throwing punches at the other. The other man didn't hit back. Strange. The older man hit time and time again the other was bleeding from his nose and some other place on his face. Holding his arms over his face the hits now concentrated on his stomach. The older man began to bang the man's body against the door of the truck. Each time the beaten body was slammed against the truck the dent in the door grew deeper and deeper.

The younger man was nothing more than a rag doll. The only thing holding him up was the grip from the other man.

Mira had seen enough. She headed out to confront the man. "No hit!!!"

The older man looked in her direction. She was now half way across the street. I began to run toward Mira.

"You no hit! It bad!" her hands were on her hips. Headed across the sea to save the weak.

The old man leaned the other man up against the truck his head rolled to the side, his eyes closed. It was Adam.

Mira had made her way to stand beside the old man. He glanced down at her, then raised his arm back ready to take the final swing at Adam. Mira jumped into the air and swung on his arm like a monkey.

Sirens neared. I grabbed for Mira holding her around the waist. She was my only concern in the whole scene. Her grip gave loose and we tumbled to the ground. A car skidded to a stop. An officer jumped out.

"Lou step back. Leave your boy be." the officer approached with caution.

The officer in the other car radioed for help.

"Lou I mean it! Let the boy be."

Once the old man stepped back and the officer helped Adam to the ground. The old man staggered backwards. He shook his head. Looked down at his trembling hands. Then his evil eyes settled on their next victim. Mira.

"What are you lookin at. You retard! Get the hell out of here!"

"Lou back off. Get in the squad car. I don't want to have to cuff you but I will. Get in the car you're going in this time." The officer came to our aid and helped us up. "Did he hit you?"

"No. he didn't hit us we fell. She, this is Mira Appleton. She went running at the man. She jumped on his arm and I grabbed her off. That's when we fell."

"Well you girls look OK. You better be going home. Go on now."

Mira was not content to leave well enough alone. Walking past the incarcerated man she shook her finger at him. "You bad! No hit!"

I tugged on Mira's sleeve leading her back into the safety of her world. Out there was not full of treasures. Not this day. Mira managed to forget the event once back in the confines of her yard. The leaves continued to kiss her softly. She favored one in particular and had to give it the honor of being part of her box.

Destiny looked at this man grinding the shifter into gear. Deriving such pleasure from a simple thing. This bubble of a memory that had just popped on the surface. Hopefully this event would remain at the bottom of this man's sea of memories. Hopefully this was a once in a lifetime event in his life. Once was forgettable, once was forgivable. There was a dark cloud that shadowed the memory. A feeling that this was not the only memory of this nature. The time and details varied but the story was the same. With so much to forget, how had he survived to be the man he was? Destiny thanked God for the time that healed all wounds.

Adam looked up from his focus on the engine now purring. Still alive with excitement. "What is it?"

"What?" Destiny hadn't realized she had been staring at him.

"You look worried. It's not going to blow up I promise. I'm not that bad of a mechanic."

The woman changed her expression to meet the events of the present. With a smile she got on the bicycle. "I don't doubt your abilities. Thanks for the air."

It was true his abilities were not in doubt. Especially his ability to forgive.

Back at the little house that night nestled in the easy chair the box lid was removed. The memory of the chalk was brought to light. And now the leaf. The chalk was such a joy to remember. But the leaf held fear and sorrow. Gazing at the other contents of the box she wondered would there be more joy or sorrow?

Chapter 31

Beep! Beep! Beep! The lightning bolts still li[t] the room . She had with each beat of her heart. Mira knew Destiny could seen it before. When she had something worth fighting And what better to fight for than your life, your existence and th istence of love.

Adam came back in the room after a couple of ling hours spent with the lieutenant. A room too small for sensit senses. A scene right out of a detective novel. Empty room exce or a table with two opposing chairs. Steel door with a knob on the side only. One small window too high to look out of even on oes. Wire between the glass that once was clear now frosted wit imy film. The one light in the room strategically placed to shine ne eyes of the one being questioned so as not to see the pers sking the ridiculous questions.

Adam relayed this picture to Mira as he filled in on the affair.

"What did he want?" Mira expressed concern.

"Other than to show his superiors he was diligent orking on the case and to through some of that excess weight arou haven't a clue. He didn't get any records back from India in th enty four hours he waited. He didn't have any leads as to who mi have tried to harm Destiny. And I was the common denominator who was with her both times. So he thought I might have been the e trying to take away this precious life I am working so hard to save

"Sounds like that pretty much sums it up." Mira s ed.

"It does doesn't it."

"Why did they let you go?'

"The lieutenant stepped out for his third smoke a ame back wearing mud on his face. A file had just arrived, Fed illed with licenses, diplomas, commendations from the deans of r cine. You name it, it was in the packet. And every piece of paper my name on it. Even this very hospital wrote a letter stating my p on here as temporary, esteemed visiting physician. Pro bono of cou

"Wow. How did you swing that? I thought that d of thing

182

was again   e rules."

He   sed his eyebrows. "Oh it would definitely be against the rules. So   s going to ask you the same thing. How did you swing that?"

"N   'm no rule breaker."

Th   urned to their patient. The halo on the monitor beeped playfully.

Chapter 32

The old truck sat outside Faye's early that morning. Purred like a kitten. All it wanted was a little attention. The paint didn't even look half bad except for the big dent in the driver door. Adam paid no mind to this. A work truck was just that, a work truck. It would look worse before it looked better.

Cranberry orange muffins. The aroma escaped out the exhaust fan behind the café, caught an updraft, held close to the roofline and cascaded back to earth in front of the café door. Adam thought he might have to indulge in a muffin. The taste buds pleaded for satisfaction.

Ed and Ed sat next to the kitchen as usual. The only ones up at such an hour.

"Morning Adam." Ed had his mouth ready to wrap around the cakes giving off the heavenly aroma.

"Ed, Ed. How are you?"

"Good. You're up awful early."

"The dog wouldn't let me sleep."

"That your dog what runs with Mrs. Walker."

"Yea. Digger. For some reason she couldn't let herself out this morning. So she came and woke me up."

The muffin was still warm and fogged Ed's vision.

The Wall Street Journal was unfolded and propped up. Faye brought a cup and banged it on the table. Coffee sloshed over the sides but no one noticed. "Hell." she muttered walking away.

"Rough night Faye?"

"Two for one. And where were you Ed and Ed?"

"I was home rubbing the little woman's feet. Five months pregnant and she decides she wants to turn back."

Ed looked through his steamed glasses at Ed.

The door bell chimed and Whitey held the door open for Mary Clare and followed in after her.

"What do you mean she wants to turn back?"

The cast of coffee characters took their seats one by one. Destiny as usual was the last to arrive. She slid into the seat at the table, next to the window, opposite the Wall Street Journal. Quietly as possible not to disturb the conversation in full swing. The corner of the paper flipped down. "Careful, Faye had one too many two for ones last night." He gestured to his cup sitting atop a pile of brown stained napkins.

"Put a sock in it." The coffeepot had a will of its own that morning and it willed itself to pour on the table instead of in the confines of the cup. "Oh, Hell again. Sorry Destiny. Ed reach around the counter and get that rag. Here Destiny, could you mop that up for me? I got something in my eye. I got to go to the little girl's room and get it out."

"Sure Faye. Thanks." Destiny grabbed the sacred box off the table before the hot brown fluid made its way across the table

Ed returned to the previous conversation with Ed. "You didn't say what Cindy wants to turn back on."

"The whole thing."

"What whole thing?"

"The baby thing."

"She can't."

"That's what I told her but she just keeps saying I've changed my mind I don't want to have a baby no more."

"You mean she wants to give it up for adoption?" Whitey chimed in.

"No she doesn't want to have it period."

"That's crazy. That's impossible. That's the one thing in life you don't turn around on. Once it's in there, it has to come out. No two ways around it. And you can tell her I said so." Faye had added her expertise to the subject at hand from the open door into the ladies room.

Destiny had a different take on the situation. "Maybe she's just going through some hormonal surges." They all turned around and stared at her in disbelief as if she had just revealed to her parents at the dinner table she knew all about sex. Cowering down she added. "You know maybe she's emotional. Pregnant women get emotional. I've heard."

Father to be Ed answered, "Nope, that's not it. She says there just no place to put it once it gets here."

"Babies don't take up no room at all. Why hell they don't weigh more than say ten pounds. That's a big sack of flour." Nearsighted Ed put his hands out in front of him and estimated how big a sack of flour was.

"It doesn't matter the size of the kid. It's all the baggage that comes with um. You know the crib, the highchair, the playpen, the swing and that's just the inside stuff." Mary Clare threw her coins of wisdom into the collection plate.

"How would you know Mary Clare, you don't even like kids." Ed squinted across the café through his spectacles.

"I've visited my sister and her brood."

"Anyway," soon to be dad Ed continued, "Cindy said there just ain't no room in the trailer for a kid. I told her we could sleep on the fold out in the living room and give the bedroom to the baby. But that didn't help her attitude any. She just wailed all the more, I'm not bringing a baby in to a one room trailer. She give me four months to sort it out or else."

Ed was completely confused now, "Or else what?"

The dad looked confused now too. "I don't know. I didn't ask. She didn't say."

Destiny spoke quietly to the back side of the Wall Street Journal. "Am I hearing this right? They live in a one bedroom trailer and they have a baby on the way?"

The corner of the paper bent down and two eyes peaked over the fold. "A camp trailer to be exact."

Some wheels began to turn in Destiny's head.

The paper was laid down all together. "Did the box get bombed by coffee?"

"No I saved it just in time. I guess I could leave it at the house. But I'm getting sort of attached to it."

"Sort of like a pet rock?"

"Weird?"

"What?"

"You think it's weird? To carry around a box. Hoping it will conjure up some memories?"

"I didn't say that."

The coke bottle glasses turned on the swivel stool to face the table. "I think he's saying, 'what ever blows your skirt up' miss Destiny."

Her eyes turned to saucers. So much for talking in a whisper. "Excuse me?"

"You know he's saying whatever makes you happy."

"What's with that expression anyway?" Mary Clare seldom spoke unless something caught her particular attention.

"It's from Marilyn Monroe, you know, that picture where the wind is blowing her skirt up and she's trying to hold it down. But you can tell she's enjoying every minute of it." Ed informed the café.

Mary Clare was not satisfied with the explanation. "And just how's that supposed to make a person happy? Trying to hold their skirt down."

Ed pondered a moment. "Well if it don't make the skirt wearer happy it sure makes the crowd happy."

"Jackass." daddy Ed said.

"You got a story for us this morning Miss Destiny?" the Ed turned to Ed. "Don't call me a jackass. You're the one that lives in a camp trailer."

"Don't go talking about miss Destiny's skirt blowing up then or I'll call you more than a jackass. Jackass."

Faye was back with a full pot of coffee and the obstruction gone from her vision. "You two pipe it. If Destiny has a story she's not gonna have time to tell it if you keep yapping."

Destiny got a grin on her face.

"Faye, better fill up the cups I think she remembered something." Adam couldn't help return her smile.

Reaching in the box the piece of candy was pulled out. "Trick or Treat."

The wind was icy walking home. Passing by Pearl's house I heard banging. Upon investigation I found Pearl in the back of her house trying to push the windows down in their slots further. To make a tighter seal. The wind and weather over years and years had changed the size and even the shape of the windows and their sills. What used to be a perfect fit was now a misfit. After she had the windows down as far as they would go she was trying to nail plastic over the whole outside of the window. Pearl took a worse beating from the plastic than she was offering the window with the hammer. I grabbed the loose end and held it out the best I could while she nailed a strip of wood down one side of the window to hold the plastic in place. I had never seen Pearl untidy but her hair was a true mess.

Pearl looked at me with appreciation and yelled, " I guess the time for this is not in the middle of a wind storm, but on one side of it or the other. Let's get out of here!"

I followed her into the house through the back door. Mira was waiting just inside the door to get the progress report.

"Too much wind Mira!" Pearl reported to her.

Mira stroked at Pearls hair and replied, "Mess."

"Well I don't doubt that!" Pearl laughed at her. "Let's have some cocoa and I'll go comb my hair, if I can." She headed for the bathroom still talking to us. "Isn't this weather a shame what it's doing to all the wonderful decorations around town. I saw Mrs. Lake frantically trying to take down her witch and scarecrow. She left out the pumpkins but I bet no one has candles in them tonight. Are you going trick or treating Destiny?"

That was the question of the day. Pearl obviously didn't assume I was too old to go trick or treating.

"Oh, but you are in high school, I forgot, forgive me, you probably have a dance or a haunted house or something fun like that to go to." Pearl added. "Surely the school is having something for the older kids aren't they?" Pearl interrogated.

"Yea, but I've already made up my mind I'm not going to that. Besides I don't know what I'd be. My mom and dad are going to a costume party at the mine. So I'll probably just hand out candy at home." I was planning my words of exit when Mira came over and grabbed my hand.

"I go wit u" she said starring up into my eyes. Her puppy dog eyes. Her slightly raised eyebrows in dog fashion, the only thing she lacked was panting with her tongue hanging out with an occasional drip on the floor for realism.

"You like to trick or treat Mira? Yea, it's fun isn't it. But, well, I'll have to let you know, you see I don't know if I will be going. OK?" I tried to pacify her but didn't seem to be doing a very good job.

"I go wit u" Mira insisted. Stomping her foot.

Pearl stepped in to save me and I was grateful. She said not to

188

worry about it. In fact she didn't have a costume for Mira anyway. I told Pearl I would let her know. On the walk home I couldn't help thinking what I would dress Mira up to be. I wouldn't want her to get scared. Her costume would have to be safe for her so she wouldn't trip. But why was I even thinking such thoughts? It wasn't like I had said yes I'll take you trick or treating. I hadn't made any definite decisions. But, surely I had an old costume packed away somewhere. Something that would fit   Mira just right. Why shouldn't I go ahead and take Mira.

Five o'clock came on a dark and blustery night. The witching hour, time to turn all little children into unrecognizable creatures so the witches couldn't carry them off to their caves and castles to suck the life out of them. Huge bowl of candy in place with a note to help yourself, I started out for Mira's. Pearl nor Mira offered any suggestions as to what Mira would like to be. I brought several costumes for her to choose from. One year I was a puppy, I thought that quite appropriate for Mira. She already had the eyes. A witches costume was big and long. Mira could be dressed warmly underneath. Somehow, her personality didn't strike me as a witch. My own costume of choice was a pirate, which I brought along. I didn't want to scare Mira right as I came through the front door. I'd put it on at her house so she could see me transform one step at a time. That way she would believe it was me under the eye patch and makeup. I was loaded down. It felt like I was bringing our whole attic.

The north wind was not being too helpful in getting me to Mira's on time. It argued with me the whole way and nearly won, till at last the gap in Pearl's fence was in sight. The wind gave up completely and went on to torment some other pour soul trying to make their way across town. The top of the box had blown open several times. The last time I had given up on putting the box down on the ground to secure the top again. I let it wave as if it were taunting the wind. The sleeve to the mad pirate suit had found its way out of the box and was also giving a greeting to all. Not to mention a royal beating to me. It was a true accomplishment to have arrived at Mira's at all. Still never once had I felt it was an omen. Something trying to tell me to turn back, retrace my steps. I looked at it rather like the mountains I climbed. Not easy, always a challenge, definitely not impossible, but always adventurous with a reward waiting at the end.

"Guess you always liked the mountains around   huh miss
Destiny?"
"I guess so Ed. I really don't remember any e   rations in
particular but yea you're right."
"Ed I'm gonna post a sign on the wall. No Int   pting The
Mira Tales!"   Faye shook a spatula at him.
"OK. OK Faye. Go ahead Miss Destiny."
*The clocks had been turned back so by the time I   arrived at
Pearl's the sun was well asleep and the stars started to ;   ner. Mira
however was more like the sun than the stars. She was s   umbering
from her afternoon nap. Pearl thought it best to let her   p as long
as she would, an exciting evening lay ahead. Pearl   ted going
through the costumes. She found the puppy dog to be he   orite. But
she was determined to let Mira decide for herself. She h   mera and
film waiting on the table. There came a knock on the do   hosts and
goblins already out for the evening. Pearl treated the   ira came
sleepily out of the bedroom. She gasped and pointed at tl   ests.*
    "Wha da?!" she questioned shockingly.
    "Those are children Mira. They are pretending   ght. They
are pretending to be somebody else and people give   n a treat
because they appreciate how much work they have gone   dress all
up."
    Pearl was still deep in explanation when the do   as rapped
on by a fairy and a little Pinocchio. This time when P   answered
the door Mira was right at her side. Mira began to laugh   laugh.
    "Dey Funye" She explained.
    Mira saw the children get candy from Pearl and   n the next
group of   costumes arrived she rushed to the door a   ave them
each a huge fistful of candy.
    "Goodness!" Pearl said, " at this rate we'll be o   f candy in
half an hour. We better get you dressed up and on your v   "
    I called Mira over to start the selection of a c   ne. "Look
Mira, I have all these costumes, which one do you wo   o wear?"
Mira looked at me, cocked her head from side to side.   go" said
Mira.
    "Yes I know you want to go, and we will, but fi   e have to
get dressed up. What do you want to wear?"
    I held out the witches costume and put the poin   at on her

head. She | e me a blank stare, folded the costume up and put it back
in the box
"N | o." she said this time stamping her foot.
I | d out the puppy costume. Brushed the soft fur against
her cheek | asked her if she wanted to be a soft cuddly puppy.
" | o" was her only reply besides folding up the puppy and
putting it | in the box with a gentle pat on the puppy head.
Pe | came to the offer some clarification. "Mira, darling
these are | es you put on and then go out trick or treating, like the
children | are coming to the door. Then other people give you
candy. De | has brought these costumes for you to choose from and
so what d | u want to dress up in?" Pearl raised her eyebrows high
and waite | d waited. Finally she gave Mira her choices again and
waited for | ply.
M | ave a deep sigh, she put a hand on either side of Pearls
face and | ezed hard, I could tell she had quite a grip for it didn't
take long | Pearl's lips to start turning blue. "Me Go!" Mira said
with all th | thority she could muster.
"I | w you want to go, but what do you want to go as?"
Pearl said | mbling through Mira's hands.
Fi | Mira made herself clear as a summers rain she said,
"Me." M | ropped her grip on Pearls face as if in surrender. If
she hadn' | ten her point across this time she would try no more.
So | a and I ventured out into the cold bleak Halloween night
with our c | to protect us from the north wind, as ourselves.
W | ossed the street to Mrs. Lake's first. Mrs. Lake's house
was by fc | e of the most decorated in town. She had large bats
hanging f | the trees. Pumpkins lined the walk and she had spider
webs dan | from the limbs that would reach out to grab anyone
that came | close. Mrs. Lake herself even got into the spirit of
things. Li | ly the spirit. She stood out by the gate dressed as a ghost
giving ou | dy. She claimed she was protecting her yard from all the
little beas | d goblin footprints. I think she was just having a good
time. Mir | s not frightened of Mrs. Lake in the least.
Sh | nt right up to her and said, "Tic, teet"
M | vas braver than I for Mrs. Lake's costume gave me a
chill. She | l her eyes painted dark black and the pieces of white
gauze ma | up her costume flowed in the wind giving her movement

191

as she stood still. Her hands were exposed   and she had old garden gloves that were caked with years of dried mud mixed with sprigs of decaying grass. She was humming a mournful "woooooooooooo" as we approached. She briefly stepped out of character, "What are you supposed to be?" she asked Mira.

Mira simply grinned and said, "Me, me"

"Best costume I've seen all night." She complimented then went back to her "Wooooooooo" as more rustling bags approached.

I had in my plan to take Mira to Mrs. Lake's, go back across the street to Pearl's, maybe to Pearl's back door, back to the front door and call it a night. I had a change in plans. Mira was now ten steps ahead of me and gaining fast. She was done with the neighbor house before I could get to the steps. All the houses were the same with the same question, 'What are you supposed to be?' By the forth house Mira had it down, she knocked on the door, when the owner answered she said, "Me! Tic, teet!" Then off she flew to the next house leaving them all shaking their heads with confusion.

She was impossible to keep up with before I knew what happened she had crossed over onto Maine street and was hitting the houses one right after another. She crossed the side street between houses and businesses and there on the corner sat the T-N-T Bar. The neon lights must have attracted her, they did look a little festive. She burst in the front door, stood in the smoke filled bar, held out her bag and said, "Me, tic, teet!" And waited patiently for the customers to fill it up. I came through the front doors just in time to see the owner, Tom coming around from behind the bar.

"What the hell is this, you kids get outa here! This is a bar we don't have no candy and we don't allow kids in here."

Mira just looked up at him and smiled, repeated her request. "Me, tic, teet!" with much more emphasis this time.

A woman sitting at the bar with starched blond hair stuck her foot out in front of Tom as he was nearing Mira. She was already several sheets to the wind. When Tom bumped into her foot she about went to the floor. He reached her arm just in time and righted her on her seat again.

"Ah, Tom let the kidz haff their fun," slurring her words, she motioned to Mira curling her finger, "here lil girl, here's some peanuts."   Mira went over to her and the lady emptied the bar nuts into Mira's sack. The woman moved her head around in a spinning motion as she, asked Mira what she was supposed to be.

"Me, me." Mira replied.

The woman stared at Mira for a while, the woman with her mouth gaping open and her eyes crossing and uncrossing. If she was trying to focus on Mira's eyes I could tell her quest was futile.

"Thas good," replied the woman, "now therz two of us, cuz I'm me too, and this here glass is empty. So Trick or Treat Barkeep. What do you know, I'm a damned poet."

Mira smiled and moved on to the next victim down the bar. She wiped Tom out of bar nuts that night. As we were leaving someone caught her attention. It was someone sitting all alone, all by himself at the very end of the bar. The poor soul was all hunkered over his drink glass. He held a cigarette in his hand, which he was ignoring. The smoke curled up from the cigarette and playfully swirled around the old man's hair. He was shaking gently, almost like a mother rocking her baby to sleep. Everyone in town knew him as Goose. He looked up as Mira neared, but he didn't look at Mira. He sat there just shaking his head back and forth.

"Hu yo," she said softly to Goose.

He acknowledged her being there but no words were spoken.

"You funye costume," she said gazing at Goose.

"Hey kid." the old man held out his hand to Mira. I tried to pull her away. She had never heard the rule don't take candy from strangers. He held out a tootsie roll. I knew it was her favorite candy of all time. This was going to be hard to get her away.

The old man directed his attention to me. "Please missy, I'm not going to hurt her. I had me some kids once. Some grandkids too. Halloween was always their favorite."

"Kids all gone?" Mira asked.

"I heard you down there telling them you was just you. Well I forgot who I was for awhile and it cost me my family. So you take this here candy. And you don't eat it. But you keep it as a reminder to be yourself. Always be yourself. You go on home now. It's getting late." he returned to his lost gaze and his half empty glass.

We headed back to her house. She took my hand as we walked slowly back. "Be me, better" Mira said as she looked up at me. And on that moonless night in October, I looked into her eyes that sparkled *brighter than any star in the heavens and I was suddenly struck with the realization of what Mira was trying to tell me all night.*

"Yes Mira, I guess it is better to be yourself."

"Me, me, better." was her reply.

Destiny put the petrified tootsie roll back in the box and replaced the lid. With a smirk she gave a nod of accomplishment to Adam. He was somehow proud of her accomplishment too but he didn't know why. Right on queue his cell phone rang. He answered it gave a few comments of confirmation then rose from the table. "Thanks for the Mira Tale. I gotta run." half way to the door he turned around and headed back. Stopping beside Ed and Ed he laid a set of old keys on the counter.

"I was going to junk the old truck. But thought you guys might be able to put it to good use."

The two Eds looked at the keys, looked at each other, their eyes welled up with tears. Dad to be Ed rose and gave Adam a hand shake. He just kept shaking his hand up and down, up and down. It reminded Destiny of Mira's hand shake. So much could be said without uttering a word. Ed rose slowly, removed his glasses and just exploded into full fledged blubbering. "Nobody ever gave me nothing so fine. I don't know what to say." He hugged Adam and tried unsuccessfully to contain his emotions.

Destiny watched the scene and realized what was so appealing about this place. What was so wonderful about the people here. They might not have much money, they might not have much education or sometimes manners. But these people were real. These people were totally unmasked, what was shown was what they were. No fake, phony airs, no pretending to be anything other than what they were. And they didn't care who knew it. Just a town full of Me's. And she knew without a doubt that coming to Bendline was not a mistake. It was just what she needed. At a time when everything was so uncertain in her life, this was the surest most stable place to be. In a town so steady and solid there was no way she could lose her balance completely. There was no way she could fall.

Chapter 33

Beep. Beep. Beep.

The officer still occupied the chair outside of Destiny's room. Mira went for a quick stroll out in the hall just to resemble a normal person that needed to get up and stretch from time to time.

Adam gave Mira an approving nod as he pushed the heavy door open. Mira tried to catch his attention but he was a man on a mission.

"Oh. I didn't know she had a visitor."

James sat in the chair usually occupied by Mira. He wasn't reading. He wasn't even talking just staring at the woman in the bed beside him. He was equally surprised to see the doctor. "I had some time this afternoon. I thought I'd check in on her. Is she getting better? I can't tell."

She was getting better. Extremely better in Adams way of thinking. But it wasn't what her husband meant. "Her recovery will be slow. You have to expect that."

"So she's not dying anymore?"

He wanted to say we are all dying instead he offered, "if she keeps this upward momentum I can take her off critical soon. Provided there are no surprises." by surprises he meant powers trying to disconnect her from this world. Extinguish her existence.

"Damn it Doctor is she gonna die or not?"

This man's compassion was amazing. Adam wanted to spill the whole truth right then and there. Tell him he was keeping her connected in this world just long enough for her to work through a few last issues and find her way back. Then it was, out of here. We're going home. Instead he offered, "It still looks rather bleak. In all honesty if she fully recovers it would be nothing short of a miracle."

"Fully recovers? You mean she could come too and there could be complications?"

"Yes. Definitely."

"She could be like what a vegetable or something?" the horror look on his face when he looked down at his wife made Adam cringe.

"She could have some motor skill problems and some speech

195

problems. She could even have some memory problems. Those are things that we won't know until she wakes up."

James rose from his seat. Shook his head in disbelief and walked out of the room. No goodbye.

When Adam was sure he wasn't coming back he took Destiny's hand in his own and bent down to whisper in her ear. "I know you are on the right track now. But if there is any way you could hurry this along. I don't know if I can take another visit from that man!" he stroked her cheek and saw the sparks jump back and forth between the tip of his finger and her skin. The halo turned crimson. He rose and headed for the door.

Turning he added, "I got a message from the council. They know there was some manipulation going on down here. Some paper files appeared out of nowhere. They sent a strong warning that there is to be no manipulation of events! Or Mira and I will have to leave immediately and you will have to continue on your own. I assured him there would be no more interfering."

The crimson halo faded to nonexistent. A lump welled in her throat. She stopped working on the wall. She was so close to the light on the other side now the warmth seeped through. But to not have the light on the other side any longer to beckon her on. It would be no use. The reason for the struggle would be gone. From out of nowhere the light became a beacon again.

He was beside her again to whisper one last word before Mira returned. "By the way Destiny, thank you. For the files. Now keep dreaming!"

The halo returned to crimson.

She struck the wall another blow.

Chapter 34

The door closed with a click. Loaded down with extra baggage this trip Adam looked up to see the runners returning. The pace was a slow walk at best and both were limping on the right leg.

Destiny opened the gate to let the injured Digger enter first. The dog walked up to his master in injured fashion, sat at his feet and held the right paw out for him.

"What happened to you guys?" the baggage tossed to the side in the lawn. The master knelt down and started a thorough examination of his friend. Starting at the paw Adam squeezed gently, working his hand up the leg and into the shoulder area.

With nonchalance Destiny began the account of the accident.

"We were just jogging along not really pushing it yet just getting warmed up and both of us at the same time just sunk in the dirt. I went up to my ankle. I didn't see how far Digger plunged."

The man's head snapped up from the examination. "Damn it Destiny! You've got to be careful out there!"

"It was no big deal Adam. Just a rabbit den or something."

"I'll bet my life that was no rabbit den."

His tone was scolding and Destiny shrank down as if she were a child.

"These hills are covered with old mine shafts. You know that!"

"I guess I didn't. Or didn't remember."

"Well don't forget it now! They tried to barricade off most of the shafts. Or blast them closed but that didn't always get the airshafts. Some of them went straight down into the mountain for a mile."

His immediate anger at thinking what might have happened took precedence over realizing she was just beginning to remember anything about the area.

"OK. I'll be careful I promise." she remained in place in case there was further tongue lashing to be had.

It appeared he was done. He grabbed Digger's face and gave it a squeeze. "I think you'll live."

Bags again once in hand he was to the gate. Destiny still had not taken a step.

"Destiny." his tone still stern, as a father trying to show the seriousness of a situation. "I'm going to be gone for three   four days. Could you keep an eye on Digger?"

Destiny was facing Digger corners of the mouth   ooped and eyes were wide as if they had both been in big trouble. "I   lad to."

"I'm sorry. About getting upset."

"It's OK. And I will be careful."

He stood with the hatch opened tossing bags in.   th runners were leaving the yard limping to the beat of the sa   drummer. "Destiny?" he called after her.

"Are you Ok. Your ankle?"

Her shoulders perked up, she turned to face hir   Just fine." She would live, he wasn't mad anymore.

Chaptei 5

Be   Beep. Beep.
A(had been gone for the day. Had to take care of some
details in   her dimension he said. Mira was in full charge. So she
barricadec   door with a chair. No one got in on her watch. She and
Destiny w   getting along fine. Mira was two thirds the way through
with <u>Gon</u>   th The Wind. How could this not be someone's favorite
book of al   le?
M   ook a break and put the book down. Studying Destiny as
she lie the   o still. "Doesn't this book just make you want to get up
and do so   ling Destiny. You have always been so active. Or maybe
you don't   ember. But you were never someone to just sit still. You
loved you   liet time but when there is something that needs doing
you are th   st one in line."
M   noticed tiny beads of perspiration forming on her
forehead.   bent close and softly blew against Destiny's forehead. "I
hope you   't getting another fever Des. Not now. Adam is gone for
the day it   ust you and me. So don't get a fever. Ok?" she blew
again.

De   y stopped dead in her fight against the wall. The light on
the other s   was not as bright as usual. It was friendly but just not the
same as t   ther light that attracted her so much. Then the strangest
thing hap   d. She felt air movement. Could that be possible in the
state of si   nsion she was in. could there be air? And further more
could it b   ving? There. There it was again!!! This was a good sign.
A very g(sign. It just had to be. The wall was definitely getting
thinner. S   orked double time.

199

Chapter 36

The wind blew. Then the wind blew some more. Then the wind really blew. The desert wind always blew in threes they said down at the café. But the trouble was if it blew for a fourth day it was sure to blow for six. The third day and counting. Destiny had put cleaning the old place up till mother nature was satisfied with where she had moved everything to in the yard. Piles of trash was spread around the yard again. Trees that had been trimmed back by man were further trimmed back by nature. The Two Eds grinned bigger and bigger each time they drove past the place in their new truck.

Destiny was on her fourth kind of homemade cookie when a loud crack hit the side of the house. Jumping out of her skin she dropped the sheet of cookies on the floor. A rattling noise came from the back of the house. Roof metal perhaps. Daring to meet the wind demon face to face, a firm grip on the door was barely enough to hold it on the hinges.   A hard slap on her face brought her sleeping mind back to consciousness and the memory of another windy day. A special windy day. Running into the little house she grabbed something out of the precious box. Scooped up some cookies into a plastic bag. The next thing she knew she was banging on the door of her landlord.

"Destiny? What are you doing out in this. I can't even see across the street. Is something wrong? Did the roof blow off?"

"No. Look." her hand raised in the air showing the bag of cookies.

"Chocolate chip. My favorite." he grabbed for the cookies.

"Not the cookies. Look."

There was still something in her hand. A small vile or clear bottle. It looked familiar but she would have to fill him in.

"What am I looking at?"

"The bottle, from Mira's box!"

"A memory? Come in. sit down." he could use a break in the day. And listening to this woman with knots in her hair she would be hours combing out, reveal an enchanting memory was just the perfect break in the day. And the chocolate chip cookies didn't hurt either.

"I'll grab a glass of milk. You want one?"

"No thanks. I'm good."

He returned to the comfort of his sofa, chocolate chip cookies, and good company.

"Shoot. I'm ready."

"OK. Pearl had asked me to watch Mira. Seems like it was going to be for quite a while. I remember taking a sleeping bag and an overnight suitcase.

The wind was blowing fiercely which added to cold temperature. Pearl made sure I knew how to run the heater and how to light the hot water heater should it blow out as it was prone to do every time the back door was opened in a windstorm. Old houses develop little personality traits and this one's personality was the most colorful I had ever seen.

The house had a language all its own and was speaking to me earnestly. The windows all whistled in the wind. Each one had its own pitch so it sounded like a chorus. The metal on the roof creaked and banged back into place when the wind let up for a moment. The floor was the most talkative, it moaned and groaned as if all the years of standing caused it great pain. I prayed for Mira to wake up early to put a silence to the house's complaints. The house would still be making all the same noises, I just wouldn't be listening to them. My attention would be focused on Mira. I walked around to the windows trying to close them tighter.

After making enough innocent noise, Mira woke from her slumber. She Came out of her bedroom rubbing her eyes. "Hu yo."

"Good morning. Are you surprised to see me?"

"Hu yo." was her only reply.

The explanation that Pearl was gone fell on deaf ears. She seemed to not care, or not understand. I told her Pearl would be back tomorrow. If she had any concept of time. Maybe to her she was just living one long day and she took naps when she got tired.

Once awake Mira earnestly requested a trip outside to see the source of all the commotion. The wind was still blowing with determination. The leaves were completely striped off the tree limbs. Gone was any indication they had ever been alive the past spring. There was enough of a fence around the yard to harbor the dead leaves. However the fence didn't contain them after they piled up to the top. The leaves looked like escaping convicts scaling the wall and dropping to freedom on the other side. They blew and swirled up the pile on the inside of the fence then they would double their speed of decent as they went tumbling down the other side. Mira and I stood at the fence and threw the leaves up in the air for the wind to catch and whisk away.

Mira squealed with joy and excitement. I wished the time could continue for her just this way. That day didn't have to give way to night for her.   The more excited she got the harder it seemed for her to breathe. I supposed it was from the wind and dust. Her breathing became more of a wheeze. The fun needed to stop for a while so she could catch her breath. We headed into the house.

Mira caught her breath. she opened her eyes wide. "Wha ou dar!" she questioned me with excitement still in her voice.

"Leaves are out there, you remember the leaves used to be on the trees but now they're on the ground."

"Na eves" she stated, "wha ou dar, dis" and she began vigorously messing up her hair with her hands. "Wha dat?"

The wind I thought, she wants to know what the wind is. "That's wind, it's air, only it's moving real fast."

Mira disappeared into her room. She brought out her 'out there box'.

"Win in heya." she demanded and headed for the front door.

She was pulling and pulling on the handle when I sprang over to stop her. I could see her life's collection of treasures sailing away into space. Now I had to make Mira realize that wind couldn't be held in her box.

"Win in heya?" she was looking at me puppy dog style. How could she do that? It wasn't fair to give a child such an expression. On the other hand,   yes it was. And I loved seeing that expression on Mira's face. It was warming to the soul. It gave me the feeling that she thought I could do anything. All she had to do was plead hard enough and I could perform miracles. But how do I capture the wind?

"We can't put the wind in your box Mira. It won't stay. The wind would leave your box and take all your treasure with it. The wind doesn't stay anywhere. It's in constant motion."

"Win no stay?" She questioned.
"No the wind won't stay and believe me you're the only person on this earth, I think, that wants the wind to stay."
"Win in heya" she said, with the look.
"Oh, how do I get you some wind?" I was at a loss. I stared into Mira's face as if the answer would suddenly show itself. The teachers from first grade had been telling us, 'well don't just stare at me the answer isn't written on my face'. But I was breaking with traditional thinking, if I stared long enough, maybe. "We have to have something the wind won't get out of Mira. We have to lock it up in something." The answer was coming, the teachers were wrong, there are answers on people's faces, if you had the right question.

I began rummaging around the house, looking in cabinets and drawers. I searched the bathroom and found what I thought might work. A large aspirin bottle. I dumped the aspirin into a glass in the kitchen and put it on the top shelf. I peeled off the labels and washed the bottle clean. I was trying to move as fast as possible for the whole time Mira was hopping and dancing around me chanting. "Win in heya, win in heya, win in heya!"

I took her hand and we headed outside.

I gave Mira the bottle to hold and held her hand up high and pointed the open end of the bottle into the wind. We could hear the whistle! The wind whipped my hair and stung my eyes. Was this in protest of being captured? It whistled across the open end of the bottle to Mira's delight. Just to make sure we had the wind from all directions we held the bottle high in the air and circled the whole house. The whistle would have different pitches on different sides of the house so we were sure it must be a different wind. When we were satisfied we had enough wind we capped the bottle quickly.

Mira was so happy I thought she would burst. She grabbed me around the neck and squeezed so tight I thought I would lose my breath.

She whispered in my ear "Win in heya, Desti my favit"

I felt a sting on my cheek, it was the rapid drying of saltwater. My tears turned to mud as they mixed with the desert dust. How could

203

anyone be so happy to capture the wind? I didn't need an answer to my question, I knew. I just sat there on the porch and hugged her back, and marveled at the miracle we had done.

Inside we gave the wind it's proper place in Mira's 'out there box'.

She was completely exhausted. I didn't realize how tired she got and so quickly, she must have been really out of shape. Off to bed she went, but not without the comfort of her special treasure box beside her.

Destiny looked through the bottle at Adam stuffing the last cookie in his mouth. As if by magic, the wind outside stopped. It would not blow for three more days. It had done what it came for. Destiny had captured it in a bottle.

"So you captured the wind?" Adam broke the silence, the calm in the eye of the storm.

"That we did."

"It sounds like she also captured your heart."

"That, she did."

Chapter 37

Beep. Beep. Beep.

Adam returned to find the two woman engrossed in the final pages of Gone With The Wind. The door to the hospital room gave more resistance than usual. The explanation was clear when he saw the chair he had slid out of the way with the door.

"You afraid of the boogie man Mira?"

"Just the boogie lieutenant." Mira said as she closed the book with a thud. The end.

"How's our girl?"

" She had some sweat on her forehead earlier today. But it seems to have gone away."

He put his palm on Destiny's forehead. The halo on the monitor when ballistic. Sparks went back and forth between his hand and the woman's skin. "She doesn't have a fever. Not now anyway."

"Like I said. It seems better now. You might have something to do with it." she smirked at the doctor.

"Any visitors make it through your barricade?"

"No. and I've been here all day. How did your trip go?"

"The council sent a pretty grave warning. Things are heating up here. Fast. Seems the light that Des brought to this world is being swallowed up faster than anything they have ever seen. Like some gigantic black hole. They are trying to find the source but no luck yet. At any rate we have our orders. Something's coming and its coming fast."

Mira took one big gulp and looked down at the sleeping beauty in the bed. "what if she isn't ready Adam?"

"She'll be ready. She has to be. Or I take her anyway. I've decided that. I told the council. They gave their approval."

"Then let's go now. Why wait the forty eight hours. You know it's only going to get worse. And more dangerous for Destiny. If there's a force swallowing up the light you know it will soon come to the source that radiated it. That is still radiating it. She might get entangled in something she can't get out of."

"I want to wait Mira. I understand your concern. And it's not

safe for any of us. Our defenses are limited in this dimer   . You can
go back if you want. I, we will totally understand. But   i going to
give her as long as I can. But I've got to step up her emc   al state so
she can break through to find her way home."

He bent down to whisper in her ear. The breatl   s like the
fire of a dragon. "I'm sorry to have to do this Destiny,   se forgive
me. But you have to DREAM HARDER!"

Chapte

A(left earlier than usual. Tom waited for him as the airport
with the j   ieled and ready for takeoff. The sun hadn't peaked yet
but flying   ight east he would have a sunrise within minutes.
"C   morning Tom. Sorry to make you get up so early this
morning.   e was an extra stop I wanted to make. Did you get my e-
mail."
"S   did Mr. Barnes. And I've got it all programmed and
input into   flight plan."
"C   it didn't look too much out of the way I'm just not sure
how long   ousiness there will take."
"N   oblem here, I got no plans till tomorrow. We could stay
the night i   u need to. I brought an overnight duffel just in case."
"A   ys thinking Tom."
Th   t rose to cruising altitude in nothing flat and Bendline
looked lil   group of dots. Somewhere down there was two dots
heading o   r a morning run around the mountains. He wrestled with
the idea o   pping by Destiny's house for quite some time. Still not
positive h   ouldn't turn tail and run he left himself an out. If he
didn't fee   it about it he would just rent a car, grab a bite to eat then
head back   he airport. Simple as that. To ensure he didn't waste time
he had ha   m schedule Lakehead for their first stop, then on to New
York for   neeting. He thought it would be better to take the time
from the t   ining of the day instead of the end.
A(found the address with no trouble. 780 Swan Drive. He
parked th   r in the circle drive. Wiped his sweaty palms on his
jacket as l   imbed out of the car. The air felt cool and moist against
his flushe   eeks. He had acclimated to the dessert and wasn't sure
he could e   make the transition to the east coast again.
Hi   ide was slow taking in the surroundings. Every detail he
wanted in   ited on his brain. The yard was manicured to a tea. She
must have   ught his was an eclectic menagerie. Perfect was the one
word to s   ip the whole. The place was uncomfortably perfect. The
lawn was   ved to an exact inch and a half, the shrubs were trimmed
to a perfe   ll. The trimmers must have been nose hair trimmers. The

flowers were color co-ordinated red, then white, then blue. Then the pattern repeated all around the circle drive. He walked around back and saw it at once. The reason he came.

The only thing she had mentioned about living here. The only thing that was missed. A white wicker chair. The cushions covered in an all over rose pattern. The temptation to sit in it was overwhelming. To feel the arms that had wrapped themselves around Destiny and given her such comfort in her time of need. It would be too much, and it would be an unexplainable offering to show up on her doorstep with the chair. It might drive her away. And they had just begun to be friends. Just begun to talk, to feel comfortable in each other's presence. To jeopardize that would be unthinkable. He had done things in the past without thinking. He vowed to use his brain instead of his animal instinct.

"Excuse me."

He turned with a jerk.

"May I help you?"

Obviously the neighbor watching over the place. He was caught. Red handed, peeking into Destiny's life. Seeing what he was not supposed to see. An uninvited intruder. He felt criminal. The urge to take flight was strong. He needed a story.

"I was looking for Mrs. Walker. I was close by (within three thousand miles) and I wanted to offer my sympathies. I'm an old friend of the family."

"I'm sorry Mrs. Walker is out of town."

Adam began backing away before the woman gathered enough wit to ask him his name. "No problem I'll just drop her a note when I get back home."

That was close. The perspiration dripped from his brow by the time he got back to the car. He'd have to use the extra change of clothes he kept on the jet. His shirt was soaked. At the highway he paused for a long time. Viewing the place where a hand had reached down from heaven and changed this woman's life forever.

The car found its way over every street in the town of Lakehead. As a school was passed he wondered if Destiny's children had gone there. The grocery store nearby was surely the weekly stop and they probably knew her by name. The post office carried packages sent to her and her family. The local clinic that healed the family's wounds.

The cell phone rang.

"Tom."

"You OK boss. New York called the phone onboard, said they were waiting the meeting."

"I'm on my way now. I got held up."

He thought about apologizing. But he owed no one any apologies. He owned the jet, the pilot worked for him and the meeting was the weekly one he called to see how each department head was progressing. He had thought about selling the whole publishing house but still couldn't break away. He had made a promise to Roy when he left it to him that he would make sure everybody had the means to the answers to their questions. He just hadn't found anyone with the same ideals yet to trust with the keeping of his promise. But he was getting weary. The traveling was wearing him down. And sometimes he longed for a life. A life like the one that was lived at 780 Swan Drive. It might have had its problems, its ups and downs. No life is perfect but he was guessing it was as close as it gets.

Headlights streaked across the front yard as if the sheriff were spotlighting the house looking for prowlers. But Sheriff Al had made his midnight rounds and hour ago. The trip had been exhausting. The side trip to Lakehead, New York had taken longer than he anticipated. The meeting was chaos everybody wanted a piece of his time, one on one. Then skirting around a thunderstorm over the plains took a while too. He never could sleep on the jet. So he got in plenty of reading time. Two manuscripts down and four more waiting in his briefcase. It could all wait till tomorrow. The ignition was killed. He would come back for his bags and computer in the morning. The only thing Adam wanted was to fall into bed.

The driver's door flew open, the sudden blast of light hurt his eyes.

"Where have you been?!"

It was Destiny. She had been pacing the road from her house to his all night.

He unfolded from the driver's seat and shut the door. The light from the full moon was enough to see the worry, or lines of pain on her face.

"I just got back. It was a long flight. Sometimes I get back late. I'm sorry were you worried? Is it Digger? Did something happen to Digger?" his panic began to rise as his imagination started cataloging all the tragedies that could have taken place to cause such an outburst from Destiny. But of all the tragedies that came to mind paled when she opened her mouth.

"I want to talk."

"Destiny please, I'm beat. We can talk tomorrow OK. I've been up for, going on twenty two hours now. I won't be good company."

Fire leapt from her eyes. "Why are you being nice to me? Why is everyone being nice to me?!"

In that moment he knew. The moment he had been anguishing his whole adult life now stood staring him face to face. His past, and she knew. With his back against the car he slid to the ground in a heap. There was no turning back. It was time to take the first step of this journey. No matter the consequences the time had come to empty the closet. Release the final monster that plagued his peaceful sleep. All things would come to pass in their own time. The time was now. It had been long enough. He put both palms on his forehead, lifted his own head back by his hair. A thud sounded when his head hit against the door of the jeep. He looked up at Destiny, her shadow casting across him, his eyes grew moist. In a whisper all he could say was, "tell me what you remembered."

Each word she spoke was a dagger through his heart and he sat there bleeding to death.

"I was in the lunchroom sitting alone. I wasn't sitting with any friends. Up until now the only memory I've had was of Mira. I haven't remembered any friends. That's because I didn't have any. I was sitting at the table alone writing in a spiral notebook. My God I was weird!"

A whisper was all he could manage for the time being. "You weren't weird, you were, different."

"Oh, I was weird alright, in fact I believe it was a direct quote from you."

He opened his mouth to protest again.

"Shut up! This is my memory! I'm just sharing it with you to see if I have all the facts right. You can give me a simple yes or no when I'm finished. Isn't that how the rule of this game goes?"

She began pacing back and forth in front of him untangling a web that had been strung long ago. Releasing all matter of disgusting creatures that had been trapped for too long. The moonlight was as bright as day then he was in total darkness once again as she came between him and the source of light.

"I was writing. I had a passion for writing. I guess since I didn't have a life of my own I turned to writing down a life. It was my way of experiencing the things I thought would never be within my reach. This guy came up behind me, his name was Adam. He was the most popular guy in school. Captain of the basketball team. A real star player. He was a senior, I was a freshman. Being a freshman had its own pressures but I added to mine by being weird. Adam tapped me on the shoulder. I jerked around. I couldn't believe my eyes. The most popular guy in school had just touched my shoulder. I hid my tablet from view and did what any self respecting freshman would do. I pretended to be disgusted and annoyed.

"This guy named Adam grabbed my note book. He turned back a few pages and began reading at the beginning of the chapter. I believe it was where the handsome prince showed up. His voice got louder and louder as he read my words aloud to the whole lunchroom. His friends and teammates gathered around my table and a pretty blond squeezed through the crowd and snuggled up beside him. His words grew more dramatic as he read on. My cheeks grew hotter with every word. I was sure I was going to vomit, which would have added more humiliation to the moment. He swung his arms around wildly as the prince fought off the foe. Then it came time for the kiss.

"Adam drew the details of the kiss out saying each word as if it were its own sentence. The crowd begged for more so Adam obliged. He looked into the eyes of the blond beside him. Dropped the notebook on the table. Took the blond, I think he called her Sandy, dipped her low across the table her hair touching my lunch tray. And right before my eyes he kissed her long and hard. Her mouth parted and their tongues caressed each other. I thought they would never come up for air. The jibes from the crowd were obnoxious. Adam started caressing

her stomach. Her blouse moving up farther with each stroke his hand came closer and closer to her breast. I closed my eyes tight.

"To the complaints of the crowd he drew the girl back up to her feet and patted her on the butt. Then Adam turned his attention back to the weird author. He sat down close beside me. Ran his index finger back and forth across my knee. He leaned close to me. His breath moist across my face. He asked, 'is that about how you pictured it? How about you, Destiny. Have you ever been kissed?' Words wouldn't co-operate with my vocal chords so I shook my head no. Our noses brushed each other. I'd say it's high time then. He said. He ran his fingers through my hair and reached around to the back of my head. Held my head tight then pressed his lips hard against mine. Then he stuck his tongue in my mouth! I couldn't breathe. I thrashed and kicked at the table. He released me then doubled over in laughter. I fought my way through the crowd. He called after me yelling to me to come back and get my notebook. He threw it after me I heard it hit the trashcan as I hit the bar to open the door.

"I looked back before leaving, Adam stood in the middle of the crowd both hands held high yelling something about two points. I ran all the way home. I had never missed an hour of school up until that day. My mother called me in sick the rest of the week.

She glared down at the heap of a man still pacing back and forth in front of him like the lioness over its kill.

"You can talk now. I need to know if I got it right. Did I remember it correctly?"

"Yes." a sorrowful confession.

"Did I leave anything out. Some tidbit that you would care to add?"

"No."

"You! You stuck your tongue down my throat! After you'd stuck your tongue in Sandy's mouth." Her rage grew stronger. "Then took my stories, my life, my passion and threw it in the garbage with no more regard than throwing away a piece of used toilet paper. Say something! Damn It! Say something and not just yes or no. I want words. You hated me. You all hated me. Is that why you're being so nice to me now? You feel remorseful? Because if you hated me then you might as well hate me now because I'm still the same. Guess what. I'm still weird!"

"I know you're the same."

She kicked at the dirt hard as she turned to pace back toward him. A cloud of dust hung in the space between them.

Anguish filled each word as he chose them slowly. He had to express to her how he felt. But mere words seemed so insignificant. Nothing but air passing over tightly stretched cords in the throat producing different pitches of noise. If only he could open his heart, show its contents. "You're not weird. You're not weird now and you weren't weird then. You were just different. And we didn't hate you. I didn't hate you. We were afraid of you I guess. It is always the first instinct to fear that which you don't understand. And we didn't understand you. You were good. You were perfect. The perfect example of a human being. You didn't drink, you didn't smoke. You didn't go to the dances. And until that day you had never even been kissed. Hell I didn't know one girl that was still a virgin till you hit high school. You made us uncomfortable. We didn't like being close to you because you were the measuring stick of goodness. When you were in the room we were aware of how far from goodness we were. And we thought it was an impossible gap to cross. And we thought we would never want to try. So we overcompensated by shunning you.

"I know it's not worth anything. But I'm sorry. I've been sorry since the day it happened. But we didn't know. I didn't know, you."

Her rage had extinguished and her pace had slowed. "And now I know, you."

Instead of turning back at the end of her pace mark now worn in the dirt she continued straight down the lane. The passing eye would assume the shadow following close behind held no threat, no concern, no sorrow or despair. Only a dark spot on the ground as result of the woman's form standing between the ground and the orb in the sky.

Adam rose to his feet a defeated slump to his shoulders. As wished for prior he fell across his bed not bothering to undress or pull back the covers. But sleep didn't come. Instead a pounding of a drum sounded in his head. Unwanted memories burst in his mind like a battlefield. She had remembered one horrible incident. One of many. She remembered perhaps the worst but the rest were sure to follow. At 4:30 he had given up his attempt at sleep and began pacing the living room floor. He had done some horrible things in his life. If each were a pebble he'd built a mountain. But the pebble that mattered the most

to him was what he had done to Destiny. In comparison scene was
mild. Any other girl would have enjoyed the attention, e llished on
the encounter. But Destiny had been different. She hac vays been
different. And that made all the difference.

One thing he had learned on his quest. His searc 'r answers
as Destiny had put it. Was that a person was allowed 't the past
haunt them. They could feel bad, guilty, ugly about s thing that
happened or something that they did. But, they didn't : too. The
past could be let go. And they could feel for the present ead of the
past. It was free will. Adam didn't know if he could let t)art of the
past go. It didn't hurt bad enough yet.

The clock on the microwave changed to 5:00:. D 'r brushed
past him and let herself out the back door. Standing in 1 hadow he
looked out the window toward the road. Destiny waite the gate.
She roughed the hair on Digger's back then they starte nning. He
wondered if it was a different pain she was transferring tl 1orning.

Faye pulled down the Wall Street Journal to p a cup of
coffee in front of him. "My God. You look like shit."

"Why thank you, Faye."

"How long since you slept?"

The man turned over his wrist and counted in his d. "Going
on twenty-eight hours."

Faye reached to take the coffee cup back but the n grabbed
it before she had a chance. "Just keep it coming." he snaj .

Destiny stood next to the empty chair at the table he corner.
After a moment she cleared her throat.

The man lay down the paper and stared at he itstretched
hand. Destiny said, "No harm. No foul. You were you 'ou didn't
know what you were doing."

He just shook his head. "I don't deserve that."

She slid into the seat opposite him. "I recalled e more of
my past last night. You didn't deserve the beating from y father."

"That's debatable."

*After Destiny's father had gotten home from wc ind heard
the horrible story in the lunchroom he headed over to , 1's house.
He intended to give the boy a lesson in manners b,)und only
Adam's father at home. His dad assured her father he w take care
of the matter and it wouldn't happen again. The matter y aken care*

214

of the onl   y he knew how, with his fists. Taking care not to injure
the boys   ooting arm for basketball. So he kept his blows
concentra   o general vicinity of the face.

By   nday morning the swelling had gone down. Adam was a
fast heale   estiny ran into him in the hall during class. The hall was
empty he   ed his locker and had to walk past her on his way to
class. He   ped her shoulder and her books spilled on the floor. He
stopped b   e her as she picked up her books and a paper that had
come loos   m his load as well.
"7   one's yours." she held it out to him.
He   k it from her and stuffed it in his pocket.
Lo   g at the bloody cut on his lip and the bruise under his
eye. "Doe   ur face hurt?"
"Y   '
"I   happened?"
"I   do you think happened weirdo. Your dad is my dad's
boss. You   t to kiss it and make it better?"
Sh   wered back. "No."
"I   ss we'll call it even then."
Sh   ached her hand out to him. "OK. Even then. No harm.
No foul."
He   glared down at the offer and walked away.
"Y   didn't deserve the beatings from your father. No one
deserves t   '
He   ugged off the past as if it were a pesky fly he was tired
of dealing   h. "He was old, he didn't know what he was doing. It
was life. Y   didn't deserve what I did to you."
"S   ' The hand reached across the table one more time. He
did what   should have done years ago. An act that could have
changed t   whole course of his future. Perhaps it wasn't too late to
change th   ourse now. He held her hand in his for an elongated
moment.   he darkness drained from him as the light from Destiny's
soul flood   n to fill the void. For the first time in his life he could let
the past g   e was ready to live for the present. "No harm. No foul
then." He   rds were manna to his heart.
"S   ls good to me."
Th   nile spread across her face. "Good then. I've got some
cleaning t   and some more memories to uncover. See ya." She rose

215

from the table.

"You are one incredible person Destiny."

"Just weird." She shrugged. "But I think I'm OK with that now."

Faye came around with the coffee pot. "No thanks Faye, I'm headed home. I've got some sleep to catch up on."

Chapter 39

Beep. Beep. Beep.

"How did sleeping Beauty do last night?" Adam looked official in a long white coat this morning. He even found a stethoscope to wrap around his neck and tuck in the breast pocket.

"If you mean me," Mira raised up from her chair "you know I don't sleep. But I'm sure you refer to the other beauty in the room." she smiled. "She's the same."

"Did you hear the news? Huge storm coming. Brewing out to sea. Could hit us head on it looks like."

"Should we be worried?"

"That depends."

"Depends? On what?"

"Not what. Who. But I'm sure there's nothing to worry about."

The door opened to allow the first visitor of the day. The inspector entered already or still wreaking of cigarettes.

Mira looked to Adam, glad he was in the room. "There's always something to worry about."

The lieutenant's eyes narrowed and honed in on Mira. "What did you say miss uh whatever your name is."

"Just talking to the doctor about the patient, there's always something to worry about."

"Yes. Exactly why I'm here." The inspector turned to Adam.

Perhaps if he didn't insist on wearing a suit coat in the middle of the summer he might smell better Adam thought.

The visitor continued. "Any more events I should know about. Has there been any more attempts on your patient's life."

"None Inspector. You have the room and hall patrolled quite well."

"Yes. About that. You have no doubt heard about the storm coming. If it hits, I'm going to need every available person. That could mean the post outside."

"I understand, and am sure Des, Mrs. Walker's family will understand as well."

"If the storm hits. There could be many injuries. What is the condition of Mrs. Walker if I might be so bold as to inquire?"

"What do you mean?"

"I mean…Do you think the room will still be occupied?"

His bluntness was unforgivable. And his question unanswerable. So Adam did just that and answered him with a forceful glare instead.

The inspector raised his eyebrows and turned to leave. "I see. Well."

Once the door closed Mira came to stand beside Adam. She asked once again. "You're sure there's nothing to worry about?"

He patted Destiny's hand. "I'm sure."

Chapter 40

The Bendline's Prospector's Day was a gala event in Bendline. There had been a jar set on the counter at Faye's for fireworks donations since Destiny arrived. Everyone put their change in. Tips were off for Faye but she wasn't in business for the tips anyway. It was the company.

The coffee clique was at a minimum that morning. Adam was out of town he was supposed to be back by nine for the fireworks. Ed and Ed had the job of hauling all the fireworks up on the hill. Whitey was the pyrotechnic expert. Since he was a blaster in the mines it seemed only right. Mel was out chilling the kegs of beer. The town put on a pot luck and all the beer you could drink for five dollars a head. Destiny tried to do the math in her head, but figured they would barely break even if they limited the beer to three apiece. Faye was holding down the fort alone, Earl had gone to Vegas for supplies and extra plates and eatery for the pot luck. And tri-tip for him and Gus to barbeque. Hal always wanted to help but the one year he did they hardly got any takers for the food. No one was sure Hal washed his hands good enough after working on septic tanks all day.

"What are you taking to the pot luck Destiny? You are going aren't you?" Faye asked in a rush.

"Oh yes. Sure I'll be there. I thought I'd take a macaroni salad."

"Just as long as it's not pies. That's always Mary Clare's specialty."

"No pies for me. She can have them."

"Do you need a bowl to put your salad in. I got extras in the back."

"Oh, thanks I thought I might scour Adam's cupboards for a bowl. But if I can't find one I'll come back."

This comment drew a raised eyebrow from Faye. No comment just an arch in the brow. "Guess we'll see you at the park then. Don't forget a blanket."

"Right good idea."

Try as she might she could not get the seven pound salad and bowl to attach to the bicycle. Nor did she feel balanced enough to steer one handed while holding the bowl with the other hand.

Digger met her at the fence as she walked past. "Hey girl. I'd take you but this isn't like our morning runs. I don't know if your master wants you to go or not."

Digger gave her a woof but couldn't convince his running partner that it was OK if she went along. The forlorn mutt went back to the porch to await her master.

The food was too good. Destiny could not stop at just one plate full. She had to try a little bit of everyone's dish. Then came the pie. Mary Clair should have had a bakery. The best apple pie ever to pass over the taste buds. A hint of vinegar in the crust was what she told Destiny when she took her to the side.

Destiny spread out her blanket in at the edge of the park. She didn't feel the center of the park was her place. She didn't feel in the center of these people. They were all so friendly toward her but still she didn't feel a part of them. More an outsider looking in. So the edge of the park fit her the best. From here the scene could be viewed all at once. Like a giant movie screen the whole event could happen right before her eyes and she could witness it all at once.

The smiles got bigger on everyone's faces. The words got louder with each trip to the beer kegs. The night sky began to lose its color. Flood lights cast bright halos underneath their aim then diffused into shadow in between. As the sky became black the stars turned to diamonds. Children played in a circle in the center of the crowd. Running in no particular pattern and following no leader. Each on their own course. Letting their feet carry them where they willed. They waved sticks that exploded with light on the ends. Some tribal ritual dance. Worshipping the maker of the light and pledging their allegiance through the next year.

Dancing on a makeshift floor to the music of someone's truck backed up to the park with the doors open. A few young people lurking in the shadows whispering confessions of their love. Only to be interrupted by the crack of a cherry bomb thrown at their feet. This brought boys out of the shadows tucking in their shirts cussing at the air.

The scene unfolding in front of her made her miss her own family. The event was different than the way they had ever celebrated but the feeling of closeness, of family, was there. And that was what she missed. The feeling of belonging.

The night drew on. The mood dimmed as the effect of the beer dulled senses. The awaited hour arrived. All the lights were turned off. The sky began to explode with color. A siren streaked into the air to explode with a boom spraying sparks of light in all directions. Then to give away to total darkness once again. Then the sky would crack open once again this time with red white and blue lights drifting slowly to the earth. A cloud of smoke drifted toward the park the smell of sulfur somehow pleasant mixed with the smell of barbeque, pie and fresh green grass. The grand finale lit the sky solid for five minutes straight. The last explosion creating the shape of the flag in the sky. Then all was black once again only the smell lingered giving evidence of the display.

Voices called out for the lights to be turned back on. Other voices called out to leave the lights off. Destiny sat in the darkness for a while. It appeared the latter was going to win out and the lights would remain off. The blanket was damp to her body as she folded it and prepared to leave. Telling Faye and the coffee group good night would be difficult in the low light. A street light a block away gave a beacon to head for. Cars and trucks lined the street on both sides. Destiny walked close to them.

Shuffling steps came up behind her. Turning to look, her arm was grabbed and her body pushed up against the side of a truck. Thick beer breath was moist on her face. The heat from the truck door radiated through her skin. The jolt threw her head backward to hit the closed window on the truck. A sharp inhale. The air too afraid to escape her lungs. The dim glow from the distant street lamp reflected off thick glasses.

Only a whisper could release. "Ed! Ed let me go." the sound was not a command, more of a plea.

The body pressed up against hers shifted the weight from one foot to the other. Taking turns trying to keep his body upright. The body was sweaty. "Mrs. Walker. Fancy meeting you here."

Her head turned to the side to keep from getting the full strength of his breath. His mouth found her throat. He began to press his lips against it. She filled her lungs to capacity ready to scream but when her lips parted a pitiful sound came out. Barely audible to the distance across the street. A whimper. "Let me go."

"I just want to feel those toned muscles of you   That tight
butt." One hand released her shoulder and was mov   down her
body. His lips moved around her throat. She squirme   d pushed
against him. His hand gripped her shoulder harder. Fi   s felt like
they were separating the muscle from collarbone. Water   le its way
from the corners of her eyes to the corners of her mout   low could
this be happening?

A force hit the side of the man at shoulder hei   His hand
released from her shoulder but tore her shirt as he fell   le ground.
Destiny jerked away from the falling man and held her s   der where
the hand had been. Once her eyes focused the man lie o   : ground a
few feet from her, staring eye to eye with a dog.

"Digger!" Her voice was back.

Adam walked up next to her and stood betwee   r and her
assailant. He reached his hand out to Ed to help him u   Wow, Ed.
Sorry about the dog. I don't know what got into her. Are   OK?"

Ed staggered to his feet, righted his glasses. "   ought to
keep that dog on a leash." he stomped off.

Adam turned back to face Destiny. Her whole b   trembled.
"You OK?"

She put the blanket over her shoulder where her   was torn.
Her chin wouldn't quit quivering. It was as if she we   eezing to
death and it was ninety degrees. " I don't know. I don'   ow if I'm
OK. I don't know if I'm going to be OK. What am I goin   do. What
would I have done. I feel so violated. So helpless! I don'   w if I can
do this. I don't know if I can survive. On my own."

He inquired as to her immediate physical well   g. But he
knew she was talking much broader.

Her body shook. The horror of what could have l   ened. The
ugliness of what did happen. The man's wet mouth on l   roat. The
hands grabbing at her. She wanted to run home and t   a shower.
Stay under the water until all the ugliness went down th   ain. Wash
all the fear away. But water alone wouldn't be enough.   longed to
be held. To be protected. Just for a moment. Couldn't   man feel
that. She needed to be embraced. Told that everything w   oing to be
alright. The danger was gone. She was safe now. No harr   uld reach
her. But he stood his ground. There was an uncrossable   r between

222

them.

To   love was the hardest love. The woman longed for
comfort. /   n longed to be the one to fill her need. But this was her
life, one t   lemanded her own inner strength. She had always been
strong in   entle way. The life style of a widow demanded the
strength o   varrior. Being invincible on one's own. Dependent only
on oneseli

"C   : on we'll walk you home."

Di   " was nuzzling her hand rubbing up against her. Dogs
were luck   hey didn't have to practice tough love. Their love was
unfettered   rules applied. Adam wished to be a dog, if only for that
moment.

Sh   l into step beside him. It was amazing how easy she was
to walk w   Usually the pace needed to be adjusted slowed, speeded
up. But it   as if the same drummer played inside both of them. Step
for step th   ythm was the same. Nearing the gate Adam spoke.

"H   on't remember a thing in the morning you know."

"P   bly not."

"A   ou?"

"C   think I'll remember!"

"Y   robably so huh" he wanted to apologize . for what he
wasn't su   id for everything. Everything that had ever happened to
her to cat   liscomfort or pain. "It's not something he would have
ever done   er. He's had a rough go since his wife left him. He's not
a bad per: Just too much beer. They might need to rethink that all
you can d   policy in the future though."

"I   w. No harm no foul. Digger saw to that." she ruffed
Digger's   "Thanks Digger. I don't know what I would have done
without y

"Y   vould have been fine."

"Y   hink?"

"I   w."

"I   l I was so sure."

"V   ll have a strength inside us. We can handle anything put
before us.   e only reason a person fails, is defeated, is because he
doesn't us   at strength. The only reason he doesn't use it is because
he doesn't   lize it's there."

" '   the Force Luke'" she smiled.

"Hey, they were on the right track."

The glow from inside her house met the running shoes.

"So you think I could have overpowered Ed?"

"Overpower? I don't know but I'm sure you could have outrun him."

"Funny, the thought of running away never occurred to me."

"No I doubt it would. You are not a coward."

She gave Digger another scratch on the top of the head. "To show my appreciation I'll take it easy on you tomorrow girl."

"I think you'll be safe inside."

"I'm sure. Thanks Adam."

"I didn't do anything."

"Thanks for being there. Being here. And for being my friend."

"My pleasure. Believe me."

Chapter 41

Beep. Beep. Beep.

The feeling in the maze became more and more intense. Destiny could not see or feel in the physical sense of the word. So she was convinced whatever or where ever she was it was a mental state. And the feeling or intuition in this mental maze was one of urgency. An hour glass fast approaching the final grains of sand. She threw every mental thought at this wall of separation. A dark cloud began forming at her back.

"Do you think I could have a few minutes alone with my wife?" James stared down the simple minded woman curled up in the chair in the corner pretending to be asleep.

"I'm not supposed to leave her alone." the reply came from behind closed eyes.

"Well if I'm here she won't be alone, now will she?"

Mira opened her eyes. Stretched like a feline. Her boots clunked across the floor toward the door. "I'll tell the doctor you're here."

The open door spread new light on the situation. Somehow made it seem more real. Not a dream anymore. "Could you close the door?" Too much realization at once was more than he was willing to take in.

James took Destiny's hand in his. He traced around each unbroken nail. It was such a shame their lives couldn't have remained as unbroken. But there was too much in the recent past to ever have what they had once had. But how did they continue from here?

"I guess the best place to start Destiny is with an apology."

The halo on the beeping machine warmed ever so slightly. But it still had a ring of caution.

"I was doing a lot of thinking last night. That's a first huh? Anyway, I just wanted you to know that I wish things would have been different. There were certain times in the past when we had the opportunity to become closer but instead I turned away. When the house got so empty I guess I got scared too. I know now you tried to talk about the changes but I wasn't ready to talk. I wasn't ready to change, to get older or move on to a new plateau in our lives. I know you turned to your religion, or enlightenment or yoga ,whatever the hell you called it. You tried to discuss it with me but it was all Greek to me. Guess I rebelled. Ran like hell was more like it. I'm not saying I wish I would have studied or meditated with you. I'm just saying I'm sorry you had to be alone through it all. I could have at least given you an ear when you were so elated or given you a kind word when you were down. A lot of good it does me to realize that now but I'm getting it. Slowly but surely. I'm getting it."

He patted her hand. Laid it back on the bed. "I gotta go. So in case I don't see…well…I gotta go."

Light filled the room. An abundance of light, the door found its own way to close without being persuaded.

Destiny paused in her determination to give attention to something else. What it was she didn't know. But the effect on the barrier was miraculous. With the slightest urge she broke through. She was on the other side! She was free! And to her dismay she could see. Actually see!   Sky, trees, birds, a road. Not another road. How many roads did she have to come across. Fatigue took over. As if beckoned a rod iron bench was at her side.   Easing down slowly not trusting the reality of this side of the curtain she found the bench to be quite sturdy.

Where was she now? Oz, Narnia, The Rabbit Hole? Did those places really exist? Of course they existed in someone's mind, in their imagination but was there some link between imagination and an actual dimension?

Her surroundings were magical. In full HD color. Colors were heightened, more vibrant than anything she had ever seen. The clarity of the scene was obvious. Not one speck of dust to cloud the vision. But everything had an inner golden glow to it that gave off a halo. Heaven maybe? The trees were rimmed with light. The pigeons fluttered down to greet her pecking at her toes. Cooing, cocking their heads. Birds sang, a breeze kissed her cheeks. It felt like a park. Thick forestry foliage all around but the grounds were too well kept to be in the middle of nowhere. Through a clearing in the trees rooftops were visible and the muffled sound of life being lived came from that direction.

There was still a heaviness in her chest. A need as of yet

unfulfilled. Perhaps this was nothing more than another maze. She rose to begin another journey. Thankful for the addition of sight and surrounding. But still forlorn as to how to get where she needed to be.

A woman approached wearing something out of a storybook. Large boots with striped socks that did not match. A skirt with a shirt wrapped around the waist in case of a sudden weather change. Her hands tucked inside sleeves that were too long but she held fast to a leash outstretched by a dog nearly half the woman's size. The woman reined the leash in, in stagecoach fashion. A strand of hair was blown from the path of sight before speaking. The dog circled around and came to a seated position on top of Destiny's foot. The woman beamed a smile in Destiny's direction.

"Beautiful morning." the woman exclaimed.

Destiny looked skyward then nodded in agreement.

"Can I help you ?"

A slight shake of her head, "No. I don't think so." Destiny looked left, then right, straight ahead then back from where she thought she came from. A crease formed above her brow and she bit her bottom lip.

"Are you new around here?"

"Yea. Yea you could say that."

"You look a little confused or lost. I've been here quite a while. Maybe I could help you. Where are you going?"

"I don't know where I'm going I just have a desperate feeling I need to be there."

"Where is there?"

"Home? It feels like I need to get back home. But I don't know where home is and

I don't know where to start looking. Which direction to go." her breathing quickened and she became more anxious by the minute. With a slump to her shoulders Destiny said in defeat. "I honestly don't know."

"You get thumped on the head or something?"

"I don't know. To be honest I don't know how I got here or where I'm going"

"I've been there."

"You've been there? Here? Where?"

"Oh yea. Believe me all of us here have been there. Or we

wouldn't be here now would we?"

Destiny was more confused now. She shook her head to clear some of the clutter.

The stranger gave Destiny's shoulder a quick pat. "I find the best directional compass is the heart. Just close your eyes and let your heart lead the way."

Destiny's head was spinning now. In desperate need of a chair before her knees gave way and her brain went back to sleep. The enormous dog was putting her foot to sleep and maybe it was affecting the circulation to her brain.

"Hey, there you guys are." A deep voice came up from behind the confused new comer. Destiny whipped around to see a man closing in from behind. He was wearing sweat pants but not a drop of sweat graced his brow. Deep steel blue eyes looked down at her first before entering into conversation with the older woman. Welcoming eyes. Eyes that made a person feel safe while under their gaze.

"Mira," he directed his voice but not his stare to the older woman. "I've been looking for you and Digger. Here Digger, get off this nice ladies foot." He tugged on the collar but there was no moving the dog.

"Adam. This is…I'm sorry I didn't get your name?"

"Destiny. Its Destiny." Or at least she thought that was her name. That was the only name she knew herself by.

"Hello." he didn't extend his hand as one does with a first introduction. And to be honest it didn't feel like a first introduction. More of a re-acquaintance. Seeing an old friend after years of being apart. But the feelings take right off from where they were left prior.

Destiny studied him for some clue. Tilted her head. "Do we know each other?"

Adam smiled. "It would appear my dog thinks she knows you. She only does this to people she likes."

The old woman watched the two converse as if watching a tennis match. Then abruptly she handed the leash to the dog's owner. "I got stuff to do. Here's your dog. Maybe you can show this lady around. I think she's confused." Her legs looked short but she was out of site before Destiny could blink.

Destiny rubbed her eyes. "I think she's got that right. I am a little confused."

"Mira's a special one. A bit abrupt at times but she's priceless. I think you're doing pretty good considering you made it here."

"Do you know something I don't know, does everyone know something I don't know?"

"Not everyone. Here maybe we should walk. Get your circulation going. Digger get up. We're going for a walk."

The dog took the end of the leash in its mouth and walked out in front of the two.

The trail wove through trees and shrubs, over a stream as clear as glass. "I feel like the cliché "I'm not in Kansas anymore."

His laugh was soft and gentle. He shook his head. "No. definitely not Kansas."

"Then where?"

"You need to take it slow. It's going to be a lot to take in all at once."

Her eyes grew grim. "But you don't understand. I have this intense feeling inside of me that's burning me up. I have to get somewhere. Home. I have to get home. So the sooner I can get through this leg of the journey the better."

He turned her around to face him. Both hands on her shoulders. His gaze dove deep into her eyes, searched her soul. "Believe me I do know."

A calm washed over her, the eye of the storm perhaps but a calm none the less. Time stood still. And where there was confusion there was now calm and understanding. An understanding that everything was going according to plan and purpose. That her world was evolving just as it should, all in its own time.

Similar to a hypnotic trance her eyes blinked slowly. Her voice direct and measured. "OK. Where am I then?"

"Just a little further ahead. It will be easier to explain there."

They walked in silence. The path now lined with flowers. The air had a tropical feel. But the trees were aspen and ash. The birds were sparrows, finch, quail and pigeons.   The more she looked around and the farther they walked the more different species of plant and animal life she identified. In fact there was just about everything she had ever seen right here in this one place. Whatever this place was.

A structure began to take shape. Built more into the side of a mountain. It looked as if the mountain was white marble and the

structure was carved out of it. Well worn steps led up all pillars.
Behind the pillars was a wall of glass. Not a wall individual
windows but a wall of solid glass. She could not see thr the glass
only the reflection of where they had been walking was ble. There
were twelve pillars at least twenty feet tall. In the cente the pillars
were two thick wood carved doors. The carvings di resemble
anything she had studied in her night class of archite re 101. It
looked like angels and demons sharing the same pi . Perhaps
symbol of harmony. The guide reached out to unlatch door. She
would guess her companion to be well over six feet tal t his head
only came half way up the door.

Only the right door gave way for their entry. He tioned her
ahead of him but she preferred to follow. Once inside waved his
hand in gesture for her to take it all in. And take it in she A crystal
cave. Every square inch of the interior was refracting l streaming
in from the windows as well as through the glass ro The white
marble floor was laced with gold, so shiny it reflected images of
the rooms contents as if it were build on top of a still r tain lake.
The interior was round as near as she could tell. The wall y from the
door went straight to a huge circle in the center. Withi is circle a
comfortable seating area which included a table an verstuffed
chairs. Out from the table area like spokes of a wheel w shelves of
books. These nearly reached the ceiling. Down each side each shelf
were library ladders that wheeled on tracks for accessing books on
the upper levels. Her jaw fell open and did not clamp s till Adam
led her to the center of the room and asked.

"What do you think?"

Blinking back tears, "I think I am in my own p e heaven.
All of my loves are here. White marble, books, overstuf chairs and
sunlight."

"You're close. Here why don't we sit down." h d her to a
very worn overstuffed chair that hugged her tight as she nto it.

"Are you ready?" he asked

"Explain away."

"This," he waved his hand around the room. you." he
checked to see if she was ready to stand up and bolt. S so good.
"This is one of your deepest levels of subconscious. W ve several
levels. We reach them at different times. Sometimes ill like in

meditatin   ometimes while sleeping. This deeper level is not usually
reached b   rdinary people. This level is absolute knowledge and
understan   of truth. There is no question that will go unanswered
here. The   no limit to what you can learn or achieve." he regarded
her cautio   . "Any questions so far?"

"Y   say this is me. My level of consciousness. If that's so
then what   you doing here? Are you in some way another side, that
is to say a   ou my alter ego?"

"C   question. No I am not a side of your ego. I am a
separate i   idual with an ego all my own. I am here because first
visits mus   chaperoned, guided. Whatever you want to call it. In the
presence   osolute truth and knowledge it can be too powerful. Like
coming to   ose to the sun, it has to be monitored, taken in metered
doses unti   a build the strength. It is such a feeling of elation that for
the first fe   mes a person doesn't want to break away. That's where I
come in fc   ou. I have to tear you away from paradise."

A   le turned up the corners of her mouth. "So, this is my
Camelot!"

"It   /hatever name you want to give it. But yea this is yours."
"D   everyone have their own."
"C   urse. It exists in the mind."
"D   ey all look alike?"
"N
"V   about yours?"
"N   hat?"
"Y   Heaven, your Camelot, your Paradise, what does it look
like?"

Nc   he corners of his mouth turned upward. He turned from
side to sid   idying the details of the room. With an approving nod of
his head h   olied, "Similar. I prefer black obsidian on the floor."

He   idied her cautiously. Her enthusiasm of this place
increased   i every breath she took. Many souls could only stay at
this level   matter of seconds or minutes the first time. Their ego or
part of tl   iind governing their physical reality would fight the
existence   is level too strongly. But this woman had a miraculously
strong cor   of her ego. She was an exceptional person. But he had
always kn   that.
"C   look around?"

"Of course."

Walking in between the aisles of books. Letting her fingers brush over title after title as if drawing all the information out of the books and into herself. He followed behind. Not too close to interfere but close enough to intervene if she became too overwhelmed.

She stopped near the end of the aisle. Turned to face her guide. Tears welled in her eyes. "Am I. Am I finally home?"

Standing beside her now he whispered. "Close." Then reached out and caught her before she hit the marble floor.

Chapter 42

The four way blinking red stop light always gave Adam the same feeling. No place like home. But especially when he came to a stop in the middle of the night. The trip had taken, as most of them do more time than he had planned. He pulled the jeep up to the edge of the thick white line painted at the intersection. Blink, blink, blink. Light gave a red glow to the surrounding intersection. The walls of Faye's Café were rosy red instead of white. The glow also enhanced the Municipal Building's front steps and pillars showing the way to pay a traffic ticket or file for a marriage license or divorce, pay your taxes or utility bill or attend a local town hall meeting. No need to waste a lot of office space when everything could be taken care of under one roof. The gas station windows reflected back the red light as if there were some secret message being sent back and forth. The buildings were safe and sound, tucked in tight for the night being watched over by this sentinel.

The blinking light always gave Adam the sense of home. This light was the heart of the town always constant. Always beating.

As he turned down the drive toward his house exhaustion settled in. It didn't matter what time of day or night he got back he never felt fatigued until he made the final turn toward home. An unusual glow came from his house. The glow sent shards of light cutting through the darkness of his yard. He must have left the light on. How nice to come home to lighted walkway but ridiculous to have it illuminating the way for three days and nights.

He pushed the door open with his foot and let his shoulder bag drop to the floor in a heap. He would unpack tomorrow. He turned and gave the door a shove. Usually Digger greeted him right about…now. The faithful companion had to have time to stir from his slumber and make his way from Adam's bed to the front door. No Digger. Hmmm. Adam looked around, whistled. Then he spotted them. Destiny sat cross legged on the floor in a nest of books. Her head bent back against the easy chair, jaw dropped open, eyes closed. Digger nestled beside her with his head resting on a pillow she had taken from the sofa. The pole lamp spot lighted her and her studies.

Before he could catch it the door shut with a bang.

Digger leaped to attention, started running in place on the wood floor. His nails making a clicking noise as he tried to gain traction. His bark could wake the dead. And if not the dead at least the dead tired.

Destiny jumped to her feet as well. Looked around confused at first, wiped a bit of drool from her chin and then began her apology. "I'm so sorry. I thought you were still out of town till tomorrow."

Adam put his hand up to stop her. Ruffed up the guard dog that now recognized him as a friendly. "Don't be sorry. I just got back.   In fact depending on when you got here it probably is tomorrow."

"What time is it."

"Three thirty. Have you been here long?" he made his way to the living room and plopped down on the sofa, Digger still at his heels.

"I. I don't know. I went to bed about ten. I had the weirdest dream. When I woke up I ran straight down here." This statement hung in the air. She looked down at herself slowly. Fearing what she would see. Her fears confirmed, she was still in her pajamas and fuzzy slippers. Her cheeks turned the prettiest pink Adam had ever seen. Readjusting the robe she continued. "Sorry, again. Anyway I just ran out of the house to see if you had any books on dreams. And..." she gestured to the floor around her. "you do."

He gave a chuckle. Her color was coming back to normal. "I recall picking up a few along the way. Find what you were looking for?"

"You mean one that tells me the meaning of all the symbols and events in my dream and tells me I'm not crazy?"

His fatigue was fading, he could sleep all day tomorrow if need be. "Tell you what, why don't I make us some hot cocoa and you can tell me about your dream. That is if you want too?"

"Sure. Are you a dream annalist along with your many other talents?"

"Not hardly. But I've had some real doozies as far as dreams go."

The steaming cups were placed on the floor between them as he threw down a couple of pillows to sit on.

"So tell me. What did you dream?"

Holding the cup with both hands letting the steam swirl around her features she closed her eyes and relived the dream. Not leaving out a single detail or actor's name. Mira, Digger, Adam, the crystal room filled with light and overflowing with books. The reference to the room as being absolute knowledge and understanding of truth.

"So what do you think. Am I crazy?"

"Wow! I'd say you had an awakening not a dream. Damn, people wait lifetime after lifetime to have something like that happen."

"Maybe, as you say I've been waiting lifetime after lifetime."

He raised his eyebrows in 'who knows' fashion.

"But what does it all mean?" Her eyes were pleading, looking for something to clear the fog in her consciousness. Her long fingers combed through her hair pulling it back into a ponytail, wrapping it into a loose knot that gave way as soon as she let her hands reach for another sip of hot cocoa.

"Awakenings like that or any awakening are a personal thing. For me to venture a guess or give you some sort of response would only cloud or alter the real meaning for you. Everyone's journey is a personal path. Each seeking what they need. That is the real fallacy with organized religion. How can one or a handful of men interpret and tell us what truth is. Religions true purpose is to give us guidelines, rules, or disciplines if you will, to physically live by to keep in harmony with the laws of nature, or the universe this denser physical plane, making the path to our awakening easier and perhaps quicker. But to encourage, not discourage our individual seeking of life's truth.

"But in my dream you are my guide. I expected some answers from you."

"Sorry to disappoint you. Maybe I'm a guide to protect you, but not sway your course. "

A quietness filled the room. A quietness heavy with disappointment. Her eyes focused on the pile of books around her. Adam knew how she felt. So many times he had been burning up inside for answers, but with his quest as with all quests answers came at their own accord. "I wish I could tell you more. The only thing I can honestly say is your answers will come. You will know what your dream was all about. All in time. But I can also say as soon as the answers to this quest are found it will be followed by more questions. It is truly never ending. It was told to me by one of my teachers that

God himself is still expanding, still learning. Get used to the search for answers for therein lies not only the answers to life's burning questions but life itself."

Her face became a little brighter. Lack of sleep finally got the better of her curiosity. With a yawn she rose from the floor and started picking up the mountain of books.

"Leave them. You're tired. Let yourself rest and digest. They can wait till tomorrow. You might decide you need to look at them some more."

"Well sorry for the mess." Another huge yawn. "Guess I'll head down the road. But I'll be back to put these away."

"They'll be here. But not too early. I wasn't planning on getting up before noon."

Digger accompanied her to the front door of her cottage. There was the palest glimmer of light on the horizon where heaven met the earth. Was this a sign? She said good night to her guardian and sent her home.

Chapter 43

Beep. Beep. Beep. Mira paced back and forth along the foot of the bed. Pushing the button in her pocket. Pace. Push. Pace. Push. Where was he? Destiny's husband had left ten minutes ago and when she came back into the room there was the strangest halo to her monitor. The patient in the bed showed no signs of breathing even though the machine was still forcing air into her lungs. There should be a feeling of panic, or urgency but there was not. The only feeling in the room was harmony, bliss. The halo turned from violet to crimson. Adam must be close.

Mira pushed the button in her pocket one more time just to get his goat.

"Mira, how many times do I have to tell you once is enough?" he found himself ranting at a mischievous smile.

He had to smile too. "OK lets have it. What's the emergency?"

She smiled, but she didn't know why. "You tell me." gesturing to the sleeping beauty in the room. "There's a difference. Look at the halo, well its back to crimson now with you in the room." The doctor smirked. "But it was violet. Neon even. And just feel the energy in the room."

He could feel it. There was a difference. A calm. Peace. "Tell me everything. What happened?"

"Her husband was here. He was different somehow too. He still didn't want to be here you could tell that. But he took her hand, not like before but in a gentle way. He told me to leave so I told him I would go tell the doctor he was here. Only the doctor wasn't listening! He only stayed for a couple minutes. Then he left. But he actually came up to me and said thank you. He was calm like he had made peace with the situation. With Destiny."

Adam took Destiny's hand. There was a rush of breath in her lungs, a babe's first breath of life. He squeezed her hand with excitement. "Now we're getting somewhere!" bending down he kissed her forehead. "Keep up the good work." he whispered.

Looking up at Mira his smile was uncontainable. "We're almost home Mira. We're almost home. Keep an eye on her. I have to go call a meeting."

The door closed without a sound. Mira pulled her ir close to Destiny patted her hand. "Did you hear that? We're almc ome?"

Sparks flew in every direction. It was a of July extravaganza. The excitement welled up inside her. Her ions were a huge balloon ready to pop. But if they popped she wo just be all the more joyous. Her awareness seemed to be expandi long with her emotions. She was limitless, there were suddenly no ndaries to herself. She was everywhere. Destiny couldn't tell the rce of the sparks as they were raining down, coming upward, sid side. The only one true thing was she seemed to be in the middle The light the sparks gave off was more than a child's sparkler ore like a welding rod. At first she hesitated looking directly at light then remember she wasn't looking through normal eyes. But r an inner eye.

"Quite a light show you're putting on. You t be very happy." A mans hearty voice.

That voice was so familiar. But where was it cor from. As she concentrated on looking for the voice the sparks begt fade.

"Sorry didn't mean to interrupt you."

He came into view. Crouched beside her. Her h seemed to be resting on his hand.

"Adam?" She questioned. Looking around tl oom now coming into focus. The glass ceiling, the towering books cool floor on her back.

"Yea. You checked out for a minute. This place do that to you."

He helped her to a seated position. Her back rest gainst the spines of books on the bottom shelf. He sat opposite e to spine with the books on the other side of the aisle.

"I fainted?"

"If this were your physical reality you could sa u fainted, but this isn't so you just checked out."

"I saw lights. Everywhere. They were beautiful here were they coming from?"

He laughed quietly. She loved this sound. Like rr from a cat. So rewarding to hear it.

"It | s coming from you. We are all just concentrations of
energy. In | dimension the energy is more visible if you are paying
attention."
"It | so good. Such a rush like nothing I had ever felt before.
an uncont: | ble joy."
"Y | were with your, for lack of a better word, God Self. That
part of yo | at is the God definition. In this dimension. This part of
your con | isness your true self emerges. It is untouched and
unaffectec | the physical or ego. You are with God. It's like you are
in your fi | mental state. A beam of light. As you saw. When our
physical r | takes the reins it focuses on other things other than our
true self a | ur true tendencies. This puts a filter over our light. So
the more | sed or obsessed we are with the physical realm the more
filters we | over our light."
"V | How long can I stay?"
Th | ugh again. "As long as you like or as long as you can
keep your | at bay. For some it is milliseconds. For others a few
minutes. | for the masters forever. For they have learned and it is
everyone' | al to learn to coexist. To be in the physical realm and
keep the l | unfiltered or in other words focus only on the God Self."
Sh | died what he was saying. "So what's next? How do I
get there | here?" then she laughed remembering what the rather
odd wom: | d told her when she first arrived. 'we've all been there,
if not we | ldn't be here' and 'follow your heart' made no sense at
the time. | didn't but neither did any of this right now. She just had
to trust h | eling or rather her heart and her heart was telling her,
screaming | er she was on the right track.
"V | ll have a guide inside us. The same force that brought
you here i | same force that knows all the answers to your questions
and the w | your God Self. The hardest part for most is to trust in
their inne | de. So many feel they are imagining things. A thought
pops in th | ead, an answer to a question you've been pondering and
they brusl | ff because their physical mind didn't think of it. It was
just there. | your best friend is your imagination and your faith or
belief in y | imagination. The force once set into motion, by you, by
your will | t to your God Self uses every physical and non physical
force to g | u to your destination. There are no chance meetings, no
coinciden | nothing is a mistake. There is a message or lesson

happening every second of your life. Pay attention.

"But it is not all fun and rose parades. There is a dragon, a demon, the greatest foe you will ever come up against. You must do battle with this foe before you can be with your God Self forever. This foe blocks the way. This foe is yourself. Every tendency you have perfected that is not of the God Self must be challenged and overcome. But this foe is tricky, this foe wants to keep all of its non God tendencies, some are not bad as in the evil sense of the word, gentleness is good unless it is too gentle, strength is good unless it is too strong and becomes domination, fear can be a good thing to keep our common sense but all tendencies keep us separated from our God Self because God has no physical tendencies. God just is. God is life, but God is pure life.

"Some people beginning the battle with their tendencies come to a screeching halt. They fear if they continue they will lose themselves. But they cannot be further from the truth. You will always be you, you have always been you, just as God has never not existed. But once you conquer your physical tendencies you become a greater you. A purer you."

"Wow again. But where or how do I start." She drank in the words. So thirsty for the truth and it tasted so devine.

"You already have. By your being here your true self has willed this journey. Just stay in this dimension as long as you can and each time you go back to the physical dimension you'll take a piece of this with you. It will be like a memory. Not always a clear picture of details but the main point is clear." he waived his hand toward the surrounding books. "And these are real. They are lessons, information, you must have a passion for books for your truths to manifest as books. Some people have people, sages, teachers, some people prefer their truths to manifest in video form. The information is the same it is what you need to know. So read while you are here. Explore. And don't doubt what you read here. But when it is time to go back to the physical realm don't despair. There are just as many lessons to be learned in that dimension as in this. Pay attention, and remember it is the balance that you are after."

She sat silent. So many questions yet to ask. But her head was throbbing

Chapter 44

She would miss a lot of things about Bendline but the wind was not one of them. She was finally done cleaning up the mess from the first wind. Then another mighty wind took an equally mighty toll on the cleanup project. The damage to the old chicken coop was bordering on total destruction. The house lost half of the good shingles and all of the bad. A branch sailed through the front window and the newly repaired gate was broken off the hinges once again. Destiny rallied the Two Eds for a meeting.

"How's business Ed?" she began as they walked around the yard surveying wreckage.

"I got to say. We got six calls within an hour after the wind stopped. But you are our preferred customer Miss Destiny. So we told everyone they'd just have to wait till we got your account taken care of. Cuz we know you are on a time frame."

A time frame she had all but forgotten about. The project had surpassed all her estimates by so far. When the family called anymore she would just say. I don't know when I'll be done. Progress is slow. I'll see you when I see you. "Well that's nice of you Ed. Let's take a look shall we. I'm wondering if maybe the back shed should just come down all together?"

"Oh it's not that bad really Miss Destiny. I think once the broken walls are shored back up it will be right as right." dad to be Ed said.

"Well you are more of a positive thinker than I am. Do you know of any carpenters that could do the roof and maybe fix the coop?"

"Ed here's looking for some side work. The little woman been on him again for a bigger place. So he might be willing to work a few hours into the night."

"That's right I remember they're going to have a baby. Is he looking for another place, something bigger?"

"Oh I guess he is. Maybe. It's kind of hard to come up with the cash though."

"Yea. I suppose." An idea was bubbling in her head.

Destiny found the other Ed inside the coop pulling down a couple of loose boards.

"Ed? Ed tells me maybe you might be willing to take on some extra work? Would you be able to do the roof repair and fix the coop? That is if you think it's worth fixing?"

"For sure Miss Destiny. I could start today if you want."

"Whenever. That would be great." She turned to leave then added. "What kind of a place are you and your wife looking for Ed?"

"I'm fine where I'm at, but she's looking for something. She just says a roof and at least two bedrooms."

"Kind of like this place?"

"Yea. Except you don't have a roof anymore."

"Well if I had a roof do you think this would be OK with her?"

"Oh I know it would. This would be right next to a mansion in her book."

"Well, Ed. Maybe we could come to a deal."

Ed didn't say anything he just stared up at the hole in the coop.

"Do you understand what I'm saying Ed?" she asked again.

"No. not really Miss Destiny."

"I'm saying maybe you and your wife and I could work out a way that you could buy this place from me."

"I don't know Miss Murphy."

Nearsighted Ed entered the coop to give some business advice to his partner. "Ed. Don't be a jackass. She's saying she'll sell you the place. And I think she's saying that she'll make it possible for you to buy it."

The light bulb came on. He turned to Ed "Don't call me a jackass"

"I wouldn't call you one if you weren't being one."

"Miss Murphy that would be a miracle come true. A real miracle come true." Dad to be saw his little woman giving him the biggest bumping belly hug ever.

"Selling it had always been my intention. So how bout I write up a paper, you can make payments to me. We don't have to get a bank involved and that way you get a house and I can go home."

They started a vigorous hand shake. "Sounds good to me. All except the you leaving part of course. You are our best customer."

"Nothing lasts forever Ed."

They all worked double time that day. There was a new incentive to get to the end of the project.

Chapter 45

Beep. Beep. Beep.

The storm watch was about all that was on every local television channel.

Satellite pictures from above gave life to the storm. A Cracken with a long whipping tail. Black as coal with red stripes showing the places with the most energy. At least it gave Destiny's husband an excuse to stay away. Conserving fuel in case of a state of emergency. Mira clicked the television off. Books were better. Pulling the chair next to Destiny so she didn't have to speak as loud.

"What shall we read today Des?"

There was no answer of course. Only the beep of the machine.

Destiny found she could stay in her private palace, as she came to refer to it as, almost indefinitely. It took deliberate attempts to return to her physical life now instead of the other way around. Adam was convinced she would be fine unaccompanied. She had to admit she did miss the company. Or perhaps she missed his company. But there was studying to be done for the present.

A different aisle of books was chosen this time. And just to mix things up a bit she climbed to the top of the library ladder, pulled down a book and opened it up. A peculiar thought hit her. Since this place, dimension was all mental anyway. She wondered if the book she opened would be the same no matter what shelf she chose from. Since the books were what she needed to know at that given moment as Adam had explained the process.

Even though it felt like she had just arrived. She wondered how long she would be in this place or have access to it. Forever. Her mind was still stuck in the state that nothing lasts forever.

Chapter 46

The run was brutal. It was as if Destiny knew her runs were numbered. Making the deal with Ed to buy the house had given a new tone to her being in Bendline. What was once a dream world, an existence with no barriers, now was pushed into the reality side of living. And the reality was that there would be a leaving of this place a going back to her prior life.

Heels hit hard on the dirt, toes dug deep into the side of the hill as the accent went straight up the mountain instead of the easy path of side hilling. It still didn't hurt bad enough. But she had to be sure she fit in all the hurt before she went back home. If she could leave all the pain here on these mountains then she could return to just memories in New York. "Come on Digger." she cried out. "It still doesn't hurt bad enough."

Knees trembled from overexertion as she sat at the table. Box by her side.

"Heard you sold out." the corner of the paper didn't turn down. It couldn't yet. More composure of his feelings needed to be reached before he showed his face.

"News travels fast." she replied.

"Digger OK?'

"Yea. Why?"

"Looks like you had a killer run. Your knee is shaking the table."

"Sorry. Yea it was quite a run. It felt good though. Actually Digger was ahead of me the whole way. She's really getting in good shape."

"I wonder what she's going to do when you leave?"

"Maybe you'll have to take up running."

The paper folded down. "Maybe."

From the box Destiny produced the bright shiny penny. And just stared at Adam.

"You look like the cat that ate the canary. Is it worth a lot."

"Your thoughts."

"My thoughts."

"Yes, didn't you ever hear the expression, 'a p / for your thoughts'?"

He shook his head. Something catching in his th| Not now. He couldn't reveal what he was thinking at this mo| And he hoped she couldn't read his mind. Faye glanced at h| Faye was perceptive. Too perceptive. She had always been. ways the matchmaker trying to get people together that really lo\ :ach other but didn't know it. She always knew.

"My thoughts. Let's see. I've got to get the is mowed before I head out of town next week."

Faye cleared her throat. He gave her a sideways g e. "Mira's thoughts were more profound than that."

Destiny began her memory of the penny. And A was glad for the reprieve. All eyes and ears turned to Destiny. Th| /ere going to miss these stories. They had all come to love this littl| :cial child just as much as Destiny.

I had been busy at school for a while. M| tests or something. Pearl called my house and asked if I cou| ome over. Mira had been in bed for a week. She wouldn't talk t| arl or go outside. It was all Pearl could do to get her to eat a fe| tes a day. She thought maybe I could get her to come around.

I entered her room slowly. The blinds were clos| 4 lump of covers was in the middle of the bed. Under the lump wa| ra. I tried to get her to play a game of peek a boo but she wouldn'| for it. She was not in the mood for fun. I had never seen her that wc|

Once she came out of her cocoon I saw she had b| crying.

"What's wrong Mira? Why are you sad?"

She wouldn't tell me anything. I tried smooshi| ier mouth together the way she would grab my face sometimes wh| ie wanted me to explain something to her and I was taking t| iuch time thinking of a Mira explanation. But it was no use she \ | 't talking. She just stared deep into my eyes like there was no tomoi|

I asked her if she hurt somewhere. She didn't tal| ly pointed to her heart.

I put my hands in my pockets and began pac| the floor. Fingering a coin I had in my pocket as if rubbing it w| grant my wish. Then as luck would have it, it did.

I pulled the coin out of my pocket. It was prett\ | v and still

246

shiny I ste d close to Mira, her head just looking at her own hands
folded in l ap. "do you know what I have?"
A it movement of her head back and forth was the only
answer I g
"L Mira. Look at what I have."
Sh oved her head up slightly. I put the shiny coin in front of
her eyes. crossed so I moved the coin back a bit.
"I da?"
"7 is a one of a kind magic coin. Whatever is troubling a
person or hering them or making them cry this coin can take it
away."
Sh oked on still wide eyed.
"L ou want to feel better Mira. You don't want to be sad
anymore (ou?
A it shake of her head again.
"I take the coin then and you will feel better."
Sh ached for the coin. I pulled it back before her fingers
closed arc it.
"(one thing though. You have to tell the coin what is
making yc d. The coins magic won't work unless you tell it what to
work on.'
M vas quiet for a long time. Destiny kept turning the coin
back and letting the light reflect off one side then the other. Back
and forth, k and forth.
In hisper only meant for the coin to hear Mira said, "Don't
go Destiny
De v was confused. "Did you say don't go?"
M odded in confirmation.
"I ot going anywhere. I'll stay right here."
"Y eaving. You moving far away."
"N o I'm not moving anywhere Mira. You must have had a
bad dream
Sh t defensive. "No dream! You leave!"
De v tried to calm her down. "Well maybe someday I will
leave you right Mira. But not soon. We still have lots of time
together. still have lots of todays. We need to think about today.
Not what it happen in the future.
"Y o leave."

"I no leave."

Mira snatched the penny out of Destiny's hand so quick she didn't have time to close her fingers.

"Magic penny. You right. I happy now."

But seems it turned out that Mira knew something I didn't know. I didn't know how but within two days my parents set me down and told me I'd be moving. I don't know which was more surprising the fact I was leaving a place I'd spend my whole life in or the fact that Mira knew.

Adam studied the penny. Still shiny. Still reflecting the light as Destiny turned it back and forth. A magic penny. To take away all sorrow. If only that was true. If only it could take away his sorrow. He knew exactly what Mira was feeling. She was quite the kid. She knew Destiny was leaving. Moving away and she knew it was going to hurt. Some things never change.

The crowd at the café was somber. It was as if they all felt Mira's pain.

Finally New Dad Ed stood up to make an announcement. "I just wanted to tell everybody there was going to be a dance at   Mel's tonight. To celebrate me and Cindy buying the house from Miss Murphy. So we want everybody to show up and bring your dancing shoes cuz we're going to have live music."

The applause only lasted long enough for Ed to sit on his stool again. Then he stood back up quickly. "I forgot. 8:00 music starts. See everybody there. Come on Ed we got work to do."

Ed gabbed the last swig of coffee before Ed pulled him off his seat. The bell rang a little merrier that morning.

Destiny dropped the penny back in the box then got up to follow her partners out the door.

"You going to work too?" Adam inquired

"Sure. I told Ed I wouldn't sell him a rundown place. So I'll be staying long enough to see the place fixed up. That wind set us back some we've got some catching up to do. Then I've got to find some dancing shoes I guess. See you there?"

"Maybe. I don't know if I'll be back that early." Then he did something he had never done before. He prayed for wind.

Once the place was cleared out it was down to Faye and Adam. She brought around the coffee pot. He declined saying he had to go.

She turned to leave pouring a handful of bright shiny pennies on his table.

"That's all the pennies I got. But maybe there's a magic one in there somewhere."

Chapter 47

Mel's Place was filled to capacity. The crowd spilled out onto the sidewalk as Destiny walked near. The sky was giving up the light of day and giving in to the light of a full moon. All manner of stories surrounded the full moon. Anywhere from surges of energy to insane (lunatic) actions. A full moon paired with two for one at Mel's had trouble written all over it.

There were no dancing shoes packed for the trip out west so freshly washed running shoes had to be substituted. The box accompanied Destiny to the dance. Why? She didn't know. Digger also wanted to come be her dance partner. Her paws hung over the gate, the barrier of her world. Destiny stopped to confide in her friend. Digger was the one out of the whole town that knew her best. Nothing was held back from Digger's witness. No tear left unshed. Digger consoled her with a nudge, a wag of the tail and when Destiny needed it most a kiss on the cheek.

Digger woofed in a whisper as her right ear was receiving a scratch. "This is going to be quite a test of my constitution tonight girl. This will be by far the hardest run so far." Her face buried in the dog's fur on the back of its neck. "I wish you could be with me too."

As if out of nowhere a familiar hand reached down from the heavens and grabbed the door handle of Mel's.

"You're back!" Destiny followed the arm up to meet the eyes of the gentleman holding the door. Adam was at the other end.

"I moved some stuff around on the schedule. Let my cell phone do the walking. How could I miss Ed and Cindy's big night. It will probably go down in the history books of Bendline. I thought that was pretty amazing what you did for Ed by the way."

"It wasn't anything. Just business."

"Right." with a raise of his doubtful eyebrow.

"Hardly history making anyway."

"You don't know Bendline."

"Apparently not. But I'm getting to know her better all the time."

"Got your memory box I see."

She gave the box a little shake. "I don't know why I brought it. Some people keep their memories in their heads. Me. I keep mine in a box."

The minute eyes could be adjusted to cut through the cloud of dust, smoke and all manner of foreign particulates in the air of Mel's, Destiny was nearly knocked to the ground. A woman the size of a five foot linebacker embraced her with a bear hug that threatened to squeeze the life out of her lungs. A hard basketball came between them and full body contact. Once the attacker pulled away from the embrace she introduced herself as Ed's Mrs.

First impressions caused one to wonder if she had grossly miscalculated her date of conception or she were having twins, perhaps even triplets. Because if there was just one baby in that gargantuan belly, they might be celebrating more than the purchase of a house that very evening.

Cindy held tight to Destiny's hand with both of hers and with tears in her eyes tried to express her appreciation and excitement about the house. Cindy headed for the back of the bar, Destiny in tow. Adam headed for the bar.

The bartender, presumably Mel shouted out "free round of drinks!"

The establishment was more of a glorified hallway. The ornately carved oak antique bar ran along one wall for half the distance of the space. Behind the bartender was a large mirror. So patrons could see for themselves when they had had enough at the bar. On either side of the mirror were larger than life paintings of women draped in shear fabric hiding only the parts of a woman's anatomy that didn't matter. Namely their stomachs, the other parts were in plain sight for the whole world to see. Each woman lay upon a red velvet fainting couch. One facing north the other facing south. The paintings gave patrons incentive to have another round even if the reflection in the mirror told them otherwise.

The opposite wall was lined with small tables pushed up tight. A neon glow lit up the faces of the patrons sitting at these tables. Each table top was an electronic gambling machine that ate money faster than it could be fed into the slot. Bells and chimes sounded when the correct combination of figures showed up on the screen. But the bells and chimes were over exaggerated for the amount of money that poured out of the hole in the side. A single file walkway between barstools and tables led to the back of the building that opened up to a large room filled to over capacity with tables and chairs. The tables were either four person square or four, six, eight or however may person could be squeezed around a round table. The chairs were a menagerie of: kitchen chrome, wood carved, sawed off barstools or metal folding. The place legally, according to fire code would probably hold fifty people. But seeing how there was no back exit to be found legalities went out the window and the management stuffed them in till a good fight erupted to thin them out.

A postage stamp dance floor was being shared that night by a husband and wife band. Both standing close to a microphone and each playing a guitar. They closed their eyes, as their lips nearly met professing undying love for each other. Or the songwriters undying love for someone. Or the songwriters imaginative undying love for an imaginative lover. When the songs last note was being sent out to fade into the land of fairytales someone shouted out. "Now give us something we can dance to."

Before the final note faded the performer's eyes popped open. Both struck a quick loud note and partners grabbed each other out of their seats. Boots started stomping and butts started bumping.

Adam showed up behind Destiny and handed her a clear drink with a lime green straw. Shouting into her ear. "Thirsty? I didn't know what you liked."

A sip on the straw revealed 7-up. "Perfect. Thank you."

"They were out of umbrellas."

"I'll bet they were." Destiny laughed. This. Being out at night, in public, without James might not be as hard as she had built it up in her mind to be. Friendly faces made it easier to bare. The antics on the dance floor were too much to watch with a straight face.

"Where's your guide?" Adam inquired.

Destiny pointed to Cindy in the middle of the dance floor. Everyone giving her more than her share of space.

"Maybe we should sit while everyone's out there it's easier to move when the tables are empty. Cindy pointed to that table on the side. I think they were saving room." through the deep dark labyrinth of Mel's Place they wove. The memory box rested at Destiny's feet for easy access.

When the song was over the crowd looked like the song had just ended in a game of musical chairs. People shoved each other from one side to the other vying for the chairs. Cindy pulled on Ed's collar, bending him in half so she could shout in his ear. He raised up looked the direction of Destiny and Adam and gave a wave resembling the swishing of a fly. Brown curls bouncing Cindy waddled toward the table with Ed in tow. A mental image of Cindy towing a stair step line of kids behind her flashed into Destiny mind. They're going to need a bigger house she thought.

Ed shook Adam's hand briskly. Tipped his head to Destiny. "I'm glad you showed up Miss Destiny. I asked the band to play a song for you. Hey Lloyd!" Ed got the attention of the musicians and he started to point downward at the top of Destiny's head.

Lloyd nodded confirming the gesture. Then the band broke out in 'Thank You For Being A Friend'

Destiny was speechless. Her cheeks warmed but it was just residual heat from her heart. How could people be so full of gratitude. Then she was struck. "Oh, my gosh!" she grabbed the box. "I need some air. I have to go outside for a minute."

Adam made up some corny but believable excuse to the table and bumped his way through the crowd. Destiny was sitting outside on the street curb. The running shoes didn't make it very far. The box was hugged to her chest. The red glow from the four way light at the intersection of town was the only other heartbeat outside. Adam sat down beside her.

"A Mira Tale?"

She looked up. She had been crying. "Just a little one."

Sitting down beside her. He looked up at the moon. Bumped her shoulder lightly, "it's a nice night for a story."

The comment brought a smile, so she began. She thought for sure these stories must seem trivial and insignificant, even boring to him. But still he gave his ear, his attention each time her heart needed to pour open. "My Dad's mine put on a dance once a month at the old Town Hall. It's the big wooden building by the sheriff office." she laughed softly. "What am I saying you have a better memory of the town than I do."

I picked up Mira for the dance. Pearl wasn't coming to the dance she wasn't feeling well. But she felt well enough to have Mira

253

dressed to a tee. Her hair was springing ringlets all o   her head.
And starched to just one degree short of cement. Mira h   on a shiny
green water taffeta dress with a full skirt that stood stro   out when
she twirled. Mira had to show me her twirl three times   re we left
the house. She had been practicing all day. I   s terribly
underdressed in jeans and tee shirt.

Since my dad was the super at the mine I got in t   'ance free.
At the door was the secretary of the mine taking money.   ther large
woman who could double for a bouncer if things got c   f hand. If
anyone demanded entry without paying their fifty cents.

"Who's this you have with you, Destiny?"

"This is Mira."

"I twirl." Mira demonstrated bumping into the cl   re box and
knocking it into the door woman's lap.

"Watch out!" the woman yelled.

She refused my offer of help and suggested we sti   an out of
the way corner inside. Just as we were leaving she cc   l us back.
"Just a minute. You need your fan."

"Our fans?"

"Yes we used the proceeds of the prior dance   buy each
person a little gift at the next dance. Last month is w   o hot and
stuffy in the Hall we thought it would be a good idea to l   veryone a
fan." out of the box she extracted two fans. One with a   en ribbon
and one with a pink ribbon. She proceeded to tie the   with the
green ribbon on Mira's wrist. Mira got a wild look in hei   and tried
to pull her arm free from the woman's grip. The woma   ld tighter
and it was the start of a tug of war. "Hold still I just nee   tie this on
you!" the woman was getting exasperated. But Mira v   tarting to
panic.

I stepped in and grabbed the fan and Mira's ai   "I'll tie it
on."

The woman glared at me. "Better keep a close   h on that
one."

We walked into the Hall. That one? What we   he talking
about that one. I looked down at Mira. Eyes as big a   ucers. My
fingers were going numb her grip was so tight. From   tement or
fear, I didn't know which.

We did find a couple of seats at the advice of the   nan in the

254

far corne
opened a
closed he
catch the
faster bac
on her dr
stayed all
When she
to find ce
"I
Th
touch the
kept creep
to its prop
body any
floor. To
other dan
and she w
Th
our chairs
twirl orbi
hooked. S
Af
men my d
The man
defeat the
H
surmise w
"My dad
M
Hi
at me.
I
my diary
wanted to
I was det
at Mira. I
M

tied the fan on Mira's wrist and showed her how it
'osed and how it moved the air in front of her face. She
es and moved her head back and forth as if trying to
'ze as it went past. Her head began to move faster and
d forth. Her curls stood out from her head like the skirt
But her curls weren't individual they were so stiff they
mected and moved as one. I stopped fanning her face.
ned her eyes they were still moving back and forth trying
again and something to focus on.
fan."

nd got things started and Mira lit up. Her feet didn't'
r so she bounced up and down on her chair. The chair
out of the line up so I had to keep pulling her chair back
lace. She couldn't contain the energy racing through her
'. Jumping out of her chair she went twirling onto the
imazement she maneuvered perfectly in and around the
on the floor. The song over, her chin fell to her chest
d back to where I was sitting.

xt couple of songs I tried to keep her a little closer to
tood just a few feet from our seats and let her twirl and
ound me. After the first trip to the punch bowl Mira was
ould twirl, then drink. Twirl then drink.

he third or fourth trip back to our seats I saw one of the
vorked with having a serious conversation with his son.
ited in our direction. After giving the floor a kick in
headed in our direction.

od in front of us. Mira looked at him as if trying to
manner of beast he might be. His mouth finally opened.
? me come ask   if you want to dance?"

eyes flashed.

es flashed and he clarified. "Not her. You?" He looked
at me.

ed to dance in the worst way. I had dreamed, written in
special my first dance would be. But this guy no more
ce with me anymore than he wanted to dance with Mira.
ned that my first dance was going to be special. I looked
red back at the boy. "No thank you." He left.

rabbed my hand and said "We twirl."   We twirled. My

255

first dance was with Mira and it was special.

After a few more twirls she exclaimed. "Go hon." We took our fans and left.

I helped Pearl get her into bed only after she had gone through the ritual of putting her fan in her box. Any time anything new was added to the box all the other contents were taken out. Laid on the dresser, bed or sofa and handled gently. Looked at. Remembered. Sometimes she would caress them to her cheek. Then satisfied that all her treasures would coexist in the box, they were put back in and the lid replaced.

I tucked her in. she gave me a big hug and said. "Thank you. You my friend."

I didn't understand her magnitude of appreciation. I didn't do anything. To deserve such gratitude. I had sat with her and watched her twirl for all of an hour. That was it. That's all the longer we were gone.

But walking home that night I realized there are key moments in life. Chances to do the right thing. And if you do the right thing it can make all the difference in the world. Sometimes they are big things, sometimes they are small things that take no time or effort at all.

Destiny pulled the fan from the box and moved the air in front of her face. Closed her eyes and moved her head back and forth as if trying to catch the air as it went by.

"Had I not been so lame and had a few conversations with you when we were young… it would have saved me a whole lot of headaches." Adam shook his head and laughed.

"I don't even remember the boy's name that asked me to dance." Destiny didn't show any sign that she had heard his comment.

"It wasn't me." He raised his eyebrows.

She looked at him and laughed. "I know. You were in the cars outside the dance with all of your friends. Too cool to come inside and have a good time."

"Like I said a whole lot of headaches."

Adam decided to call it a night and go home to Digger. Destiny went back in to watch the twirling. Adam wondered as he walked home. He wondered, yet again and still, at this woman. She spoke of the attention she gave Mira as nothing at all. No time and no effort.

For people truly good at heart maybe it was effortless to do goodness. To make all the difference in the world to someone else. Without even realizing it.

Chapter 48

To her surprise Adam was retrieving some papers from his car and met her face to face as Destiny was looking toward the yard to call her running partner.

"Good morning."

"Oh! Good morning. You surprised me. You're up early."

He waved a thick book of papers in the air. "I've got some work to finish."

"Is Digger running. Or is she keeping you company."

Digger cleared the fence with a woof and headed out in front of Destiny. "I'd say she answered that one for herself." Digger looked back over her shoulder and woofed at Destiny.

"She's been very competitive lately. She likes to be out in front. She gives me the workout now instead of the other way around."

"Have a good run. I'll have the coffee on when you get back if you need a cup."

She was off answering his invitation with a wave of the hand and a swing of her chestnut ponytail.

Digger must have had her energy drink. She was up the hill double time. Destiny was lagging behind keeping more of a jogging pace. The late night at the bar had taken a toll. Usually she and the Two Ed's worked half a day on Saturday. But the last thing she told the Eds when she left at 1:00 a.m. was she was taking the day off. The Two Eds seemed pleased or inebriated. They just smiled and waved goodbye.

Ed had gotten up early none the less. He still had one more haul to empty from Friday. He had told Mary Clair he would help her haul a chest of drawers to her niece in Vegas. Ed pulled over on his way back from the dump. Just to have a look around the hills. His window rolled down rather stiff in the newly acquired truck from Adam. Two dark tunnels panned the surrounding mountains. Then jerked back to pan an area again. Stopped, sharpened the image. There she was. Only her pony tail wasn't swinging and there was no bounce to her step. She wasn't moving at all. She was seated on a rock. She hadn't stopped running or keeled over for months. Ed reached for his phone. Flipped it open ready to make the emergency call. He kept looking through the tunnels. The beast that attacked him was there with her. Destiny was seated on a rock. They were playing fetch. Then the woman put her hands behind her head and reclined against the rock behind her.

A hangover was not entirely dependent on alcohol intake. The lack of sleep and general party atmosphere would produce the same result. Destiny hadn't had anything stronger than a light beer. A glass of Chardonnay' was requested but the bartender said they was fresh out. She ordered the alcohol thinking it would help her relax and sleep better. The joy of the celebration was contagious. And Destiny came down with a full dose. She didn't remember having that much fun just watching people enjoy life, in, in forever. These people didn't hold back a thing. Be it their opinion or exuberance.

A wave of guilt kept trying to overtake the evening but it was held at bay until her head hit the pillow. Then it kept her awake for nearly the rest of the dark hours. Just as exhaustion was engulfing her the alarm went off and it was time to hit the hill to see how bad it could hurt today.

Digger didn't mind the break. The stick dropped at Destiny's feet and so did the dog. Sleep came fast to the animal. Destiny's head cradled in the perfect pocket of a rock. Worn smooth over long eons of years by wind and weather, waiting till the day it would be called to service to give a lonely runner a few moments of rest. Eyelids closed to shield against the days first rays of the sun. And there it was. A Mira memory.

The weather getting colder Mira wasn't getting enough exercise. So I had offered to give Mira an exercise program to wear her down before bed time. We went outside. We walked around the yard several times to limber up. Then we would touch our toes and lift our arms way up high in the air. Mira's shirt pulled up and the icy breeze brushed her tummy, she laughed.

"Code", she said.

She spotted something on the ground by the house that captured her interest. I looked in that direction but could see nothing. She slowly crept toward the house, putting her finger to her lips and telling me to "Shush."

She reached the house and bent down. There, lying stone cold and dead was a bird. Mira nudged it with her foot, no response. She bent down and poked it with her finger, nothing. She picked it up and tried to open its wings. Waving it in the air she held it high and went round and round in a circle. Mira had the right idea, she knew the bird was supposed to fly, she just couldn't get it to understand. She brought it over to me.

"Fit it." she commanded.

"Fit it, fit it? Oh fix it. I can't fix it Mira, it's dead." I replied, thinking this was going to be a hard one to explain. She only smiled and pushed the bird at me requesting me to 'fit it' again. Then she put the bird down and put a hand on either side of my face and held my face close to hers. She repeated the request. Her small chubby little hands felt warm on my face. Her heater motor was running great. I could usually tell with what intensity Mira wanted me to understand something by how hard she pressed her hands against my cheeks. This situation was of the strongest importance I had felt yet. Mira was pressing my cheeks together so hard my lips pushed out like a big fish. I had to pry her hands away from my face.

"Mira I can't fix it, it's gone away, it can't work anymore, it's like it's broken."

Mira made the wings stretch out again, and shook her head, "not boke" she said.

"Not that kind of broke Mira. How can I make you understand?"

Why was death such a difficult concept. How is death explained. When something dies, what dies and what lives in Mira terms. I took my own understanding of things too much for granted. Mira brought my understanding to a new depth. She would make me dig deep into my own soul to explain this one.

"When we are born Mira," I began slowly, "we get connected to God, he is like our power source. He turns on the light in us. And when something happens to hurt us real bad, it's like the power cord gets unplugged from God. Like when you unplug the vacuum on Pearl. The vacuum stops working. We can't plug the cord back into God by ourselves, just like you can't plug the cord into the wall. Pearl tells you not to plug the cord in, she has to. Well when we die it's like we have to go back up to heaven to have God plug us back in. We have to go back to God for help"

I didn't know if Mira understood. She just stood there blankly staring at me. Her eyes drifting in and out of focus. I didn't know why it even mattered to me if she understood. But it seemed that I wanted her to understand. It was something she would have to experience someday and I didn't want her to be afraid. I just wanted her to understand. Then she put her hands on either side of her face and began to rock back and forth slowly. This was what she did when she tried to make herself understand something. She rocked for several minutes. Then a tear rolled down her cheek. I knew she understood.

"Dead" she said, "is sad."

"You don't have to be sad Mira," I said

"No sad? Happy better?" she asked

"Yes," I said rather astonished, "happy is always better."

"K, happy den," she said with a smile, "happy, happy, happy."

Destiny didn't know if happy was better. She was happy for the first time in a long time last night and it didn't feel better today. She felt like a traitor. A traitor to grief. She could do better than that.

"Time to run Girl." Destiny jumped to her feet and began the run again. Straight up the mountain. No side hilling. No zig zag to gain altitude slowly. It didn't hurt bad enough. Not yet. Not today. Toes dug into the rock. Shale slid out beneath one foot just as the next was taking hold. The mountain was assaulted in jumps rather than footsteps. Sweat rolled from her face. Muscles called for oxygen that lungs could not produce. Eyes lost focus. Ears rang announcing to the brain the state of emergency. Using the final bits of oxygen to scream at the heavens. Destiny stopped. A relieved Digger stopped panting beside her. Maybe it hurt bad enough. For today. The two walked home.

Destiny unlatched the gate so her partner didn't have to jump over. The workout was harder than it had ever been. It was the least Destiny could do for her companion. Adam came from the side of the yard pushing a lawn mower. Digger ran up to him as if to tattle on Destiny for giving her such a hard work out. Adam scruffed the fur around her neck. She forgot all about the torture.

"There you two are." he directed his comment to the one wearing shoes. "I thought I was going to have to send out the search party."

"I'm sorry. Guess it was a little longer than usual. I sat down to rest and sort of nodded off."

"Looks like you got in some running too."

Destiny didn't know it but her face was still fl   d and her shirt though dry had rings under the arms where the   from her perspiration had collected. Her legs brown, stained in du   rned mud from mixing with the sweat. And her hair needed no tie   ld it back it was starched to her head. The term she would ha   sed upon viewing herself in a mirror would have been nothing sh   f, a mess. Lucky there were no reflective surfaces at hand or she   ver would have sat down for a glass of ice tea.

"I've thrown out the last of the coffee but how   some ice tea?"

"That sounds pretty good right now."

Destiny sat on the porch rocking in a new ch   Adam had found the last trip out of town. The chair ran a close sec   to the one she had at home. It was the closest Adam could find any   . The cool tea began to work and a normal color returned to the   an's face. She thought about the memory she had of Mira. Had   explained death correctly. The being connected to God. Now   she had experienced it firsthand would she explain it differ   y? If she changed any part of the explanation it would be the addit   of the fact we remain connected to God, just in a different di   sion. Just because our physical body or coat of many colors dis   ects from our being, doesn't mean our amness, she heard it referre   one time, disconnects from God. But on the other hand that would   e been far too complicated to explain to a little girl especially a   like Mira. Simple was better with her. Perhaps with everyone.

Regrettably James and her had never had that   versation. Did he even believe in God? She didn't know. It was a   ct that he shied away from.

"You believe in God." it was an observation   question directed to her companion on the porch.

Adam cleared his throat. The answer to this no   lestion. If she in fact was requesting an answer. Was obviousl   s. As he believed everyone had a belief in God, it was the def   on of that belief that varied. The definitions in fact were limitless.   mitless as God. But in all reality or in the reality he came to believ   there was no definition for God. For to define something was   it it in to

262

boundarie | nd God is boundless. To define something is to say what
it is and i | mething is something then it, on the other hand, is not
other thin | 3ut God is all things. The best he could hope for at this
particular | nent was to give this woman a simple yes and if the
discussior | nt further it would be entirely up to her.
"Y

Th | ords flowed out of her like a gentle stream. Meandering
though a | en meadow. Not sure where they would end up just
following | path of least resistance which would ultimately lead to
the final (| nation. "On our run this morning I sat down and had a
memory (| ira. She had found a dead bird on the ground and was
trying to ; | t to fly again. I tried to explain to her it was dead. Then
she wante | know what dead was. I'm afraid my explanation fell
short of \ | I wanted to convey to her. But the explanation was
limitless ; | unexplainable. Trying to define death is like trying to
define life | ried to explain that the bird was no longer connected to
God or as | ld her a power source. But I should have told her that it
was just tl | rds body was disconnected. Not the bird itself."

A | pause formed as the words got stuck temporarily in a
level vall(| Adam decided to give Destiny a few more moments to
gather mc | houghts to push the words along their way again. "I
believe in | l. I think I always have. But I don't think my realization
of God is | at most people think. Or anyway I used to have a hard
time sittir | rough Sunday school listening to them define God as
some gra | uper human sitting on a golden throne casting down
judgment | he peons inhabiting the earth."

He | iled. Deep lines formed at the corners of his eyes.
Dimples] | nthesized his mouth. Had he always had dimples. Did
they emba | s him when he came of age? Was it something he might
have thou | unmanly? Or did he play of them knowing it was an
irresistibl(| ute to the opposite sex? Enhanced his gift of charm. Her
thoughts \ | rambling.
"S | ls a bit farfetched. I'll have to agree."

Sh | arly forgot what she had been talking about. Letting her
mind wan | on such things as dimples. "I just had such a hard time
thinking t | f God was supposed to be so loving why did bad things
happen to | ple? I just knew it had to be us that formed our fate and
not a supe | man being past the stars doling out events."

"I think we think along the same lines."

"I'm no good at explanations. What I think has a hard time coming out the way I mean it to. Like mortal words are so incompetent. Trying to explain the color red to a blind person. Trying to explain a beautiful symphony to a deaf person. What do you think then? What do you believe? I'm looking for details."

Another one of those questions. The answer was not a simple one. The answer was complex, multifaceted and might take well into the night to even pass the first goalpost. He had time. All the time in the world for whatever this woman wanted to discuss. He raised his eyebrows high and blew out a big puff of air. As if to request confirmation that she wanted him to continue. Destiny raised her eyebrows back prompting him to continue.

"I'll have to agree with you. It's an almost impossible subject to discuss. Because it deals with what you know. What you feel. It deals with truth that has no physical concrete proof, or anyway none that mortals have come up with yet. But they are working on it. But when someone does manage to write about the truth it's like water to a man dying of thrust. The words jump off the page. Or a thought hits you like a ton of bricks. The voice inside your head yells and screams at you. This is it! Keep reading! But the problem with that voice inside everyone's head is that it gets ignored. We have it as a child. But soon learn that we shouldn't be listening to anything inside. What is real is only on the outside. So. The voice locks it's lips. And leaves us to listen to the opinion of other people. We need to trust ourselves. It's all inside of us. When did we lose faith in ourselves?"

"It's easier to doubt. It's easier to not believe than it is to believe in ourselves. We are animals after all. Following the path of least resistance."

He didn't know if she was talking about the subject of God or had strayed to darker matters in her past. He would keep to the current subject until she was ready to talk of other things. "I think we all believe. Even those that say they don't believe in a deity have some sort of deity they do believe in. It's just the defining of that deity that causes all the trouble. I think of all the blood that has been shed over time because of our difference of thought on the subject. Our belief evolves over eons and just as we become more civilized so does our belief in a deity. I do think however that the state of the church needs to step up. I think they know more than they give out. Only small portions at a time to keep us hungry. Which is good, keeps us searching for more manna. But civilization as a whole is so scientific today. The proof to everything is right in front of our eyes. Things that seemed impossible only decades ago are common place now. I think when the church finally gives up fighting science, and science gives up fighting the church and they decide to join forces, there will be an explosion of comprehension of what the deity is. For God is both sides, logic and faith joined together to form thought. And that thought can create and run and be the limitless physical universe and the limitless non-physical all at the same time. God is the existing force. Whenever we say I am. The amness is god. One might call it a life force but it goes beyond our interpretation of what living is. Existing. Most of what we think we are is just that. Apparitions brought into being by our thoughts. We are really magical creatures and we don't even know it. The whole of existence is one big continuous bang or chain of events. All rippling in different vibrations and degrees of light. And speaking of light. If God is existence then all that exists is, because of a variance in the degree of vibration. Anything that vibrates fast enough will eventually turn into light. Ergo the higher we raise our vibration of understanding the more light we become thus the term illuminated! God is light. The ultimate destiny we are heading for. But the journey must be slow. We must evolve one step at a time. Or else it would be like suddenly becoming the sun. We would disintegrate. Too much light too fast. I think we need to spend more time being with God than trying to define God."

"OK. Yea." She looked dazed. "Well maybe we aren't totally on the same wave length. Maybe on the same trail but from what you just said I might be a few hundred miles behind you."

"No. I think you've been ahead of me the whole time." Anyway it had always been her light that kept him moving forward on his journey. Whenever he thought of how different she was from other people it was because of the light that radiated from her. Could she really not have known? Could she really not know now?

The rambling on of this man had been overwhelming but at the same time comforting. Like he had said that voice inside her head seemed to be saying listen, this is truth. But there was something more when he spoke. When they carried on a conversation. It was as if they had known each other for years. Living 25 years with James had never felt this comfortable.

"It feels so strange. Sitting here talking like this. That wasn't a subject ever brought up between James and I. I don't know what he believed. Of course our conversational subject matter was really not very broad now that I think back on it. There was so much I don't know about him. And never will know now. Are you sure we weren't friends before?"

"Let me put it this way. Not before in our current lifetime. I don't know about before that, another lifetime. And I don't know about the future."

"Well, I'd like to call you friend in the present." The words came hard. It might have hurt James to think of her asking another man to be her friend. But James was not here now. And she needed a friend.

"I'd like that too."

"Well the time is flying by. I better get going. Thanks for the tea. And the conversation."

She got to the gate and turned at the mention of her name. "Destiny? The memory about Mira? Was it the feather?"

"Yea. You have a good memory."

Mira and I dug a hole in Pearl's flower bed and wrapped the bird in a napkin. I threw a big shovel of dirt over the napkin. Mira screamed. "No!"

"Don't you want to bury him Mira? The dirt. The dirt will keep him warm and protect him."

She was on her hands and knees pulling the moist soil away from the bird one chubby handful at a time. "Not yet. Not yet. Not yet." She muttered with each handful.

Once the napkin was visible the bird was ceremoniously unwrapped. She examined the corpse as if doing a crime scene investigation. Then taking the longest feather on his tail between two fingers she yanked it out like plucking a whisker from an old woman's chin. "Dirt now." She ordered.

Obeying orders I covered the bird with the mound of extracted dirt. Patted it down firm so the evidence of our tampering in Pearl's flowers was gone.

"Code." Mira said as we walked hand in hand back to the

house. She stroked her cheek with the tail feather, pulled me down to her level and stroked my cheek with the feather too. "No forget him." she smiled and looked up at me. "I no forget Desty."

"And I'll never forget Mira."

"But I did forget her." She admitted.

"But not forever."

He watched her walk down the lane wondering, like she did with her explanation to Mira, if he explained himself correctly.

Chapter 49

Beep. Beep. Beep.

The storm was closing in fast. The threat shown in the atmosphere. Even with no clouds in the sky it was grey. As if there was a permanent eclipse. The threat reflected in the faces of the people as well. Worry, fear, even anger the latter for no apparent reason. People were just short tempered. A powder keg waiting for a spark.

The hospital had been put on alert. Truckloads of supplies arrived hourly. If the storm hit they would be supplied for the next five years. But that would be the better scenario to pray for.

Adam had gone from esteemed doctor to box carrying laborer. He didn't know it was possible but his muscles ached. A sure sign he had been here too long. The council had told him the previous night that the estimated time limit was down to forty eight physical hours. They were pushing it to the wire. Adam still felt there was nothing to worry about. Nothing as far as Destiny, Mira and himself were concerned. The rest of humanity, that was a different story.

He sat holding the hand of his special patient. As he did in the wee hours of the night when he was sure there would be no one showing up that might object. The door opened. Sure that it was Mira he didn't turn around.

"Doesn't look like any bedside manner I've ever seen Doctor!" The words came out in a loud slur. Legs of his chair gave way as hands grabbed the back of it and jerked hard throwing it across the room. Adam jumped up in time to right himself and spin around to meet the aggressor.

"What the hell are you doing Mr. Walker. You could have hurt your wife!" Adam spoke in an exaggerated whisper.

James didn't bother to whisper instead raised his voice for the whole floor to hear. "What the hell are you doing?"

Quickly Adam recovered. "I was checking your wife's pulse."

"That's not what I saw.' in a volume turned down a couple notches.

"It looks and smells like you're not seeing clearly. Go home. Sleep it off."

Slurring and blubbering at the same time James continued. "I need to talk to my wife. I've had enough, the pressure is too much. All this." he started grabbing tubes and wires. Adam pulled his hands away just before an IV came loose. "I have to talk to her. I went to a lawyer, I've signed the papers. Forty eight hours. That's what the papers say. Then all this comes out and the machines turn off. And it's done. Now would you let me say good bye to my wife." suddenly he seemed sober.

Adam turned to leave. He owed this man that. He owed him some privacy. "very well. But just for the record. I think the hospital will fight it. They will have to hear from the attending physician that the prognosis is hopeless. That would be me. And it's not. We are never without hope."

"Leave!"

Darkness filled the room but a new shade of darkness. Destiny felt the walls to her palace holding strong but the storm threatened to break through.

James righted the chair he had thrown and put it back in its place beside his wife. He sat. His beard was more than a five o'clock shadow. But it was well past five o'clock.   He began. "This is hard Destiny. There's a lot I got to say. Cuz well I don't know if you heard or understood, but this can't go on. It isn't right. Not for you not for the family. I think you would agree with my decision. But since this is the last time we will talk there's some stuff I got to say. They say confession is good for the soul. I don't know who's soul it refers to the one confessing or the one being confessed to. But here goes. There's been, there is, still is someone else in my life. I didn't mean for it to happen. Honest. Just like you didn't mean for this to happen. But it happened and so we go on. Change our course maybe but move on just the same. I was going to tell you. I was in fact coming home to tell you when I got the call about you being hit by a truck." he cleared his throat. Stood to leave.

"Well if it's any consolation it doesn't feel better yet." as he reached the door he turned again. "I want you to know this decision doesn't have anything to do with the other woman. It's just so hard to see you like this. You were always so full of life, now like this, it's not fair."

Destiny looked up toward the ceiling of her palace sure she

heard the roof crack. Adam appeared beside her. "Look: : a storms coming."

"Yea. A bad one from the feel of it."

"Don't worry Destiny. All storms will pass."

M(   )f the work done so far had been on the yard, fence and
the outbui   gs. Ed and Ed were repairing the roof on the shed in the
afterhours   ice making the deal with Ed to buy the place Adam had
a friend c   up some legal sounding papers that scared Ed just to
read them   estiny decided to trust him to pay for the house on his
word of h(and trashed the paperwork.

To   sfy her conscience Destiny just had to rework the inside
of the hoι   is well to make it somewhat inhabitable.   The three of
them atta   l the house with a vengeance. Ed and Ed found
themselve   be pretty good handymen too. They painted, plumbed
and even   some minor electrical. They were thinking of adding a
line to the   e of the truck instead of just Eds Hauling it would read
Eds Hauli   nd Handyman Service.

Th   iad started at the back of the house and were nearly to
the front ι   As they would finish a room they would close the door
and move   ) the next. They were at Mira's bedroom.

Th   irpet was rotted and coming up in long strips. Destiny
carried a   strip out to the truck. A familiar vehicle approached.
Adam sto]   beside her and rolled down the window.

He   eted her then gave his full attention to the transformation
of the hou

"V   . You guys have been busy. I had no idea the house
looked thi   eat."

"It   oming along. Just one room left. Mira's room. I was
saving tha   om till last. I think it will be the new baby's room." She
nodded ir   ifirmation toward the house. "I think Mira would have
liked that.   you want to look around. Ed and Ed do some amazing
work. Ma   you might want to hire them some time."

A(turned the ignition key off and unfolded from the Jeep.
"Sure I'd   : to see the accomplishments." They walked toward the
house thr(the gate that actually worked on the hinges. He turned
and sprint   ack to the car grabbed a package from the passenger seat
through th   )en window. "I almost forgot this came for you. Just as I
was leavii   ) I thought I'd drop it off."

"Oh? Thanks." she took the fat manila envelope and turned it over in her hands. The return address didn't have a name, just a P.O. Box. All the mail was being forwarded and the postmark on this one was three weeks ago. She hoped it wasn't anything important.

Borders of marigolds led the way to the front door. Newly planted grass was peeking through the mulch behind that. The door swung open to reveal a miracle. There was no way anyone would have believed what the old house could have looked like. The floors were stripped and the rich wood grain swirled from the door way through the kitchen. The walls were painted a biscuit with dark mahogany trimming the windows and base and crown molding. Adam looked around in amazement. Ed and Ed came through the side door with one long roll of carpet in tow.

"This is unbelievable. What you've done in here. It's beautiful." Adam complimented

Ed and Ed bowed their chest with pride. His comment was directed at Destiny but redirected to Ed and Ed.

Destiny noticed the pride popping out of her work companions. "Oh, hey Ed and Ed why don't you guys show Adam the bookcases you built in the back bedroom. I have a feeling he'd love to see them."

The carpet was dropped with a thud. Everyone entered the newly remodeled house. "We found this old used walnut in the shed in the back. Must a been from some cabinets or an old barn or something. Anyways we sanded it down and oiled it good and it turned out pretty decent." their voices trailed off with Adam following behind them ooohing and ahhhing as they pointed out details along the way.

Destiny stopped in the kitchen and turned to the package in her hands. Mail from home. She couldn't imagine what it must be. The manila envelope was padded with little air cells. But there was definitely some concentrated bulge in the center. She squeezed and felt trying to guess what it might be. She loved surprises. Especially when they were wrapped up. And this was sort of like being wrapped up. The suspense was too much she tore open the seal.

Her hand thrust into the opening and pulled out a man's wallet. There was a folded letter inside. The wallet fell to the floor as eyes scanned the writing on the page.

Destiny was right. Adam loved the bookcase. The raised panels were used for the sides of the cases and the borders of the doors were doweled together to make the shelves. The shelves were different depths and they graduated up the wall from large to small. Old brass hinges were polished and inset at the connections between the shelf and the rungs.

"These are wonderful." he ran his hand over the wood so smooth the nerve endings on the tips of his fingers could hardly feel it.

"Ms Destiny come up with the design. We just put them together."

"It's great! Is there any more of the wood out there?"

"Yea, there's a few more. We could maybe make one more about half this size."

"Could you work me up a price for one?" The bookcase would go well in the miners shack.

Ed stuck his tongue in his cheek and gazed at the ceiling through his glasses. His hands drawing something in the air. The other Ed stuck his thumbs under his suspenders and gazed blankly at Ed.

"I don't mean this minute. I don't need to know now. Just when you have time. You can tell me at the café."

"Oh! OK good cuz I think I'm gonna need a calculator."

Glass shattered somewhere in the front of the house. The three men bolted out of the room. In shock they stared into Mira's room to see Destiny ripping and pulling at the carpet. Glass littered the floor from a broken window. She looked like the Tasmanian Devil hard at work.

Adam picked up the envelop to reveal the wallet on the floor. The letter began: *They say confession is good for the soul...*

He read no more. Pieces fell into place. "Ed you two go get a broom."

"Destiny." he approached her slowly as if coming upon a wounded animal. Would it flee, would it fight?

She was tugging and pulling at a stubborn piece of carpet. It just wouldn't let go. Blood dripped on the floor from punctures on her hands from the tacks along the edge of the flooring. She looked up at him. Wildness in her eyes. Every nerve in her body trembled. Her jaw chattered.

She opened her mouth and whispered. "I. I have to go."

The stubborn piece of carpet was abandoned and the woman bolted through the door. Adam followed calling her name. A half a block down the road leading to nowhere in particular he caught her arm and turned her around.

Tears of anguish streaked her cheeks. "I have to go. Let me go." through hiccup sobs.   He held her close to his chest.

"OK. Come on we'll go." he walked her back to his jeep and gently put her in the passenger side. He dialed his cell phone as he walked around to the driver's side.

"Tony. I need you to change our course for today."

They drove to the airstrip in silence. Destiny watched the sagebrush pass by an occasional rabbit scurried ahead of their path only to dart off the side of the road just in the nick of time. The world was passing by her window but she viewed it void of emotion. Dust boiled up behind the jeep as it sped down the dirt road. Soon the dust would settle and there would be no indication that they had passed this way.

A small Lear Jet stood at attention awaiting orders from its commander. A man's form filled the open doorway as the crunching of gravel under the tires indicated the arrival of the passengers.

Adam stopped the Jeep came around to the passenger side and opened the door for Destiny. In an almost hypnotic trance she let him lead her to the stairs of the jet. An introduction to the pilot was made and she entered the plane.

Tony was used to last minute notices. He kept the jet ready at all times day or night. He was even used to destination changes, even in midflight. But Adam to have a female passenger was a first. He looked to Adam for instructions but not an explanation. That was the way things were.

"Thanks Tony. You have the route OK."

"Sure thing Mr. Barnes."

"I've just got to make a couple phone calls. Could you show my guest around and tell her I'll be right in. Oh and Tony,"   there was a long pause as if he didn't quite know how to say what he wanted to say. "I was just wondering. Maybe if, well your wife cleans the jet for me. And I know you and your family have taken it on trips. I was just wondering if your wife might have left any cloths on board. Maybe something that might fit Destiny. She was working on a house remodel when I picked her up and I just thought she might like to change into something else. We're going to lunch in Monterey."

"I'll check Mr. Barnes."

Destiny was standing in the middle of the cabin when Tony entered. There was a child's doll in the cushion of the seat. She pulled it out of hiding. "Oh. I'm sorry." Tony took the doll from her. "My little girl comes to play in here when my wife cleans the plane. She must have forgotten her doll.

"She might be missing her."

"You're probably right. She gets pretty attached to things. Anyway. We'll be taking off pretty soon. Mr. Barnes is just making some phone calls. The bathroom is just past the kitchenette on the left. There's coffee or tea and there are a few cold drinks in the fridge. My wife made some cookies if you'd like to try some. They're in the microwave. Keeps them from landing on the floor during takeoff."

"I'm fine thank you."

You can sit wherever you like there are seatbelts in all the chairs. The floatation devices are in the compartments overhead and in case of emergency the oxygen masks come out of these little doors. A fire extinguisher is beside the door. I guess that's about it. I'll be up front doing the flight check."

They were certainly prepared for any disaster. If only she could say the same for herself.

The letter tucked neatly inside her husband's wallet was from a woman. The woman he had been with before heading for home. She was wrought with guilt over the death of Destiny's husband and her lover. She needed to cleanse her soul. Confession is good for the soul she began, but good for who's soul. Not Destiny's. The mistress worked with James. In the same office. They had been seeing each other for about a year. As far as she knew James had no plans of leaving Destiny. And he loved his wife very much. Destiny found this a very odd thing to say. But the real punch to her heart was the final paragraph. The mistress was pregnant. Six months pregnant. She had told James the day he died. Now was overcome with guilt thinking James might have done something stupid because of the news she had given him.

Destiny thought his stupidity might have started long before the day he died. The true intention of the letter was a plea to monetarily consider the child she carried. According to the person that penned the letter, James had promised to take care of the child. Not to marry her, but to take care of the child.

The door of the jet slammed shut! Destiny jumped.

"Oh. Sorry. Didn't mean to scare you."

He took his bag to the back and opened a closet door.

"Do you want to sit down. I think we're ready to get started."

Destiny looked from one seat to the next. One chair was well worn a small table in front of it. It was assumed the frequent flyer usually sat there. The remainder of the seats were equally worn. In other words looked like new. The seat on the opposite side of the table was chosen. There was another window in which she could watch her world go by.

Adam took his usual seat and buckled in. "Do you want anything? Coffee? It's not as good as Faye's but it keeps me awake."

Destiny shook her head. "No. Thanks."

The engine wound to a shrill whistle. Her body was thrust back into the seat. Looking out the window she willed God or whatever force there was in the universe that moved people around to take her away. Before the wheels lifted off the ground she was asleep.

"Thank you God." Adam whispered.

"Destiny." a hand was on her shoulder giving it a gentle shake. The dream continued even after her eyes opened. There was no look of recollection in her eyes.

"We're about to land."

Adam was shaking her shoulder telling her they were going to land. That must mean they were in the air now. Out the window was water. As far as the eye could see.

"In the water!"

"No. look out the other window." he laughed.

A city on the bay. They banked hard, bumped a couple times, skidded tires on the tarmac. And Tony's voice came over a speaker. "All set Mr. Barnes."

"Where are we?"

"Monterey."

The tilt of her head and the lines between her eyebrows indicated more explanation was needed.

"Canary Row. Steinbeck."

A smile graced her mouth and her eyes opened a little bit wider. "I love Steinbeck!"

A sigh of relief exhaled long and slow from his body. She could still smile. "I thought you might."

"I need to go." she pointed toward the back of the plane. "Does the bathroom work. Is it OK or should I wait."

"No. it's fine go right ahead."

Adam poked his head into the cockpit. "Tony any luck with some extra cloths."

"Sorry Mr. Barnes. There's nothing on board except my daughters doll."

"OK. Thanks anyway."

Emerging from the bathroom patting down her freshly wet hair. "I can't go. I'm sorry. I'm a mess. What was I thinking getting on this plane. Looking like this. I wasn't thinking!" she sat back in the seat and started strapping the seatbelt back on.

"Ok. Alright. I just thought it might be good for you to get out of town for a day. So something different. Monterey just popped in my head. I just love it here. The ocean air. The relaxed pace. It's sort of like stepping into canary row and living there for while."

"Thank you. I'd love to see it. I really would. But..."

"Then let's go. Throw caution to the wind." he stood sweeping his arm toward the open door. Like a matador tempting the bull.

"I'm in my painting cloths. My shirt is ripped. My face is a mess."

"So we'll make a quick stop along the way."

Within an hour she were spit, polished and speeding toward Canary Row in a rental car.

They strolled down small streets. Past the big canning houses. They pet stingrays, starfish and clams at the aquarium. Picked up some favorite shells from the beach that were special enough to put in an out there box if Destiny had one. The seals begging for snacks along the waterfront made Destiny think of Digger.

"I'm hungry. How about you?" Adam asked.

"Yea. I could eat. What do you suggest."

"I know this place that makes the best clam chowder. In fact they all make clam chowder but this place puts big hunks of bacon in it." He lead her to a small café on the wharf. They walked through a covered hallway with shops and eateries down each side. The whole group floated on the water. All the floors were just boards from the

dock. Water could be seen through the spaces in the boar They were
seated outside at Adams request. Red and white check ablecloths
flowed in the sea breeze welcoming their guest. Come a it a while.
Breathe in the air. Forget your cares. Forget the world ou e. Destiny
fell easily into the spell. The waiter brought a huge brea wl full of
clam chowder. Eyes wide with anticipation, "I can see w ou love it
here." She was smiling again.

The soup was attacked as if she had been strand n a desert
isle with no food or water for weeks. When the soup wa ie and the
top button on her pants bursting she pushed the dish av eaned her
head back so the sun could shine full on her face. "Tl as been a
great day!"

"Has it?" his tone was glad yet concerned.

She looked him eye to eye. Hers filling with tear he opened
her mouth then shut it again. Opened her mouth agai en shut it
again. Looked away. Out to sea.

He could wait.

She began slowly. Like a thread coming loose. I ng go one
stitch at a time. "You know sometimes how you just k things. I
knew." she took a deep breath and blew it out slowly. "I w. When I
heard the awful crash at the end of the road. I knew. \ n I had to
keep reheating dinner. I knew. When there was the sour a strange
car pulling up in the driveway. I knew. When the do ell rang. I
knew. When I opened the door. I knew. And where h is coming
from. I knew. That was the one fact, the one detail t was never
discussed. Where he was coming from. It was assumed rk. But he
gets off work at 4:30. He was turning into the drivewa 7:00. Not
that he had to account for his whereabouts every mint certainly
didn't. But it was just out of the ordinary." She raised eyebrows
high. "There are some things a person just knows. Some igs a wife
just knows. I didn't know for how long. I do now. I didn ow who. I
do now."

"I guess I don't blame him. Not one hundred p nt. It was
our life, as in two. If there is blame it has to be shared. I w I didn't
feel the same about him as I did twenty-four years ago e is hard.
Change is hard. Our life was so busy, kids, dinners, so ing going
on all the time. Then it started slowing down. It got slow id slower.
There was this empty void. A void that we didn't talk ut. Maybe

278

we shoul(
didn't talk
when you
"I
suspected.
They wer(
do while i
out about.
from then
the kids g
life."
"Y
leaned clo
"I
reveal hov
room like
lately that
the situati
me wrong
dead man
He has."
"Y
easy thou;
Ot
back in. li
boat fadec
take over.
But easy?
got our w(
her nose b
He
back. "Tii
be a thous
to be OK.
Sh
"N
going to f
"I

ve. Like I said before. There were certain things we
)ut. That was one of them. It's hard to change. Especially
hanging in different directions."
n't ask him about it once I knew, or should I say
idn't want the kids to find out. He loved them so much.
. world. Imagine, there are all these little things the kids
are growing up that they don't want the parents to find
;y haven't a clue there are things the parents are hiding
hought or I was hoping he would grow out of it, the way
out of their shoes. I viewed it as a phase, a chapter in

;eem quite composed. Are you? Is it all show?" Adam
o her, inviting her to continue if she wanted to.
't think it's show. I feel I know you well enough to
'eel. You saw me bolt out of the house. Race around the
iad woman and then slip into a daze. I have discovered
ck, grief, numbness imitates composure. And the truth of
; there's nothing I can do about it. Not now. Don't get
;el betrayed, hurt, angry. But it's so damn hard to hate a
, like he's done his penance. I have to move on. Don't I?

ou're right. Not everyone would let him off the hook so

the ocean past the row of boats the fog began to roll
. monster engulfing whatever was in its path. Boat after
. of site. She could not let this new revelation in her life
illow her whole not without a fight. "I'll have to let it go.
:re won't be anything easy about it. Digger and I have
:ut out for us." the water filled to the brim of her eyelids
:d. The weather wasn't cold, just her heart.
iched for her hand across the table . She didn't pull it
eals all wounds? In time all things will pass? There must
clichés out there. Guess what I want to say is, it's going
i're going to be OK."
dded and swallowed hard. The taste of saltwater.
she wants money. For her, their child. Guess the kids are
)ut now."
k it might be easier on them coming from you. Rather

279

than chancing them finding out another way, the way you did. And telling them some of what you just told me. How much he loved them. How life gets hard. If you can be forgiving, I'm sure they can too."

"You're right. They are wonderful people." after a pause for contemplation. "Probably the sooner the better. Huh?"

"That would be your call. I don't think it will get any easier."

"All the more reason to get cracking on the house I guess."

His heart was aching seeing this woman go through such torment. Now his heart was aching because of his own torment.

"Can I ask you a question?" she didn't look him in the eye. Kept her focus on the corner of the napkin she was twirling around her finger.

"Anything."

"Do you think I should give her child money? Morally what is right?"

"I don't mean to pry. But you need to look at your own financial position first. You and your husband built for your future. You need to make sure you are secure."

"That's not a problem. No. he had enough life insurance. I guess you could say I'm a damn millionaire." another attempt at sarcasm. "He did love his children though. I'm sure he would have loved this one. I guess I owe him that I think."

It was the decision he thought she would come to. Knowing her, her heart, he couldn't see her deciding any other way. This woman had just received the worst news anyone could hear. And yet in the middle of such anguish she was letting her heart lead the way.

"Do you think a DNA test would be too much to ask?"

"Not at all." He affirmed.

"How do they do that? They wouldn't have to dig..." Destiny closed her eyes not
wanting to see the horrible picture of her husband being exhumed and samples of him being taken back to a lab to analyze. If it came to that she would just give the child a settlement and be done with it. Money was not that precious to her.

"No. no I don't think so. Surely there is some of his items around the house they could use to test. A hairbrush, razor, his clothing, toothbrush. I could ask the researcher at the office to check it out. Discretely of course."

She just nodded not really hearing the last part of his offer. Remembering the house so far away. A world away from this café table on this wharf under this western sun. she muttered. "Yea. There's still a house full of stuff that was his."

Destiny missed the sites on the flight back as she missed them on the flight there. Rest was the best thing for her. Wounds heal faster when you sleep.

He gazed out the window. The clouds were below them. Everyone continuing with their normal daily activities while they streaked above them. Some were working, some were sleeping, some happy some sad, some lying some loving some living and some dying. Life went on. It was a challenge of his own mental constitution not to hate this husband of Destiny's. how could he do that to her? Didn't he know who she is, how special she is. Didn't he know what he had. The world right in front of him. But then why would he know. The town of Bendline didn't know what they had all those years ago. Himself being the most ignorant of all. Treating her the worst out of the whole school. Adam's final thought or rather prayer was that he hoped James realized the truth before he drew his last breath.

Watching her sleep. The only movement was a slight rise and fall of her chest. She had been becoming more stable, more grounded each day. Coming to terms with her new life. She had done a remarkable job of dealing with her situation. Now out of nowhere to be hit with this news. Just like James she had been blindsided. It was no easy quest for her to climb this mountain of grief. Just as she seemed to be reaching the summit a blast of wind came up from the other side to send her tumbling back down the hill. She climbed it once, he had faith she could do it again. Still, how much could one soul endure? He thought of his hike up the mountain years ago and he could hear the voice of Ram. As plain as if he were sitting beside him.

"How could you ask a question you know the answer to."

"I don't know the answer to this one Ram."

"Of course you do."

"Why don't you make it easy on me and tell me the answer just for old times' sake."

"A soul can endure as much as it takes."

"It takes for what?"

"Why to turn these human lumps of coal in to diamonds.

That's each and every one of our objectives. That's the end we are seeking. And we ourselves order up whatever events it takes to produce enough heat and pressure to transform us into something that can reflect the light instead of absorb it and keep it hidden away. That way we never have an event or situation we cannot handle. Because we are the ones doing the ordering. Subconsciously we know what we are capable of."

"Look at the light she has. She lights up a room just by entering it. Why would she need such tragedy?"

"Maybe it is not tragedy to her. It's not for us to know. Maybe the ones being transformed are the ones around her."

He knew the process of transformation was continuous. Never ending. And he could feel himself transforming each day he was in her company.

"Good night Ram."

Chapter 51

Destiny had not looked so over run since the she first started beating the mountains around Bendline. Double pain called for double running. Water poured from every pore in her body. The clothes still damp and her face flushed. Small unruly locks stayed motionless around her face. The salt from her sweat had a starch effect, stiffer than any hard to hold moose. Her hand trembled with exhaustion as she turned the knob of the door to the café. The friendly jingle was starting to sound comforting.

The morning paper was immediately folded and placed on the table at first site of the marathoner. He worried for her health. She sat opposite him. Still breathing hard. Eyes bloodshot.

"How's my dog?"

This brought a smile to her face. His concern for her was felt. She appreciated the respect he had for the boundaries of their friendship. Always careful not to overstep, be too caring. She couldn't deal with someone being too caring of her at this chapter in her life. She didn't have to worry about that with Adam. Grabbing his ice water before hers arrived she answered before gulping the contents empty. "Better than me." the hand holding the glass still trembled.

He slipped a paper to her. The name and phone number of a DNA lab.

She mouthed "thank you." while Faye filled her cup.

"Boy don't you look a site this morning. You must have overdone yourself this morning. I'll get you some eggs and bacon to go with your muffin. You need some protein girl."

"Feels like I need some more water please." Destiny still spoke in short chops taking in extra oxygen between word groups.

"Coming up." Faye stuck a order slip on the clothes line stretched across the window to the kitchen. Handed a glass of water and a pitcher to Ed to pass across the aisle to Destiny.

"Here you go Ms Destiny. Say, me and Ed was talking. Maybe you should enter one of those marathons. We see them on the sports channel all the time. You look a lot more fit than a lot of those runners." he turned his attention to Adam. "Mr. Barnes you might know, do they allow betting on those events. Coz, if they do me and Ed would be willing to throw down a twenty apiece on Ms Destiny here."

"I don't know about that Ed. I think most of them are for charity. You know the runner gets donations or pledges. The money is sort of an entry fee for the runner. And they give the money they bring in to the charity specified. But this is Nevada. I wouldn't doubt you could find someone to cover your bet."

"How bout it Ms Destiny. You want Ed and I to find a race for you to run in."

"No thanks Ed. I only compete against myself when I run. Horses run. Maybe you could bet on horse racing."

"Naw. That's too risky. Betting on you would be a sure thing."

"Thanks for the vote of confidence but the answer is still no." She had thought about it years and years ago. It was always in the back of her mind. Things she wanted to do before she died.

The two Eds returned to their fried eggs and bacon. They'd have to think up some other way to make a quick buck. Something other than backing a runner.

Destiny ate her muffin in two bites. Fueling the bodies need for blood sugar. The protein didn't sound that good to her she took it to go. Left some cash on the table. Her money was always kept in her shoe. Today it needed to be dried out. She stood to leave sliding the note off the table.

"I've got to leave myself." Adam took the last swig of coffee and deposited his paper in a wooden rack Faye kept by the door.

The door jingle announcing their departure. Faye looked up to wave goodbye but they were already talking outside.

"Some things just go together." she mumbled.

"What's that Faye?" Mary Claire had sharp ears.

"I said some things just go together." Faye answered, louder.

"You mean like eggs and bacon." Ed asked.

"Hot dogs and sauerkraut is another one." Whitey added.

"You can't beat beans and franks. Did you ever taste my beans and franks?" Mary Claire inquired looking at Ed.

"No. I don't like beans and franks I'm a steak and potatoes man. Hey that's another combination Faye." Faye rolled her eyes and Mary Clare shot up out of her seat slamming the door behind her.

"You jackass. That's not what she's talking about." Ed jabbed Ed.

"It's true I've always liked steak and potatoes. And don't call me a jackass."

"Faye's not talking about food and if you ask me Mary Clair wasn't either."

Ed got up from the bar. Slapped his partner on the shoulder. "Let's get to work. Least wise then I know what everybody's a talkin about!" The door slammed behind them.

"Don't know if that bell can take anymore misunderstandings." Faye mumbled again.

"What's that Faye?" Earl hollered from the back.

"Nothing! Just a whole lot of nothing."

Destiny and Adam stood out front of the café. But it was hard to carry on a conversation with all the patrons storming out of Faye's. They watched Mary Claire march off up the road toward the school. Ed and Ed burst out of the door bits of gravel flew past them as the truck got turned around and headed toward the house on third street. Once the dust cleared they resumed their conversation. Faye watched from inside.

"The name on the note. Our head of research said he would be a good contact. The office is close to you and they come highly recommended. They've done a lot of legal cases. If it were to come down to that." Adam began.

"Thanks. My dad insists I at least go that far with it."

"You told your family then?"

"Yes. I thought the sooner the better. I called them last night."

"How did they take it?"

"The reaction was varied. My dad was furious at first. I'll always be his little girl. He still sees me in pigtails. But he calmed down. Then said he'd contact his lawyer first thing in the morning. I told him to hold on. At least till I got back home and got settled. Then he told me the sooner I got home the better. What was I thinking flying all over the country with someone I hardly knew?"

"You told him about lunch then?"

"Yea. It was just in the course of the conversation. I mentioned a few comments made between us and then he started drilling me like I was on the witness stand."

"He's just concerned about you I'm sure."

"Yea. Lance took everything pretty good. He's   rock. He never drifts too far off center. He said we'd work it all ou   /hatever it took. Oh and then he said 'way cool Mom I've always w   :d to go to Monterey!' then I called Hannah. She is miss dram   :r brother always called her. She ranted and raved. Cried then got n   Then told me to get a grip. I haven't even been a widow for a year.   last thing she was talking about was the fact that I didn't (her first. Then…my phone went dead. I'll call her back tonight."

"Maybe it would have been easier to wait to tall   them face to face."

"No. I'm glad I called. We've always been a clo   amily. We tell each other everything. Well almost everything.   at sounds hypocritical now doesn't it?"

"It sounds like a great family."

There are some things in life that will never be e>   enced. He had conceded to this fact.

Be   Beep. Beep.
Sv   dripped from Adam's brow. The last truck had been
filled witl   ra blood. The fluid of life. It had to be unloaded double
time as th   nperature was critical. The inspector found Adam at the
loading d(
"S   ge place to find a doctor with so many achievements to
his credit.
"V   can I say inspector? I do what needs to be done."
"I'   oticed that. And you seem to have made an enemy in the
process. I   Walker. The brain dead patient's husband called the
hospital t(quite upset."
"I   n't report she was brain dead in fact she has a
consideral   mount of brain activity for someone in a coma."
"Y   ;o you reported to the hospital when they needed the
patient's   lition. And with that report they have staved off the
unpluggin   the life support for Mrs. Walker. This seems to be the
catalyst fo   r. Walkers rage. He has of course threatened the hospital
with endl   lawsuits. But it is the personal threat against you that
gave me c   : for alarm. Did the hospital authorities inform you of his
threats."
"Y   something was said."
"A   ou are not concerned."
A(thought briefly. "No."
"T   you don't think Mr. walker capable of doing bodily
harm?"
"P   iatry is not one of my licenses."
"B   f you were to guess. Given the description of the man
you saw g   g onto the elevator?"
"Y   suspect him of trying to kill his wife? I don't see the
motive?"
"N   e or not, I don't rule out anyone as a suspect. And I
advise you   be cautious."
A(headed into the truck for one more load. "Noted
Inspector.   right now we've got a truck to unload."

Chapter 53

Out of the corner of his eye he saw his mountain bike cruise by void of a rider.

Peeking out from under the open jeep hatch he watched it crash. The fence never knew what hit it. Looking back in the direction from which it came running shoes caught the balance of their wearer. Out of breath the woman came to a halt beside him.

"You're finally home. I've been riding by about every half hour."

"What's up?" hoping his tone didn't relate his mood. He tried to add a smile. The whole morning had been spent arguing with a team of editors trying to cut the guts out of an authors story. Publishing could be so unfair to writers. They poured their soul into a story, conveying a point. And if the wrong editor got a hold of it the story could be lost for the sake of the editors trying to give the readers what they thought, the readers wanted to hear.

Destiny started grabbing his bags out of the back of the car. "There's something I just have to tell you."

"Here give me those you don't have to carry my bags."

"I've got these, you get the rest."

At least giving in to Destiny's stubbornness was easier to take than the editors at the office. At least the heavy bag had been left for him. His masculine ego could only take so much.

She practically pushed him into the house. "Is this OK right here by the door?"

"Sure fine anywhere."

The chair cushion released a puff of dust from the force of the person plopping into it. "So, wait till you hear this."

"Whoa Destiny. Can you give me just five minutes. I'll put this in the other room then I'll be right back and we can talk."

From the bedroom door he glanced back into the living room. A form was walking back and forth. Bouncing up on tip toes. The bathroom was just down the hall to the spare room but she knew that. Hands clapped together in the front of her then swung wide. Her face was radiant with excitement. He should go back in there but it was too enjoyable to just stand there and see the excitement boil out of her every movement. No father could feel joy any deeper at his child's first step than Adam was feeling that very moment seeing this woman's joy for living be rekindled.

Destiny glanced in his direction. He was caught watching her. One finger flew up into the air. "Be right there." She certainly knew how to change his mood. The sour mood was a faint memory along with the catalyst it was formed from. He couldn't wait to hear the good news.

The chair puffed again at the pounce, he sat opposite on the sofa.

"Let's have it."

Saucer eyes widened, "I made an unbelievable discovery this morning. I was going through your books. I borrowed a couple today."

"Fine."

"It was right over there third shelf up, in the middle."

He squinted in that direction. The classics shelf.

"There it was To Kill A Mocking Bird! I love that book. My favorite book of all time I think. In fact I have a rating system. I have a journal of all the books I read. When I'm finished I write a little blurb about them in my journal and I rate them. I hold them up against To Kill A Mockingbird. And rate them accordingly they get mockingbird's"

"What?"

"Yes one for not so good, four for great and five for equal to or better."

"Has any book gotten five?"

"Not so far but I'm still looking."

"What did you like about the book?"

"You've read it? Surely you've read it? Everyone has."

"Yea."

"Yea? Just yea? Didn't you like it?"

"Loved it. But I want to hear what you liked, or obviously loved about it."

"We're getting off the point I was headed to, but I love to talk about books so I'll get to my point latter. I loved everything about the book, it was a complete circle of perfection."

"Explanation please?"

"It was a book enjoyed by women, enjoyed by men, and young readers alike. It was edge of your seat excitement, but not horror. The writers voice was pure poetry that carried and held the readers heartbeat in the palm of his hand made it race or calm all with the use of a mere combination of twenty six letters. It was wrought with life's lessons and conscience. The first time I finished reading it I raced out to get everything written by Harper Lee. But, nothing. The only book she ever wrote. But why write more when perfection had been reached. It was like the author was saying ' that's all I have to say, but you must be a smart girl. You found the book. You can figure out the rest on your own'. I could go on and on, but do you get my drift?"

"Yes. And I agree, but I've never heard it put so passionately. Why don't you come to New York and work for me. We could start you a book review column."

She waved off the invitation nonchalantly."I love the book." the pause was accompanied by the sigh of joy, "But on to my point. I saw it sitting on the shelf. And pow! It hit me. I have always loved that book."

"So you said."

"I have ALWAYS loved the book. Every since I can remember. And today I remembered when I read it. I was here. It was right after I started watching Mira for Pearl. It meant so much to me. Because it helped me understand the way people viewed Mira. It painted the whole picture for me not just the ugly stares she got or the whispers behind her back. It showed me that just like Bo living inside the dark house, people feared him. They feared him and hated him, because they didn't know him. If they could step out of the shadows for just long enough and get to know Mira they could have seen what I saw. They could have seen what Scout and Jem saw. And it might have changed their life too. I just didn't know how to show people Mira."

He leaned back. Studied her face. Studied her soul. The discovery being conveyed to him through this passionate display was how amazing it was that the memory of the book would stay with her and the memory of the circumstances at reading it would not. But there was a different even more amazing discovery that formed in his thoughts. She didn't learn to be understanding of people, forgiving and caring. It was her, it was inherent in her. A natural state of being. Back in school she came across as weak, but it was strength that she possessed. Her gentle understanding was strength in disguise. And she was stronger than all of us.

"Isn't that incredible?"

"Unbelievable! I'm sure there's some explanation, probably to do with selective something or other. Sort of like why do you remember how to brush your teeth or your times tables." She waved him off it was not scientific explanation that was sought but understanding.

"You're probably right but I was just so excited to discover that something I cared so much about my whole life, that book. Had come from here. It was like this time frame was with me all along. Like I never did lose it all together."

"Yea. I know what you mean." he was not trying to give her the reaction wanted, the understanding was true.

"Actually there was two things I wanted to talk to you about. The other thing is dreams."

"Still having those dreams?"

"Yea. Do you believe in dreams?"

He hesitated. Maybe she would keep talking before he had to answer. He was beginning to know her pretty well.

She got impatient waiting for his answer. "I keep having the strangest dreams. It's not the same dream. You know how some psychic people have the same dream over and over again. Anyway mine are different dreams but it's always the same scenario."

"I'm all ears."

She smiled. "I'm in a hospital. Comatose. And you are a doctor. My doctor. And you're trying to save my life."

He raised his eyebrows. "Interesting. I'm a doctor , I'm a spiritual guide. I promise you give me far too much credit in your dreams."

"Yea and it gets even stranger. Mira is this, I don't know. She's not a nurse but she is always by my side."

"Hmmm." he didn't know what else to say. But he was sure she would think of something.

"I was just analyzing the dreams trying to make sense of them."

"What did you come up with."

"The weirdest part is when I'm dreaming it's like that is every bit as real as this. Talking to you right now. Working on the house. And when I have a memory of Mira it's just as real just as present. Like there is no time difference. No fog to the memory. Every detail is sharp and vivid. So I get confused. What is real. What is the true reality."

"Maybe it's all real. Maybe there is no time and space. Only thoughts and everything can exist at the same time." He contributed.

"So, maybe I am in a coma somewhere in my mind. And maybe you are trying to save me. Are you trying to save me Adam?"

He thought long and hard. Lost all concept of the illusion of time. All his eyes registered were her ocean blue eyes. And he was diving deeper and deeper into the ocean. There was no space or time between them. Their thoughts touched each other in the dimension of true reality.

She repeated her question. "Does my dream have any basis? Am I psychic? Are you trying to save me?"

"I think there is always someone there for us. Someone always willing to save us. If we let them." He paused giving her a turn to speak. "However, if you needed saving. I would be happy to oblige fair lady."

Ocean blue eyes smiled at him. "That's what friends are for right? Because if it were in my power. And you needed it of course. I would try to save you." Her attempt at trying to tell him how much she appreciated him being there was falling short of what she intended. Why was it so hard to just come out and say what was on a person's mind. Why couldn't she just say. *Hey I don't think I could have gotten through these past days, weeks, months without you.*

She didn't know she already had saved him. The thought and memory of her, the very essence of her goodness had pulled him through the deepest tar pits of his mind. He was trying to save her. Call it favor for favor. But it was more than a favor to him. It was a privilege and a pleasure.

"Careful. I might have to hold you to that some day."

"I'll be up for it. Well I've got some thinking to do. As usual when I get done talking to you."

The chair cushion was left to resume its original form. "I'll let you get unpacked. I just had to tell you. I didn't think anyone down at the café would understand where I was coming form with this one." The blind on the window beside the door banged as the door was slammed.

Destiny was gone but the feeling from her excitement lingered in the room.

It was becoming clear to him that he was going to miss this woman. He was going to miss her too much. There was so much in her life that needed to be worked through at this time. He had come to know his place in the universe, in the grand scheme of things. But even with all this knowledge born of pain he couldn't find his place in Destiny's life. So that brought him to realize there wouldn't be a place for him there. He had done what he could for her. Lent her an ear. Rented her a miner's shack.

Everyone dealt with their pain and difficulty in their own unique way. Destiny ran herself ragged in the hills. Faye kept a bottle under the counter for the quiet afternoons, Ed bought himself a spyglass to view the world with. He on the other hand chose to disappear. Leave civilization behind so he could sort out his thoughts. Just him and God. He was never any good at goodbyes. So for now, he needed to disappear. He didn't even unpack. He called Tony on the way out to the airport. Tony wouldn't mind. He never did. Perhaps he had his own issues he was flying away from.

Chapter 54

Ed turned out to be a fair after hours roofer and [...] to be a fair friend helping Ed with the new roof after h[...] house was going to be Ed's in just a matter of days Ed t[...] would do the labor of the roofing at no charge if she w[...] the materials. The other Ed on the other hand agreed to [...] no charge as a favor to Ed.

This was the subject of conversation when Desti[...] Café. Mary Clare was accusing nearsighted Ed of bei[...] after all.

"I'm just getting some favors in the bank. My[...] going to last another year or two at best and then it's no[...] to have a few people around you that you've done a favo[...]

"Is that why you fixed my fence last year?"

"I didn't fix your fence I fixed my fence after [...] street fell on it. I couldn't help it if your side of t[...] happened to be attached to my side."

"Good cuz I'm not wanting to owe you a thing."

"Good. But if you keep that kitchen fan running[...] baking much more I'm going to have to fix your side o[...] you'll owe me some fresh cinnamon rolls."

"Well I wouldn't do too much fence mending if I [...] rolls are Pillsbury."

"Even Pillsbury would be better than what [...] microwave."

"What do you two got your fur standing on end [...] came around with the coffee pot.

"Mary Clare's accusing me of being nice."

"Oh, why don't you two just admit you lik[...] Everybody in the whole place sees the way you lo[...] counter at each other every morning."

Eyes bugged out behind thick glasses. Mary Clar[...] noises that would never be found in any dictionary no m[...] language. They both got out of their chairs and hit the d[...] time. Two bodies were wedged momentarily in the d[...]

enough fo
New Year
W
down ove
Th
except fo
Wall Stre
read pape
Fa
to clear a
Besides it
around it.
"Y
"T
full coffe
landlord?
"I
there whe
it?"
"N
De
curiosity.
Adam ha
They did.
Not unlik
disturbing
"N

popped them to the outside like a champagne cork on
ve. Ed turned left and Mary Clare Turned right.
put some bills on the counter turned his cup upside
mouth for the last drop of Faye's Café coffee.
ll on the door rang again leaving the place deserted
woman sitting at the table by the window. The un read
urnal lay on the opposite side of the table. In fact the un-
re stacking up.
ok the chair opposite Destiny. "Well, I sure know how
m don't I. Nobody ever accused me of being subtle.
e they got eyes for each other. Time they quit skirting
y aren't getting any younger."
hink they'll be back?"
rrow for sure if not tonight. It's meatloaf." putting the
t on the stack of papers Fay inquired. "Where's your
asn't been in for a few days."
't know. I haven't seen him either. His car hasn't been
icked up Digger for our run. But that's not unusual is

just thought you might know where he is."
y felt there was more to Faye's inquiry than simple
question reeked of undertones that perhaps Destiny and
re communication between them than landlord, tenant.
their communication was nothing more than friendship.
ye and Adam. But to have someone imply to more was

wouldn't know."

Chapter 55

Two and a half weeks in New York City. That's how long it took Adam to find his answer. Roy had told him, you don't need to go into the mountains in complete solitude, you just have to find complete solitude inside yourself. And if you can find that solitude in the middle of New York City then you can find solitude anywhere. So that was his place of solitude. He had turned his phone off for and told the office he was on a sabbatical. It wasn't the first time. They knew not to disturb him. They knew what ever broke while he was away could be mended on his return.

The answer didn't come all at once in one quick blast of lightening but rather a slow seeping in. like a sponge taking on water. For the first week all he could think about was Destiny. He would go for walks hours on end. At least a dozen people a day took him by total surprise thinking they were her. The joggers in the park especially. His heart ached. Then it turned to anger. Anger at life. Why did she even show up in Bendline? If everything in life was a test what was this testing? Or maybe this was the working out of his eons of years of karma. There were no mistakes, no happenstance. Everything in the universe was one giant precise formula being played out. The end result impossible to reach for there was a constant change in the quotients, each free will decision made by every human being changed the formula. But still in all there was no chance involved. It was all as it should be. The positives he had acquired in meeting her again after all these years were infinite. But that didn't mean the intersection of their paths would or were supposed to stay connected. At one point in a deep meditation he had seen a picture. It was golden illuminated threads all branching out and intersecting each other, an endless web woven out into infinity and it all started from one single point. He was that point and this particular web he was seeing was his life. He wondered which intersecting point was Destiny. If the vision could have lasted longer he knew he could have picked out which thread was hers, it would have been the one that shone the brightest.

Then he finally realized what he was doing was mourning for her leaving. He needed to transform this mourning energy to happiness for having had the chance to spend time with her again. Every time a sorrowful thought entered his mind her would replace it with a happy memory. He found there were plenty. More than plenty: a smile, a laugh, a smirk, a look of shock at seeing Trixie for the first time, tone of excitement in her voice, how her eyes opened so wide when she was telling a story about Mira. Whitey was right she should be a writer. For seven days the sorrowful thoughts were beaten off but there were plenty of happy memory pictures to take their place. He still had a whole storehouse full of happy memories. But after that week it was just the joyful memories that took control of his mind, the sorrow was subdued.

He became anxious, he had to get back to Bendline he had to explain to her what he had gone through. The system he had devised for dealing with this pain. Perhaps it would help her with dealing with her pain. But then after thinking about it he was sure she already knew. She had been through so much more than his pain. And yet she could still shine and give her light to others so that they could have happy memories to hold onto. Yes she already had a system.

Chapter 56

Faye was sporting a brand new hairdo. Instead of being backcombed and starched to death her hair was cut shorter and swung loose around her face. Brushing lightly on the top of her shoulders as she swung the coffee pot around the café. The seating order had changed. Whitey was moved across the center island and Mary Clare took up camp next to Ed. His glasses were fogged but it wasn't the steam from the coffee. She had taken off her ball cap to reveal a beautiful head of red curls. The other Ed had taken up reading the Wall Street Journal. Or at least part of it. The only part that really mattered in Bendline.

"Says here the DOW is up." Ed exclaimed.

"What do you care if the DOW is up or down. You don't even know what the DOW is." Ed retorted.

"Just trying to stay informed."

"OK Mr. know it all what's the DOW."

Ed put down the paper and turned to Ed and Mary Clare. "The DOW is the Dow Jones to be exact. One of several stock market indexes, created by the nineteenth-century Wall Street Journal editor Dow Jones and Company co founder Charles Dow. Dow compiled the index to gauge the performance of the industrial sector of the American stock market. It consists of 30 of the largest public companies in the US." he ended with a smirk.

Faye had to pick up her chin to close her gaping mouth. "Where'd you come up with all that?"

"Just cuz I work with a Jackass doesn't mean I am a jackass." Ed replied. Then went back to reading the paper.

"Don't call him a jackass." Mary Clare warned.

Destiny was making some last minute notes at the table by the window. The Wall Street Journal's were piled so high they had to start stacking them on the floor.

The bell on the door chimed. Everyone turned. A man dressed in brown called out for Ed.

"Which one?" they both looked up.

"Ed Sweeney."

"That would be me." The soon to be home owner stood at attention.

"Need your signature this one's overnight with a signature required."

Ed puffed up like he had just been elected mayor. The brown suit was no more than out the door than Ed had the envelope opened.

"Miss Destiny! This here's the papers on the house. We just signed them yesterday."

The call of her name broke her concentration. "Oh, you got them good."

"But they didn't have to come so special delivery."

"I wanted to make sure you had them in your hand before I left. So I requested overnight from the court house."

"What do you mean."

"Well, I'm leaving tomorrow afternoon. If everything wasn't in order it would be a hassle making any correction clear across the country."

"You're leaving tomorrow?"

"Yes. Tomorrow."

Everyone in the whole place turned to stare at her. Earl came out of the kitchen to stand in the doorway of the swinging doors. It was as if they had never heard the words uttered before.

"You knew I was leaving."

"I guess we just didn't realize it was tomorrow." Faye explained with a quiver to her voice. "That doesn't leave much time for a going away bash."

"Oh, no. No bashes. I've still got packing and this whole list of things to do." actually she was looking to avoid any going away tears. Even from little old Bendline.

"We can at least all meet down here tonight for dinner. Earl what's on the special?"

"Whatever Destiny wants." Earl pulled the corner of his apron up to wipe his hands.

Destiny shook her head. "I'm going to cry. But how does spaghetti sound?"

"Spaghetti it is. I'll start the sauce." Earl disappeared into the back.

"I'll get on the phone." Faye said. "What about Adam? Has

anybody seen Adam?" No one responded. Destiny shook her head. "I hope he hasn't gone off and gotten himself killed. Flying around the country everyday in a jet. You know it's just a matter of time."

Destiny felt sick. It was true. It was just a matter of time. She looked around the room, everyone chattering who they were going to call, what they were going to bring. It was just a matter of time for James. And it was all just a matter of time before every chair in Faye's Café was permanently empty. The hills were calling her name. She had to go for a run. She had run earlier that morning. It still didn't hurt bad enough.

Digger didn't accompany her. Perhaps her master got home and was giving her some well deserved attention. That would be Destiny's prayer. Instead of the ominous statement Faye had made. Hopefully Adam's matter of time was not up yet.

The rocks gave way under her feet. The rocks were only temporary too. Only held in place for a brief moment of time. The hold on the mountainside might be weathered away by rain and wind. The rocks might dissolve into gravel, later sand. The shrubs and sage were only temporary. They would grow, bloom, reseed and eventually they would die, decay and return to the elements from which they were formed. The rabbit setting the running pace in front of Destiny would soon run its last race. By some form or another it would inevitable meet with its demise and become a meager meal for the continuing food chain. The remnants left to fertilized the soil. Everywhere she looked all manner of life and element, the trees, the springs, mountains the stars even the sun itself was destined to return to whence it was formed. Everything was in a constant direction of change perhaps slower than the average eye would detect but none the less everything was changing. And not to sound dreadful but it was all headed in the direction of demise. But not death. All the basic building blocks remained they just changed form. What really existed, the part of everything, everyone that stayed the same, ever constant, would never die. The spark of life was absolute. James's body had changed in chemical makeup, his matter of time had come. But the spark behind his body's make up, the animator to his arms, legs, his heart was still in existence. That did not and would not ever die.

This was perhaps what Adam was talking about. There was a voice inside her head screaming. Yes you've got it. That's the truth.

She couldn't wait to tell Adam.

Destiny screamed out in burning anguish. Knees buckled as the climb was halted. She laid down in the dirt, a rock for a pillow. Pulse whooshed in her ears, it was as though ever inch of her body jerked with each heartbeat. The sky spun around in slow motion. If her arms would have been big enough she would have embraced the whole sky. She finally understood. James was gone but he was by no means dead. His spark was still ignited.

The decent down the mountain was slow and methodical. Every blade of grass observed every rock stepped over. The world was alive. And it was OK if she took her time to appreciate every moment of everything. Because it finally hurt bad enough.

Chapter 57

The little house two blocks up and four blo
transformed to a cozy cottage for two and a half people
game of chess was nearly a checkmate. The papers sign
the sale to Ed and his wife. The kids, family and friend
York had been running Destiny's phone bill up. It was
to Swan Drive and use some of her new found knowled
It would be possible now to build up a life back there
finally hit the ground and she was ready to take the fir
journey.

The bags waited by the door. As if knowing s
different about this day Digger came clear down the di
up with her. The mornings were getting cooler but it still
long to build up a sweat.

Destiny gave Digger a kiss on top of the head.
miss you girl. I just might have to get me a dog back l
won't be anything like you."

The run began. Slow at first. The climb w
morning. The pace wasn't as pushed. The pain wasn't i
of her thought. Up, up, and still up further. The highest
so far. Digger began to pant heavy. Destiny decided to
and start the circle. The rocks were unfamiliar. Jumping
came down hard on her tailbone when she lit. "Crap.
make for an uncomfortable plane ride."

The two dropped down in elevation to where
looser and less rocky. The race was on. "Come on girl le
Digger stayed right at her side. Droplets of drool
animals tongue splashing on her partners leg. All she
laugh and yell as the pleasure mounted. They leaped r
bush after bush. A rabbit took the lead for a moment but
fast for him he gave up and let them pass.

A newly painted door with the words 'Ed's Hauli
Man Service' framed a man sitting by the side of the roa
mountains with spy glasses. There they were. Her pony
out straight behind her. Her leg muscles had toned s

over was
e life size
complete
ck in New
to return
ack home.
r feet had
ep on that

thing was
e to meet
ldn't take

going to
. But she

asier this
forefront
had gone
the turn
er one she
t's gonna

soil was
ck it up."
from the
d do was
after rock
were too

nd Handy
tching the
was flying
ey didn't

jiggle. Ed
Bendline.
        Th
they were
lens hopir
waited. N
He lookec
The old C
        Th
turned on
and they \
hands wri
had a harc
was a holo
were dow
        Th
        Fa
"Adam. It
        Hi
        "E
paramedic
        Ac
about the
        Ru
make it. F
the runwa
        Hc
out of bre
a stretche
sloughed :
got closer
        Fl:
put a strar
back and s
        "C
swing. Kio
        Ac
same trea

going to miss waking up early to watch the hills around
final show was playing, he kept the glasses to his eyes.
inners disappeared. One second they were there. Then
e. He waited for a moment straining his eyes through the
) see a glimpse of them climbing out of a washout. He
in of them. Something inside told him this wasn't right.
und the perimeter of the mountains and got his bearings.
on mine! He called the paramedics then he called Faye.
ifé was empty. Faye and Earl held down the fort and
two way radio. In the kitchen. They made an exception
both in the back, Faye had crossed the line. Eyes wide,
g, glued to the speaker. It didn't sound good. The trucks
e reaching the scene. There was no longer a road. There
out six feet in diameter, it went straight down. Two men
: hole on ropes. But no word yet.
int door Jingled. "Hey Faye? Where are you?"
ame through the swinging doors in the back. Face white.
estiny and Digger. The Crimson mine."
nd found balance on the counter in front of him. "How?"
vas watching through the glasses. He called the
verybody's up there."
pushed off and swung open the door. "Shit! I warned her
ts."
ig up the hill on foot was faster than the jeep would
illed Tony on his cell as he left. Tony was at the end of
idy to take the jet to Vegas. Adam told him to sit tight.
s right about getting out there faster. He didn't even feel
He searched the faces in the crowd. The paramedics had
: up on the ground next to the hole. It gaped and still
et stepped too close the edge. He heard screaming as he
ie paramedic unit. It was Destiny's voice. She was alive.
g her arms in the air screaming like a hurt animal. They
her and she would tear it off. They tried to make her lie
iunched one of them in the face.
:t her! Leave me alone! Go get her!" she took another
. the man closest to her, he tumbled to the ground.
reached the side of the stretcher but she gave him the
it. Pushing him away time after time. Tears streamed

down her cheek forming mud packs. If they could only understand they had to go back in, they had to go get her. She was not the only one down there. She made another attempt "Go get HER!!!" Dirt flew up from her every time she took a swing. Blood gushed from a knee and a scrape went clear up the leg into area too high for her modesty. One cheek bone was beginning to swell and a cut by her eye dripped blood blurring the vision.

She managed to break free from the team trying to tie her down. She made a run for the hole in the ground. Adam caught her around the waist just before their feet gave way. The mad woman spun to face him and started beating his chest screaming. "We have to get Her! She's still down there! Destiny dug her fingernails into Adam's face trying to get him to understand. She raised up as high as she could to stare him eye to eye. "We have to get MIRA!"

The breeze caught chestnut colored silk and pulled it gently from her face. All eyes were on her. The squawk on the radio the only audible vibration breaking the tomb of silence. The door was open all the way. Memories flashed before her like pages in a book caught by the breeze. Her mind recorded the events to be remembered at any time she chose now. She chose one out of the thousands to relive in this moment. Their eyes were one and they saw the same scene.

Pearl had let Destiny take Mira exploring. Once they hit the outskirts of town Destiny let Mira be the leader. A walking stick in one hand and a lunch box in the other. Mira had insisted on carrying her own lunch. And Mira could be very insistent when she wanted to be. Since her attention span was so short it would no doubt be discarded in a matter of minutes once the great outdoors captured her interest. March, march, march. Up the mountain they climbed. Mira sang a song as they marched but Destiny was not familiar with the words.

When Mira got winded they stopped to rest. Destiny instructed Mira to sit very still and she would sneak up on a lizard on the rock and catch it.

Mira put her finger over her mouth and "Shhhhhed." being quiet was one of her favorite things to do because she loved to make the "Shhhhh."

Destiny began to creep. Slower, slower, quieter. Each time she looked back to check on Mira she got a "Shhhhhh."

Eyes forward, closer, almost there. Her hand reached out. At the same moment she looked back to see the expression on Mira's face.

Mira had a puzzled look on her face she looked down at her feet. Something was wrong, something was strange.

Destiny saw Mira's feet sinking . She jumped up, ran, grabbed Mira around the middle and they both plunged into the earth followed by hundreds of rocks. The ground all around shook. The earth continued to belch dirt and rock after them. They fell for what seemed eternity. A feeling almost like flying. Then nothing. The earth caught them in her hand but she was not gentle. The limbs of their bodies bent and twisted out of normal position. The earth blanketed them with itself.

Adam was in the miners shack. His father found displeasure with his performance at the basketball game the prior night. He lay across the bed throwing a basket ball into the air. The lines spun to a blur then fell back into his grasp. The curtain across the hole in the wall reached out into the room releasing a cloud of thick dust. Did he hear a scream?

Slowly he sat. The air was thick. Too thick to stay in that hell hole of a shack.

Another noise? He pulled the tail of his shirt over his mouth and nose, pulled back the curtain, listened, nothing. A couple steps back into the mountain the air was too thick to enter. He hated that hole anyway.

Climbing the side of the mountain soon answered his questions as to what had taken place. The air shaft had caved in. What used to be a three or four foot diameter hole going straight down was now a twenty foot wide sink hole. The sides slanting down into a cone. Small rocks still rolled down to find a new place to rest at the bottom of the cone.

Then he saw it. A child's lunchbox.

He ran to the house. His father was still passed out. He slapped both sides of his face. He came up swinging.

"A cave in! Get up dad call somebody there's been a cave in!"

His father sat, rubbing his eyes. Adam held him upright by the front of his shirt.

"I think it's Mira."

"What's the matter with you?"

"I think it's Mira trapped in the shaft."

His father still looked disoriented.

"The retarded girl!"

"What do I care?"

Adam threw him back against the bed. "You Bastard!"

Adam yelled for help up and down the street. The neighbor came running to the door out of breath, Adam instructed her to call for help. He headed back to the shack.

A flashlight revealed little and got worse the further back in the tunnel he went. The air so thick it could be chewed but the grit wore at the teeth. He hit a wall of dirt and rock. The beam from the flashlight revealed it went clear to the top of the tunnel on a slant. The rays covered the wall inch by inch deciding which would be the best course to take. The light flashed for a moment of something that looked out of place. A different color than the rest of the dirt. The beam went back. A shoe about two feet from the roof. And a hand scraped and bloody not a foot away.

He began pawing at the soil. Pulling the dirt from under the body. As he pulled the limbs began to loosen. The leg was exposed to the waist. But the head would be the most important end. The body was face down. The shoulder now exposed. Rocks and boulders went rolling down the mound. There was a large boulder wedged at the roof and the mound just above the bodies head. If it gave way the skull would be crushed. Carefully he pulled the dirt back. A face was turned in his direction. Destiny! No air was felt from the nostrils. Time was precious. He dug and dug, his fingers bleeding. His lungs aching for oxygen. More than half of the body was uncovered. It felt loose enough to pull. He might dislocate some joints, he'd have to take the chance . He held one arm and one leg and pulled. Slowly inch by inch the other limbs sucked from the grips of the earth.

She was lifeless in his arms. He lay her on the ground outside the shack. He could hear sirens now. Still no air escaped her lungs. Gently he laid her head on the hard ground. Bent her head back. He traced her lips. wet with blood with his thumb. He bent over her, opened her mouth and exhaled into her body. Both palms pushed the air back out of her lungs. He breathed into her lungs again. And repeated the sequence.

"Come on Destiny!"

He turned his head away from her, inhaled as deeply as he could as if taking in a different force from nature. With lips against hers one last time he pushed the air out of his body with all the force he had and breathed life into her.

Eyelashes caked with mud fluttered then opened.   "Mira!" she whispered. Then her eyes closed.

The ambulance arrived followed by two sheriff cars. The attendant ran toward them with an oxygen tank in hand. They strapped the mask over her face. Loaded her up in the ambulance and she was gone. He would never see her again.

"You." she whispered. "You saved my life."

Eyes not wanting to look away even afraid to blink for fear she'd disappear down into the earth again. "Yes."

"And Mira?"

His head barely moving just a slight back and forth. "No."

"I. I loved her so much."

"I know. She knows." He wanted to add he was sorry but there would be time to fill in the blanks later. She melted into his arms her head buried deep as if she wanted to open up his chest and climb right into his heart. She didn't know she was already there. He held her tight. The world continued to spin, the sun rose, the breeze blew. He didn't care because they were in a world all their own and for now time stood still. Not caring how long it took how long she wanted to stay. He would be right here for her.

The words were muffed from pressing so hard into his chest. But he understood them all the same. "Digger?"

"Digger's just fine."

Chapter 58

All the regulars showed up for the morning coffee at Faye's. No one wanted to miss Destiny's send off. The accident had changed her travel plans. Adam had insisted Tony fly her home on his jet. Her leg was still tender and the stitches hadn't come out of her head. The private jet would be more comfortable, walking around was even an option. Faye poured a final cup of coffee. The steaming genie rose in front of her face and danced a final dance. "Now this one's definitely on me." gave her a hug.

"Thanks Faye, I'm going to miss your coffee. In fact I'm going to miss everything about your place."

"Just don't forget us this time." Faye winked.

Adam was late to coffee. He had taken a drive into Vegas. Some last minute business before heading back east. Ed and Ed had to head off to work. They had an employee now so they had to keep close tabs on him.

The door jingled and a familiar face peeked around the corner. Adam had taken a few extra paces outside before entering the café. In a matter of hours this woman would be starting her old life back up again. He would no longer be in the daily routine of it. And she would no longer be in his. Could a heart hurt this bad and still remain beating? He thought not? This was what Destiny must be feeling. He planned on buying a pair of running shoes the first chance he got. Maybe they would help. He stared into her crystal eyes from across the cafe and gave in to their gravitational pull.

"Looks like you're about ready." The words were slow passing over his vocal chords to keep the quiver from escaping. Long deep breaths. He felt like the man in an old western getting a bullet removed without the aid of anesthetic.

"I guess. It's hard to leave though." The whole time she had spent in Bendline, in the company of these people, this man. Words had never been so hard to come by.

"I don't like good-byes and I don't like good-bye presents so that's not what this is. It's just something I thought you might use." From behind his back he withdrew a spiral notebook and slid it across the table. "I took this away from you once. I wanted to be the one to give it back. I think you just found a bestseller in your head. When you get it done give me a call. I know a guy that wants to read it when you're done."

"I'm speechless."

He raised his eyebrows and smiled. "That's not a good start to your book."

"Did I. Did I ever thank you?"

"For what?"

"For saving my life."

"You didn't have to."

The door jingled again. No one came through. Instead Digger rounded the edge of the door. In her mouth was the end of a leash. At the other end of the leash was a miniature Digger, a big red bow around her neck. Digger sat beside Adam and the new pup headed straight for Destiny's feet and laid down on top of them.

She couldn't hold back the tears of joy, nor did she want to try.

Chapter 59

Tom couldn't remember a clearer day for flyi   across the
country. Adam had asked him to be a tour guide on the   . At each
point of interest he would turn on the intercom and tip   jet to one
side or another to give Destiny a good look. She could   he figures
on Mt. Rushmore without the assistance of binoculars.

The great plains went on forever. Never had she   land that
went on forever without a mountain or trees to define bo   ries.

Adam disliked this part of the trip the most. Bu   ay it held
even a darker cloud. The expanse of nothingness was lik   e distance
that was growing between them. Each space of   between
conversations grew longer. In a matter of a couple of h   he would
be walking her to her door. Unloading her belongings. G   her back
to the arms of the chair she loved so much. To tell h   w he felt
would be too much of a burden for her to know. But   had to do
something. He had to make sure the distance between t   remained
crossable.

The pup lay sleeping on Destiny's lap. Eyes fc   d out the
window at the miles of land being crossed. There were   any miles
of the same that it felt like she was suspended in time a   pace. Not
moving forward or backward. It was as if her life were   ned up in
that one moment of realization. She was stuck. And did   now how
to move. Tears welled in her eyes for reasons she   n't know.
Perhaps out of habit alone. Would her life ever be norma   in.

He chose his words carefully. "I just want you to   w Destiny
that I'll be here for you. I'm only a call away. For any   son at all.
Just call."

A few quick blinks made the tears disappea   t not the
emptiness. "In case I fall down any more deep dark hole
"In case of anything."

"Thanks I'll keep your number on my cell pho   Her gaze
went back to the miles crossing under them. "I didn't   it would
feel like this. Going back home. I thought I would be ha   . But each
mile we cross retches at my stomach more and mor   m afraid.
Afraid of what I'll find back home. Or what I won't find.

"W   ould turn back. I haven't put the shack up for rent yet.
It's there   s long as you need it. If you need more time. Just say the
word."

"I   t do that either. It's like I'm stuck. I've crossed the point
of no retu   nd I don't want to move forward. I'm just suspended. I
don't sup   you could ask the pilot to just stop right here?"

"I   ld ask. But I think your bordering on asking for a
miracle."

"D   't hurt to ask I guess." The pup moaned and stretched in
her lap. "I   s just starting to feel grounded in Bendline. Just starting
to feel ha   gain. I don't know if I can find that back home."

He   s without comment. Because he knew exactly how she
felt.

Th   lence grew with only the high pitch of the engines to
keep it fro   eing a complete void.

At   instruction he pulled around to the back of her house to
unload he   gs. A pain in his heart sounded as they neared the chair
with soft c   ions and rose print.

De   y stopped in front of it. "That's the one. The chair I told
you about

"L   s as comfortable as you described it."

Th   or stuck not wanting to open, it mirrored the feelings of
the keepei   he key.

Sh   rned to face the man behind her burdened with her
possessioi   Would you like to come in? I could offer you some
coffee. N   s good as Faye's but I promise it's not stale I put the
grounds ii   freezer before I left. But that's all I have I'm afraid. The
first thing   ed to do I guess is grocery shop." But her rambling was
what she i   zed to be as a waste of breath.

To   ay the inevitable seemed pointless and a waste of both
their prec   breaths. She had some major obstacles to overcome in
her life. N   nlike every person in the world. The only difference he
didn't lov   ery person in the world. Only this one. So her pain had
become h   in. But the battles she faced now were battles only she
could wag   ly victories she alone could claim. There was no sense
keeping h   om her destiny.

"I   er get back. Tom wanted to keep to the flight schedule."

He   nd stretched out to his. He took it in his not wanting to let it go.

"Thank you for everything, thank you for saving my life. I know I don't have to say it but I want to express it."

"Well, thank you for bringing life to Bendline. Don't be a stranger. Call me some time."

"I got your number."

He couldn't help himself he pulled her into an embrace. She didnprotest. If she could have heard his thoughts she would have heard. "come home. I'll be waiting. No matter how long it takes."

He released her back to her life. Slowly walked back to his car and his life.

The passing eye would assume the shadow following close behind held no threat, no concern, no sorrow or despair. Only a dark spot on the ground as result of the man's form standing between the ground and the orb in the sky.

Chapter 60

Beep. Beep. Beep.

The worst storm of the century the television had said. On the fourth floor of the building the people below hurried into nearby buildings to avoid being hit by blowing debris. It resembled a war zone. Nature against mankind. And nature was winning. The power went out three times in the course of the day. And now the hospital was solely running on generator power. Branches broke loose from trees and hurled at any moving object in their path. The only good thing about the storm that Mira could see from her perch was the injured didn't have far to go if hospitalization was needed. The hallways however were quickly filling up. The alarms and calls for help were constant on the PA. Adam had only been in once to check on Destiny. As he put it he had to do what he could while he was here. It wouldn't be right to just stand by and watch.

Whack! Mira jumped backwards. Something, she wasn't sure what, had hit the window. A hole the size of a baseball was now letting in wind, cold and rain. Glass pieces sprayed as far away as the door. A few landed in Destiny's lap but she was otherwise unaffected. But the temperature in the room was quickly dropping. The hole needed to be covered. She would only abandon her post for a few minutes. Adam was far too busy to bother with this trifle event. She went in search of something to patch the hole. Minutes ticked by.

The officer posted outside Destiny's door had been called away to deal with more urgent events. The noise in the hallways was almost deafening. Alarms for every level of emergency rang out. Calling all that could help to report immediately.

The door to Destiny's room finally opened once again. The wind being let in through the hole in the window had made the air in the room damp and cold. The blinds slapped the side of the wall hard as if being held against their will. Striking out to be released from their captor. The scene was studied by the new visitor. Eyes coming to rest on the other captor in the room. The one still sleeping in the bed. The visitors shadow drew a curtain of darkness over Destiny's face. The halo on the monitor turned to panic. The heart rate increased. Even in her deep sleep she felt the danger coming ever closer.

The dark shadow circled the bed. A wolf toying with its prey. Eyes traced the machines power source. Last time the tubes had been pulled out. But the power to the machines were still connected. Once the tubes were replaced Destiny was back on life support in no time. The shadow would not make the same mistake again. Pulling the plugs out one by one a scalpel was drawn from the pocket. As sure as a surgeon the cords were severed from the plugs.

An attempt at an explanation and apology was carried on a whisper to Destiny's subconscious. It was met by shock and confusion. The last words she would hear from this physical world. The door to her room opened one last time. The halls still in a state of chaos. The shadow went unnoticed as the door to the elevator closed.

Back in the quiet of the room. The damage had been done. There was no turning back. It was over. Destiny became weightless. Floating. Free. The freedom gave her just enough strength to utter a few words. "James. Thank. You."

Mira entered the room puffing hard from her search. Cardboard and ducktape hit the floor as her eyes took in the disastrous scene. Hands traced the machine cords to their decapitated ends. There was no halo around the light on the monitor. A hand on Destiny's chest felt no heartbeat. Water welled up in Mira's eyes, one last blink released the dam. She reached for the call button in her pocket. Not knowing whether Adam would want to go now or wait to help this race of people some more. She would abide with whatever he decided. Destiny would be in good hands now.

Adam came through the door just as the backup generators gave out. The room was black but he knew what was before him.

Somewhere between the second and third floor the elevator came to a stop. A man crouched in the corner of the cube and began to weep.

Chapter 61

"WAKE UP!"

Destiny shielded her eyes against the intense light from inside the palace. Forgetting at first where she was. Then the feeling of bliss sank in. A stack of books at her feet. More on the table before her. A huge open book in her lap. A hand still rested halfway down the page marking the place before exhaustion took over.

"Oh. Wow. I must have dosed off." Destiny reached out and stretched. Rubbed her eyes and yawned.

Adam had just slammed another stack of books on the table. "No time for that. You have a lot of reading to do. Come on."

"What? What's wrong? Are you mad? Did I do something wrong? Am I not supposed to fall asleep? I don't know how long I was out but I don't think it was very long. The book didn't even fall off my lap."

"I'm not mad. You just need to hurry. Get to reading. I'll bring you some more coffee."

I. I thought there wasn't any hurry in this place. I thought I could go at my own pace. You know digest along the way."

"When you came there was time. What I thought was ample time to get what you needed. But events have changed in your physical world. Now you are out of time. So you need to hurry and get as much out of this level, as you can."

She looked around. The cases of books were endless. Her concentration was fading. Anxiousness grew. What was he talking about. This new attitude of his was completely contrary of her last memory. She rubbed her temples to try to stay focused. The light around her was dimming.

He grabbed her arm. Hard. "Stay with me. Do you understand! You have to stay clear. Fight. Fight to stay conscious."

"I'm suddenly so tired. Adam I just need to sleep just for a little while. You said it was too much for some people. This place needed to be taken in small doses." eyes blinked slower and slower. Staying shut for longer periods of time.

"I won't lose you. Destiny do you understand?" he was shaking her shoulders now.

Eyes popped open but she didn't know for how long. She felt heavy all over. Looking around at the books. It was the last thing she wanted to do. Read a book. "What do you mean you won't lose me again? There is so much I don't understand Adam. But right now…"

He shoved a book in her face. "Look! Read the book. I'll read with you." he began reading at light speed. Turning page after page. His voice was like fluid. A rambling stream. She was a leaf floating and bobbing along. Going where ever the current would take her. Her chin hit her chest.

Her cheek hurt. Stung. He was slapping her face. Her eyes saw red. "What are you doing? Just let me sleep and I promise I'll read double time when I wake up. But I can't right now."

"You don't have time Destiny. Events have been set in motion that are unstoppable. You need knowledge and understanding to make the final jump. Or stay for another cycle. You don't want to stay another cycle."

She looked around the room again. If the books represented all she needed to know and understand in a matter of minutes. It was impossible. She didn't know why or even what it was he was talking about but she just knew she didn't want to stay another cycle. Another cycle would mean the labyrinth again. Tears welled in her eyes. She didn't want to go back not on single step. She had come so far.

She looked into his eyes. Plead her case without saying a word. "Can you help me?"

He nodded slowly. In a whisper he spoke. "Sometimes the greatest lesson of a lifetime is to learn to ask for help. It is the final realization that you are not in this world alone but part of the whole." with that he stepped toward her placed a hand flat on either temple.

Her eyes grew heavy once more but for a different reason. The last thing she saw were his eyes. Deeper, deeper, his eyes drew her. She closed her eyes. And. Let. Go. Let go of all the chains, obstacles, memories. And she began to expand. Bigger. Bigger. Bigger. Extending out in all directions. She didn't grow in physical size but in understanding. Knowledge and understanding poured into her from everywhere. All things past, present and the chance of being was within her realm of understanding. Faster and faster the information poured. Faster and faster the expansion continued. Instead of feeling tired it was the exact opposite. Her alertness heightened. Nothing or place escaped her awareness. Faster, faster, faster. The complete expansion, working of the universe were before her eyes. Objects were no longer finite but merely concentrations of energy. The energy was atoms with millions of miles between them yet how could that be when object she was looking at was a flower. Electrons orbiting the atoms nucleus just like planets orbiting the sun. Destiny opened her eyes as if on cue but Adam hadn't uttered a word. His hands still on her temples his eyes still locked with hers. Then it happened.

A blinding flash. Then calm. Absolute calm. The peace that passeth all understanding.

All things fell away. The glass ceiling came crashing down falling all around them only to be shards of light upon closer examination. The walls were the same as they crumbled. The floor beneath their feet gave way but instead of falling they remained suspended on the beams of light. There was nothing but her and Adam. Standing face to face. Reading each other's thoughts Destiny said "Did I make it?"

Adam replied. "You did".

Chapter 62

It was raining in Bendline. It hardly ever raine(Bendline. Digger lay curled up next to the wall of windows in t ffice. Her master hard at work pouring over manuscripts. A fluff il began a steady beat on the floor. A soft woof.

"It's just the rain girl. You're not used to the : d." Adam assured his companion.

No response came from the second knock at the (. The jeep was in the drive a positive indication he was home. Th in sheeted off the porch roof. It was like looking out from behind a erfall. The door was open. It always was.

"Adam?" Destiny called softly. A rush of m(ries came back. She couldn't count how many times his name h; een called out in this manner.

Digger's head popped up from her paws she star t the man. Why was he still sitting there?

He set down the reading glasses put both palms (le arms of the office chair.

"Shall we go save the fair lady again?"

"Woof!"

She was closing the door behind her, drippin in on the hardwood floor.

"Destiny."

The room was dark from overcast sky. The li cascading from the wall of windows backlit the silhouette of a m; \ thin line of vibrant light formed between the space where his n met the light.

"Hello there." Her voice was almost a whisper. hint of a question at the end. As if she had woken from a dream a ecognized the person in front of her but needed a moment to get her rings.

He crossed the room and stopped short of the pi e of water dripping from her hair forming at her feet.

"What are you doing here?"

"You're heading out." Her eyes looked down is packed bags that waited beside the door.

"N
flying in t
De
deep, brea
Lisa smile
"I
"S
The phon
hour. Yet
"H
"K
"T
Sh
shock or a
it by ear.
I've know
with you a
do that yo
can't be o
transferred
you didn'
soon, aga
compellin
through q
You survi
After all o
life and ev
"N
was with
when I wa
me to con
smiled. A
"E
"A
mean actu
real? Was
full of ligl
with Mira

called Tony and canceled. It was just the usual, no sense

y let her eyes trace the details of the room. She inhaled
g in the warmth. Her eyes came to rest in his. The Mona
ned up and filled the room with light.

l to ask you a question."

Anything." He wondered what the question might be.
had given her still worked. He checked it every half
she was in person to ask her question.

long have you known?"

n what?"

was dead."

new. She was calm. Composed. He couldn't read any
r in her voice. The truth, the whole truth? Or maybe play
nd is only a state of being. But to answer your question.
nce the millisecond it happened. I knew before. I was
lly. You had to let go of the physical ties completely. To
nd to uncover all your memories. You see the crossing
lete without the total mind and all its memories being
ou were stuck in between. It was my fault last time that
eak the ties completely. I didn't want to pull you too
couldn't bear to see you in pain." his tone soft and
e same as when he told her this before. "We put you
a bit. Hammered your brain with everything we had.
you died so to speak. But I wouldn't say you are dead.
is," he waved his hand around the room, "don't you see
leath are just a state of   mind. How did you find out?"

She came to see me. I was just waking up and there she
hand outstretched to me. The same as I always saw her
re. Only this time I knew what she wanted. She wanted
ith her. I told her I couldn't that she was dead. She just
knew. I knew everything."

thing?"

ure of speech. I still have questions. Where was I? I
? Where did I exist? Was I in the hospital? Was that
Bendline with you and Digger? Was I in a crystal palace
ams and knowledge for the taking? Or was I in the past
ng down a mineshaft? Or was that the past. I don't even

know on a time line which events came first second or last. It all seems equally real, equally now. Or was it all just in my mind?"

"Everything is real and everything is in your mind. The only place you were is the only place you will ever be. Right here. And the only time there will ever be is right now."

"I recall there being an impending cataclysm I was trying to wane. Did it work? Did we save the end of the world?"

"Destiny. Nothing ever ends it just transforms."

"Then did we transform the world?"

"We transformed your world. That's what all of this was ever about. Was transforming your world. But your world and the whole are one and the same. So in transforming your world we transformed the whole world."

"But I remember a horrific storm. Scores of casualties."

He shook his head and smiled. "Define casualties. If nothing dies then there can be no casualty. There was a fair amount of suffering. But in time all wounds will heal. There are those that choose to advance only by the path of pain. Still multitudes although not realizing it, subconsciously accepted the aid of those, like you, that have a heart so vast they would do almost anything to avert the pain and suffering of others. So the suffering was not as severe as it might have been. What I'm trying to say, is the world was better for you and your compassion having been in it. "

She took a long pause to ponder, digest this. The room, the books. "I want to thank you for rescuing me."

A slight bow of his head. "A pleasure my lady."

"That sounds familiar. Have you rescued me before?

His smirk revealed the answer. "Always, a pleasure my lady."

"When? Where?"

He shook his head. "It would fill volumes."

"Today's my birthday. I'd like to go home. And hear a good story."

Stepping out of the water toward him her arms wrapped around him as his lungs took in a sharp inhale and held it. Her head rested against his beating heart. His unique spark of life. She was the rib that was taken from his side at the beginning of time. He pulled her closer in and their souls became one again.

There would no longer be a shadow following close behind, no longer standing between the ground and the orb in the sky. She had finally become one with the light.

Epilogue

The lights came on in the lecture hall. Sniffs and outright blubbers could be heard. Long sighs. Finally someone in the front row honked his nose to rival any diesel on the highway. The mood was lightened but not forgotten. Like the mood at a funeral. The undertone is solemn, but even though comic relief is offered everyone still knows why they are there.

"So that's it. That's the end, but one main rule for a writer is that it's not necessary to input 'The End" it is understood. And with the case of some stories the last page could just as easily be the first page of the second volume. Because let's admit it, time never ends and neither does the story.

"Time is out. Are there any brief questions?"

One young woman rose in the front row. "Is any part of the story true? Are you Destiny?"

A smile. "All stories are true to me. Somewhere out there I'm sure the story was lived. And I think if a writer stops to think about it and be truthful with himself he is all the characters in the story. The writer has drawn from his or her self what he could do or be in any given situation. It's not to say that the writer is a priest, a nun, a prostitute, father, mother, child, even murderer. But, it also holds true that he has the potential to be all of these. Each of us contain all characteristics. What makes us unique is which ones we choose to bring into the spotlight and which ones we choose to hold back. But the writer knows himself well enough to describe to the reader that character so that the reader can relate to the personality on paper."

Somewhere off the stage a person cleared their throat indicating there was just no time left.

"Thanks, I really have to go and so do you. So happy writing. Oh, wait a minute I have to hear what you have to say."

A young man in the top row third seat from the left was on his feet. His voice carried loud and strong without the aid of a microphone. "And God said, *it was good.*" He began a slow steady clap that resonated off the walls. A clap that was in no hurry to get to any destination. Every student stood and joined in the applause.

The writer stepped to the microphone one last time. A sparkle in her eye reflected the overhead lights back at the crowd. "I'm speechless. You see the magic of words. All I can muster is theologically speaking. God Bless You All."

Made in the USA
San Bernardino, CA
03 April 2015